About the Author

Quite early, Kathrin Brückmann developed an interest in the history of Ancient Egypt. In consequence, she chose to study the exotic combination Egyptology, Archaeology and Judaism.

After giving birth to two children, realization dawned on her that digging Egypt top to bottom and being a single parent might not go together all too well. So she tried something different. In 2011, she started writing and, in doing so, returned to her roots. The novel Sinuhe, Sohn der Sykomore (Sinuhe, Son of the Sycamore, so far only available in German) is about a young Egyptian scribe in Twelfth Dynasty Egypt and tells the famous story of Sinuhe as recorded on numerous papyri. The book was received so well, she decided to become a freelance writer. Some short stories in various genres followed her debut novel, one of which won a writing contest by a well-known publisher.

In 2013, she developed the concept for a historical mystery series about two young physicians investigating murders and other crimes in Ancient Egypt—not exactly of their own free will. Apprenticed to Anubis (Verborgener Tod in German) is the first novel in this series. Edith Parzefall translated it into English.

Read more about it on http://hori-nakhtmin.jimdo.com/

Also by Kathrin Brückmann

Shadows of the Damned: In Maat's Service 2

The Bitter Taste of Death: In Maat's Service 3

Apprenticed to Anubis

In Maat's Service
Volume 1

Kathrin Brückmann

Original title: Verborgener Tod
Hori und Nachtmin Band 1

Copyright © 2014 Kathrin Brückmann, Rigaer Str. 102,
10247 Berlin, Germany
E-mail: kheper@gmx.de

Translation: Edith Parzefall
Editor: Les Tucker
Cover design: Hannah Böving

ISBN: 1501028812

ISBN-13: 978-1501028816

Map of Ancient Egypt

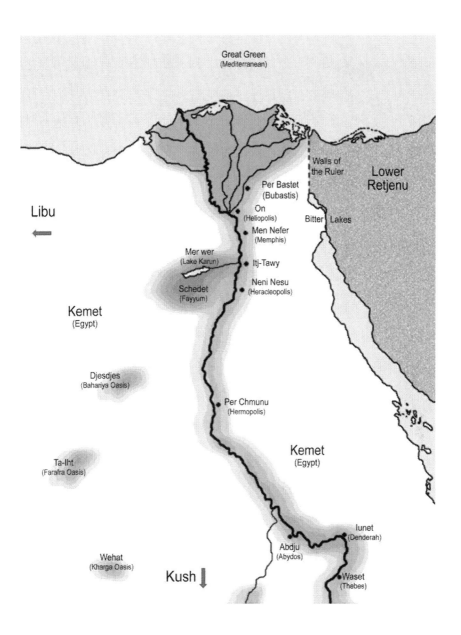

Great Green
(Mediterranean)

Walls of
the Ruler

Lower
Retjenu

Libu

Per Bastet
(Bubastis)

On
(Heliopolis)

Bitter Lakes

Men Nefer
(Memphis)

Mer wer
(Lake Karun)

Itj-Tawy

Neni Nesu
(Heracleopolis)

Schedet
(Fayyum)

Kemet
(Egypt)

Djesdjes
(Bahariya Oasis)

Per Chmunu
(Hermopolis)

Ta-Iht
(Farafra Oasis)

Kemet
(Egypt)

Iunet
(Denderah)

Abdju
(Abydos)

Wehat
(Kharga Oasis)

Kush

Waset
(Thebes)

Principal Characters

Historical persons are set in bold characters, followed by pronunciation pointers in parenthesis and the translation of the names in italics. The letter combination 'th' is pronounced like an aspirated 't'.

THE ROYAL DYNASTY

Senusret III. (Senusret) – *husband of goddess Useret* – A young pharaoh with an ancient secret.

Khenmetneferhedjet II (Khenmet-nefer-hedjet) – *joined with the White Crown* – Although the Great Royal Wife is called Sherit, the younger, she is older than her brother Senusret.

Nofrethenut (Nofret-henut) – *beautiful mistress* – Second royal wife, who hasn't much to say for starters.

HORI AND HIS FAMILY

Hori – *name of god Horus* – As a physician, he wants to help the living but soon finds himself among the dead.

Sobekemhat (Sobek-em-hat) – *Sobek is at the top* – Hori's father and a treasurer, who doesn't treasure his son.

Nofret – *the beautiful* – Hori's mother rather caters to the wishes of her husband than to the needs of her sons.

Teti and Puy – Hori's brothers are chips off the old block, no doubt.

AMENY AND HIS FAMILY

Ameny (short for Amen-em-het) – *Amun is at the top* – The second prophet of Amun has a willful daughter, so he gets her a minder.

Isis – *name of the goddess Isis* – Ameny's wife notices a lot but rarely wastes a word on anything.

Mutnofret (Mut-nofret) – *(the goddess) Mut is beautiful* – The daughter who gets her own way with a sharp tongue.

Hetepet – *the content* – The daughter who can't say anything anymore.

Huni and Bata – Twins who become unmistakable in the course of this story.

Penu – *mouse* – A servant who proves mice also have teeth.

A goat who gave its heart's blood for the cause.

AT THE HOUSE OF LIFE

Nakhtmin (Nakht-min) – *Min is strong* – Feels much weaker than his name indicates, still he takes on a hard task.

Meriamun and Weni – Physicians who show little collegiality when it is imperative.

Imhotepankh (Imhotep-ankh) – *Imhotep shall live* – Head of doctors with an acute awareness of tradition.

Inpu – *name of the god Anubis* – Head of the House of Life, a principal with principles.

NEBIT AND HIS FAMILY

Nebit – *mistress, name of a goddess* – Vizier with punchy arguments and peculiar affections.

Sitamun (Sit-amun) – *daughter of Amun* – His wife, who is hardly affected by him.

Neferib (Nefer-ib) – *beautiful heart* – His oldest son, who had an unfortunate fall.

Shepses – *the noble* – His second son. Unfortunately, many women fall for him but not the right one.

Hotep – *the content* – His youngest son and a case of bad luck.

Henut – *the mistress* – His daughter, a stroke of luck, but not for everyone.

AT THE HOUSE OF DEATH

Hut-Nefer – *beautiful house* – The head of the embalmers has a knack for dramatic appearances.

Kheper – *formation* – An embalmer with a good heart although he likes to remove other people's hearts.

ADDITIONAL PERSONS

Thotnakht (Thot-nakht) – *Thot is strong* – The king's first scribe scribbles on scrolls and in the end gets rolled over.

Bastet – *name of the cat goddess* – She cannot tell her father Thotnakht anything anymore.

Merit-Neith – *loved by goddess Neith* – Daughter of a harem official, but her heart has gone cold already.

Ankhes – *she lives* – The king's ward, whose name tells a lie.

Isisnofret, Beast-Merit, Nofriti and several other Merits and Nofrets – spoiled young women without inhibitions.

Khonsu – *name of the god Khonsu* – Innkeeper of a tavern with a haughty name. He has much to laugh about.

Nebet-Het – *mistress of the house* – His daughter, who has little reason to laugh.

PROLOGUE

Year I of Pharaoh Senusret, the third of this name to ascend the throne of Horus.
Day 12 of month Rekeh-wer in Peret, season of the emergence.

The winter sun radiated little heat, and Bastet pulled her shawl tighter. A gust of wind blew through her clothes and urged her to haste—her least favorite time of the year. The air smelled of mud, and the cold forced inhabitants of the capital Itj-tawy to stay indoors, where the gloom dispirited Bastet. This year though, not even the cold could keep her inside. She hurried on, while her thoughts leapt ahead. Her lover awaited her, and she was on her way to see him.

A hot wave of excitement surged through her as she recalled their previous tryst when he smuggled her into the garden of the Amun temple. She could almost feel his hands on her body again. That time they didn't stop at kissing and fondling. While she lay on the ground, he pushed up her dress, squeezed his knee between her thighs, so she opened up for him, like a flower in bloom. Yes, her first time, and she'd wanted it, wanted him! His erection was enormous and he penetrated her with so much force it hurt. She'd imagined joining with a man would offer more pleasure and passion. Instead, he'd thrust into her hard.

For a moment, she wondered if he even cared who lay beneath him. His lust had a desperate quality. So what? They loved each other, and nothing else mattered. Her friends had assured her the act would become more enjoyable. Were they right? She could hardly wait to find out, to surrender to him once more.

Clamping a hand over her mouth, Bastet giggled. Would he take her to the holy realm again, the zone reserved for priests? Meeting in a forbidden place sure made their rendezvous even more alluring. Would he mention marriage this time? Her monthly bleeding was overdue. Maybe she carried his child already.

She turned into a narrow alley rimmed by the walls of two properties. Although she didn't like the gloomy, deserted lane, it offered a welcome shortcut taking her to the man she loved much sooner.

A figure stepped from behind a protrusion in one of the walls and blocked her path. She started, then recognized the face and laughed with relief. "It's you! Oh, you scared me…"

The arm moved fast, fist clutching a strange object. A thud. Brief, intense pain in her chest. She touched the left side. Her heart cramped. She stumbled. Why? Again the arm lifted, and she recognized a weapon. Run! Get away! She dashed back the path she'd come but her strength dwindled. At the sound of sandals slapping over the compact ground behind her she imagined the vicious tip piercing her flesh again. Fear for her life allowed her feet to fly along the path. At last, she reached the end of the alley. The park there promised safety and hiding places. "Help!" she yelled. "Help me!" But no people roamed the garden. Her heart raced. She could hardly draw a breath but had to move on, hide among the bushes. She panted and hardly felt the branches whipping her skin. Her shawl caught in the thorns. She released her grip on it. Ahead she saw dense shrubs and ducked into their shadows. Need to get away! The brushwood clasped her, and she couldn't muster the strength to tear away. So she crouched in a trough.

"I can see you; I can hear you. No use hiding from me," the voice purred.

Unable to suppress her gasps, Bastet listened to the rustling noises of her approaching pursuer. The twigs above her parted. She wanted to jump up and run away, but her limbs no longer obeyed. Black spots dotted her vision. No, don't! Don't lose consciousness…

EFFORTS BEARING FRUIT

Day 5 of month Renutet in Shemu, season of the harvest

A new morning dawned in Itj-tawy. With the first rays of the sun god, the inhabitants of the capital stirred and left their houses to start their daily chores. In the district where the royal officials lived Hori stood wavering on the threshold of his parents' house. He lifted his face toward the sky and took a deep breath. Tense anticipation seemed to permeate the city. Or was it just his own excitement?

He smoothed his *shendyt*, a wraparound skirt of fine linen, and made sure the wig sat properly on his shaved head before he strode through the garden and into the street. The walls surrounding the villas still cast their shadows onto the compacted mud and dipped the path in cool gloom. Hori turned toward the harbor. Now Ra's glistening rays cast his grotesquely elongated shadow ahead of him as if the god meant to goad him on. In the craftspeople and fishermen's district, a bustling crowd swallowed him. No choice but to adjust to the throbbing pulse of this busy quarter and go with the flow until the narrow alley spilled into an intersection, releasing him like a jug being unplugged.

Relieved, Hori drew air deep into his lungs. The breeze dispersed the vapors of sweat, garlic, rotting fish entrails and cooking smells to replace them with a faint hint of incense surrounding the temple district like a protective cloak. Hori's sandals, made of braided rushes, slapped over the cobbled boulevard leading to the temple of Amun. The mighty pylon dwarfed the narrow passage to the temple area. Had the builders intended to impress on people how tiny they stood before the gods? As always, Hori held his breath when he entered the dark tunnel and let the power of the supreme god pervade him.

Like a blossom, the temple's large vestibule opened up to the rays of the sun god. Hori shied from the bright terrain and stuck to the shadowy path along the wall although he had no reason to hide. He hardly noticed the gorgeous reliefs depicting Amun and his divine family.

Picking up his pace, he passed through a gate next to the main temple building. In this secluded area, the House of Life, he'd spent most of his time over the last few years studying. These premises harbored the secret knowledge reserved for adepts. Priests, scribes, physicians and sculptors received their training here, where the scrolls describing the mysteries of the gods were stored. In one section of the House of Life, the physicians performed their craft and tended the sick.

Hori had achieved the lowest degree of consecration since it was a prerequisite for being trained in these halls. To learn the medical profession, he had to be at least a *wab* priest of Amun. As the son of treasurer Sobekemhat, he would have qualified for the highest offices, but he'd set his mind on medicine at an early age—out of spite or true longing? Hori couldn't tell. His father's self-righteousness always prompted him to contradict. He had to admit that their troubled relationship often brought out the worst in him. Whenever generations of treasury officials showed in Sobekemhat's reproachful glare, Hori felt sick. Numbers didn't interest him except when measuring the correct dose of medicine. He shrugged. His choice of profession might have originated in a need to rile his father, but now his studies gave him a sense of fulfillment, and he liked the work. Today he'd take his final exam. None of his brothers had expected he'd make it this far, and certainly not his father. With determination he shook off these depressing thoughts. He'd prove to his family, who deemed him a good-for-nothing, what he was made of. If he excelled, maybe even passed the exam top of the class, would they be proud of him at long last?

His fellow students already waited in the arcade before the head of doctors' office. For three years they'd been learning together, shared joy and misery over their tough training. Hori greeted and joined them. His gaze swept over the faces, all showing the same tense expression. *Likely, I look just like them.* The thought made him grin. Only Shepses displayed his usual self-important countenance. The vizier's son was the only classmate he didn't like. Too arrogant. Wasn't it enough that he came from a noble family and learning never posed any difficulty for him? Did he have to boast about it? *His* family did not scoff at his choice of profession but supported him. On top of all that, the guy looked great. Hori ground his teeth. Shepses often bragged about his female conquests. If he were to be believed, he'd plugged every flower at court. Wishful thinking, more likely…

The door opened, and a servant called, "Shepses, you will demonstrate your knowledge first."

Appalled, Hori averted his gaze. Why did the fellow grin like that? One might think he'd bribed the examiners to guarantee his graduation. As soon as Shepses left, the excited medical students started chatting.

"What did you prepare for, Hori?" Nakhtmin asked.

"I mainly focused on remedies, diseases of the anus and the *Book of Wounds*. Oh, and I looked at eye complaints as well as female disorders," he replied.

His friend's dark complexion changed to a muddy gray, and his shoulders sagged. "I mostly studied the books on instruments and remedies. Didn't they say the exam mainly focused on fundamentals?"

Hori felt sympathy for Nakhtmin. His lowly origins had made things difficult enough for him all these years. The boy from Upper Egypt was the orphaned son of a minor priest of the god Min and had drawn attention because of his sharp mind. Unfortunately, he was at quite a disadvantage compared to the offspring of nobility, who had access to education from an early age on. Nakhtmin first had to learn how to learn. Hori tried to calm him. "Right, that's what I've heard. I probably revised too much. And look what happened—I totally forgot the medical instruments. Sure hope that won't bite me now."

"Don't worry, you know these by heart," Nakhtmin assured him. "I envy you for your quick grasp on anything. You seem to remember every text you've read. I wish I were as smart as you."

"But you appear to see through a patient's skin. No one else finds out which demon has befallen an ailing person as fast as you do."

Nakhtmin grinned sheepishly. "That won't help me much if I flunk the exam."

Hori froze. Flunk the exam? No way! If he were a regular medical student, he'd be able to repeat last year's courses. He could deal with the mockery of his classmates and wouldn't mind the teachers hassling him some more—if he did get the chance. His father, however, would scrunch up his face and take the youngest son's failure as something to be expected, then force him into a civil service career. What a struggle it had been to convince the mighty treasurer to even let him try. As long as Hori couldn't provide for himself, he depended on father's support. Allowances would cease immediately if he didn't pass the exam today. He wiped his sweaty hands on his shendyt.

That moment the door opened, and Shepses approached the group with his arms spread wide. "My parents have arranged for a banquet to honor the best of new doctors. After all, my success must be celebrated. You're all invited."

His fellow students cheered but Shepses's self-confident airs annoyed Hori. How could he be so sure he hadn't failed? The guy acted as if his getting the best results were the only option.

A nudge in the ribs drew his attention. "You'll come to my graduation party as well, right?"

"Sure." Hori forced a smile. Nobody could afford to alienate the vizier's son, no matter if he was an arrogant prick or not.

While the young men still inquired which questions Shepses had been asked and when the banquet would start, Nakhtmin was called into the head's room.

Hori noticed his friend's shaky knees and called after him, "Good luck! You'll do fine."

Nakhtmin's exam took longer than Shepses's. Maybe it only seemed that way to Hori because he couldn't stop wondering what was going on behind those locked doors. Despite his encouraging words, he wasn't so sure Nakhtmin's knowledge of diseases sufficed for him to pass. Hopefully, their teachers had recognized the boy's talent. Any knowledge he lacked, he could still acquire, but such an intuitive sense for ailments couldn't be learned. It came easy to Nakhtmin. Shepses, however, would never become an equally skilled doctor, no matter how well he'd done in the exam. He was so full of himself that other people only served as a mirror for his grandeur.

Finally, the door opened. Nakhtmin kept his gaze to the floor as he staggered into the corridor.

Oh dear, that didn't go too well. Hori placed an arm around his friend's bony shoulders but Nakhtmin shook him off.

"Leave me alone." With a scornful gesture, he wiped over his eyes.

Hori shrugged. If Nakhtmin didn't want consolation, he wouldn't impose. Let him deal with his distress on his own.

Next, Meriamun was called. One after the other, the prospective physicians faced their finals and most of them looked relieved when they'd put the test behind them. Hori was happy for them or cheered them on, while he grew more and more nervous. If only he'd brought his transcriptions of the medical papyri to make best use of the waiting time. Now it was too late. While his mates relaxed and settled in the shadow of a tamarind in one corner of the adjoining courtyard, he leaned against a column and brooded. Snippets of conversation wafted to him.

Did the head of doctors intend to unsettle him by calling him last? Hori knew old Imhotepankh didn't like him much. Whenever Hori connected what he'd learned with what he'd experienced to gain new insights, his comments raised the head physician's hackles. For Imhotepankh, only the written word counted. He dismissed Hori's ideas, without recognizing the chance to find new possibilities for treating the sick. Keen on traditions, Imhotepankh wouldn't make it easy for him to pass the exam, but he too was bound by the laws of Maat, the divine world order, and by those of the temple.

When the call finally came, Hori's legs turned wobbly and shook. His heart pounded like it wanted to jump out of his mouth. With sweaty hands, he stood before the men whose questions he'd have to answer. Imhotepankh, head of doctors; Inpu, head of the House of Life; and Ameny, second prophet of Amun.

"Hori, son of Sobekemhat, are you ready?"

"I'm ready," Hori mumbled and swallowed. He didn't feel ready at all. All of a sudden, everything he'd learned had vanished. His mind resembled a blank sheet of papyrus.

Imhotepankh cleared his throat and recited in a droning voice, "If you see mucilage in a man's neck, and he suffers in the joint of his neck…"

Relief flooded Hori. This case he knew well. With haste he gave his answer and finished with, "A disease I will fight against."

The satisfied nod of his examiner restored some of his confidence. The supreme doctors asked further questions, and he was able to answer them all. What a relief. His reason had not abandoned him. At last, they led him through a door into an adjoining room, where three patients lay on wooden cots.

"Hori, son of Sobekemhat, tell us which diseases these people suffer from."

In his nervousness, he clenched his clammy, cold hands into fists, then quickly wiped them on his shendyt before turning to the first patient. The middle-aged man's chapped hands covered in chalk, and his split nails, gave away the stonemason. The tip of his left thumb was swollen and showed blue coloration. Carefully, Hori palpated the injured digit to determine whether the bone was fractured. The man groaned with pain.

Hori announced, "I find a man whose thumb has been bruised. No bone is broken. No open wound is showing on him."

The three examiners appeared content with the diagnosis. "Which treatment would you suggest?"

Now, Hori found himself in a pickle. The traditional method called for a cooling compress soaked in aloe juice. However, the injury would cause the thumbnail to peel off, which would hamper his work for quite a while. If instead he used the heated tip of a puncture needle to smelt a tiny hole into the nail, the collected blood could drain and the nail be preserved. Additionally, this procedure would spare the man pain. Once he'd tried this on a servant in his father's household, and the result turned out very satisfying. Hori took a deep breath before he recited the common treatment. Then he explained his method and its advantages for the patient, whose dull gaze brightened at his words.

Imhotepankh displayed a smug smile. "Your thoughts aren't relevant at this point," he droned. Hori suspected the man had set a trap for him.

The second prophet, Ameny, however, bent over and scrutinized the wound with visible interest. Then he asked the sick man, "Would you be willing to let this young man here, Hori, test his idea on your finger?"

"My lord," the stonemason stammered. "I'd be very happy if I could go back to work very soon. I have a wife and seven children to feed. Let the young man try, please!"

From the corner of his eye, Hori saw Imhotepankh press his lips together in scorn. He reined in the grin trying to conquer his face and set to work. With quick moves, he heated the tip of his lancet over a charcoal basin and performed the treatment. Carefully, he caught the oozing blood with a piece of linen and afterward wrapped the thumb with a soaked compress.

The other two patients he also diagnosed without difficulty. The rash of a child he swabbed with oil of black cumin seeds. No physician in the Two Lands, though, could cure the swelling in an old man's abdomen. In this case, he prescribed an extraction of poppy juice and willow bark to ease the pain.

Hori believed he had solved all problems well. Leaving the room, he felt light— light and strangely empty. For a moment, he lacked orientation when he found himself at the end of the long path leading to his graduation as physician.

Soon all examinees were asked to gather in the room.

Imhotepankh rose and announced, "Students of medicine, I'm very pleased to elevate you all to the rank of doctor. Shepses, top of class, please step up."

The haughty grin of the vizier's son aggravated Hori. He couldn't help feeling others deserved the honor far more.

That moment priest Ameny spoke up, "That is not quite right, venerated head of doctors. We agreed doctor Hori has proven himself most knowledgeable today. Not only were his answers flawless, he thought beyond his training, with his patient's best interest in mind although he knew such demeanor might endanger his graduation."

Hori couldn't believe he'd heard right. With quivering fingers, he took the golden amulet featuring the *udjat* eye, which would designate him as physician from now on. Imhotepankh's scowl couldn't dampen his joy. When he turned around, he believed he saw contempt flare up in Shepses's eyes. So he couldn't resist granting him a bright smile. "Today, we truly have reason to party! I'm looking forward to the banquet in honor of your and my success."

Shepses managed a lopsided grin. "Sure, we'll thoroughly celebrate the accomplishments of the two best students of our year." Moving rather stiffly, he accepted the insignia and stomped off without further comments.

Soon the ceremony ended, and the fledgling doctors swarmed into the courtyard of the House of Life, where the sick awaited treatment. The dignity of their new office forgotten, they sent cheers into the deep blue sky.

Entering the twilight of his parents' house in the afternoon, Hori found his father as well as his older brothers at home. Teti and Puy had already established their own households but often visited their family. Had they come because of him? Hori could hardly believe it. If so, then only to laugh at his failure. Well, he'd have to disappoint them.

For a long time, he'd been living in the shadows of his brothers, both true offshoots from the paternal roots. Hori was the only colorful flower in the uniform green of their family tree. Sometimes they looked at him as if he were a weed that needed to be pulled. Today he'd prove his worth to them! He quickly took off the necklace and hid it in his fist.

Puy noticed him first. "Look, there he is."

Sure sounded like they'd been talking about him.

"So, how did it go?" his father asked.

Mother darted him a shy smile. "At least he's finished his training. Don't be too hard on the boy."

Her appeasing words pained Hori. Not even she had faith in his abilities? He knew not to expect anything better from his father, who wanted to see him push numbers in the pharaoh's treasury, where he and his two other sons served. Hori's refusal had caused a deep rift between him and his family. Since then, Sobekemhat found fault with everything he did. His father liked to claim Hori's recalcitrance showed his immaturity and called him too fickle to learn an honorable profession. At least Nofret, his mother, understood him but rarely dared to defy her husband in this matter.

Hori wanted to throw the amulet at their feet but restrained himself. Such a spiteful gesture would only confirm his father's opinion of him, not change it. And he was proud of himself. He'd achieved so much! He opened his balled fist to reveal the Eye of Horus, which had left an imprint on his palm, and pulled the necklace over his head. Warm and heavy, the metal lay on his bare chest. "I passed the exam. Not only that, I was declared best of class by the examiners. From today on, I'm an accredited physician in Kemet." He beamed at the strained expressions on his brothers' faces.

You thought your own light would shine even brighter if I failed, didn't you? How gratifying!

"Hm," his father breathed. "Well, that was the least you could do since you refused to take on a position at court. Physicians! Nothing more than educated craftsmen. I can only hope you won't bring more shame on your family."

"Sobekemhat! The boy has achieved a lot. Doctors are highly respected, and he graduated top of class!" Pride briefly flashed in his mother's eyes, and she blinked away some tears.

Hori couldn't resist pointing out, "By the way, father, if the vizier of the Two Lands deems a medical career suitable for his middle son, the disgrace can't be that horrible for you. Don't bother planning some kind of celebration tonight. I'm invited to the vizier's place—for a banquet in *my* honor—and Shepses's of course."

He cherished how Teti and Puy gaped at him. Leaving the room, he heard his father's indignant snort. His shoulders tensed. Even if he'd been stupid to believe Father might show some appreciation, his reaction disappointed him. He longed for parents who loved *him* and not his status in the world.

Reaching his room, he peeled off the starched linen. Naked, he threw himself onto his bed. He'd nap before the banquet because he'd have fun tonight for sure. He deserved it! His head comfortably placed on the wooden headrest, he soon drifted away into wholesome sleep.

A BANQUET WITH CONSEQUENCES

Day 5 of month Renutet in Shemu, season of the harvest

In the evening, Hori donned his best shendyt, starched so intensely that the front stuck out. After some consideration, he chose a neck collar with pearls of lapis lazuli and carnelian, broad enough to cover his shoulders, and picked up the amulet with the Eye of Horus. Had this been worth alienating his family?

"Whatever." He pressed his lips together and slipped the golden necklace over his head. Diligently, he circled his eyes with kohl and extended his eye line to his temples. The curly wig, cut in steps, and the sandals made of artfully braided bulrush completed his outfit. He left his parents' house without saying good-bye.

The sun had already set, but it wasn't far to the vizier's place, and Hori knew the way. The scarce light of torches mounted to the gates of noble premises sufficed. Turning a corner, he glimpsed the Nile. The mountains at the western bank loomed dark against the dark blue sky. Glowing dots marked the buildings on the other side of the river, the temple complex of Anubis. Farther downstream lay the separated compound, in which the dead were prepared for their journey to the Beautiful West. A dog howled, or maybe a jackal in the desert. Their cries sometimes carried from afar across the water. The noise sounded eerie and made Hori pick up his pace on the last stretch. He reached the enclosing wall of Nebit's premises.

The vizier's house stood in an expansive park adjoining the river and boasted its own jetty. The gate was brightly illuminated. As soon as Hori stepped through it, the day's lingering warmth and laughter enveloped him. Torches stuck into the ground lined the paths and showed his feet the way with their flickering light.

Finally, he reached a grassy area surrounded by bushes and trees. Lanterns fixed to branches illuminated long tables laden with dishes. Chatting guests stood around and laughed. At first, Hori felt blinded and strangely apart—like in a dream. For a while he hung back, thinking he didn't belong here.

Somebody welcomed him cheerfully. "There's Hori, the guest of honor. Come on over, we've been waiting for you."

Hori recognized the caller and forced a smile. "Nakhtmin!" The face of the young doctor from Upper Egypt glowed with a reddish tinge in the lantern light. Likely, he'd already enjoyed some wine and seemed relieved by Hori's arrival. Nakhtmin might feel even more out of place than he did.

Together they stepped into the illuminated area, and their host turned to them. The high official darted him a most unwelcoming look, then an amiable smile slid onto the vizier's face. "I greet you, son of Sobekemhat. You and my son…" He pulled Shepses closer. "…are my guests of honor tonight."

Son of Sobekemhat? Why can't he use my name? Am I nothing and only worth being noticed because of my father's position? Despite his misgivings he bowed. "Thank you, noble Nebit, for your invitation to the banquet this evening. Every single one of the young physicians well deserves this celebration."

Nebit cast a glance at Nakhtmin, then at his crumpled, spotty shendyt and wrinkled his nose. He opened his mouth as if to say something, but reconsidered and waved his arm to call the young doctors to the tables. Hori was assigned to sit between Shepses and a young man who resembled him, likely his older brother Neferib. The seating order made very clear who was the real guest of honor tonight. Shepses sat to his father's right side. Nebit's gaze held warmth as he took in his family: his beautiful wife, the three sons and little daughter.

Curious, Hori appraised the table. In Nebit's household, they really knew how to celebrate! Servants brought platters and bowls with steaming food. The view alone made Hori's mouth water. Condensed water glittered on the jars of wine. Obviously, they'd been taken from the cooling wraps just now and promised refreshing contents. Hori took a tentative sip. Soft and sweet, the wine caressed his tongue. With relish he took a big gulp, and soon the alcohol went to his head. He'd better be careful and restrain himself.

The food was more delicious than anything he'd ever been served at home. His family ate far simpler meals. Hori savored the feast and forgot all his resentments against Shepses. He'd love to be part of this family with easy manners and openly displayed affection. Quite the opposite of his father's strict reign. Over and over again, he filled his bowl. The food was very spicy and hot. To soothe the burning in his throat, he had his mug refilled as soon as he'd emptied it.

Conversation turned more lively at the table. Nebit's wife, noble Sitamun, dominated with her easy chatter. Her husband hung on her every word. Although she flirted with her son's young friends, the vizier didn't show a hint of annoyance but gently stroked her arm. Whenever her mouth spilled pearls of laughter, he joined in. Otherwise he didn't contribute to the small talk—perhaps it didn't interest him.

Shepses's mother enchanted Hori. She seemed so young. The full lips often parted for an enticing smile. When she bent forward, the shoulder straps of her dress hung loose and granted him a glimpse of the tips of her henna-colored nipples. He certainly appreciated the starching of his shendyt hiding his erection.

Wine and beer flowed like water. Some of the young men already needed to throw up into the bowls discretely presented by servants. Hori too felt drunk and hot. A group of young women emerged from the shadows of the trees—the entertainment commenced. A blind musician intoned a cheerful melody on her harp, and when the drums and sistrums set in and pounded the rhythm, the dancers, wearing only thin belts on their naked bodies, swayed with the beat.

Sitamun placed a hand on her husband's arm and whispered in his ear. At the same time, her eyes glazed and her lewd gaze wandered over the young men until it met Hori's. Had she winked at him just now?

Nebit rose. "I will retire. Tomorrow important tasks are awaiting me. But you should enjoy the evening as long as you like."

As if on cue, the music grew louder and more gleeful. The guests settled on the lawn. Hori joined Meriamun and Nakhtmin, the two classmates he liked best. Lazily, the two enjoyed the performance of the dancers, while Hori, spell-bound, focused on fascinating Sitamun. The music seemed to carry her away. Shepses handed her a beaker of wine, which she quaffed down. Then—Hori didn't trust his eyes—she stripped off her dress and joined the dancers. How her body swung and bent! Never had he seen a more desirable woman; he wanted to drag her into the bushes—or if not her, any woman would do right now just to get relief.

The other young men also stared at the vizier's wife with lust-filled eyes. Faster and faster the music churned; the dancers' moves turned ever more titillating. The naked girls approached the guests, circled them with cooing calls. Sitamun noticed

Hori's gaze and wove toward him. Imagining his fantasies might become true, he moaned and almost ejaculated. That brought him back to reality. He swallowed and quickly sobered. If he'd got carried away with her, he'd be facing severe consequences! Did Nebit know how his wife behaved? His erection dwindled as fast as it had come.

Sitamun stood directly in front of him. This close, he saw the wrinkles in her face despite the thick layer of make-up and the diffuse lighting. They revealed her true age. She sat on his lap astride and slid a hand under his shendyt. No, that couldn't happen! She was married! The world spun around him. Nauseated, he pushed her off, jumped up and ran from the revelers. Sitamun's now shrill laughter followed him. In the shadows of the trees, he threw up.

Trembling and gasping, he leaned against the trunk of a palm tree. He felt dirtied. His hands were sticky, but he didn't want to wipe them on his shendyt lest he rub the stink of puke into the cloth. Were the servants still around? He peered across the clearing toward the tables. No, but maybe they'd left bowls with water so he could wash his hands. His throat burned. A sip of water would be real nice now. He staggered around the meadow toward the tables.

Where was Sitamun? Ah, there she danced around Meriamun, ensnaring him with her lascivious moves. The woman wanted to be satisfied. Hori shook his head in disbelief. Meriamun obviously had fewer qualms or was too drunk, because he pulled Nebit's wife down to him. Soon the two were passionately groping each other. Hori couldn't bear the view any longer. A pinch of jealousy seeped into his disgust. He almost stumbled over another lump of entangled limbs. The dancers pleasured his friends. The music was quieter now but seductively urgent. It accompanied the gasping and moaning of the copulating couples. Only moments ago, Hori had wanted nothing more than to shove his pulsing member into a willing body, now the view disgusted him. Sitamun's outcries of lust rang far too loud in his ears. Didn't Nebit hear what was going on in his garden? He glanced around.

Sweat glittered on Sitamun's body. She'd finished with Meriamun and turned to another young man. When her new chosen one turned his face, Hori recognized Shepses. His mother bent over him and took his cock in her mouth. At first it looked like Shepses wanted to stave her off, then his eyes rolled upwards with pleasure. His body obviously reacted to the skilled tongue. Now his mother straddled him and guided his manhood deep inside her. In an almost violent ride, she took him as if Meriamun hadn't been able to satisfy her.

Hori's face burned with embarrassment. Didn't anybody notice what was happening right before their eyes? How could a mother do something like that—with her own son! Shepses, however, didn't seem to find her actions out of the ordinary, enjoyed them as if such things were normal. This *was* normal for him, Hori realized to his horror. She'd done it before and not only once. Now he noticed the looks of Shepses's brothers. The face of the older Neferib as well as that of the younger Hotep reflected his own revulsion. Had they known? Now, Hori was really glad not to be part of such a family. Underneath the deceptively smooth surface, reflecting the image of Shepses's family, lurked a crocodile. He went to the table and turned his back to the proceedings. Hopefully he could blank out the images with wine. He poured his beaker to the rim.

He didn't remain alone for long. Neferib and Hotep joined him although Hori hadn't spoken to them before. Neferib held an administrative position, that much he knew about the older brother of his classmate. He not only resembled Shepses, but also showed his cocky demeanor. Hotep, however, was lanky. The stooping posture and darting gaze gave him a skulking air, which Hori couldn't really define. Instinctively, he took a dislike to Hotep. The youngest of the brothers hadn't contributed at all to the conversation during the feast and appeared like a foreign body in the harmonious fabric of his family. But then he wondered how harmonious this family really was. Hotep lifted his beaker and toasted. The next moment, Hori realized why Nebit's youngest acted so shyly. "To th-th-e -p-ph…"

"Yeah, yeah, to the pharaoh—life, prosperity and health," Neferib interrupted and set his beaker in front of Hori. "Please excuse my brother, he's a bit slow."

"I-I-I'm n-not sl-l-ow."

With a patronizing smile, Neferib mocked him. "I-I-I'm n-no-o-ot sl-l-l-l-l—not, certainly not, Hotep. Everyone needs that long to say one sentence." He burst into laughter showing how drunk he was already.

Hori felt uncomfortable witnessing such humiliation. While Hotep only lowered his head in resignation, his own cheeks burned with mortification. His vague dislike of the young man changed into sympathy. With relief he welcomed Nakhtmin and another young doctor called Weni to their table, giving their talk a new direction. Nakhtmin reiterated the exam and soon a lively discussion of symptoms and diagnoses unfolded. Naturally the vizier's sons had nothing to contribute.

After a while Neferib complained, "There's nothing going on here anymore. Let's go to the harbor and party on. I know a drinking hole that's open all night."

Leave the celebration? Indecisive, Hori turned around and swept his gaze over the meadow. The remaining guests busied themselves with the dancers. At first glance, he couldn't make out Sitamun. Had she retired? Looked like it. Relieved because she spared him and others further embarrassment, he faced Neferib sitting at the table's opposite side, which allowed him an unobstructed view of the scene in twilight. Rage and hatred distorted his features. Hori checked the clearing again. This time he spotted Sitamun between Shepses and another young man, and his eyes almost popped out. Shepses lay on his back, while his mother rode him like before, but the second man… Fascinated against his will by the strange view, Hori watched as the guy shoved his cock into Sitamun's anus. Until now he'd had no idea this orifice could be used for sexual intercourse. His medical mind analyzed the implications. Would the man's semen work like an enema? He giggled.

A rough hand grabbed his arm and pulled him off the chair. "Isn't it a view for the gods when my noble mother gets stuffed like a goose?"

Hori averted his gaze. Obviously Neferib didn't appreciate that he and others witnessed the scene. Best to distract the brothers so they wouldn't have to keep watching and listening to their mother, while she acted like a whore. He couldn't tell which of the brothers he pitied most. The act of love-making honored the gods—in theory. What he'd experienced tonight, though, was rather a perversion of love. Pharaohs married their sisters to transfer the royal blood line to their sons and daughters, but this—mother and son—was something different. The openly committed adultery alone was unheard of! Hori recalled the fairy tale of the two brothers. The one who was cheated fed his unfaithful wife to the dogs.

What would happen if the family of the highest official of the Two Lands were shattered by such a scandal? He didn't want to imagine. Even worse how noble Sitamun used and abused her middle son. Did Shepses enjoy the special attentions of his mother or was he only a reluctant toy for her to satisfy her needs? A new question popped up in his heart. Was his mother's behavior the reason for Hotep's stutter?

With feigned nonchalance he said, "So what? Now, how about that den of thieves at the harbor?" He linked arms with Neferib and Weni. A short while later, the five of them staggered through the nighttime streets of Itj-tawy, laughing and joking.

As soon as they entered the tavern *Golden Ibis,* Hori found himself in a different world. No breeze dispersed the stench of stale beer, vomit and rancid fat mixed with the odor of sweat and foul breath. Sooting torches mounted to the walls only offered dim lighting. The air in the hot room was stifling. A few late patrons sucked their beer through straws so they didn't have to swallow the dregs of grain. The innkeeper, a portly baldhead in a blotchy apron, lifted his head. A sleazy smile pushed up his fat cheeks and narrowed his eyes to slits.

Obviously, he recognized a fine shendyt right away.

The fat man squeezed between the rows of seats and welcomed them with many bows and even more words. He led them to a table and, with a swipe of his forearm, cleared the surface of rubble.

"Daughter," he shouted over the heads of his guests. "Bring these noblemen our best beer!"

After a short while, a weedy young girl—almost a child still and close to collapsing under the weight—carried over a pitcher and mugs. Neferib stared at the blossoming breasts of the girl, barely covered by her threadbare dress.

As soon as they'd downed the beer the next pitcher stood before them. Hori restrained himself but felt the beer getting to his head anyway. The brothers quaffed the frothy drink with greed. No surprise there. The two had much to wash from their minds. Nakhtmin's eyes turned glassy, and his head sank onto the table.

When the innkeeper's daughter brought the third round, Neferib dragged her onto his lap. The young wench writhed playfully at first. She had to be used to cheeky patrons groping her. When Neferib didn't let go, she struggled against him but the nobleman held her tight.

"Let me go!" she called. Hori noticed the pleading in her cry.

Neferib laughed hard. "Little slut, I'll fuck you harder than your fat father ever did."

The scorn in Neferib's voice startled Hori. He looked around, but couldn't see the innkeeper although the man must have realized what was going on here. Hori turned back to Neferib, whose fingers had pushed up the girl's dress. With horror-struck eyes, she looked straight into Hori's heart. Too much! He couldn't take it. This guy simply took what he wanted. Unchecked rage at the whole depraved family seized Hori. He jumped up but had to grab the table's edge. The room spun.

"L-let her go, N-neferib," he slurred and thought of Hotep's stutter. He laughed. *I'm drunk.*

The sharp scream of the girl sobered him fast. Neferib had forced her thighs wide enough apart to penetrate her with his fingers. She bled, had still been untouched! Neferib had no right to force himself on her. Hori lunged at the vizier's son and pulled him around.

The attack surprised Neferib. He swung his right. The girl seized her chance, slid under the table and into safety.

"What do you think you're doing?" Neferib yelled. "She's mine!" He attacked.

Hori blocked the poorly aimed blows without difficulty, but he too had drunk too much. Neferib punched him in the stomach. The pain took away his breath. He curled up like a hedgehog. More blows rained down on him. Shouts cheered on the fighters. From the corner of his eye, Hori spotted the innkeeper's stout calves. Why didn't he intervene? All his furniture might break in a bar brawl. Hori struggled to his feet and shoved Neferib. Stumbling, arms flailing, the guy tripped over the legs of a toppled stool. All movement seemed to slow. Neferib's wig slid from his head, while he fell. In the silence not even a gasp could be heard.

Then the ugly noise of Neferib's neck hitting the corner of a table with uncanny precision. His muscles slacked immediately as he slumped to the ground. Slowly, blood pooled around his head. Hori's medical mind told him with ruthless clarity what his heart refused to accept: Neferib died instantly.

The surrounding patrons stared in silence. Hotep ran to his brother, clutched his head and howled. In accusation, he lifted a blood-smeared hand. "Gr-rab hi-im! He k-killed m-my b-b-brother!"

Hori stood with drooping shoulders and limp arms. This couldn't be real, couldn't be happening to him. He must have watched somebody else do it, someone he didn't know. In a dream-like state, he let them drag him out into the cold, dark night. Without a will of his own, he stumbled along between his two captors and only came to his senses when the men pounded on the gate of the pharaoh's lawmen. Hori feared what lay ahead once the *Medjay* had him in their custody. Stories flashed in his frightened heart—of beatings with batons that broke the skin or cruel executions and damnation to perpetual oblivion, which awaited those without a grave for eternity.

"Open up!" the trailing crowd screamed. "We've got a murderer!"

"No," Hori mumbled. "That's not true." But deep inside, he sensed the validity of their verdict. He, who only wanted to help other people, had killed a human being!

WHAT DO YOU HAVE TO SAY?

When Hori woke, his head ached. Still, he remembered what happened with shocking clarity. Even before he opened his eyes, he knew he wouldn't see the whitewashed walls of his bedroom, but the rough bricks of his cell, in which they'd thrown him last night without much ado. The sound of footsteps in the corridor outside made him fear the worst. He sat up.

Bad mistake. Stars danced before his eyes, and his stomach cramped. He'd have to throw up any moment, no matter if fear or hangover had turned his insides to water. The screeching of the cell door was too much. He jumped up and reached the hole in the corner serving as toilet just in time.

When the retching stopped, a tall Medjay addressed him. "Hori, son of Sobekemhat, you will give testimony before the Small Kenbet now." He and a colleague grabbed Hori's arms and dragged him out of the cell.

After only a few steps, the guards opened a door. Blinding sunlight stabbed Hori's eyes. Slowly, he adjusted to the glare and saw a small courtyard. At the opposite side, several figures sat under an awning—the judges and assessors. Right before him stood a block of stone—for punishment. Hori felt sick again.

After the trial, they might bend him over the block and hold him down while one of the Medjay beat him. His legs gave out, and he stumbled. His guards caught him and dragged him the last steps. When the men released their grip, he couldn't stand upright and collapsed in front of the pharaoh's officials. *Please, oh gods, let this all be a bad dream. This isn't me!* Would the immortals listen to his plea?

The voice reading the charges against him made his head jerk up in horror. It really was Nebit, whose mouth spit accusations at him like venom. Next to the vizier sat some officials he'd seen before, but recognizing his father among them struck hardest. Of course he was a judge—not only at the Small Kenbet but the Great Kenbet as well. Sobekemhat's face looked carved in stone. His father witnessing his shame and humiliation almost weighed heavier on him than his own regrets and self-blame. He groaned.

"What do you have to say to these accusations?" the vizier ended.

Hori parted his lips to reply but his tongue lay in his mouth like a dead animal: fat, furry and unmoving. If only he could get something to drink. At a blow to his back tears welled up in his eyes. "I…" he stammered. "I'm so sorry." Then he wept.

"So you confess your crime?" Satisfaction dripped from Nebit's voice.

Had his verdict already been rendered? No, that couldn't be. "Please, let me explain. It was an accident," he pleaded.

"Guards, place the convict on the block!"

Strong arms pulled him up. Black dots filled his vision. Through the fog in his head he heard his father's words. "Hold on, without verdict nobody is punished in Kemet. Also, I would like to hear the full story."

Carefully, Hori opened his eyes. Some of the officials nodded, others whispered to each other. For a moment he met his father's gaze. Worry and fear showed in his eyes. Did he care for his youngest son after all? Hori felt consoled and energized.

"Speak up then," someone prompted.

"I'm no thief in the night, who steals from his fellow man, nor am I a villain, who batters someone to death…" The words came to his tongue now as if of their own accord. Hori related the events of last night but omitted the role noble Sitamun had played. He couldn't say why—maybe he feared to enrage the vizier even more, maybe he felt dirtied by what he'd witnessed.

The longer he spoke, the more his father's features relaxed, and that encouraged him. Was there still hope for him? During the interrogation he felt like his winged *ba* hovered above him and watched the proceedings carefully, while he answered questions. Finally, silence spread in the courtyard. The judges weighed his statement in their hearts. Tension gripped his own heart while he waited for what lay ahead. Only the vizier kept his hate-filled gaze fixed on him. Of course he couldn't expect any understanding from him. No matter if by accident or intentionally, he'd caused the death of this man's oldest son—possibly the bearer of all his hopes.

"Hori, son of Sobekemhat, after thorough deliberation, we realize your case shall go before the Great Kenbet. Until then, you remain in custody."

For a moment Hori's breath caught. He'd have to account for his actions in front of the Lord of the Two Lands. His thoughts tripped over each other. Was that good or bad? And when would the next Great Kenbet convene? In the worst case, he might have to spend several moon cycles in a cell. What was harder to bear— uncertainty of his fate or spending the last hours of his life in full knowledge of certain death?

When the Medjay pulled him from the block, whose pitted roughness he'd come so close to feeling against his chest, relief flooded him.

Dumped back into his cell, Hori welcomed the isolation of the shabby abode like a home. He spotted a jug of water next to the bed and drank greedily. The pounding in his head lessened and gave way to fear. After a while, footsteps grew louder, and muffled voices sounded. When the door opened, his father entered.

"Make it quick," the accompanying Medjay admonished.

Sobekemhat ignored the man and sank onto the cot instead. To see his father so dejected and—yes, old—stabbed Hori's heart. "Father…" he whispered.

In the dim light seeping through the narrow slits in the wall, Hori recognized the usual mix of disappointment and contempt in his features.

"Why did you have to disgrace your mother and me like this? What were you thinking, prowling around in such a disreputable quarter and getting into a fight like a stray dog?"

Hori buried his face in his hands. Then the all too familiar defiance welled up in him. "I told the truth. Neferib was about to force himself on the girl. I only wanted to prevent such a crime, but he was drunk and fell in a most unfortunate way. I didn't…fight like a stray dog. My intentions were honorable. If you only knew what a depraved family this is!"

"Don't you dare pour dirt over noble Nebit. You've hurt the man enough!"

"I'm sorry. Oh father, I don't understand how all this could have happened either." Pleading, Hori reached out to him, but Sobekemhat snorted with contempt.

"For your mother's sake and to protect my reputation, I'll see what I can do for you."

He stood and pounded on the door. "Hey, guard! Open up."

Of course. To save his reputation. How could he have been so naïve to think his old man worried about him. For a long time, Hori stared at the door through which his father had left.

The days dragged on in dull monotony, and just as inevitable as the sun god taking his course over the horizon, Hori's thoughts circled around the same questions. At night he jerked awake from horrible nightmares of his Judgment of the Dead. If the scale tipped to the side in which his heart lay, weighed against the feather of Maat, and if the devourer's mouth opened, he'd know what fate awaited him. No more visitors came, so the only diversion in his drab existence happened once a day when fresh water and a simple meal of lentils and onions were brought to him. Gradually, the realization that endless uncertainty was worse than a quick death turned into a bitter lump inside him.

Therefore, he felt immense relief when the Medjay, bringing his meal, announced, "Tomorrow, the Great Kenbet will convene. Then you'll be condemned!"

That night, sleep escaped him. In his mind, he pieced together his statement. Would his words even carry any weight? If the witnesses testified against him... But why should they?

Hotep's cry rang in his ears. "He k-killed my b-b-brother!"

What if Nebit bribed the innkeeper to say the same? No, the Vizier of the Two Lands would never do something like that. More than anyone else, he was obliged to serve Maat, the divine order. His heart, though, was filled with hatred for the murderer—as he thought—of his son. If it had been up to Nebit, he'd have sentenced him to death at the first trial without much ado. Now, everything depended on the pharaoh. Senusret, the third of this name, had only recently ascended the Horus throne. His father had been a fair ruler. Hopefully, the gods had also gifted his son with prudence and circumspection.

Hori rose from his cot and paced the cell. Through the slits in the wall he could see a bright star, and it seemed to wink at him. The notion consoled him somewhat. *Oh gods, don't let them to punish me for something I didn't do. Maat, feather of truth, you know my heart. It lacks evil intentions. Let me survive tomorrow's trial and I'll devote my life to you.*

24

A Tempting Offer

Nakhtmin left the House of Life as one of the last doctors and headed home. Nothing drew him to his crude hut in the paupers' district, so he liked to work as long as possible. Today a patient gave him the generous present of a bale of fine linen. He'd trade it for copper. As soon as he'd saved enough, he could buy a better house. Maybe in the craftsmen's district? Then his reputation might also spread, and he'd attract wealthier patients able to afford more valuable presents. Nakhtmin hadn't imagined it would be so hard to start out as a physician.

When he was still a student from out of town, he'd been accommodated in the House of Life. His living expenses he'd covered with the remainder of his inheritance left to him by his late father. Only during the last months of his training, had he been allowed to treat the sick and receive some small presents, affording him to buy the ramshackle hut he had to call his home. He sighed. Still a long way to a carefree life.

He turned into the alley, where his dwelling stood. Tomorrow he'd have to give his statement before the Great Kenbet. Hori... What a streak of bad luck he'd had with Neferib. Nakhtmin didn't remember much. He'd been too drunk. If only he could recall the events and exonerate his friend!

A hand fell on his shoulder. He spun around.

"You're Nakhtmin, the doctor?" The man was dressed like a servant in a rich household.

"Yes," Nakhtmin stammered. "Who are you and what do you want?"

"Follow me. My master needs your services."

A patient, and a wealthy one too! Nakhtmin rejoiced. Maybe he'd work his way up faster than he'd thought. If he could help the man, he might get recommended. "Lead the way, I'm coming," he replied.

The servant strode ahead as if he couldn't leave the paupers' quarters soon enough. He turned toward the riverbank, lined by stately mansions. In a public park, he stopped. "Wait here."

Very strange. Why wasn't he brought to the ailing person? Twigs snapped behind him. A robber? He scanned the area, parted the shrubs with his arms. That was ridiculous. Who'd want to rob him and with such effort? He turned toward the path and saw a man—the vizier of the Two Lands. Nakhtmin dropped to the ground in reverence.

"Get up, doctor. I'm pleased to see you followed my invitation."

Nakhtmin rose. Nebit had aged visibly during the two moon cycles since the banquet. Losing his oldest son must have been a hard blow for him. "Can I help you somehow?" he asked. "Are you sick?"

The vizier waved dismissively. "No, I want to offer you a deal. Can't be easy for a young doctor of humble roots to make his way in life."

These words echoed Nakhtmin's own considerations earlier but what could he give the mighty man in exchange for his support? Something smelled fishy. "N-no," he admitted reluctantly.

"Tomorrow's trial weighs heavy on my heart," Nebit said. The sudden change of subject surprised Nakhtmin. The vizier continued, "Noble Sitamun and I are heart-broken over the loss of our beloved son. Can you envision the extent of our woe?"

"I don't think so." Nebit's outburst seemed a little exaggerated but who was he to judge? People grieved in different ways.

"What if the scoundrel responsible will be acquitted?"

Nakhtmin took a step back. This scoundrel Nebit referred to was his friend, and he wished for a favorable verdict. But then, he had no idea what really happened. Hori might have committed an abominable crime. Sometimes he was filled with rage, and his temper flared quickly. Nakhtmin trusted in the justice of the royal court to find out the truth. What did the vizier want from him? Learn what he'd say tomorrow and in whose favor his statement might tip the scales? "I'm really sorry for your loss, believe me, but I don't really know what happened. I…" Ashamed, he lowered his head. "I was very drunk and fell asleep on the table. When I woke, it was all over."

"Hotep, the physician Weni and the innkeeper of the tavern saw how this Hori clobbered Neferib. My son, my poor son! He couldn't defend himself."

"If it is as you say, the Kenbet will certainly come to a just verdict," Nakhtmin mumbled in a noncommittal way. This whole conversation made him uneasy.

"Oh!" Nebit bent over and picked up a handful of dust. As a symbol of his grief, he let it trickle over the hair of his wig. "Didn't you see how Hori stood upright, while my son lay dead on the floor?"

"Sure, but…"

"Isn't it reasonable to assume Hori attacked Neferib? Drunk he was and filled with scorn. I heard he quarreled with his father. One inconsiderate remark may have sufficed to set him off. They say he rioted, toppled tables. My son only want-ed to restrain him."

The vizier's words evoked images before Nakhtmin's eyes. Hori's face distorted in disgust. Hori lunging at Neferib. "You're probably right."

A smile sneaked onto Nebit's face. "I'd feel much better if I knew you'd confirm this chain of events in front of the judges tomorrow. Then noble Sitamun could sleep soundly tonight. I'd show my gratitude for your courtesy. With a few gold *deben*, you should be able to afford accommodations more suitable for your profes-sion. I'm only asking you to embellish your statement a little, then ten gold deben will embellish your arm."

Dizzy, Nakhtmin swayed. Such an incredible amount he wouldn't be able to earn in three years of hard work. He'd be rid of all his worries in one fell swoop. The more he thought about it, the more likely Nebit's version seemed. Hori had been angry. No way could he speak in Hori's favor, and if the vizier already had three witnesses lined up, he couldn't make it any worse. "Deal," he heard himself say.

Nebit patted his shoulder. "Good man. Tomorrow evening the gold will be yours."

COURT DAY

Day 20 of month Khenti-khet in Shemu, season of the harvest

Sometime after sunrise, the door to Hori's cell opened. To his surprise, his brother Puy accompanied the Medjay. He avoided Hori's gaze and handed him a clean shendyt. Grateful, Hori donned it. At least he wouldn't have to appear like a ragged tramp before the pharaoh. When he looked up, Puy had vanished. *Looks like he doesn't want to have anything to do with me.* For once he could understand his brother although he'd probably have acted differently.

The Medjay grabbed his arms and escorted him outside. He inhaled the fresh air deeply. An eternity seemed to have passed since he'd smelled the Nile. Then he realized it might be his last time. His legs buckled. Without mercy, the men goaded him on, and he quickly recovered.

Their way led along the broad boulevard to the palace. A large crowd had gathered along the road and stared at him. A rumbling murmur wafted in the air. Not a good sign. People already condemned him although the pharaoh hadn't even heard witnesses yet. Hori appreciated that his life didn't depend on the judgment of these folks. Instead, highest royal officials attended the trial. Far too soon they reached the double gate.

The palace's interior felt strange today although he'd often been here—as a guest invited to a banquet. They took him to the large hall, which he'd last seen illuminated by torches, filled with the sounds of laughter and celebration. Today, the slaps of the Medjay's sandals echoed from the painted floor. The tall, decorated columns reminded him of silent guards. The judges sat in the gallery. Dragged in front of these men, Hori dropped onto the floor in reverence.

"Get up, Hori, son of Sobekemhat."

The disembodied voice hovered in the large room. Hori couldn't tell who'd spoken. In one lithe move, he rose and straightened, then gazed at one judge after the other. To the very left, he recognized the first prophets of Amun and Monthu. Next to them sat his father, the treasurer. The first scribe Thotnakht and the vizier flanked the pharaoh. Then came the first prophets of Horus and Ra, followed by further dignitaries Hori didn't know. Perhaps they'd traveled to the capital for the trial?

He'd seen Senusret since he became his father's successor but never close up. The ruler over the Two Lands had only lived to see nineteen floodings, barely older than himself, but deep creases were carved into his face from his nose to the corners of his mouth as if the weight of responsibility dragged them down. His lips were thin, the eyes shadowed by heavy lids. Even the outer corners of his eyes drooped slightly. Maybe he didn't get enough sleep. Hori wondered whether he too looked like that after lying awake all night.

The pharaoh's scribe rose and read the arraignment. "Hori, son of Sobekemhat, physician, you are accused of the following. On day five of month Renutet, you visited a tavern at the harbor with Neferib, son of Nebit. There you started a quarrel with Neferib, and in the course of this fight he died. Noble Nebit, father of the deceased, presses murder charges against you."

Hori had listened carefully and noticed Thotnakht distinguishing between the vizier's charges and the mere facts. Very encouraging.

Thotnakht continued. "First you shall get the chance to state your case."

All eyes fixed on Hori. His heart raced; his hands sweated. He cleared his throat. "It wasn't like I provoked noble Neferib to start a fight. Instead..." As during his first trial, he recounted the events of that fateful evening in detail while mostly seeking eye contact with the pharaoh for he was the one he needed to convince.

The ruler's face remained unreadable. Nebit, however, showed signs of agitation. Several times he looked about to interrupt, but the first prophet of falcon god Horus nudged him each time, reminding him to keep silent. Grateful for the priest's intervention, he took it as a good omen that the man was devoted to Hori's patron god.

When he ended, Thotnakht spoke up again. "Now the prosecutor, noble Nebit, Vizier of the Two Lands, may speak."

Neferib's father shot to his feet as if he'd been sitting on a thorn. "Hori is a liar!" he shouted and sprayed saliva. "He sneaked into my house like a thief at night. Because he envied my son Shepses for his success, he wanted to take revenge. So he convinced Neferib, my oldest son and close to my heart, to leave with him. He lured him away from the protection of his family home—to beat him to death. Numerous people can attest to that." After this muddled statement, he sat down again.

Hori wanted to contradict him but only managed to say, "That's a l—" Then a guard's baton struck his back. Searing pain took his breath away and cut off his speech.

"Keep silent!" Thotnakht thundered. "You have stated your case, now witnesses will be heard. First, innkeeper Khonsu may testify."

The fat man appeared taller today than back in his drinking hole. He wore a shendyt of finest linen, and his collar looked expensive, too. Khonsu had turned a wealthy man, while Hori sat in prison. As soon as the man opened his mouth, he realized what that meant.

"The night in question, this Hori here came to my tavern with two friends and the two sons of noble Nebit. At the *Golden Ibis* we serve the best beer in all of Itjtawy, and..."

"Not relevant," Thotnakht admonished. "Stick to the events leading to Neferib's death."

"Certainly, certainly. The young men had already imbibed considerable amounts of my excellent beer when the accused, this Hori fella..." He turned to point at him with a fat finger. "He'd already been drunk when he entered my place and quaffed more beer. Suddenly he jumped up and threw over tables, like drunks sometimes do. I feared for my precious furniture. You should know they are made of the finest—"

"Witness Khonsu, your tables aren't of interest to us. What happened then?"

"Certainly, certainly. Noble Neferib wanted to restrain Hori, who molested my daughter. A very young thing and the support of my old age, the apple of her mother's eye, the paragon of virtue..." Before Thotnakht had to admonish the fat man again, he caught himself. "So, when Neferib pulled back Hori, that fella clobbered him until he sank to the ground—dead."

"That's a lie!" Hori shouted, received another blow from the Medjay and gasped.

Thotnakht sent the witness away and called for Weni to enter. Hori took a breath of relief. His former classmate would speak the truth for sure.

"Weni, son of Iruwer. You are a physician, and on the evening in question you were also in the tavern *Golden Ibis*. Please tell us in your own words what happened there."

Weni briefly turned to Hori and darted him a crooked smile. Then he cleared his throat. "Hori was already drunk when we entered the tavern. He drank more jugs of beer, and at some point, he jumped up and started throwing over tables."

"Weni…" Hori gasped, shocked by his friend's lie. Had Nebit bought him as well? Of course, he must have.

"Then Hori molested the innkeeper's daughter, and Neferib tried to restrain him. Hori clobbered Neferib until he sank to the ground. Dead."

Nebit faced the king with a satisfied smile. "You see, both witnesses say the same. Hori is guilty."

Now, Sobekemhat cleared his throat. "Noble Nebit, please don't jump to conclusion before we've heard all witnesses. And yes, indeed, these two witnesses said the same—to the word almost."

Hori didn't trust his ears. His father standing up for him? Well, likely to protect his reputation.

Nebit bared his teeth and hissed, "Sobekemhat. Of course, you'd defend this murderer."

"Naturally, just like you want to see him punished. But neither you nor I decide the verdict alone."

During the exchange, Senusret had looked from one man to the other. His brow furrowed. "I will render judgment, but only after we've heard all the witnesses and I've consulted all the judges in this committee."

Hori breathed a sigh of relief.

"Doctor Nakhtmin, please enter," Thotnakht called.

The sight of his friend encouraged Hori. He'd definitely say the truth. Again, Thotnakht explained what they wanted from him.

Nakhtmin nodded and began, "Neferib asked us to leave the banquet with him. We followed him to the tavern, where we kept drinking. Hori was upset and threw over tables—" He fell silent and turned to Hori. His eyes pleaded understanding.

Hori realized Nakhtmin had been bribed as well. He swayed. If the Medjay hadn't caught him, he'd have fallen. In the ensuing silence, only the swish of Thotnakht's bulrush stylus on papyrus could be heard.

Nakhtmin faced the judges. "No, I cannot do it. I must speak the truth."

Had he misunderstood? Did he mean…?

"I'll tell you what really happened. I'm not used to so much beer and wine, so I fell asleep. I didn't see how the fight between Hori and Neferib started. I only came to when they were already wrestling. Neferib hit Hori, who pushed him back. Neferib tripped and fell. The back of his head crashed against the edge of a table in such an unfortunate way he died. It wasn't murder but an accident as far as I could see."

Hori's legs turned rubbery again, this time with joy though. "Thanks," he whispered under his breath.

A murmur passed through the ranks of judges.

Thotnakht rose. "Hotep may enter now."

Neferib's youngest brother emerged from the shadows of the columns and stood before the panel of judges. His hands kept balling into fists, then unclenching again. Sweat glistened on the youngster's bare back. Hori wondered why he was so nervous. His statement would certainly not help his case. Did he have a bad conscience because of it? As soon as Hotep started talking, he remembered.

"Th-th-this H-hori h-h-has..."

"Speak louder, Hotep, and clearer," Nebit interrupted. "Nobody can understand your stuttering."

Hotep gulped audibly. "I c-c-can n-n-n-..."

The pharaoh turned to the vizier and whispered in his ear. Nebit looked surprised but nodded and said, "The king wishes to question you. You only need to answer 'yes' or 'no'."

Hotep hung his head, and his shoulders drooped in resignation.

"Were you in the tavern *Golden Ibis* on the fifth day of month Renutet together with Hori and the doctors Nakhtmin and Weni, as well as your brother Neferib?" Pharaoh had come well prepared since he didn't need to read the names from the papyrus Thotnakht had shoved in front of him.

"Y-yes."

"Did your brother molest the girl..." Now the king quickly referred to the notes. "...Nebet-Het, daughter of innkeeper Khonsu?"

Hotep seemed uneasy. He kept glancing at his father, who slightly shook his head. "N-nn-n-no," he finally said.

Hori watched a satisfied smile curl Nebit's lips. *What a bastard! He told Hotep exactly what to say.* Apparently, the pharaoh had noticed Hotep's hesitation as well since he warned, "Young man, consider what happens to you if you give false testimony. At the Judgment of the Dead such a misdemeanor will weigh heavily against you. However, the pharaoh's court will burn your tongue with a scorching hot stick today if we catch you lying."

Hotep shrunk under the king's serious scowl. "D-don't b-b-burn!" he cried. "Y-y-yes, he d-did it."

Nebit groaned.

"Did the girl struggle against your brother Neferib's attentions?"

To Hori's relief, Hotep nodded. The threat had hit its mark, the most sensitive spot of the vizier's son. He appeared willing to speak the truth despite his father shooting him looks that promised far worse agony as soon as they returned home.

"Did Hori attack your brother without cause?"

Hotep shook his head.

"Hori claims Neferib tripped and died of injuries his fall caused. Is this true?"

Nebit hissed, "Hotep, I warn you..."

The young man squirmed and his shoulders shook. Hori guessed he cried, but the king's threat outweighed his fear of paternal rage. "Y-yes."

"We've heard all witnesses. The committee will retreat for consultations." Thotnakht's voice sounded as dry as the papyrus he rolled up.

While the mighty of the Two Lands exited the hall through a door in the back wall, Hori contemplated his chances. Who would the judges believe more? Whose statements carried more weight? Two persons testified against him, two in his favor. His legs shook, and he desperately wanted to sit. Maybe the Medjay would let him. He asked, "May I sit down?"

Shrugging his shoulders one of the men gave his consent, and Hori gratefully sank onto the cool stone.

Consultations took a long time. Hori imagined Nebit fighting for the guilty verdict he coveted. Would his father show as much fervor in his attempt to save his son's life? Had the other judges and pharaoh noticed how Nebit had influenced witnesses to give false testimony? To Hori it seemed obvious, so he thought everyone must have realized. But if the king suspected his vizier of such a crime, what consequences would that have for Nebit? He would likely lose his office. Hori swallowed. The man didn't deserve that although he'd done him wrong. Pain must have blinded him. Still… Should someone like him hold the highest office after the pharaoh?

Finally the door opened, and the judges filed back to the table. Hori jumped up immediately. They should see him standing up straight when he received judgment.

Thotnakht unrolled the papyrus and read, "Hori, son of Sobekemhat. The Great Kenbet finds you guilty of causing noble Nebit's death…"

Hori's ears rushed. Impossible! This couldn't be happening! He almost missed the rest of his sentencing.

"…not intentionally or with malicious purpose. Your majesty, King of Upper and Lower Egypt, of the Sedge and the Bee, Senusret—life, prosperity and health— therefore decided in his benevolent wisdom that you will lose your privilege as a doctor in the House of Life. Instead, you will serve in the House of Death from today on. You're not allowed to step on the shore of the living. You shall perform the holy ministrations for the dead to atone for your wrongdoing."

Hori didn't trust his ears. The *weryt*, the embalming hall! Not a death sentence but as good as. For the living he'd be dead, and for the dead he'd be living. Incredulous, he stared at the judges. Nebit and his father both looked glum. Neither of them seemed content with the verdict. Nebit would have preferred him suffering a disgraceful death followed by eternal oblivion, and Sobekemhat's dignity would only agree with an acquittal. But why should he care about the sensitivities of these two men?

He had no idea about the proceedings in the weryt. The rituals turning corpses into bodies for eternity were highly confidential. Curiosity sneaked into his horror. He'd gain unique knowledge off limits for all inhabitants of the Two Lands. But what good would that do him? He could never share his learnings with anyone. The king had ostracized him.

The real meaning of his ban slowly sank in on the way to the harbor. No matter how unwelcome he'd felt at home, he did have a family. His parents, his brothers, he'd miss them all. Even more though, he'd miss being a physician. He only wanted to cure people. Those he'd be tending to in the future were beyond all medical help.

THE WERYT

Day 20 of month Khenti-khet in Shemu, season of the harvest

A ferry already waited at the quay. In this season, with the water level at its lowest, crossing the Nile didn't take long—not long enough for Hori. Ruefully, he watched the magnificent metropolis shrink. It hurt to think he'd likely never walk the streets of Itj-tawy again, never inhale its scents once more.

The weryt had its own pier a short distance downstream of the capital. Usually the dead arrived here, but today Hori was rudely pushed onto the planks made of gnarly wood. The Medjay dragged him to the gate and pounded against it. Soon a bald man peered through the hatch in the door.

"Only the dead get access. What do you want, guards of the pharaoh?"

"We bring someone, who is dead to the living. His majesty—life, prosperity and health—sentenced this man to serve in the House of Death for the rest of his life."

The man's eyebrows arched. "Really? How unusual. Do you have the written verdict with you?"

One of the two Medjay pulled a roll of papyrus from his shendyt and handed it over. The gate guardian skimmed the lines with a speed giving away the skilled scribe.

"So be it. He may enter the hall of the dead." Releasing an eerie cackle, he pushed the hatch shut.

The gate opened, and rough hands shoved Hori through. Inside, the scent of decomposition hung heavy and sweet in the air. Fortunately, he'd grown used to the smell of festering wounds, or else he might have felt nauseous now.

"I'll take you straight to Hut-Nefer, the *mer-ut*. He doesn't like it if he isn't informed. Come to think of it, he doesn't like changes either. I'm Kheper, by the way, one of the *utu*."

"Hori. My name is Hori." Curious, he glanced around. The weryt and its staff inspired numerous myths and legends although nobody knew what was going on behind its walls. Nobody *wanted* to take a closer look. Enough to know that the bodies of the dead were prepared for eternity. The rituals and conjurations, the magic and dark forces at work here—better to stay far away. After only a few steps, they reached an expansive courtyard almost completely occupied by a pavilion made of rush mats. Only a narrow path allowed them passage. Despite the open air, the stench seemed more suffocating here. He heard trickling water and murmuring voices from behind the rush mats.

"That's the *ibu*, the place of purification," Kheper explained. When Hori darted him a questioning look, the man added, "Inside, the dead are being washed. I guess that's going to be one of your tasks."

After quite some time, they reached the other end of the courtyard and stepped into the shade of another building. By now, Hori hardly noticed the smell anymore. They walked down a corridor past several doors until Kheper stopped in front of one. Somebody had painted the word MER-UT, head of embalmers, in black ink onto the wood. His companion knocked. A few moments later, Hori found himself face to face with Hut-Nefer, his highest-ranking superior from today on.

Like Kheper's, the man's head was shaven as well. At first sight, he appeared ageless, but the moment his face became animated, a web of fine lines revealed he must have lived a few decades. Kheper explained the situation and handed over the papyrus. Hut-Nefer skimmed the content and waved Kheper away. When he fixed a strict gaze on him, Hori quickly bowed and stretched out his hands at knee level.

"Well, well. Hm, hm," the mer-ut issued. "So, you're Hori and you've been sent here to make amends for a crime you committed. The king's request is most extraordinary. When he informed me of his plans, I made the consequences for you very clear to him. You should know: who enters the weryt leaves as a mummy. The utu are born and raised here. We are trained in these halls and stay until death claims us too. Even the lector priests come from here. Our art is the most secret in the Two Lands. Only a few outsiders were allowed to learn it. Since we are procurators of the highest mysteries, we need to remain secluded lest knowledge be passed to the unworthy."

While listening to this lengthy lecture, Hori let his gaze sweep over the room with its whitewashed walls and plain furniture. Now he nodded in resignation. "I know, noble mer-ut. I can never leave the weryt. That's how the pharaoh—life, prosperity and health—ruled in his wisdom and benevolence."

"Well, I wonder, though, why you stand here in front of me, Hori, instead of breaking your back in a quarry like other criminals do. Naturally I'm also concerned for the safety of my people with a criminal among us."

Hori felt like Hut-Nefer's penetrating gaze reached to the bottom of his heart, while he recounted how the accident happened.

The old man clicked his tongue. "You're a physician? You can read and write? And we're supposed to use you as a servant..." Thoughtfully, he placed his chin in his hands. "We'll see. Kheper will show you your quarters."

Hori took a deep breath. The mer-ut seemed less strict than he'd feared. He must have managed to convince him he wasn't a bad person. On stiff legs he left the room and stepped into the corridor. The mer-ut called for Kheper but didn't keep him for long. When the bald embalmer returned, he led Hori away.

Behind another door lay an even larger courtyard than the one with the purification tent. Here the houses of the utu, the embalmers, and their families stood squeezed together. The whole setup reminded Hori of a small town behind walls without exits. No gate led to the river, and he wondered how the inhabitants obtained water. Likely they had a well somewhere.

Kheper pointed out some larger houses with small gardens further away from the others. "The head of the embalmers lives there, and the *heriu-heb*, the lector priests. You're lucky one of the smaller houses isn't occupied. Doesn't happen often. The owner recently died and left no sons, who could claim it. His only daughter lives in her husband's house."

Hori felt blessed indeed. He'd expected to share communal housing with other servants. He stumbled after Kheper, crossing streets and rounding corners, and soon lost orientation. The walls surrounding the weryt blocked his view at landmarks that might give him a sense of direction. So it felt like they'd walked much farther than they probably had until they reached a square. Small children played in the dust. Hori's eyes widened. They actually played funeral procession! This truly was a different world.

Here, he also spotted the *shadoof* with a large pole—weight on one end, rope and bucket on the other—balanced on a crossbeam. Work seemed to be over for the day. From all directions men and women hurried toward the square. Many headed for a larger building.

"What's happening there? Is that a meeting place?" Hori asked.

"That's our *ibu*," Kheper explained. Judging by his grin, he'd cracked a popular joke among embalmers. In response to Hori's questioning look, he added, "After work we need to wash off any residue of the dead. Just as important is shaving all the hair on our bodies every day, because evil spirits might take hold on them otherwise. You'll be able to give your wig a break. Only when we're thoroughly cleaned do we enter our houses."

Hori nodded. "Cleanliness is important. Physicians also need to take care. The demons of diseases hide in dirt."

"You're a doctor?" Kheper darted him a puzzled glance.

"No, not anymore," Hori replied. "From today on, I'm only the lowliest servant in the weryt."

Kheper winked at him. "What happens in the weryt, stays in the weryt. Even the pharaoh—life, prosperity and health—knows nothing about it. Your knowledge might come in handy since we don't have a physician here."

Hori laughed. Maybe life behind these walls wouldn't be as bad as he'd feared. "What do you do when one of you falls sick or gets injured?"

"Of course we have priests here. They know their incantations."

While Hori had respect for magical amulets, magic alone rarely cured the ailing in his experience. He furrowed his brow.

"And some of our women are well versed in the use of medicinal plants," Kheper added. "We get along. Still, to have a doctor within our walls… Ah, there we are. This is your house."

Like most buildings in Kemet, his new home was built of adobe. In the utu's settlement, where space was limited, they'd even erected two-story houses. On the ground floor weren't the usual airing slits in the walls. Probably because no breeze could enter anyway, but the smell of decay would penetrate. Only the top floor, closer to the rim of the surrounding wall, had some. As common, a ladder allowed access to the roof, where people slept, cooked and ate for the major part of the year.

He followed Kheper through the low door into the almost pitch-dark interior of the ground floor. Gradually, he recognized jars and boxes holding provisions. One of the jugs seemed to contain beer. A privy had been built into another corner. Back home servants emptied the low buckets filled halfway with sand. Here he wouldn't enjoy such luxury. "Where do I get rid of the refuse?" he asked Kheper.

"Glad you're asking, because that would have been one of your tasks if the merut hadn't decided to make better use of your talents. Excrement and rubbish are collected at the square in large baskets. Once a day they are laden on donkeys. Servants from outside the weryt receive the animals at the gate and lead them to a pit in the desert where the waste is disposed of, like everywhere else."

"Ah." Hori certainly appreciated using his skills in other areas. In these halls, plenty of stinking dirt would accumulate. Not a task he'd have enjoyed.

He climbed up the ladder through a hatchway to the upper floor. Here he found a cot and chest for clothing, but he climbed higher to the roof, wondering if he'd see the Nile from up there—or at least the skyline of the capital. Everything was so foreign to him, he'd soon long for freedom. "Do you never feel the urge to get out of here?" he asked.

Kheper stuck his head through the hatch, looking puzzled. "Here's my life, my family, my home. Why should anyone want to leave the weryt? We have everything, suffer no want—unlike many other people in Kemet, because the pharaoh generously caters to us."

Hori rose onto his toes and craned his neck, but beyond the wall he could only see the red mountains of the western desert or the endless blue sky. Thick black smoke rose from one building of the embalming workshop. What did they burn there? "But there's so much to discover beyond these walls. Were you never curious?"

Kheper settled onto the rush mat spread in the shadow of an awning. "Sure, when I was much younger. But we children of the weryt know exactly what we need to preserve and protect. What's in the weryt, stays in the weryt. Nobody can leave because the secrets need to be kept here."

Hori sighed. If only he could content himself with such a drab outlook on life.

The next morning Hori woke with stiff muscles. At home he'd slept on a thick sack of straw, and even the prison cot had been softer. The rush mat on the hard stone roof offered little comfort. The bed in the second floor promised more snugness, but it was far too hot this time of the year to sleep inside. In this walled village no breeze came through the north-facing window slits. The headrest hadn't fit with his body either, so he'd been lying awake for long hours, staring into the night sky. At least some luxury. He could have easily faced far worse a punishment—without the freedom to pick his sleeping place.

Why did the king devise such an unusual verdict? To satisfy both his highest officials equally? How much hassle would it have been to find a new vizier? Nebit had bribed the witnesses—the innkeeper Khonsu, his friends Weni and Nakhtmin, as well as Hotep. Hori ground his teeth even now. It had been so blatant that the pharaoh couldn't possibly still trust the second most powerful man in the Two Lands. Nebit had already been his father's vizier. Maybe reasons unknown to Hori had played a role in his leniency. Possibly Senusret couldn't afford to remove the man from his staff because he knew some secrets. He rolled onto the other side.

Senusret was still young but ruler of the Two Lands. He had nothing to fear except divine judgment. Hadn't he threatened to burn Hotep's tongue with a scorching poker?

Weni's betrayal rankled. What had Nebit offered the young doctor to make him lie to the judges and risk eternal life? With Nakhtmin it was far easier to guess. His friend hardly had enough to live, not to mention buying a place suitable for a physician. During his studies in the House of Life he'd at least enjoyed free accommodation, but now he'd likely have to return to his native Khent-min if he couldn't gather some wealth quickly. Still, Hori felt deeply disappointed by the boy from Upper Egypt even though he came around to saying the truth pretty fast. Nebit must have baited him with an excellent offer. Hopefully, the almost-traitor would get in serious trouble with Nebit. Only fair!

As far as Hori could tell, the pharaoh did notice some witnesses had lied. Nevertheless he avoided a clear statement as to which party he believed. If he'd acquitted Hori—as would have been common in the case of an accident—he'd have alienated Nebit by openly showing he didn't trust his vizier. How would his father have reacted if the sentence had been lifelong labor in the quarries? Hori wanted to think he'd have protested and thrown his full weight into the argument. Now, the treasurer's son was one of the utu instead of a murderer.

Not even the verdict was clear. How did they phrase it? Guilty of causing Neferib's death, but not intentionally or with malicious purpose. The king knew a death sentence would have offended Maat, Hori told himself. He'd recognized his innocence. The thought stirred hope. Maybe someday he'd leave these walls behind. But why had the pharaoh chosen this particular punishment? That moment he remembered his oath to dedicate his life to the goddess Maat if he survived. He snorted a laugh. Pondering the question if such an existence could be called life, he rose to face the new day.

Hori had barely finished his meager breakfast of grain porridge and beer when a knock sounded on his door. Kheper picked him up and took him to the ibu.

"First, you'll learn how to wash the deceased. I'll show you today. The mer-ut said to reveal all secrets to you as if you were born in the weryt." He lifted the rush mat covering the tent's entrance.

Large parts of the interior still lay in the shadows of the surrounding wall. In the twilight, Hori saw a long, very broad corridor with a narrow water canal running along its center. The tent's ceiling of coarsely woven linen allowed some light and air to penetrate but protected against direct sun, so it remained pleasantly cool inside. There had to be a clever airing system too since a constant breeze blew around his legs. Left and right of the center aisle, mats separated individual chambers with stone tables. Kheper led him into one of them.

"The deceased are placed on these tables to be washed. See, they are slightly tilted so the liquid can drain."

"You mean the water used for washing?"

"That—and all bodily fluids."

"Oh," Hori said. He hadn't known that a body oozed fluids after death, but then dead animals were also drained of blood. He circled the table and noticed another canal at the lower end, which pointed away from the corridor.

Kheper must have been watching him since he said, "Yes, that's the sewer. The water for cleansing has to be pure though. You'll fetch that from the canal in the center aisle. All demons and dirt need to be washed off the dead to prepare them for their journey into eternity."

"Where do you get the water from?"

"From the divine Nile. We branched off the channel." Kheper picked up two jugs leaning against the table and handed them to Hori. "Here, fill these. In a moment, we'll get the first deceased."

As if on cue, men carrying bodies covered in linen entered the tent and laid them into the various chambers.

Staggering under the water's weight, Hori returned to his chamber to find a body on their table as well. Kheper pulled back the linen. Hori sucked in air. A young woman barely older than himself and so beautiful! Still, she lay here, the thread of life chopped before it could be woven into colorful fabric. "What could have caused her death?" he stammered.

Kheper unveiled the rest of the body and showed Hori a ribbon with an ivory label on the girl's wrist. "Merit-Neith," he read. "Daughter of Tutu."

"Tutu is an official at the king's harem," Hori blurted. "I know her! That is...I knew her. How awful." He recalled the jaunty young woman flirting with the young courtiers at the last royal banquet. With him too and...Shepses. Without learning her name, he wouldn't have recognized her. "Death has changed her features so much," he said.

"Only the breath of life makes us human. Now you've discovered one of the secrets we harbor here. For the dead to live on in the hereafter, life needs to be breathed into them again. Unfortunately, many of those brought to us have died too young. The gods don't distinguish between young and old, high or lowly, beautiful or ugly." Kheper sighed. "They take us whenever they like. You'll get used to that. I'll leave you alone with young Merit-Neith now, but don't you get any ideas!"

"What do you mean, ideas?"

Kheper giggled. "Some young deceased still have enough allure for one or the other utu. It has happened..."

Understanding the hint, Hori grimaced. "Don't worry. I'll treat Merit-Neith with respect. By the time you return, she'll be cleansed and free of bodily fluids—hers and mine."

Cackling, Kheper sauntered off.

Hori studied the laid-out, naked corpse. Nothing hinted at the cause of her death. He touched the back of her skull and neck for hidden injuries no physician in the Two Lands could heal, but to no avail. Her abdomen seemed normal too, no bloating or caving in. He spotted no parasites, only something like a raw insect's sting under her left breast. As a physician he was stumped.

Carefully, he pulled the linen out from under her. Kheper hadn't exaggerated. Already excrement leaked. He wrapped it in the cloth, which he put aside. Then he set about washing her. First he removed the coarse dirt and feces, then poured water over the whole body of the young woman and washed her thoroughly with a sponge, spared no crack or crevasse. Three times he repeated the procedure until Kheper returned and handed him a bowl containing a gray, granular substance.

"That's potash. We make it ourselves in the workshops. Rub it onto the clean body to draw the remaining fluids so it won't rot." He held out a leather bag. "Put your hand in that or the potash will draw your juices too. In the future, if you need more potash, you'll find it in a large tub at the entrance."

Hori nodded. "And when I'm done, do I need to do something else with the girl's corpse?"

"No, you'll signal to the embalmer at the potash barrel. The cleansed body will be taken away and the next one brought to you."

Again Hori took extra care with Merit-Neith. Not only was she the first dead he'd treated, he'd known her and wanted to exercise painstaking diligence with her. Finally he signaled and the body was carried away. His next corpse was a man in his prime, who'd obviously died of an injury. Seeing how poorly the compound fracture had been set, Hori wrinkled his nose. This man's doctor had been a botcher, or the dead had meant to save the expenses and asked a relative to take care of it. Although patients were treated in the House of Life even if they couldn't afford a gift in return, Hori knew many were too proud to ask for free treatment.

He washed two more corpses before the day's work ended. Together with Kheper and other utu, he headed toward the cleansing hall for the living, where he scrubbed off dirt and stench. Everything was well organized. Large baskets contained clean desert sand to rub over their bodies. In another room, they could wash with fresh, clean Nile water, channeled into the tent via another canal. The wastewater flowed gurgling into a hole in the ground.

Hori felt the strain of hard, physical work and was very hungry. If only he could sit down at his parents' table now and savor a warm roast. Instead, only the same porridge of grain he had for breakfast awaited him, with onions and beans mixed in. To his surprise and joy, he found fresh bread wrapped in linen cloth, fish and a bowl of dates in his pantry. Did he have Kheper to thank for that? While the fish cooked over the small fireplace on the roof, he devoured the bread and washed it down with a jug of beer. Tired as he was, he didn't bother to sieve the barley brew and simply swallowed some of the grains. That night he had no trouble falling asleep and quickly found himself in a dream.

Sounds and colors swirled around him. He spun to the beat of music in the large hall of the palace. Behind a column stood Merit-Neith, and she waved at him. Laughing, he pulled her into his arms and danced with her. Boisterous steps took them into the garden, where a heavy odor hung in the air. It was very humid, and Merit-Neith undressed. He too stripped off his shendyt. Her laughter lured him to a lake. They frolicked in the cold water.

"I'm very clean now," she said and smiled seductively.

He pulled her into his arms and kissed her but her lips were cold and waxen. His erection throbbed and he spread her thighs. Again and again, he thrust into her until he realized she lay lifeless in his arms. Had he killed her?

The Medjay stormed into the garden and dragged him away.

Covered in sweat, he jerked awake. A cool breeze drifted over him and left him shivering despite the warmth. He'd ejaculated in his sleep. Did that mean he'd defiled a dead woman? Heat burned in his face and Kheper's cackle echoed in his ears. But the main question remained unanswered: How did Merit-Neith die?

NEBIT'S VENGEANCE

Day 21 of month Khenti-khet in Shemu, season of the harvest

Inpu held Nakhtmin back. "Not so fast. Today you'll treat the patients in the yard."

Puzzled, Nakhtmin thought it wasn't his turn to serve the poor, but he simply shrugged. "As you wish." Maybe one of his colleagues had fallen sick.

The head of the House of Life gestured his regret. "You've made powerful enemies. I've been instructed to only let you work in the yard from now on."

"What? But...how am I supposed to make a living?" Nakhtmin was flabbergasted. Usually, two doctors of the House of Life took care of the ailing poor—always different ones to guarantee everyone had to take on this unprofitable assignment in regular intervals. The meager gifts offered by these patients could barely feed a doctor, not to mention saving a little something. Nakhtmin caught a glimpse of Imhotepankh strolling past. The aged head of doctors looked rather complacent. Then everything fell into place. Shepses had always been the old man's favorite. Nebit's son had obviously passed on his father's chagrin over Nakhtmin withdrawing his false testimony.

He grimaced in disgust. How stupid of him to believe he could get away with such a thing unscathed. People who bribed witnesses certainly had no qualms when it came to asserting themselves. All right, Nebit had his revenge, and Nakhtmin would be able to deal with it. The punishment couldn't last forever.

He found it hard to concentrate on his work though. Today's colleague in the yard kept darting him curious glances but avoided him. Likely word had gotten around that he'd fallen from grace. The other doctors, usually keen to chat, evaded him as if he carried a contagious disease.

Damn Hori! Why did his friend have to mess with the vizier? By now he regretted not having told the requested lie. He could be ten deben richer and pick a beautiful house. Instead he'd have to go home to the bleak neighborhood, where his hut stood, for much longer.

With an awkward smile, his last patient of the day put a bunch of dried dates in his hand. Nakhtmin thanked him. At least he wouldn't have to go to bed hungry. Then he headed home.

It was dark inside his hut, so he didn't see the three men awaiting him before it was too late. Two held him, while the third battered him without mercy. A fist hit his nose. The piercing pain made Nakhtmin's eyes water. He yelled for help, but nobody came. The area teemed with scoundrels; people were used to it. Nakhtmin struggled free from the hands gripping him and pulled his arms up to protect his face. Bad mistake. A punch to his stomach winded him. He doubled over and sank to the ground, where kicking feet lashed out at him. A particularly hard one to his side made him scream in pain. Did they mean to beat him to death? Then please hurry up!

After another blow, his tormentor hissed in Nakhtmin's ear, "Remember what happens to those who defy the vizier. Don't you dare file charges for this or the other matter."

Nebit's henchmen, Nakhtmin thought. The vizier really hated thoroughly.

Finally the men let go of him and disappeared out the door. They didn't even bother to close it after them. Groaning, Nakhtmin remained on the floor and explored the various sources of pain. No ribs seemed broken. At least something. In the last light of day he saw the dates scattered and trampled on the floor. No matter, he didn't feel hungry anymore.

AN INCREDIBLE DISCOVERY

Hori's days grew long since he had little to think about while working. The dead from wealthy families were not only washed at their arrival but a second time after the embalmers had removed the inner organs. Then Hori had to remove the traces at the abdominal cut on the side. The head also had to be attended to because often a slimy substance stuck to the nostrils. Poorer folks couldn't afford such an elaborate treatment. They headed directly for the natron chamber after the first purification, where the rich were also taken after the second washing. All corpses remained there for forty days. Afterward they returned to the ibu for a last clean-up. Hori had to remove the remains of salt from the natron-parched skins of the bodies.

On the morning of the fifteenth day since Hori had entered the weryt, Kheper thought the time had come to instruct him on the next steps in the secret procedure of mummification. He led him to another small yard in which several stone tables stood. Servants in teams of two carried fresh, washed bodies to the tables and laid them down.

"Here we remove the inner organs," Kheper explained.

"What for?"

"Often putrescence sprouts in the entrails. Drying with natron can't draw all the moisture from the bodies. If there are juices left in the entrails, these can alter and destroy the mummy. Therefore we treat the organs separately and entomb them in special containers with the dead since they'll need them in the afterlife, of course. Naturally, we attend to the hearts with the utmost diligence."

"For the Judgment of the Dead," Hori blurted.

Kheper nodded. "Exactly. How else should the hearts of the deceased be weighed against the feather of Maat if they don't have one anymore?"

Hori thought of all the people who couldn't afford this expensive procedure. "What happens to those people, whose mummies rot because their organs weren't removed? Will the devourer open her jaws for them?" He shuddered.

Kheper flashed a sly grin. "No worries, that's what heart scarabs are for. Pretty much anyone can afford those."

"Heart scarabs?" Hori echoed.

"Oh, you know the dung beetle, after which I'm named, is the holy symbol for rebirth because it creates itself from dust."

Hori nodded.

"That's why it represents the human heart. In our workshops, we produce small figurines of the beetle, some made of precious stones, some of clay. On the bottom, the following words are engraved: 'O my heart that I received from my mother, my heart that I have had since birth, my heart that was with me through all the stages of my life, do not stand up against me as a witness! Do not oppose me at the tribunal! Do not tip the scales against me in the presence of the Keeper of the Balance! You are the *ka* of my body, you are the creator god Khnum who makes my limbs sound. Go forth to the Hereafter...'

"So even if the body should be destroyed, the deceased can still pass the Judgment of the Dead. Of course only if he or she lies in a properly equipped and inscribed grave."

"How clever!" Hori cried. "And the Gods can be tricked that way?"

Kheper cackled. "Some people don't even want their hearts to be entombed with them but request a heart scarab to be placed in their chest."

"Because they think the burden of their evil deeds will never let them pass the weighing of their hearts?"

"Why else? I'd rather live as an honest man, though, not harming anyone, and then I don't have to fear the Judgment of the Dead."

Hori wanted to agree, but then he remembered why he was here and swallowed all comments.

"All right, enough chitchat. Today, we'll work on this man here." He turned toward one of the tables and fumbled a leather bundle from his shendyt before he spread it on the stone surface.

Hori recognized several instruments wrapped in the leather. Some looked just like the ones he'd used as a doctor, others vaguely resembled medical tools, but Hori had no clue what purpose they served. There were bronze hooks of varying lengths and curves, tweezers, something that looked like a mason's scoop, only smaller, and a knife with an obsidian blade. To his surprise, he saw a leaden needle among Kheper's implements as well as a kind of spoon and an awl-like tool. Kheper bent to lift a fist-size stone from a cavity under the tabletop.

"First we need to remove the gray matter from the skull," Kheper explained. "That's the only difficult thing since the face of the deceased must not be disfigured. So, pay close attention."

Hori watched as Kheper inserted the awl into a nostril. "Now I've hit an obstruction. Here, feel for yourself."

Hori took the end of the awl and probed around inside the nose. Yes, there seemed to be a bone in the way.

"We've got to break through." Kheper grabbed the awl and slammed the stone hard and with good aim on the tool's end, producing a crunching noise. He did the same with the other nostril. "In a moment, we'll have access to the gray substance. It's surrounded by a tough skin, which I have to cut with the knife first."

Hori handed him the thin blade. Now he understood why the stone knife wasn't any broader. It needed to fit into the nose without harming the facial tissue.

For a while Kheper labored with a concentrated expression on his face, then he announced, "Done!"

Hori took the knife from him. "And now?"

"Hand me the hook with the spiral end, please. Yes, that's the one. I'll shove it up the nose and all the way into the gray matter. Here, try for yourself."

Hori took over and moved the tool around. "Feels like mash," he said.

"You must stir the mash until there are no more lumps in it. It's strenuous work, and you have to mind the dead man's nose. And don't forget to scrape off everything sticking to the skull bones. I'll leave you to it now and get started on the next corpse. Same procedure. I'll be back later. By then you should have finished, too."

Hori nodded and continued with his assignment. The mass was quite tough in places, and soon he broke into a sweat. Finally, Kheper returned and relieved him.

"In the summer heat, the mush will quickly liquefy and seep from the nose as soon as we turn the body around. But first we'll remove the organs from the visceral cavity. Get us five of the jugs stacked against the wall over there. Take care, they are heavy. Only carry one at a time."

Hori set to work and when all five jugs lined the table, he asked, "What's the white powder in them?"

"Oh," Kheper replied, "that's natron, our magic salt. It draws moisture from the corpse, like the potash you rubbed on the bodies after washing them." He lifted an arm, and a lector priest stepped from the shadows of a doorway.

"While cutting the abdomen, prayers and evocations need to be spoken, and that's what the heriu-heb are here for."

He grabbed the knife, and the *heri-heb* immediately began to drone words that held little meaning for Hori, likely spells in the ancient language.

"Pay attention, Hori. See where I place the knife? We cut along the left side. Do you feel the last rib?"

Dutifully, Hori touched the bone though he knew its exact position.

"One has to place the blade two fingers' width under the costal arch and cut two hands' width down." Kheper cut in one smooth move then put the knife aside. His hand slipped into the opening. "Intestines first."

Hori's eyes widened as he watched cubit after cubit of entwined intestine spill from the wound. At last, Kheper pulled out his arm.

"The bowel is fixed in two spots, the stomach on one end, and the anus on the other. We need to sever the connection, but first you feel around the secrets of the body. Your hands must be your eyes. Tell me what you notice."

Hori swallowed. As a doctor he'd often wished to be able to see under the skin to better recognize a disease. Today, he got the chance for the very first time. Slowly and carefully, he felt around the already fairly empty cavity, cold and slimy to his touch. The organs weren't soft and yielding but hard and unwieldy. He oriented himself along both ends of the bowel, still hanging from the cut, used them like a rope to guide him. He felt the spot where the intestine widened to a bag—had to be the stomach. "I found the transition from stomach to bowel," he called.

"Good. Before we cut, we need to knot both ends with a sinew."

"Why?"

"The intestines hold excrement. If we'd simply cut it loose, feces would spill into the cavity. The stomach bag also needs to be tied in the same fashion. Likely it still holds the last meal of the man."

"Oh, right." Of course Hori should have known that. "But I'll need both hands for that. How else to make a knot?"

Kheper clicked his tongue. "No way can we make such a long cut. You'll need to learn tying with one hand. I'll show you how. Look." With nimble fingers, he wound a sinew around a part of the intestine, using only his right hand, and formed a simple knot. "The most difficult part is getting it tight. Needs the most practice. Try it, while I prepare our friend here."

Hori managed the one-handed knot but to pull tight, he needed his left. He considered the problem. If the sinew were long enough, he could keep the one end dangling from the cut and pull with his other hand if necessary. Yes, that should work. "All right, let me make a stab at it," he said.

Kheper darted him a surprised glance. "You think you can do it? Well, you can take care of the anus."

43

Once again Hori slid his hand into the abdomen while holding the end of a long sinew between his fingers, feeling his way to the right spot. Without eyesight in the cramped, slick environment, the task turned out far more challenging than before, but after some fumbling he succeeded. After pulling tight the first knot, he tied a second one. "Done."

Kheper lifted his eyebrows, looking rather doubtful. After he'd checked up on Hori's work, he nodded his appreciation. "Not bad, my boy. I'll let you make the cuts then. Take care to chop right between the two bindings. Start at the stomach."

Removing the rest of the organs proved much easier. Soon intestine, stomach, lungs, liver and heart lay each in a different jug, covered in natron.

"We'll keep them in those for forty days, just as long as the bodies stay in the natron chamber." From the space under the table Kheper fetched small tablets hanging on a piece of sinew as well as ink stone, rush and a small water jug. "On these slabs, please note the name of the dead together with the symbols for heart, lung and so on. We want him to have his own organs in the afterlife, not someone else's, don't we?"

The heri-heb's work was also done. The murmured prayers ceased, and the priest retreated to the shadows. While Hori wrote, Kheper fetched a shallow bowl and placed it on the table. Then he took the plaques and fixed them to the necks of the jars before plugging them.

"Now you can help me turn the body around. Later you'll have to manage on your own. It's not that hard. Just make sure the face remains over the bowl because the gray matter will start running from the nose as soon as we turn the head."

"And it'll also be placed in natron?" Hori guessed.

Kheper laughed. "No, why should we do that? It's not a vital organ a human being might need. Now it's turned to mush anyway. We don't have running water here to clean the tables so we better catch the slime."

Hori marveled at the amount of liquid pouring from the man's nose. When the flow stopped, Kheper used a long hook to pull a large skin flap through one nostril. "This is the skin that envelopes the gray stuff. Removing that is very important."

Hori nodded, and Kheper lifted a funnel from under the table. "Now we need to rinse the skull and afterward pour in anointing oil. Please empty the bowl and bring it back. Over there you'll also find jars with oil and water. Bring one of each."

Carefully balancing the shallow bowl, Hori crossed the yard and dodged other utu also removing organs from bodies. When he returned with the things Kheper had requested, he watched intently as the older man rolled the dead man on his back again and inserted the nozzle in one of the nostrils. Together they lifted the jug and poured water into the funnel until it spilled out the other nostril. Then he turned the body onto its side and let the water flow into the bowl, together with the last remains of gray mush. After rolling the man over again, they poured anointment oil into the skull.

"The oil remains in the head to protect it from decomposition." He inserted linen wads into both nostrils to keep the oil in.

Hori remembered that vegetables were preserved in oil.

Kheper gestured and some servants approached. Two men lifted the prepared corpse onto a stretcher and carried him off—to the second washing, as Hori knew. The others hauled the jugs away.

With all these interesting new things going on, time flew. When Hori looked around, the shadows had already grown long.

The following days he assisted Kheper removing organs until the old man said, "You're ready to prepare your first body on your own."

Hori beamed. This treatment of the corpses fascinated him most, and his probing hands had already made interesting discoveries that spoke to the doctor in him. The organs were connected via vessels, and each body seemed to be a giant circuit. In some bodies, he'd noticed organ alterations. An ulcer had eaten a hole in one stomach bag, and food had dripped into the visceral cavity—certainly the cause of the man's death. Though he would have been powerless to save him as a doctor, such knowledge might help find cures in the future. Every evening in the solitude of his house, he took notes of his discoveries on shards of clay, which he tended to collect. If only he could share his findings with other doctors! Although he'd settled in quite well here, the closed borders of the weryt were still hard to accept.

One day the body of another young woman ended up on his table. She reminded him of Merit-Neith. Potash had already made her face look hollow, so he checked the name slab. Hetepet, daughter of Ameny. He staggered back. Oh no, not Hetepet! Not long ago, he'd seen her pick up her father at the temple of Amun.

Ameny was the second prophet of Amun and therefore responsible for the organization of the House of Life within the large temple compound. Hetepet had smiled at Hori. A whole life seemed to have passed between then and now, hers and his. Gently, he stroked her forehead. For the first time, his hands trembled as he put the awl in place. How strange that two young women from noble families had died in such a short time. Was an incurable disease spreading in Itj-tawy? No, the utu would certainly have noticed, and not only girls would fall prey to it. But young adults didn't just die without apparent cause! He'd scrutinize Hetepet's organs.

Finally, time to perform the abdominal cut had come. Intestines and stomach looked the way they should. Then he removed the heart and found what he'd been looking for. Congealed blood surrounded the firm muscle tissue as if the heart had been injured. He fetched a water jug and washed off the brownish lumps. Now he could discern a puncture where the flesh was raised and discolored, like in the case of an infection. Very odd. After an injury, such sickness demons usually didn't appear straight away. Where did the puncture come from? He put the heart aside and examined the girl's skin. At first, he didn't see anything, but when he pushed the left breast up a little, he discovered a purple bruise right in the fold. It almost looked like a blossom with a hole in its center. Hori gasped. Hetepet must have been murdered! How? What blade barely left any trace?

No, that's impossible! There's no such weapon. Such a thin knife would break. He'd hardly finished the thought when he started to feel around the wound. Maybe a piece of the blade still stuck in it. No matter how much he pressed, though, inside or out, he found nothing. His gaze wandered to his tools. If he straightened one of the hooks, shaped it like a doctor's puncture needle, he could check if the wound really reached deep enough to injure the heart. He wielded the hammer stone and quickly flattened the curve of a rarely needed hook. With quivering fingers, he inserted the needle in the center of the blossom. It slid through the ribs without resistance. Reaching into the cavity, he touched the needle tip right where the heart

45

used to be. His own heart hammered.

At the table next to him, Kheper bent over another corpse. Hori opened his mouth to call his instructor. Just in time he realized such a revelation would stir anger rather than interest. Not only had he damaged an expensive tool but also injured a dead body in a spot where he wasn't supposed to. Would Kheper believe it wasn't him who'd stabbed the girl with the needle? If he told him about his discovery, he risked being dragged before Hut-Nefer, the mer-ut.

Hori had to thank the head of embalmers' foresight or else he'd be hauling around stinking garbage instead of learning the far more interesting tasks of the embalmers. Just as easily, he could take away the privilege any time. Hori didn't know Hut-Nefer well enough to anticipate how the old man might react. He needed time to think about it, which he didn't have right now. If only he could take a look inside the heart and search for clues, but that was unthinkable. He'd destroy Hetepet's prospects of an afterlife.

Fortunately, he'd already finished work in the visceral cavity because his hands were trembling again. With quite some effort he managed to lift one jug after the other over the funnel and was glad to finish his day's work, though as one of the last men in the yard.

Since Kheper had already left, he was able to walk to the cleansing hall in silence. When he entered his house, he was still weighing his options in his heart. Should he tell Kheper about his suspicions? During his meal a thought struck him. What if Merit-Neith died the same way? What if she too was murdered? The insect bite on her breast might have been a stab wound!

He shuddered. That would imply the same man had killed both girls. Maybe he'd kill again. He might have killed before and more than once! How daring to pick the noblest young ladies as victims, daughters of the pharaoh's official and the Gods' prophet. Hori leaned back and stared unseeing into the sky. If he kept his discovery a secret, all further victims of the killer would also weigh down his heart. He had to tell someone! Would the inhabitants of the weryt take him seriously? Who else could he turn to? Walls barred his way to the outside world. He swore to himself he'd inform Kheper tomorrow. Then it would be his responsibility. However, he fell asleep with the troubling feeling he was taking the easy route.

In the middle of the night, he jerked awake and sensed a stranger's presence on the roof. The moon shone on a tall figure approaching him: a woman wearing a feather on her head. Tears streamed down her face.

"Maat!" he called.

Without a word, she turned away and climbed down the ladder. Why did the goddess come to him? What did she want? This wasn't a dream, but Hori felt dazed. He followed the slender apparition out of the house, then through deserted alleys of the settlement. Finally, they reached the part of the wall, where the canal flowed through and to the washing house. The goddess stepped into the water and beckoned him. A smile played around her lips, so beautiful—that moment Hori would do anything for her. Then she plunged into the current and dove under the wall. Hori stood with dangling arms.

When he woke the next morning, he remembered the events of the night so clearly he couldn't have dreamed them. The goddess of a just world order had sent him a vision. The scales of justice had to be off kilter! Whether his own verdict or

46

Hetepet's death had caused the imbalance, he couldn't tell. Maybe both. Either way, the goddess had shown him the way to escape his prison. He only had to brave it.

His ears rushed. If caught outside the weryt, he couldn't expect any further leniency nor hope for the stone quarries. He didn't even want to imagine how someone betraying the weryt might be punished. Hut-Nefer and Kheper had treated him well, made the best of the pharaoh's sentence. His sacrilege would be a bitter disappointment for them. Surely his body wouldn't receive the honor of mummification. He wouldn't be granted a grave as his house for eternity.

Would the goddess understand if he was brought to her as a failure that couldn't carry out her divine order? Fear of the Judgment of the Dead choked Hori. Disregarding the goddess's wish would be even worse. Then nothing could save him when he approached the divine judge someday. Anubis would feed his heart to the devourer. Hori groaned.

BEYOND THE WALL

Day 30 of month Ipet-hemet in Shemu, season of the harvest.

All day Hori's thoughts circled around one question: Could he really escape the weryt the way the goddess had shown him? Swimming and diving he'd learned as a child, but he wasn't sure if he could hold his breath long enough to reach the other side of the wall. Fortunately, it wasn't very thick, though, and should be manageable even against the current. But if he were caught… Maybe guards patrolled along the wall. He knew too little about life here and didn't dare ask Kheper about security measures, fearing he might raise suspicions. Hori had discarded the idea of confiding in him after the goddess clearly lined out the way for him. Tonight he'd make his first attempt.

Mechanically, his hands performed the already familiar tasks, while he mulled over what lay ahead. He flinched when Kheper suddenly appeared next to him and said, "Tomorrow I'll teach you the next step of our process, anointing the dead after natron treatment."

Tomorrow I may be floating belly up in the canal if I fail. Hori imagined Kheper performing all the services for the dead on his body. If he succeeded, he'd be free though. He forced a smile. "I'm looking forward to it. Hey, what happens when I've finished my training? Will I get one task assigned and keep at it, or does the mer-ut schedule people for varying jobs?"

"Since only the mer-ut keeps track of how many dead need which kind of treatment, he plans the work and assigns it accordingly." Kheper moved on to fetch a bowl, and Hori turned back to his body.

Would he really enjoy freedom outside the walls? He could go away, leave Itjtawy and move to some city where nobody knew him. He'd hardly finished the thought when the goddess's face popped up before him, crying. No, he couldn't run away, he had to find out who murdered Hetepet. That much he owed both of them. To do so, he had to go against the pharaoh's verdict, which also offended Maat. Hori sighed. He'd have to secretly investigate at night when everyone slept and return to the weryt at dawn. How could he possibly manage that? While everybody slept, he wouldn't find out much. He couldn't show his face. If someone recognized him, he'd return to the weryt as a dead man. He needed a better plan.

Nevertheless he'd try diving under the wall tonight. Maybe the goddess would appear once more and show him the next step.

Since he usually slept like a log, Hori had to stay awake while waiting for the inhabitants of the weryt to go to bed. With stealth, he sneaked along the paths he'd walked in the wake of the goddess last night. He'd decided to go naked since a bundle of clothes at the canal might raise suspicion in case someone roamed the streets this late. He cursed himself for not checking out the area this side of the wall in daylight to find a hiding place. Nothing he could do about that now. He'd only do reconnaissance, see if there were guards patrolling.

Silently, he slid into the waters of the canal. It only reached up to his crotch, just deep enough to swim. After a few strokes he reached the opening in the wall. His heart raced, so he waited a while to calm down before he dared diving. The water surged around his head as he felt for the tunnel walls and pushed forward. Only three strokes under water and he was through.

Had other weryt folk used this escape route before him? But unlike other children living at the riverbank the kids here probably never learned to swim. How could they? The canal was far too short. Apart from that, they were used to living and dying in their own narrow world. They'd have little reason to find a way out.

With caution, he peeked over the canal wall. The almost full moon provided enough light for him to see pretty far along the flat sandy stretch of the riverbank. No sign of guards. He climbed out of the water. The night air was so warm his skin had almost dried after the first few steps. Since he'd come this far, he might as well look for a way to cross the river. After all, not only the walls of the weryt separated him from the world of the living. Although the Nile's waters were fairly low this time of the year, he didn't dare swim to the other side. The current was treacherous, and besides hippos, crocodiles lurked under the surface.

Soon he reached the river. To his right, the weryt's pier protruded into the mud. It was deserted, no watercraft tied to it. Of course nobody left a boat here. Where would they go? The west, being the realm of death, belonged to jackals and scorpions. Every fisherman and every ferryman brought his boat to the eastern bank for the night. Stumped, Hori turned left. He'd rather not get close to the gates of the weryt in case they had a night watch on duty. He hadn't walked far when he spotted a palm tree half fallen into the water. All kinds of driftwood had caught in its branches. With some luck he might find a trunk he could use as a simple raft. That wouldn't protect him against a hungry crocodile but he'd have to take the risk.

To his joy he even found a partly disintegrated papyrus dinghy, either abandoned or adrift and stranded here. *Great!* Hori pulled and dragged until he managed to get the small boat out of the water. The back was frayed as if a hippo had taken a bite, but the bundles of reed should still carry him. Had the goddess sent him this craft? Now he only needed some kind of oar. Among the flotsam, he found an old plank, which would have to do. He shoved boat and board among shrubs growing along the river. In daylight an abandoned boat would draw attention. Someone might even steal it.

Having prepared everything for a nightly river crossing, Hori returned to the canal. Going with the flow, it was even easier to dive under the wall. Back at his house he found no rest. What should he do once he reached the eastern shore? He still had no idea how to find the killer when he could only operate at night.

The next morning, as soon as Hori opened his eyes, he knew the answer. He needed someone to ask questions and investigate. Someone who could visit the noble families. Someone he could trust. Nakhtmin! His former friend could hardly refuse his help after he'd almost betrayed him. He owed Hori.

Then the next problem hit him: how to find Nakhtmin? He'd still work at the House of Life during the day but no longer live there. Did he have his own little house by now? Maybe his friend had returned to Upper Egypt. Who else might help him? He considered each of his former fellow students but decided he couldn't trust any of them not to turn him over to the Medjay. With a sigh, Hori dug into his porridge. He had to try his luck, take the risk. The goddess wouldn't have shown him a way that turned into a dead end.

A little later, Kheper knocked on the door to fetch him. This morning Hori hardly listened to his teacher's chatter, barely noticed they took a different route. About to ask where they were heading, he remembered that today he was supposed to learn anointing.

This time Kheper led him to a room lit by oil lamps and torches mounted to the walls. Despite the many ventilation slits in the walls, a heavy scent of myrrh and other precious fragrances hung in the air, mixing with the sweet whiff of decay. Several bodies lay on wooden tables. Everywhere sat jugs, vials and pots, boxes of sawdust and linen sacks. The shelves along the walls held large jars, with which to refill the smaller, handier ones, Hori guessed. He picked up one of the containers and read the inscription along the neck. "Ben oil."

"Yes, and these are juniper berries. In here, we have myrrh and in the small pots with red lids is incense. Good morning, I'm glad you finally woke up."

"What…? Oh." Hori realized he'd remained silent the whole time since leaving his house. If Kheper had asked him a question, he likely wouldn't have noticed. Fortunately, the old man only thought him tired. "Why do we use strong-smelling herbs and substances?"

Kheper made a face Hori had come to think of as his teacher expression. "You know the breath of life leaves through the nose, right?"

Hori grunted his agreement.

"When it's time to return to the body, it takes the same route. That's how the gods animate all their creatures. That's why everything with a strong scent also harbors the divine breath of life reviving people."

"I see. Rubbing the body with fragrant substances allows it to reanimate itself."

Kheper looked doubtful but said, "Simply put, I guess you could say that. It only works after the secret ritual of the mouth opening though. Not even we utu know how it works. Anubis' prophets take care of it." Kheper turned toward one of the tables with a corpse laid out, awaiting treatment. After the time in the natron chamber the body had shrunk, its skin darkened, hardened and brittled.

Still, Hori recognized her at first glance. "Merit-Neith!"

"What?"

"She was the first I washed, and I knew her."

"Oh, I remember. It's really been forty days already since you arrived."

Hori felt excitement bubble up inside him. Now he'd get the chance to examine her for traces of the same injury he found on Hetepet's body. "Show me how to perform the anointment," he demanded.

Kheper grabbed the ben oil. "All these substances are very precious, so don't waste them. Pour some in your hand, then rub it on the skin of the dead until it softens and becomes flexible again. Understood?"

Hori nodded eagerly and reached for the jug. "Sounds easy."

"Good, I'll leave you to it then. Call me when you're done, and I'll tell you how to proceed afterward."

Hori had to restrain himself not to check the spot under her left breast right away. Instead he followed Kheper's example, who started with the legs of the body on the next table. The treatment took an agonizingly long time, but to Hori's amazement the skin afterward nearly felt like that of a living person. Some of its original fullness and elasticity had returned although it remained dark. At long last, he'd worked his way up to Merit-Neith's chest. The light was rather poor, and because of the coloration of the skin, he found it hard to see anything. When Kheper turned his back to him and looked like he might remain in that position for a while, Hori snatched an oil lamp and illuminated the spot. Yes! The same discoloration as Hetepet's body showed, and it might have once been shaped like a blossom. His fingers felt the puncture wound at its center. He hurried to return the lamp. He was right! Triumph soared through him. At the same time he mourned both women. A ruthless murderer roamed the streets of the capital and he'd killed more than once. This discovery hardened his resolve to begin the search for Nakhtmin tonight.

He finished anointing Merit-Neith's body. Afterward Kheper showed him the art of stuffing the corpse's cavities with aromatic cedarwood shavings to fill out cheeks and body to a life-like shape. Juniper berries were pushed into the nostrils, lichen and fragrant incense into the visceral cavity, while myrrh was placed behind the teeth. Kheper picked two bulbs from a chest and placed one in each of Merit-Neith's hands. Hori recognized the scent, a popular perfume among the noble ladies, who applied it to their clothes. The old man crossed the dead girl's arms over her lap. "This is how you pose women. Men are laid out with their arms by their sides. Only a pharaoh can go off to eternity with his arms crossed over his chest."

Hori found it hard to concentrate on Kheper's explanations, his mind spinning around the latest discovery and his nocturnal expedition. While finishing up, his gaze wandered to the many labeled receptacles, and an idea sparked. He scrutinized the room and spotted a trash can holding many broken jars. Having used up his stock already, he picked out a large smooth shard and hid it in his shendyt. Later, he'd write a message for Nakhtmin. Hopefully, he'd find someone in the harbor taverns who knew the young doctor. At least he should be able to find a messenger content with a small reward.

And there rose his next obstacle in front of him. He owned nothing of value. A few incense bits lay scattered on the table. Could he…? Nobody was watching him. Stealthily he picked up the crumbs and hid them in his left palm. That should suffice.

Up on the roof of his house, he used the last daylight to scribble a note onto the shard. He couldn't let the ink get runny in the water, so he scraped tallow from the lamp and coated the symbols with it. With luck, this was enough protection against the water. To make sure, he thoroughly greased a piece of leather and wrapped the shard and incense in it. The bundle firmly tied, he could only hope its contents would survive the short passage through the canal unharmed.

Around the same time as the previous night, he set out. He'd decided to wear his shendyt. Naked, he'd stand out even in the harbor district, and attention was the last thing he needed. With his shaved head he might not be easily recognizable even by people who knew him back in the days when his face was rimmed by the doctor's wig.

This time he didn't hesitate to dive and soon found himself outside the weryt's walls. He reached for the precious parcel and shook off the wetness before he wrung his shendyt and wrapped it around the package. Using his belt, he tied the bundle onto his head. Although he appreciated having found the boat, he didn't quite trust its reliability. If he had to swim, he needed both hands free and the shendyt would hinder him as well. The dinghy still lay in the spot where he'd hid it. He hurried to get it in the water and knelt on the reed bundles. Tiny waves spread from the boat and rolled unbroken over the silvery surface. No dangerous animal lurked nearby. With his makeshift paddle, it took strenuous effort to get across and he drifted downstream significantly. Finally reaching the other side, he dressed, pulled the dinghy on land and dragged it along until he found remarkably dense bushes around a single palm tree: easy to distinguish and an excellent hiding place should someone stroll along the river bank. And the spot was close enough to the city so he could get here quickly if someone recognized and chased him.

To his surprise, the street was deserted. After a few steps he reached the first houses of the capital. The artisans' quarter lay in complete darkness, and Hori headed toward the harbor. Here he passed several revelers far too drunk to pay him any attention. Smoking torches illuminated the doors of taverns popular not only with sailors. Hori gave the *Golden Ibis* a wide berth. Instead he turned toward a tavern in which he'd never been before. His throat dried up with tension when he stepped through the door. Inside it was gloomy and unbearably warm. The patrons looked no better kempt than he did in his stained and wrinkled shendyt. Glad he fit right in, Hori still avoided looking at anyone. The innkeeper inspired little confidence but Hori had no choice.

He approached the short, scraggy fellow with a hooked nose. "Good man, do you know someone who could deliver a message for me?"

"Sure, my son often runs errands." The black eyes scrutinized him from head to toe and reminded Hori of a bird. Then he shouted, "Hey, Good-for-nothing, get your scrawny ass over here."

A skinny boy dashed from a corner.

If he called his own son good-for-nothing, I'll probably be a lucky bastard if my message reaches its destination. Hori braced himself before talking to the imbecile child. "Do you know the House of Life?" he asked.

When the boy nodded fervently, Hori unwrapped the parcel. Fortunately its contents had remained dry. "Take this message to the doctor Nakhtmin at the House of Life. As a reward I'll give you these crumbs of incense." He took the shard from the leather and showed him the incense crystals.

The boy's eyes widened and his lips moved as if he wanted to say something, but his father reacted faster. Like a claw, his hand shot out and clutched the leather. "Certainly, noble lord, my son will deliver your message."

Hori grinned inwardly. All of a sudden he'd turned into a noble lord, just because he had something of value to offer. "It's important the message will be delivered tomorrow. No later. Do you understand?" Hori asked the boy.

"Yes, sir. I'll deliver this message to doctor Nakhtmin at the House of Life when the first ray of the sun shines." Hori had to lean toward the boy to understand him because he talked in such a low voice. Was he shy or trying to keep their arrangement secret from any prying ears?

"Good. If you carry out this task to my satisfaction, I'll use your services again," he added. Having received his reward in advance, the kid had little reason to actually take the trouble of playing messenger. For good measure, Hori fixed the father with a stern look.

The innkeeper nodded solemnly. "Any time, noble lord."

Hori left the tavern. Having set things into motion, he couldn't get out of Itj-tawy fast enough. Now, if only he could rely on Good-for-nothing!

Nocturnal Encounter

Day 30 of month Ipet-hemet in Shemu, season of the harvest

Nakhtmin brooded over his second jug of beer. Nothing drew him to his miserable, vermin-infested hut directly at the Nile. Once again, he cursed his honesty. If he'd testified according to Nebit's wishes, he could have a small property in a noble district—like Weni.

"You only need to embellish your testimony a little and these ten gold deben will embellish your arm," the vizier had enticed him, and he—at long last—had agreed.

But that would have been a lie, his inner voice reminded him. Angry, Nakhtmin discarded the objection. "Maat always grabs honest folks by the neck," he grumbled. He'd rather scratch his flea bites with a clean conscience than toss and turn on fine linen. Hori was his friend after all! Unfortunately, his speaking the truth hadn't procured acquittal. The verdict of the pharaoh and the judges still puzzled Nakhtmin. At the same time he was relieved nobody came to question him the days after. Whenever he'd heard heavy steps, he'd flinched in horror, fearing the Medjay might take him away.

Somebody tugged on his shendyt. Annoyed, Nakhtmin turned around. It was the innkeeper's son.

"You're Nakhtmin, the doctor, aren't you?" he asked.

"What if I am?"

"We got a message for Nakhtmin, the doctor." The boy ogled the copper lump Nakhtmin carried on a string around his neck. "Is that a whole deben?"

"You want a reward for delivering the message?" Nakhtmin guessed.

The boy spun around to look at his father who gestured wildly. Sighing, Nakhtmin beckoned the little man. Using a knife, he cut a thin piece off the copper deben. "All right, this is for the two jugs of beer. And this…" He sliced off another bit. "…is for your son's trouble delivering the message." He handed the precious metal to the boy. "And now I'd really like to hear it."

The youngster pulled a shard of clay from his threadbare loincloth and held it out to him with a wide smile.

What silly joke was that? They must be kidding, Nakhtmin thought. The shard was smeared with a thick layer of tallow. If that was a message, he didn't get it. Then he noticed a blurred symbol under the grease and scraped off the layer with his knife. In his corner it was too dark to read, and the ink had run, making it even harder to decipher the signs. He walked over to one of the torches and read.

To Nakhtmin, doctor. Greeting. This is a matter of life and death. Meet me tomorrow, third hour after sunset, waterfront road heading north, at the lone palm tree. A friend.

Three more times, he read the message before he shoved the shard in his shendyt and frowned. What a strange notice! A friend? He had no more friends since… He missed Hori. His colleagues at the House of Life looked down their noses at him. What was he still doing in the capital? A doctor's life back home in the province shouldn't be too bad. Every day he was reminded of his offense defying the vizier of the Two Lands. Among all his fellow students, he was the only doctor banned from events like the big banquet celebrating the harvest, banned from treating noble patients bringing generous gifts. He was only allowed to cure the poor and received very little in return. Who, then, was the ominous friend who'd sent the message? Surely none of his patients since most weren't able to write. One of his fellow students? But they avoided him as if they might catch his fleas.

What if it was a trap? The thought tore away the veil of fatigue and intoxication, which had enveloped him until now. Were they luring him to this remote spot to throw him into the river? But why? Nebit had no reason to fear he might go tell the pharaoh about the attempted bribery. By sending the thugs to beat him up, he'd made pretty clear what would await Nakhtmin if he did suffer another fit of imprudent honesty. Deep in thought, he strolled home.

Heri-renpet I, first leap day in Shemu, season of the harvest

All day long, Nakhtmin wondered if he should comply and go to the meeting. A matter of life and death, the message said and it did sound urgent. But if this was about a serious disease, why wait all day? Why meet at night like thieves? No, something smelled fishy. He recalled the servant intercepting him in the alley when Nebit required his presence. Had the vizier thought up a new ploy to punish him? Or was someone else simply planning to rob him? But then he had little to lose, except his life, since he didn't own anything worth stealing. If the vizier wanted him dead, he'd find plenty of better opportunities to get rid of him. Maybe he should go meet this *friend.*

As soon as he decided to do it, fear turned his limbs to water once more. He imagined the club already hurtling down toward his head. Waiting for an attack in the dark, unable to defend himself... No, he wasn't brave enough to take such a chance. As soon as he'd treated the last patient of the day, he set out to check the terrain, where he was supposed to meet the guy.

During the day the waterfront was bustling with people. Many men returned from the nearby fields; fishermen brought in their catch of the day at the harbor. Nakhtmin had already left the city behind and passed several lone trees. Was the unknown sender pulling his leg? How was he supposed to find the right meeting place? Then he saw a single palm tree and knew that had to be it. The trunk rose in a strange arc, which made the tree unmistakable. In its vicinity, an irrigation ditch had been dug up for the next flooding, but so far it was still dry. Nakhtmin peered in. He could hide there and observe his *friend* without being seen. Yes, that would work! He hurried back to the city.

At home he made a meal from the meager gifts he'd received as payment for his services that day: some onions, beans and a young Nile perch heavy enough to feed him the next two days as well.

At dusk, nervous unrest chased him out of the house. One hour into the night, he lay in his hideout, rocks painfully stabbing at his flesh. *He won't be on the way yet so I might just as well get more comfortable.* As comfy as possible under the circumstances, he peered over the edge of the ditch. The full moon cast silvery light onto the river's surface and seemed to turn it into liquid silver. Nakhtmin's head sank back.

A tawny owl's call jerked him awake. *Damn, I've fallen asleep!* How late could it be? Had he'd missed his so-called friend? A gentle splashing arrested his attention. Someone seemed to paddle on the river. Yes, now he could see the man. His bald head glittered in the moonlight. A priest? Could this be the man wanting to meet him? The many questions confused him even more. The boat slowly drifted past and soon disappeared from view. Nothing to do with him. Nakhtmin leaned back into the ditch. Who traveled on the divine Nile at night? Quite strange. He slid into a state between waking and sleeping.

Then he noticed a dragging sound, already close. He realized that he must have heard it for a while already because in his dazed mind he'd conjured up images of a grinding stone for doctors' knives. He scrutinized the path along the riverbank. A hunched man lugged something bulky. A boat! Had to be the priest he'd seen earlier. Nakhtmin held his breath. The stranger hid in the shadows of shrubs and seemed to wait. How stupid. He lay here and the other guy cowered over there. That way he'd never find out if the man posed danger. And he was trapped in this ditch.

Nakhtmin had no idea how long he'd been lying there and weighing his options when his *friend* stepped onto the path and gazed toward the capital. Moonlight gave his face sharp contours. Something about him seemed very familiar. "Hori!" he blurted.

The figure jerked and dove into the bushes.

"It's me, Nakhtmin."

A rustle, then they stood in front of each other. Dumbstruck Nakhtmin stared at his old friend Hori. How could he be here?

"I'm so glad you came. Let's get off the path. I've got to tell you something important."

Nakhtmin grabbed his arm. "How did you get here? Aren't you...?"

"Later." Hori led him along the path to a dirt track, which they followed for a while before he settled in the cover of bushes and pulled Nakhtmin down to sit beside him. Here he gave him a brief summary of the events since his sentencing. "You see, I had to come. I couldn't think of anyone else I'd trust more."

"Hori, I... Because of you I'm already in trouble." The words spilled from his mouth before he could bite his tongue. While listening to his friend's sometimes nebulous report, realization had dawned on him what awaited them if they were caught.

"Oh, I get it."

"No, I doubt you understand. Nebit sent his thugs to beat me up. I live in the paupers' quarters and often don't have enough to eat, because the vizier took care that I can't treat rich people. As soon as the Nile reaches top water level, I'll have to return to Khent-min." He hadn't really decided yet, but now Hori would have to accept that he couldn't do anything for him.

"What a great friend you are. Is it my fault you let him bribe you? I'm grateful you said the truth at court, but you brought the consequences on yourself."

Hori was right. Nakhtmin felt it in his heart. However, what he asked him to do was impossible. "How should I be able to help you? You need someone who is welcome in the houses of high-ranking officials." He released a bitter laugh. "I'm anything but."

Hands grabbed his shoulders and shook him. "It's Hetepet, Ameny's daughter! Doesn't that mean anything to you?"

Nakhtmin cringed under these words. They lashed him like a cane. Little Hetepet... Often he'd teased her, while she waited in front of the temple for her father. Since her mysterious death, the second prophet had been overwrought with grief. An idea began to form in his heart. "Yes, it does mean something to me. You can't imagine how shocked everyone was when she lay dead among the pillars of the vestibule."

"And nobody realized she was murdered?" Hori spluttered.

"Imhotepankh assumed a heat stroke killed her."

"Likely he didn't even look at her. And what about Merit-Neith? Do you know anything about her?"

"No." Nakhtmin's thoughts traveled back to those days after the trial. He'd still been suffering major pain after the beating when the young woman was found in her parents' garden. Only later he'd learned what happened because Shepses flaunted his grief in the House of Life. Obviously, the two had been engaged. "Listen, Hori. What happened to both women is tragic, but I can't see a way to help you. One of your brothers or your father should be in a much better position to—"

"No! I'd never ask my family for help. You don't know my father. In his eyes, I disgraced the family. He didn't lift a finger to prevent this unjust verdict. And my brothers are like him. Not a word to any of them. They'd probably report both of us to the Medjay."

Nakhtmin recoiled from Hori's vehemence. What kind of family treated one of their own like that? Likely Hori exaggerated but he didn't dare broach the subject again. That put him back in the lurch. "Maybe the killer will never strike again. What do you care? You risk your neck by leaving the weryt. Hey, how did you escape? I thought that was impossible."

"I've pledged myself to Maat," Hori explained, then told him about his vision as he called it.

Nakhtmin couldn't help feeling impressed. Hori's voice rang with sincerity and dedication. His own conscience stirred. He too had good reasons to pledge his life to Maat. He'd almost lied in front of the Great Kenbet! The intent alone weighed like lead on his heart. He had to do something, and Hori's excitement started to rub off on him. "Maybe there's a chance..." he began. "What if I confide in Ameny?"

"No way! You can't tell anyone. Consider the danger for both of us. Nothing's more secret than the secrets of the weryt!"

"But you didn't reveal those and you won't. You only left because of the murders you discovered."

"*We* know that, but do you really believe the second prophet of Amun will understand?"

"The man's devastated in his grief over Hetepet," Nakhtmin explained. "Believe me, if he knew she was murdered, he'd do much more than keep our secret."

Hori groaned. "It's too risky. Still, let's assume you go to Ameny and spill everything. He reacts as you say. What then? As second prophet he can't just walk into houses and ask people if they killed his daughter. He can't even go to the pharaoh because he'd have to explain how he knows about the murders. That's our dilemma. At the same time I'm sure Hetepet won't be the last victim of this vicious killer. We have to prevent more murders."

Nakhtmin felt dizzy. The extent of this matter was too much for him. If Hori thought Ameny powerless, what did he expect of him? He was just a boy from Upper Egypt, trained as doctor. On his own he'd get nowhere. "I can keep my eyes open, but someone will have to open doors for me, or we won't get anywhere."

"You're right." Hori's sigh sounded desperate. "We have to take the risk. Approach Ameny with utmost care. Maybe a condolence visit? I'm sure the goddess didn't show herself without reason."

Nakhtmin's skin crawled. "No, the eternal ones only show themselves to a few people. If they do, they can't be ignored. Listen, although you've found a way out of the weryt, it's too risky for you to cross the river. We need to find a way to stay in contact that's less dangerous for you. It's easier for me to get across. If necessary I can even do it in daylight. Do you know a place where we can deposit messages?"

Hori remained silent for a while, then he nodded. "A bit downstream from the weryt there's a thicket at the riverbank, where I hide my dinghy. Let's dig a small pit in the sand, ten steps inland from there. We can place messages, shove sand over them and mark the spot with a rock or branch, so the other can find it."

Nakhtmin nodded. "And the place can't be seen from the gate of the weryt? I'd rather not be observed by guards while digging in the sand. They might get curious."

"No worries, all day long they stare out at the Nile, and the bushes are right behind a river bend. You can see it from the path here. I'll show you."

The headed back to the river, and Nakhtmin made sure he'd be able to find the spot before he helped Hori launch the damaged boat. Then he said good-bye to his friend and wished him a safe return.

On the way back to Itj-tawy he felt like a changed person—so different from the guy he was when he came here. What happened to make him sign up for such an adventure? That wasn't like him at all. But he also felt new hope grow inside him, where yesterday only misery lodged. Maybe this was his chance to establish himself as a doctor in the capital and actually make a living. Back in his hut he mulled over their situation for a long time.

SHARED SECRET

Time stretched for Nakhtmin at the House of Life. Against his habit, he found himself rushing his treatment of the ailing. When he thought of what he had to do later, anxiety made him fidget. Since he didn't know the second prophet very well, he could only hope he was right about him. The man was responsible for the administrative side of the House of Life within the Amun temple compound, but he didn't really get involved in the training or work of doctors. Come to think of it, he'd based his opinion of the prophet mostly on what his youngest daughter had said about him. That's how he knew Ameny had tenderly loved Hetepet.

Nakhtmin had only seen the priest once after her body was found. Already wearing the yellow clothes of mourning and a stony expression, he'd walked along the aisles, his face smeared with dust and tears. Nakhtmin calculated. The three days of private mourning, when household members grieved for the deceased in the seclusion of their home, had passed. During the next ten days friends and acquaintances were actually expected to visit and offer condolences. His showing up at Ameny's house wouldn't seem strange at all, even if he didn't belong to the noble circle around the higher priests of Amun.

Finally, he sent his last patient of the day home with a fresh bandage and doused himself with water in the washroom. Then he headed home. Among his few possessions was a shendyt of fine linen, which he'd received from one of the few merchants requiring his medical services. He donned the garment and put on the necklace with the Horus-eye amulet before he set out for Ameny's estate, heart pounding.

The howling of mourning women greeted him at the gate of the house. A servant escorted him to the large hall, where the host, his wife and their children welcomed guests. In addition to Nakhtmin there were five other people present: a third prophet of Ra, two officials—judging by their wigs—and two women, likely friends of Hetepet's mother. Everyone had already dipped their hands in the bowl of ashes and smeared their faces and hair. Nakhtmin followed suit and appreciated that nobody seemed to expect him to tear apart his shendyt as a sign of his grief. He'd certainly have mourned the loss of his best garment.

Ameny raised his eyebrows in surprise when he noticed Nakhtmin, then a wistful smile brightened his features. Nakhtmin stepped up to him and murmured a few words of condolence, which he repeated to Ameny's wife and Hetepet's siblings: two young boys, obviously twins, and a girl only slightly older than Hetepet. She resembled her sister very much.

She lifted her gaze. "I'm Mutnofret. You knew my sister…doctor?"

"My name is Nakhtmin, doctor at the House of Life. I often met your sister when she picked up your father at the temple."

"Oh…" Her harmonious features darkened. She swallowed hard, and the corners of her mouth quivered. "She loved walking home with him." Tears rolled down her cheeks and left light trails in the ash.

Nakhtmin took her hand and squeezed. "I liked her a lot. You must miss her."

Mutnofret nodded and averted her face.

Nakhtmin felt like an intruder in such pain. What was he doing here? Then he remembered. He looked around for Ameny and found him standing at a pillar, his shoulders drooping. Nobody kept him company. Although Nakhtmin despised himself for tearing the prophet from his silent grief, he ambled over to him. "Noble Ameny…"

The priest flinched, then recognized him and grimaced in annoyance. Nakhtmin couldn't treat the man's feelings with misguided respect. After all, he was acting in the prophet's interest. "I hate having to disturb you, but I need to tell you something very important," he murmured.

"Young man, this really isn't a good time. Please come back another day. Or even better, talk to one of my deputies." His lips tightened to a thin, hard line, and he turned to walk off.

Nakhtmin noticed the gaze of Ameny's wife resting on him and realized he was drawing unwanted attention. Still, he dared to grab the priest's shoulder and hold him back. "Noble lord, I have evidence that your daughter was murdered." He only whispered the sentence but a thunderclap couldn't have struck his host harder.

Ameny spun around. "What are you saying? Explain!"

"Not here. I can only tell you what I know in confidence. If you can't get away right now for a private talk, I'll be happy to wait until you've bid farewell to your guests. Still, what I know is certainly of utmost interest for you."

Ameny's brows knitted, while he seemed to mull over the suggestion. "Fine," he said in a low voice. "My servant will take you to my study. Wait there." He exchanged a few words with the attendant who'd escorted him to the hall earlier.

Nakhtmin said good-bye to the family and followed the man out of the hall and down a gloomy corridor. After a few steps, the servant opened a portal and shoved him into a room. He could just discern his kidnapper's disapproving expression before the door closed.

Again time seemed to stand still as Nakhtmin waited. Of course, Ameny had to fulfill his duties as host. What a heavy burden the rituals must turn into for the bereft! He couldn't imagine how he might feel as the mourning father. To occupy himself, he studied the furnishings of the room. On the desk made of black, shiny ebony lay a writing palette with a rolled-up papyrus next to it. More scrolls peaked from an open chest in the corner. It looked like Ameny had quickly rifled through it in search of something but didn't have the time to replace the other documents.

With the tips of his fingers, Nakhtmin unrolled the scroll on the table far enough to skim the beginning. It was the dirge of goddess Isis for her beloved husband Osiris. He didn't dare read on or pass time with one of the other texts. Ameny wouldn't be happy to find him sifting through his belongings. Some of the scrolls might even be secret—reserved for the eyes of the highest priests of Amun. So instead he considered how to present his knowledge to Ameny. How should he begin? He couldn't be so blunt again, had to gently, respectfully reveal the source of his knowledge, proceed with care… Easier thought than done. He flopped onto cushions piled into a divan in one corner.

At long last, Ameny entered the room. His face looked even more emaciated than before, and Nakhtmin realized how much more burden he was going to pile onto the man's shoulders. Without a word, the priest settled in front of him, crossed his legs and gazed at him intently, accusation and challenge in his eyes.

"My lord, I..." Nakhtmin's voice faded. No, it wouldn't work if he apologized again. Ameny might throw him out of the house. He pulled himself together. "I have to tell you something of grave importance. Under...special circumstances, I received evidence that your daughter Hetepet fell victim to a heinous murderer. A murderer who also killed noble Merit-Neith."

Ameny wheezed. Eyes closed, hands clenched into fists, he trembled with suppressed tension. Nakhtmin feared a violent outburst.

After a while his host's breathing returned to normal. Regaining control, he asked, "Are you aware of what you're telling me?"

"Yes, sir, I am. It is a horrible allegation. Therefore, please tell me what you know about the cause of your daughter's death." Nakhtmin felt more confident now they'd swapped roles. Ameny was no longer his strict examiner. Instead, Nakhtmin asked the questions.

Ameny slumped. "I found her—my sweet little girl." He covered his face with both hands. His shoulders shook. He needed some time to compose himself. "I found her in the arcade of the forecourt to the Amun temple. She lay there as if asleep, except her mouth hung open. Like she was astonished. Surprised by death..." The corners of his mouth pulled down in pain.

Nakhtmin didn't want to see him burst into tears, so he tried for a factual tone. "What did you do when you found her?"

"I lifted her, thinking... I thought I could... I carried her to the doctors at the House of Life, to Imhotepankh, the head of doctors. He..." Now tears did well up in his eyes and roll down the Amun priest's cheeks.

Nakhtmin wished he could spare the man this pain, but finding the killer might bring him some relief. "Imhotepankh could only assert Hetepet's death?" he prompted.

Ameny nodded.

"Did the venerable head of doctors give you his opinion on the cause of death?"

"He spoke of the demons of the heat. My little girl died from too much sun, he thought, like it happens to those who are exposed to the rays of the sun god for too long. But how could that be when I found her in the shade? You!" He pointed an accusing finger at Nakhtmin. "You spoke of evidence. Show me, and I'll go to the pharaoh right away. I won't rest until the villain is arrested and sentenced." Ameny jumped to his feet and towered over Nakhtmin in a threatening pose.

"Noble lord, unfortunately I can't show you the evidence. Somebody confided in me that he found a wound on Hetepet's body, which led to her death. Merit-Neith's body had shown the very same injury."

"Who? Who saw the wound? And how could he find what Imhotepankh overlooked? Speak up, man, who is the villain? Whoever knows such things must be the murderer of my little girl!"

Ameny grabbed Nakhtmin's shoulders and shook him dizzy.

"Hold on!" he yelped.

Ameny immediately let go and sank back onto the mat. He groaned. "Forgive me, but in the name of the gods, tell me all you know."

"Nobody examined Hetepet's body? Nobody noticed a wound? A small one, no bigger than a mosquito bite. Likely it wouldn't have bled much either." Nakhtmin still shied from revealing his source of information. First he needed to make sure the powerful priest would keep their secret.

Ameny's brow furrowed. "Why? Do you think...? Who? Who could have found the wound you're talking about?"

Nakhtmin sighed. "Listen, I turned to you because I think I can trust you in this matter. Nevertheless, I need you to promise, no, I need your holy oath that you'll keep secret what I'm going to tell you. My life depends on it—and somebody else's. Even for you it might be dangerous. Are you willing to take this risk to bring Maat back into balance?" In the ensuing silence he believed he could hear his heart beat. Opposing emotions waged a battle on the prophet's face. Had he said too much already?

"I swear by Amun, the highest of gods, and by Maat, nothing you reveal to me will pass my lips except with your permission. Are you content with this oath?"

Relieved, Nakhtmin nodded. "Do you remember Hori, doctor in the House of Life? You might know—"

Ameny's scream interrupted him. "Dear gods! Are you going to tell me this convicted murderer escaped his punishment and roams the world of the living? Is he the man who killed Hetepet?"

"No. Please. Listen. Let me tell you what really happened." Obviously the truth about Neferib's death never spread beyond the king's court, and Nebit certainly would have made sure it stayed that way. Under the circumstances, Ameny's suspicion shouldn't surprise him. In much detail, Nakhtmin told him about the tragic events of the night Nebit's son died. He even confessed his temptation to accept the vizier's bribe.

When the prophet learned of Hotep's testimony and how the boy renounced his lie in the end, Ameny's jaw dropped. "Despite all this, Hori was sentenced by the Great Kenbet? It shouldn't have been anything but an acquittal!"

"I don't understand this myself, but let me continue." The account of their secret meeting captivated the priest. He let Nakhtmin finish without interrupting again. Only Ameny's contorting features gave away his indignation.

"You see, Hori discovered something crucial, something unknown until now. The goddess Maat herself appeared to show him which route to take. He could only trust me with his knowledge. I, however..." Nakhtmin let his shoulders sag. "I'm a man without power and influence. Nebit made sure I couldn't get any patients from noble families at the House of Life. Thus, their doors remain locked to me. That's why I came to you, in hopes of—"

"You did well! A murderer roams the capital. Who knows how many girls have already fallen prey to him. Who knows how many more will—if we don't stop him. First thing tomorrow, I'll go to the pharaoh and..."

Nakhtmin jumped to his feet. "Not the pharaoh! You have no idea in what danger you'll place us all. No, you of all people would know. What awaits those who betray the secrets of the weryt?"

The older man groaned. "Right, I forgot for a moment. What can we do? My duties at the temple will hardly allow me to make inquiries."

Nakhtmin saw his own helplessness reflected in Ameny's eyes. He sighed. "And I don't belong to the noble society, where questions need asking. I'm convinced the killer is to be found there. Merit-Neith was attacked in her parents' garden. Nobody

61

can easily get in there."

"To think in what danger Mutnofret might also... Of course! That's the solution. Young man, I'll hire you as personal physician of my daughter Mutnofret. You'll move into a chamber of my estate and make yourself available day and night."

Nakhtmin's face grew hot. Spend the nights in the company of this beautiful young woman?

"Mostly during the day, I guess," the concerned father added quickly. He must have read his thoughts. "Since everyone but us believes Hetepet died of a mysterious disease, it's only natural that I'm worried about her sister. Mutnofret freely enters the homes of her friends. Noble families often invite her to banquets. You can accompany her without raising questions. Thus you'll get access to the estates of the high and mighty—with time and occasion to investigate." For the first time since Nakhtmin entered the house in mourning, a gentle smile conquered Ameny's face. "I thank you for mustering the courage to come here and confide in me. I will never forget."

Embarrassed, Nakhtmin lowered his gaze. "I have to thank you, my lord, for hearing me out and giving me your word although I'm the lowliest of doctors. I'll be honored to accompany noble Mutnofret. If necessary, I'll protect her with my life."

The priest rose and grabbed his hand to pull him up from the cushions. Together they went to the private quarters, where Ameny officially introduced him to his family again and announced his plan to hire Nakhtmin as Mutnofret's personal physician.

His wife, noble Isis, appeared relieved and moved by her husband's parental concern. Both young sons cast shy glances at Nakhtmin and hid behind their mother's flap. Mutnofret's face distorted slightly, but she was too well-behaved to show her resentment in front of a guest.

For her I'm a supervisor limiting her freedom and reporting to her father. Nakhtmin winked at her to show his understanding.

Ameny instructed the attendant, and soon after, Nakhtmin was led to a spacious guest room.

"Here you shall reside. Thus decided my lord."

"Thank you... What's your name?"

"Penu."

Nakhtmin suppressed a grin. Penu meant mouse and the name fit the man, with his protruding teeth. "Thanks, Penu. I'll fetch my things from my house and should be back soon."

"As you wish."

The servant's disparaging gaze scrutinized Nakhtmin's dark skin and the quality of his clothes. Obviously, he wasn't deemed noble enough to be welcomed to his master's house, but of course he couldn't openly disregard a direct order. Nakhtmin sighed inaudibly. His mission wouldn't be easy, though certainly easier than before.

With a spring in his steps, he set out for the paupers' quarter. His few belongings packed, he returned to the Amun priest's estate. Striding through the gate once more, he wanted to praise his luck. If only the cause weren't so sad.

THE BURDEN OF RESPONSIBILITY

Heri-renpet III, third leap day in Shemu, season of the harvest

The next morning Penu brought him a stack of folded linen. "The master sends you these clothes as part of your payment." He managed to sound friendly and condescending at the same time as if Nakhtmin were a beggar receiving the leftovers of a luxurious meal.

Still, Nakhtmin was far too happy he didn't have to disgrace himself by wearing shabby clothes in front of noble citizens to get angry with the guy. New sandals with straps adorned by pearls were among the donations as well. Dressed up like this, he eagerly followed the servant to the garden, where the family had already settled under an awning to have breakfast. Their faces still showed grief. Mutnofret briefly knitted her eyebrows when she spotted him. The chair beside her wasn't occupied.

"Ah, there's my daughter's new personal doctor. I hope you found everything to your satisfaction?"

"I slept very well under your roof, thanks." Nakhtmin interpreted a wave of Ameny's hand as an invitation to sit beside Mutnofret, so he grabbed the backrest.

In a defensive move, the young woman pushed the chair up to the table. "My sister used to sit here."

Nakhtmin cursed himself. He should have asked if he might take the seat. How should he watch out for Mutnofret if he alienated her? Maybe they should take her into his confidence so she'd support him. No, girls liked to gossip and blab secrets. The more people knew about Hori's nighttime excursion across the Nile, the greater the danger for his friend. Too much was at stake. "Pardon me, I wasn't thinking," he offered. At a loss, he glanced around.

With the hint of a sneer on his face, Penu pointed to a stool standing aside. Nakhtmin fetched it and finally settled between noble Isis and one of her sons. They certainly weren't off to a good start. He felt uneasy. The silence at the table weighed him down. Not even the boys made any noise. Under different circumstances, he'd have cherished the delicious food, but now he had trouble swallowing. Finally his host rose and asked Nakhtmin to follow him to his study.

"I took the liberty of excusing you at the House of Life," Ameny said for openers.

"Oh, good." With events unfolding so fast, he'd almost forgotten his duties as doctor.

"I've mulled over things some more," the priest continued.

Nakhtmin immediately worried the grieving father wanted to abandon their plan. Maybe he had qualms about covering Hori's breach of the rules? His heart pounded.

"I'm afraid we won't be able to hide the nature of your guardianship and mission from Mutnofret. My daughter is an intelligent young woman and will soon figure out that you aren't protecting her from the rays of the god Ra."

"But...sir, please forgive me, but I'd rather not take the risk. Too big is the danger of her letting something slip. Hori would have to face the consequences."

The corners of Ameny's mouth twitched in anger. "My daughter isn't a gossip.

But I do understand your concerns. A connection to young Hori is a threat to anyone, and I wouldn't want to put Mutnofret at additional risk. When we tell her Hetepet didn't die of natural causes, I think we can omit his role. She might even be able to assist you in your investigation if she knew."

Nakhtmin sighed. "All right."

Ameny stuck his head out the door and called, "Penu! Please fetch Mutnofret."

A short time later the servant returned alone. Nakhtmin believed he saw mute satisfaction on the fellow's face. "Noble Mutnofret went to the temple of Isis to make a sacrifice for her sister."

She'd escaped him. Nakhtmin had no doubt she'd already planned to give them the slip at breakfast. Her father was probably right: as long as she saw him as unwanted company, only coming along to boss her around, she'd make his task more difficult.

Ameny swore through clenched teeth. "Penu, why didn't you stop her? Didn't I make myself understood, yesterday? I do not want my daughter to leave the house without physician Nakhtmin accompanying her. Your disobedience has earned you five cane strokes."

The priest's glare made Nakhtmin appreciate it wasn't directed at him.

Penu's lanky figure seemed to shrink even more. "Yes, my lord, I'm very sorry." Despite his demure pose, his eyes shot daggers at Nakhtmin.

"If something befalls my daughter, you'll be even sorrier. I can promise you that much. Away with you!" As soon as the door closed behind the servant, the priest released a groan of agony. "Please try to catch up with Mutnofret. I can't bear to lose her as well."

With a curt nod, Nakhtmin set out to search for her.

Dear gods, please let me find her at the temple of Isis. A horrible fear sneaked up on him. What if Mutnofret told Penu the wrong destination to send him onto the wrong track? Ameny sure had been right. She needed to know or else he'd be spending his time chasing her instead of the killer. Though he didn't believe her in actual danger right now, he couldn't be sure. What motivation drove the murderer? According to Hori, he'd left no other marks on his victims' bodies. No fight, so the villain must have gotten close enough for a surprise attack, which meant they must have known and trusted him to let him approach.

The temple of the goddess lay right before him. He strode through the large pylon into the first courtyard. Nearby, Mutnofret passed through the gate, behind which the believers' sacrifices were accepted, and stepped into the blinding sunshine.

It took a moment before she noticed him standing there, then her eyes narrowed. "You've sniffed me out then," she said in a mocking tone with a crooked smile and stepped beside him.

"It wasn't that difficult since you left a few clues. I think we'd both benefit if I didn't have to hunt you down all day long."

The notion made her smile. "Is father very upset because I simply left?"

"Noble lady, he isn't angry! He is worried about you. I'm sure you understand that. Besides, he wanted to tell you something important, so you should return with me."

"All right. Under one condition."

Nakhtmin sighed in resignation. "Which is?"

"Never call me noble lady again."

He suppressed a smile. "My apologies. How could I possibly do something so absurd?"

"Quite cheeky!" Her eyes sparkled. The next moment, her face turned serious. "Are you *the* Nakhtmin Hetepet sometimes told me about?"

"How many Nakhtmins do you know? Yes, I knew your sister and liked to joke with her. She was endearing. I liked her. Your loss really pains me."

"Thank you. We all miss her so much. If Hetepet liked you, you must be a nice guy. She rarely misjudged people. Still, I find it rather unpleasant to be under constant watch."

"I totally understand and don't want to be a pain in your neck. Maybe you can simply forget my presence and regard me as a…hm…"

"As a hand fan?" she suggested.

He laughed. "Something like that. A convenient thing to have around."

They'd reached the second Amun prophet's estate, and Mutnofret sighed. "I better collect my earful right away and get it over with."

They found Ameny in the garden. Deep in thought, he gazed at the flowerbeds. When he noticed their arrival, he seemed relieved at first, then made a stern face. "Mutnofret, your behavior disappoints me."

"Yes, Father. In the future, I will respect your wishes."

"Girl, you have no idea in what danger you are. Has Nakhtmin told you already?" Nakhtmin shook his head.

"Told me what? What danger?"

Ameny cast a glance around to spot possible eavesdroppers, then lowered his voice. "Your sister didn't die of a heat stroke. She was murdered."

Mutnofret paled and staggered. Nakhtmin jumped to her side and steadied her.

"What are you saying, Father?"

"Yes, it's true," Nakhtmin confirmed. "Did you know Merit-Neith, who also died recently? She fell prey to the same killer. Maybe he killed before, maybe he'll kill again."

"You could be in great danger, my darling."

Mutnofret looked from one to the other. "How do you know, Father, and what's Nakhtmin got to do with all this? Did he tell you? He could have made it all up to torture you." Her voice had grown shriller and shriller.

Nakhtmin feared someone might hear her. He dropped all manners and pulled Mutnofret aside. "I can't tell you how I got the information. Be assured, though, it's true. I'd never want to torture any of you or make up a bogus allegation to worm my way into your father's household."

"That's right," Ameny barged in. "I came up with the idea to hire Nakhtmin as your guardian. He didn't hint at anything of the kind. Now you may better understand my anxiety. A murderer is on the loose and kills young women from noble families. At the same time, I can't neglect my duties as prophet of Amun. Once the first phase of mourning is over, I'll have to serve at the temple again. Nakhtmin, as your personal physician, can accompany you everywhere, keep his eyes open and ask questions."

Mutnofret looked flabbergasted. Then she pushed out her lower lip. "Why don't you leave the search for the killer to the Medjay? It's their job. Why didn't you inform the vizier? Why do you want this little doctor to investigate?"

At the mention of the vizier Nakhtmin flinched. The last thing they needed was Mutnofret walking into that man's house and revealing what they knew! To his relief Ameny scolded her himself.

"Enough! I have good reasons for my decision. You only need to know that I trust Nakhtmin. The murderer, though, must be a man with free access to the palace. Or do you think a stranger could have approached your sister—on the premises of the Amun temple?"

The girl didn't give up yet. "What if the killer is a woman?" She scoffed at the puzzled face of her father.

What a sharp tongue, Nakhtmin thought. At the same time he had to admire her cleverness. Neither Hori or Ameny nor he had considered this possibility. Yes, it was possible. "Smart reasoning," he said. "Let's try to find out together. Soon you'll be visiting friends again and we can both keep our ears and eyes open. As long as I accompany you wherever you go, you'll hopefully be safe. The killer uses a thin, pointy instrument to pierce his victims' hearts. To do so, he must have gotten very close to Merit-Neith and Hetepet."

"Merit-Neith," she murmured. "Dear gods, she was supposed to marry soon! And my sweet little sister—who would do something like that?"

Nakhtmin guessed Mutnofret had still been battling the bitter truth and was now slowly accepting it. She sagged, seemed feeble. Ameny must also have realized that his head-strong daughter had given up all resistance, since he retreated to his study. Silent, Mutnofret ambled down the garden path, likely processing their revelations. Nakhtmin followed her but kept his distance, assuming she'd need some time alone.

In the afternoon the family received mourners like the day before. Nakhtmin kept to the background and tried to become as invisible as possible, while he observed the guests' behavior. The murderer might show up to feign sympathy and to avoid raising questions by his absence. If he was among the gathered mourners, his behavior might give him away.

Mutnofret would be safe among her family. In this environment, he didn't have to worry about her and could focus his attention on the guests. Whoever stabbed Hetepet, he must have been alone with her or else he couldn't have escaped without anyone noticing. In that case, the girl's death would have been examined more closely. The same applied to Merit-Neith. Nakhtmin really appreciated Mutnofret's comment the killer could be a woman. Otherwise he'd probably have only concentrated on men and possibly overlooked something crucial. However, none of those present acted strangely or seemed nervous. Well, finding a lead on the very first day would have been too much to ask for.

He thought of Hori. The prisoner of the weryt must fare much worse than him since he could only wait. Nakhtmin knew how impetuous his friend was and commiserated with him wholeheartedly. This very night, he'd cross the river and leave a message for him, he decided.

After the evening meal he briefed Ameny about his plans in the isolation of the priest's study.

"Help yourself to my writing utensils to compose a message to Hori. Our garden borders the river. At the small pier you'll find my boat for the duck hunt. You know how to handle it? Great. Feel free to use it any time, though I'd prefer if you told me in advance where you're going. If the killer realizes someone's on his scent, you might be in danger as well."

Touched and comforted, Nakhtmin realized how much he'd missed parental care for a long time now. These concerns showed the Amun priest wasn't indifferent to his fate. With quick strokes he laid out recent events on a piece of papyrus and remembered to tell Hori about Mutnofret's remark they might be after a murderess. Surely his friend would understand they had to take the young woman into their confidence. So as not to worry him too much, he emphasized several time that she didn't know anything about him. Finishing his report, he became aware how much more they had achieved than either of them could have imagined when they decided to seek an ally in Hetepet's father. He gently dried the ink with sand and rolled up the papyrus.

Ameny handed him a clay tube for waterproof storage. "You can keep the container since you'll certainly need it again."

Nakhtmin nodded and sneaked off into the darkness. He pulled one of the torches from the lawn to light his way to the pier, where he shoved it into the ground. Its shine should help him find his way back.

With trembling knees, he climbed into the small watercraft, which rocked fiercely until he found the right position. Just days before the expected Nile floods, the fairly narrow river flowed slowly. Paddling away, he quickly reached the other side of the river without drifting too far downstream. He dragged the lightweight boat through the mud up the riverbank until sand crunched under his feet. What had Hori said? A copse downstream of the weryt. He found it and measured ten steps, walking away from the river.

A cloud moved over the moon, and in the dark, he hit his foot on something hard. Suppressing a curse, he dragged in a sharp breath and waited until no more dots danced before his eyes. He'd injured his big toe. Blood turned his sandal slippery. Feeling around with his hands, he found a rock, likely the marker. He rolled the boulder aside and started digging. With the sand so loose, he assumed this spot was above the high-water level. Excellent, no need to worry about their cranny getting flooded. Shortly after, he held a long, narrow shard of clay in his hands. A message from Hori. He let the tube with his report slide into the hole and filled it with sand. Rolling the rock back in position, he realized Hori wouldn't be able to tell if there was a message waiting for him. Oh well, a conspicuous sign could be seen by anyone during the day, and Hori was only able to leave the weryt at night anyway. Now the silvery rays of the moon clearly showed him his way back, and he realized how much he'd stand out if someone walked past. Fortunately, the western side of the river was pretty much deserted even during the day. At night, nobody would dare enter the realm of the dead—for fear of ghosts. A sudden gust of wind rustled the bulrush at the waterfront. Nakhtmin cringed in horror. What if a restless soul took possession of him? No longer did he mind his injured foot but hurried to the boat as if something chased him. The paddle couldn't dip into the muddy water fast enough. To his relief, the torch was still burning. Now he had to paddle against the current to reach the priest's estate. After he'd tied up the craft at the pier, he still felt the breath of death on his neck.

Crossing the garden, he saw light in Ameny's study. Likely the prophet was eager to hear how his excursion went and whether Hori had sent news. He knocked on the wattle-covered door to the garden and was let in.

"Well?" Ameny asked.

"Here's the message." He showed Ameny the shard. In the light of the oil lamp, the smeared symbols were hard to decipher. Hori had used less tallow this time. "Oh, and I left the clay tube behind for him so he can carry the papyrus safely back home. If he uses up too much grease, people might ask questions. I told you he needs to dive to leave the weryt."

"Of course, I can give you a second tube. Now, come on, read aloud what he wrote!"

"A friend to a friend, I salute you."

"Ah, good, he isn't using names," the priest interrupted. "That way, if anyone finds it by accident, neither sender nor recipient can be identified. But go ahead."

"Nothing new here. I hope you've seen him, whom we talked about, and managed to enlist his help. Since nobody came today to interrogate me, I assume my secret is still safe. Please reply soon. Not knowing what's happening is killing me." Nakhtmin lowered the shard. "We should send him some papyrus as well. Not many words fit on these shards."

Ameny nodded. "Help yourself to my supplies."

"Well, we didn't learn anything new, but at least we know the exchange works." Then Nakhtmin remembered hitting his toe on the rock and glanced down.

Ameny followed his gaze and drew in a sharp breath. "I'm glad I've got a doctor in the house."

Nakhtmin almost burst out laughing.

In the solitude of his room, he bandaged the foot, then sank into dreamless slumber.

MORE VICTIMS?

Day 10 of month Wepet-renpet in Akhet, the season of the inundation

Hori had adjusted to life in the weryt. Under different circumstances, he'd have much appreciated the knowledge he acquired here. As a doctor he could have used these new insights—if only he still were one and not a prisoner. As is it stood, he could neither pass on his findings nor put them to good use, and that made him grow more irritable. He just wanted to smash himself against the walls of the weryt, bang his head against the stones until they yielded or his skull burst.

Not knowing what was going on in the world of the living was the worst torture though. His imagination conjured up horrific scenarios, and the more days passed without news from Nakhtmin, the more restless he became. If only he could investigate himself! His friend might overlook things, which he himself could have noticed. Seven days since Hori found the last message under the rock. Nakhtmin might have fallen prey to the murderer as well. No, he discarded the idea. They couldn't have brought his body to the weryt without him noticing.

During the afternoon wash in the cleansing house, he sometimes asked the crew purifying the corpses if any young girls had been brought to the House of Death. At first they mocked him for his unusual interest, but soon that became boring, and they realized Hori had no sexual interest in these bodies. They knew his origins and about the pharaoh's strange sentence since news traveled fast in such a tight-knit, isolated community.

Kheper once explained, "Our friend here has already had two young women from his circle of acquaintances on the table. He hasn't lost his ties to the world of the living yet, so you should understand his inquisitiveness." Unknowingly, he'd given Hori the perfect excuse for further questions and the statement was close enough to the truth.

Thus Hori learned that quite some time before his arrival, young girls from noble families, who might fit the pattern of the killer, had been brought to the weryt. Two cases seemed particularly interesting and warranted closer investigation. To Hori's dismay, his colleagues wasted little thought on what may have caused a death. Without any ties to the world outside, one corpse was like any other. So there could have been more victims of the murderer he was hunting—without anyone having noticed. His tenacious questions led the men to tell him of their own account about cases that might interest Hori: all men and women from noble families close to the palace, as well as any young people without visible cause of death.

All the information rather confused him instead of clearing things up. And it certainly didn't chase away the feeling of helplessness, which rose like the waters of the Nile.

Annoyed, Hori slipped into his sandals and headed for the anointment chamber, where Kheper already waited to instruct him in the deeper secrets of the process that turned a deceased into an *akh*, a transfigured person.

THE MOURNING PERIOD ENDS

Day 17 of month Tekh in Akhet, the season of the inundation

Everybody groaned and moaned in this heat. The house was unbearably warm. Isis and Mutnofret spent the days under the shade of a vast sycamore with water-soaked cloths hanging from its branches. These cooled the air somewhat.

In the mornings, the women took care of stitching and darning tasks. Occasionally, Isis had the weaving loom brought outside, and Mutnofret spun flax into exquisitely fine threads. Nakhtmin entertained them with stories he read to them, and sometimes he told fairy tales from his homeland.

Around noon the high temperatures arrested all life. Even flies seemed to doze through the hottest hours. That time of the day, their humming sounded as lazy as Nakhtmin felt. After an extensive rest, Mutnofret liked to set up her *senet* board game and did so today as well.

Nakhtmin admired the ivory chest with the grid of thirty squares engraved in the lid. He opened the drawer in the box and took out the pawns. As usual, Mutnofret picked the light-colored ones, while he played the dark ones—a hint at his darker skin, he assumed. She demanded the first throw of the counting plates, shuffled the four ivory slabs in both hands and threw them into the air. Spellbound, she gazed at the result, and Nakhtmin sighed. All pieces lay white side up, and once again she scored five of five possible points. The other side of the plates was red. Depending on how many whites the players cast, as many fields they could move their gaming pieces. And four whites up meant five moves. With all plates showing red, the player had to miss the turn, a situation Nakhtmin was all too familiar with. Sometimes it felt like the counting plates obeyed their owner.

Mutnofret picked one of her pawns and moved it five fields forward, while her tongue poked out from between her lips. Now it was his turn, and he cast a three.

More and more figures conquered the board and soon Mutnofret announced, "Ha! I beat you!" With a flick of her hand, she swept his front pawn from the board.

"You just wait and see, I'll get my revenge." He cast a five and chuckled with joy. "See, I told you."

"You scoundrel!"

"That's how the game works." He laughed, then quickly ducked because she threw the counting plates at him.

The longer they played, the more pieces made it to the finish line. Now they both only had one piece in the race.

He grinned at Mutnofret. "Let's see who's the lucky one." He cast, closed his eyes and prayed silently. *Please, no three!*

"Aaaah-haha," she shrieked with delight.

He opened his eyes. Of course: three. With a sour face, he moved to the field *House of Water,* so close to the finish—but whoever landed on this one had to go back to field fifteen, the *House of Resurrection.* Groaning, he moved his pawn to the middle of the board.

Mutnofret, too, shut her eyes as she cast, and now it was Nakhtmin's turn to laugh. She also ended up in the *House of Water*, and since he already sat in the

House of Resurrection, she had to move all the way back to the start. Then seren-dipity abandoned him. Three times he had to miss a turn, while she caught up with her pawn. Next he cast one. He hardly dared watch her throw. Of course, she beat him—once again. It simply was no fun playing senet with her. Far too often she cast the perfect number, while bad luck seemed to stick to him.

He preferred playing *mehen*, a game where strategy and tactics counted. But since he was much better at it than Mutnofret, she'd banned the game to the darkest corner of her chest. Nakhtmin sighed. One could learn a lot by studying mehen, but she lacked the necessary patience.

Day 4 of month Menkhet in Akhet, season of the inundation

The seventy-day period of mourning in the house of the Amun prophet had dragged for Nakhtmin. Today it ended with the elaborate funeral procession taking Hetepet's mummy—now transfigured into an akh—to her tomb in the city of the dead. He couldn't attend the ceremonious ritual since only family members were allowed to accompany her on this last journey to her final resting place. For the first time in over sixty days he wasn't with his charge, and time stretched even more.

To make himself useful, he settled in a shady spot in the garden with ink stone, writing palette and papyrus, and wrote down what they'd found out so far. This should help him sort his tangled thoughts and decide how to proceed. First, he scribbled the names of the two young women who had definitely fallen prey to the wanted killer. For the names of the two possible victims, whom Hori had reported, he used a different color: Ankhes and Bastet. When he first read Hori's message about these suspicious cases, he couldn't place the names right away, and Ameny only knew Bastet's family. She was the daughter of Thotnakht, the king's first scribe.

Mutnofret, though, recognized the name Ankhes right away and told him, "She was one of the court ladies with the Great Royal Wife. Now I remember. She was found in the palace gardens by a lake. Rumors said she'd drowned. The queen was heartbroken since she liked the girl very much. If I remember correctly, she was an orphan, daughter of a provincial prince and the pharaoh's ward."

Nakhtmin wondered whether they should first investigate these two cases to see if they really were part of the series or start their search at Merit-Neith's house. The papyrus gradually filled with his musings. Still, they knew far too little, particularly about the murder weapon. When Hori told him about the thin wound and the blos-som-shaped bruise, he couldn't think of a weapon causing such an injury. Mostly, the blossom challenged his imagination. A deadly flower? He wrote the words down. A bee with its sting popped up in his mind, and he doodled the sign for the king's title. *He of the Sedge and the Bee.* The insect symbolized Lower Egypt. Could that be relevant?

Noises in the house signaled the return of Ameny and his family. He glanced up. This last day of mourning was the hardest to bear. He wouldn't bother either Ame-ny or Mutnofret with his presence. Instead he copied his notes, not even omitting his absurdly meandering thoughts. Maybe they'd spark new ideas if someone else read them. This evening, he'd deposit the scroll for Hori.

The morning after the funeral, Mutnofret announced she wanted to resume her social life. Her decision to visit the palace first answered Nakhtmin's question where to start his inquiries. His hands turned clammy with excitement. He, the boy from Upper Egypt, visiting the royal family!

The Great Royal Wife Khenemetneferhedjet was called Sherit, the younger, to distinguish her from Senusret's mother of the same name, called Weret, the elder. Together with her children and the second wife of the king, Nofrethenut, Sherit occupied her own wing of the women's house. She was several years older than Mutnofret, while the second wife was closer to her age and a good friend.

The queens passed their time in the sweeping gardens of the palace, and that's where the servants led the two guests. Mutnofret introduced Nakhtmin as her personal physician, then seemed to completely forget about him while talking with the ladies. He felt so out of place, he didn't dare get involved in conversation. For a while, he leisurely strolled through the park before he settled under a solar sail with a good view of his charge chatting with the pharaoh's second wife under a tree at some distance. The tinkling voices of the two ladies lulled him and his eyelids drooped.

A warm voice startled him. The Great Royal Wife stood before him. "A personal physician is a wonderful idea. Maybe I should convince my husband to employ one as well. Losing her sister must have devastated Mutnofret."

"Your majesty…" Nakhtmin stammered. Holy rays of Ra, he couldn't just have a chat with the Great Royal Wife! Where was Mutnofret when he needed her? She knew how to move in these circles. Then he realized what a chance this was, and he overcame his shyness. "I heard you, too, recently lost someone dear to your heart though not a family member?"

Sherit gathered her garment and settled beside him on the lawn. "Ankhes, yes." She sighed. "She was the last living relative from the house of the nomarch of Elephantine. I was planning to wed her to a good husband."

"Oh, I heard she was your maid…"

A wistful smile played around the queen's lips. "Maid, confident, younger sister—a little of everything. She was my husband's ward as well. I'd have loved to see her married to a worthy man so her princely line would live on. A real shame she drowned. I miss her."

"She drowned? Strange. Was Ankhes alone in the garden? And was she found in the water or at the edge? How did that happen?" Nakhtmin bit his tongue, realizing he'd veered off into a rather unexpected direction. Fortunately, the queen didn't seem surprised.

"It happened on a day like this one when it was too hot inside. Ankhes had been withdrawn for a few days already, as if she harbored a secret. I think she might have fallen in love."

"Indeed? Do you know who could have won her affection?"

"She hadn't confided in me yet." Sherit's lips formed a tight line and Nakhtmin guessed the girl's behavior had disappointed or annoyed her. "She left on her own, and I suspected she was going to see her lover."

Nakhtmin's ears pricked. The queen must have had good reasons for such an assumption. So the girl likely had arranged to meet someone.

"Obviously, she remained alone or else the accident couldn't have happened," she continued. "At dusk I sent the king's servants to search for her, and they found her at the edge of the small lake on the other end of the garden, hidden in the reeds."

"That must have been a horrible blow for you. The bodies of drowned people are so awful to look at. The foam at the mouth—"

"Not at all! No, she was..." The queen's eyes filled with tears. "She looked surprised. Her eyes seemed to look at me in wonder, and her mouth was slightly open. No foam."

"Then she probably didn't drown," Nakhtmin muttered.

"What was that? I didn't hear you."

"Oh, nothing. I'm really sorry about Ankhes. Who would you have selected as her husband?"

"I had one of the vizier's sons in mind or maybe the son of the first prophet of Amun. All very promising young men."

The last words of the king's wife resonated with something inside Nakhtmin, but he couldn't identify what that might be. As soon as he thought he might have grasped the fleeting notion, it was gone. To his relief, Sherit didn't notice his absent-mindedness. She too seemed lost in memories. Soon after, the laughing and babbling flock of children and young women headed their way, and the moment of privacy passed.

Around noon Mutnofret wanted to leave and Nakhtmin was more than happy to oblige. The nightly excursion across the river took its toll. With the rising waters, it had become far more difficult to get news to Hori. Now, he longed for the solitude of his room. After a nap, he might be able to see what was lurking under the surface of his mind.

"I saw you talking to Sherit," Mutnofret said. Curiosity rang in her voice. Of course she'd want to know if he found out something.

Nakhtmin cast a cautious gaze around. Out here on the street, he'd rather not reveal his gathered knowledge. "Yes," he said. "But I'd prefer to tell you and your father at the same time. It's too dangerous here and I'm too tired to report twice."

"Dangerous, dangerous. Oh yes, I can see the walls murmuring the news to anyone passing by. There's nobody around." Her objection sounded like that of a stubborn child.

Nakhtmin sighed. "Don't tell me you've never stood at the edge of your garden and listened to the voice of people beyond the wall, like little girls love to do?" With satisfaction, he registered first her throat turning crimson, then her face.

"Bumptious goblin!"

He'd have loved to retaliate with a similar term of endearment but restrained himself. At least he'd gotten to her. Mutnofret could be tiresome, and he didn't quite trust her. In her obstinacy, she'd already slipped away once. She treated the investigation like a game. *Yes, like when we play senet and all of us are her pawns, which she can place according to her wishes or sweep from the board. Except real life doesn't work like that. One of these days her brashness is going to get her in major trouble.*

They walked the rest of the way in silence.

Ameny took a deep breath. "The king's ward—what a foolhardy miscreant!"

"If Ankhes really fell prey to the same killer. Unfortunately, she's lying in her sarcophagus now and we'll never be able to prove it."

"Unless we can draw a confession from the culprit."

Both men looked up in surprise. Nakhtmin had completely forgotten Mutnofret's presence since she'd remained unusually silent until now. "Before we can get a confession, we'll have to find and arrest him," he grumbled.

"I don't like you being dragged into this investigation, child. Leave it to Nakhtmin. Today, he learned much without your help."

"But I like it. It's more exciting than my normal life."

The anguished father groaned. "If you don't stay in the background, I'll revoke my permission. Then Nakhtmin won't accompany you as your personal gua…doctor any longer. And I won't let you out of the house on your own until this villain has been caught. That's my last word in this matter."

"Father!"

Shocked, Nakhtmin looked from Mutnofret to the Amun prophet. If the spoiled brat didn't get a grip, he'd lose access to the big houses. Father and daughter locked eyes and fought a silent battle.

At last, she demurely lowered her head. "Fine. I'll respect your wish."

Nakhtmin imagined hearing the silent addition, 'although I think you're exaggerating.' She stormed from the room, and he sighed his relief. Maybe they shouldn't have let her in on their plans, but who knew how difficult she'd have turned out then.

"Now we know more but didn't really get closer to our goal," Ameny picked up their discussion.

"Yes. And there's more. The queen mentioned something that seemed to remind me of something else, except I can't access whatever that might be. Ever since, I've been wracking my mind but it won't come forward."

"Maybe it wasn't important. In any case, you have to stop thinking about it, then the memory will surface."

"You're probably right. Before I take a nap, I want to write down everything the queen said. Hori should receive a copy of my notes."

"Then I'll leave you to it and talk to my daughter, try to make her understand my reasoning."

The next day, Nakhtmin had just settled in the shade of the sycamore, under which the ladies of the house liked to spend their afternoons, when one of the servant girls announced a visitor. A young woman with a naked toddler on her hip followed in her wake.

Mutnofret didn't seem the least bit surprised and introduced her friend as Sati. "She's Tutu's daughter and, like me, recently lost her younger sister, Merit-Neith."

When did she contrive this? Of course, Nakhtmin was happy to meet Sati, and here in the garden he didn't have to worry about Mutnofret's safety. Although Sati cast curious glances at him when she lowered the little boy, Mutnofret didn't introduce him. So he had to do it. After all, he wasn't a simple servant! "What's the name of your son?" he asked afterward.

"Sinuhe."

Nakhtmin raised his eyebrows in astonishment. "You like the *Story of Sinuhe*?" That was his all-time favorite among the stories they had to transcribe in school.

"Didn't you know Tutu is a direct descendent of Sinuhe?" Mutnofret asked in a rather condescending tone.

Nakhtmin hated it when she made him feel his ignorance of all things concerning the noble society, reminding him of his lowly origins. To hide his embarrassment, he pulled the boy onto his lap and tickled his burly belly. Squirming and squealing, the little fellow slid onto the mat where Nakhtmin played with him some more. The women only talked about household matters. Did Mutnofret expect him to question her friend, or would she try to get information from her? Of their own accord, his fingers wandered over the boy's smooth skin. Vigorous and well-nourished, he determined. "You're lucky to have such a healthy boy," he said.

Sati beamed. "Yes, I thank the gods."

"Does your husband also work in the king's house of women, like your father?"

She nodded and held out her arms. Chortling, Sinuhe crawled to her and curled up on her lap.

"Your sister, she was younger than you, right? Wasn't she supposed to marry soon?" A rather clumsy change of topic but she didn't seem to notice anything odd about it. Her smile vanished though.

She stroked her son's lock of youth and pressed him against her. "She was engaged to Shepses, the vizier's son."

"I know Shepses. We attended medical school together," Nakhtmin offered.

She wrinkled her nose. "Then you must know what a ladies' man he is. I doubt he would have made her happy. Oh well, that doesn't matter now." She wiped at her eyes.

Nakhtmin hated having to stir up her grief again. "Did she catch a fatal disease? Or was it an accident? Such a tragedy at her age. I feel with you."

Sati's lips quivered. She buried her face in the child's tuft although he struggled indignantly.

Mutnofret hissed, "Really, Nakhtmin! You're such a yokel!"

While Sati wasn't looking, he pulled a face at Mutnofret. He'd happily leave it to her to drag more out of her friend. He took the child from his mother and set him on his feet while holding one of his hands. On unsteady legs, little Sinuhe explored the flowers with him.

In the evening, Mutnofret told him Sati's sister had been found lifeless in the garden of her parents' estate. Like in Hetepet's case, the doctor they'd called had suspected a heatstroke—not unusual in these temperatures.

FINALLY A CLUE?

Hori awoke with a sense of anticipation. *Oh right, the message!* He'd retrieved a new scroll from their hiding place. For fear of someone noticing light in his house late at night, he always waited to read the news in daylight. And he had to make his tallow lamps last. He'd already used a significant amount of the fat to seal his first two messages. Each worker in the weryt received only a certain amount every year.

He hadn't really expected to receive news from Nakhtmin this soon again but had checked anyway. Maybe his friend had discovered something. He quickly counted the days—right, the period of mourning in Ameny's house had ended. In the light of dawn, he skimmed the distinct writing of his friend, then read it again more slowly. He didn't have much time before he needed to head out to the yard of evisceration and start his day's work.

By now he was privy to most secrets of the weryt, and the always-same moves bored him. How much more interesting it was to find out what ailed a sick person! The mystery surrounding the deaths of the young women gave him the mental challenge he missed during the repetitive, unchanging tasks in the House of Death. His fingers moved of their own accord, while he gave his thoughts free rein.

If Ankhes had really drowned, the *ut*, who mentioned her to him, would have noticed. A drowned body showed characteristic features hard to overlook. Wasn't it strange that two of the supposed murder victims were about to marry? There it was—the connection!

Dazed by his shocking realization, he felt like someone hit him over the head with a hammer. Merit-Neith was engaged to Shepses, and Ankhes, too, might have married one of the vizier's sons. No, too far-fetched. Hori recoiled from the thought as if it were a poisonous scorpion. Nebit's family had suffered enough because of him. How could he possibly point an accusing finger at the house of the vizier? However, it was a strange coincidence and a fact connecting both cases. They needed to spin this thread further. Even if it led nowhere, it might set Nakhtmin on the right track. He couldn't possibly hold back his suspicion, not even for fear of hurting the vizier once more. Come to think of it, what did he owe the man? Nefer-ib's death had been an accident, and the vizier had violated Maat by convincing witnesses to give false testimony. Hori was being punished for something that hadn't been a deliberate act. He'd only meant to protect the girl in the tavern. His heart was pure. Still, he felt a lump of guilt and unease in his stomach. If only he could ask Kheper to cut out the foreign matter.

Time passed slowly as he worked bent over the table. He desperately needed to tell Nakhtmin of his suspicion. If only his thoughts could fly like clouds! Eventually, the day ended. While washing, he met Kheper, who cordially invited him over for dinner.

"Thanks, but not today. I've got a headache and want to go to bed early," Hori lied. The older man's face showed disappointment, so he added, "How about tomorrow evening? I'd certainly be looking forward to your wife's cooking skills. And please give my regards to your enchanting daughter." Inaudibly, he groaned. The ut trying to hook him up with his daughter Nut was starting to annoy him. The girl was nice, pretty too, but everything inside Hori rebelled against growing roots in the weryt. Deep down, he still harbored hope his sentence might not be as final as it had sounded from the pharaoh's mouth.

Reaching his house, he went to the bedroom, where he kept Nakhtmin's messages well hidden behind a loose brick. Here he also wrote his replies. Too many people spent the evening on the roofs, and he couldn't afford to be seen. Someone might wonder what he was writing and, even more, where he got the papyrus. The inhabitants of the weryt were one large community, only he didn't quite belong. And just as he didn't fully trust the utu, they regarded him as something strange. Therefore he couldn't risk drawing any attention lest someone follow him one of these nights when he left these walls. That would be his end.

Ink dropped from his stylus. The splash almost rendered the last sentence unreadable. He cursed his wandering thoughts and quickly finished his report. What would Nakhtmin think of his discovery?

DEADLY FLOWERS

Flabbergasted, Nakhtmin dropped the papyrus. "How could I have missed this! That's what I couldn't grasp yesterday." He so wanted to wake Ameny and talk things over with him, but the priest had gone to sleep hours earlier. Although he'd rowed across the river, he hadn't really expected to find a reply from Hori in their cranny. What could he possibly tell them? There wasn't much he could contribute to the investigation behind walls, or so Nakhtmin had thought. How wrong he'd been! If it weren't so exhausting to stay awake so late, he too would check for news every night like Hori did.

Still tempted to tear Ameny from his slumber, he imagined Lady Isis's puzzlement if he knocked on their bedchamber. No, he had to ponder things on his own. Had they really found a clue?

He sank onto his bed and watched Shepses scamper through his thoughts. Why should the vizier's son kill his bride? That made no sense. If he didn't want to marry, surely nobody would force him. Gradually, Nakhtmin drifted off to sleep but these questions haunted his dreams.

The next day, Hori's suspicion caused Ameny to ruminate as well. "The vizier is the highest official in the Two Lands. Until now, I thought him and his family above any doubt, but this truly is…" He rested his chin on his folded hands. "I find it hard to believe in such a coincidence."

"Shepses is a womanizer so it surprised me he wanted to get married. That would put an end to his escapades. Maybe his parents are pressuring him? After all, Shepses is their oldest now."

The prophet regarded Nakhtmin with a thoughtful look on his face. "We should examine this connection closely. In the process, we might dig up more to further our investigation. But how? Mutnofret doesn't visit Nebit's house since the man has no daughters of her age, only one child who has lived maybe six seasons of inundation. And lady Sitamun is too old for her to consort with."

Nakhtmin smiled. "For once, I can help out. Shepses and I are both doctors and studied together. Although I'm currently employed as Mutnofret's personal physician, I still have access to the House of Life. Shepses isn't exactly a friend of mine but I could visit him there without anyone finding it strange that I talk to him. Let's see what I can glean. I'll ask Mutnofret if she can dispense with me later in the day." He rose and was walking toward the door when he remembered something. Terror made him trip, but he caught himself before he fell. "The House of Life!"

Ameny stared at him with a blank look.

"Hetepet used to pick you up there every afternoon. I often saw her, even when she still had her lock of youth."

A wistful smile spread over the priest's face. "Before I leave, I always go to Inpu and ask if he needs anything for teaching students or treating patients. She used to wait nearby."

Nakhtmin nodded. He'd noticed Ameny's daily conversations with the head of the House of Life. "Sometimes I talked to her or joked with her, while she waited for you. I still regarded her as a little girl, I guess, although she'd blossomed into a woman. Maybe I wasn't the only young doctor who noticed her. And maybe not all of them overlooked her feminine charms?"

First Ameny's face had paled, now it glowed red with rage. "Shepses! You think he could have seduced my little girl? The miscreant, that…"

Nakhtmin had trouble calming down the raging father. Except for Shepses's boasting, he had no evidence the vizier's son really conquered as many young women as he claimed. Did the guy look attractive? Nakhtmin found it hard to judge the appeal of another man. He admitted to himself that he disliked his colleague too much to find his exterior agreeable.

Of course, his plan to simply tell Mutnofret he'd be absent in the afternoon didn't quite work out.

"Oh, and where are you going?" she asked immediately.

She kept at it until she'd pried everything out of him. Could she see it in his face when he tried to hide something from her?

"Hetepet in love?" Her features distorted with conflicting emotions. "But she was still a child! I never—I mean—I couldn't see her interested in a man. A short time ago, she was still playing with dolls and loved to annoy me no end…"

Nakhtmin couldn't suppress a grin. "You mean your little sister couldn't possibly get ahead of you in something? Maybe you underrated her."

Mutnofret's eyes glistened in the gloom. He couldn't interpret her expression. "What makes you think she'd have been the first to open up to a man?" The tip of her tongue slid over her lips. She leaned toward him.

"Stop it. We both know you'll just laugh at me if I fall for it."

She hissed. "All right. Go. Get lost. Play with your tweezers and knives."

Darn, what a difficult woman! He took flight under taunting laughter. On the way to the House of Life, images of her rosy tongue swirled through his mind. Last thing he needed was getting seduced by the little minx.

He caught Shepses between two patients and cast stealthy glances around at the furnishings. He'd never been allowed to treat people in these elegant rooms. Obviously they were reserved for very rich patients.

"Hey, Nakhtmin! What are you doing here?"

Nakhtmin cringed. "Um…" He should have thought of a reason for his visit instead of contemplating Mutnofret's charms. Fortunately, Shepses wasn't one to take much interest in what others might have to say, so the vizier's son didn't even notice the lack of a reply.

"I guess you want me to speak to my father, put in a good word for you. Forget it." The slender brown fingers played with elegant medical instruments laid out on a leather wrap.

Grateful for the plausible pretext Shepses had provided, he almost nodded with enthusiasm. Just in time, he caught himself and tried for a crestfallen expression. "Too bad, I'd really hoped… It's been awhile and I didn't harm anyone, only spoke the truth. Does it really warrant a lifelong grudge?"

Shepses laughed. With derision or bitterness? Nakhtmin couldn't tell.

"My mother isn't someone to easily forget or forgive," he squeezed out between clenched teeth.

That moment, Nakhtmin noticed what had bothered him about the medical instruments, which gleamed dully in the rays of the low sun. He reached for a puncture needle and studied it. The bronze pin stuck in an ornate handle formed like a blossom.

Shepses flashed a wide smile. "Classy, isn't it? A graduation gift from my mother. A doctor without his own instruments isn't really a doctor."

Nakhtmin ground his teeth since he couldn't afford his own kit yet. "It's the doctor who heals, not the tools. And not everyone handling a knife does so to help people." Then he realized he'd said too much and bit his tongue.

Shepses granted him a puzzled look before he laughed out loud. "Oh, Nakhtmin, you've always been envious." He splayed his fingers. "To think you could have had everything if you'd done my father's bidding. But you've always been an ass."

Nakhtmin wanted to punch the arrogant grin from his face but restrained himself. Excitement over his discovery made him antsy. He couldn't get into a fight with Shepses now that he knew what the murder weapon was and who owned it. No time for mistakes! If Shepses was the killer... If? No doubt he committed those heinous crimes! But he couldn't let on that he knew. So far, only unsuspecting girls had fallen prey to him, but if cornered, Shepses might kill him. He had enough weapons at hand. Nakhtmin headed for the door. "Never mind, Shepses. I just thought I should ask. Farewell."

"Wait."

Nakhtmin spun around, his hands sweating.

"I heard you had a streak of luck after all. Mutnofret's personal physician?" Shepses clicked his tongue and closed his eyes. "If she's as passionate as her little sister, you must be having a lot of fun with her." Laughing, he replaced the puncture needle in the leather wrap.

Nakhtmin was glad Shepses had turned his back on him. He didn't think he could have maintained a straight face. Uncontrollable rage boiled up in him, almost an urge to kill. Another word and he might have lunged at the creep. With trembling shoulders, he walked through the door, then ran as if demons were chasing him down the deserted hallways. At the temple of Amun, he paused to catch his breath. The extent of what he just learned made him dizzy. How to break the news to Ameny?

Listening to Nakhtmin's report, the second prophet of Amun grew very upset indeed. Fists clenched, he paced his study. "I'll get the mangy mutt!"

"The problem is we can't prove anything. Not even that Hetepet and the other girls really were murdered. He'd been too clever. Nobody suspected anything but a natural cause of death." Finishing the sentence, he thought Shepses wasn't really that clever. His boastful, flamboyant behavior didn't fit well with a cold-blooded, deliberate killer. Still...the connection was right there. Hetepet seemed to have been one of Shepses's playmates, and the physician had the murder weapon. "I doubt anyone else in the Two Lands owns instruments with a similar handle," he verbalized his thoughts. "But somehow I don't think him capable of performing the crimes."

Ameny stopped in his tracks and knitted his eyebrows. "What do you mean? Why do you defend the son of a bitch? He practically confessed!"

Nakhtmin shrugged. "I don't know. Just doesn't seem to go with his personality.

Shepses likes to brag about his deeds, display them openly. Our murderer acts in the shadows, furtive like a snake's sudden attack. And he seemed a bit too candid for someone who has much to hide."

"I don't understand you. Sounds like you're trying to get him off the hook when we only need to reel in the fish now."

"What if someone else has access to Shepses's instruments? We have to be absolutely certain before we press charges at the pharaoh's court. The king…" Nakhtmin darted a quick glance at his benefactor. "The king—life, prosperity and health—has already shown once that he is not inclined to prosecute obvious misdemeanors of his vizier." He took a deep breath and braced himself for an outburst to wash over him.

Ameny's eyebrows formed one stormy line, his face turning a threateningly dark color. All of a sudden, pent-up air escaped from his mouth, and with it, all rage over Nakhtmin's insinuations seemed to evaporate. He said, "Today I read the protocols of your friend's trial. You're right, the verdict is a scandalous injustice. Witnesses had been bribed, and everyone should have noticed that. Unfortunately there are no records of what was said during consultation. I assume Hori's father stood up for his son, but Nebit's wish to see the young man convicted must have carried more weight. I can't imagine why the pharaoh—life, prosperity and health—" He scrunched up his face. "…turned against Maat like that."

"Yes," pondered Nakhtmin. "I got the impression the vizier had a hold over the king. How could the pharaoh be put under such pressure? What offense could be so grave?"

Ameny burst into bitter laughter. "It might not even seem serious to us. Senusret is a young man of great sincerity and high moral values. I really wonder how he could have become entangled. The house of Nebit appears to be the center of all evil, like a swamp from which putrid odor rises."

Scenes of that fateful night flashed in Nakhtmin's mind. Lady Sitamun mounting her own son. He shivered. "My mother isn't one to easily forgive," Shepses had murmured. And that although they'd been talking about Nebit holding a grudge. "Nebit has another brother, Hotep, and he really is a strange one," he said. "The gods have bound his tongue. He accompanied us to the tavern that evening, and I've rarely seen such hatred."

Ameny listened intently. "Hatred for whom?"

Nakhtmin could only shrug his shoulders. "His brothers, his mother, himself—hard to tell. I can't shake off the feeling something that happened during the banquet is the key to solving the murders. Unfortunately, I can't remember events very well. I drank too much, and then…" His tongue shied from revealing what the vizier's wife had done.

"I think it's time to meet your friend. Tonight I'll cross the river with you to discuss the situation with Hori. First I want to give you something I acquired a few days ago. Regard it as part of your payment. I feel more at ease if my resident doctor has all the tools he needs to perform his profession." He handed him a leather bundle.

Nakhtmin's fingers caressed the material before he unrolled the instrument kit. "Thanks," he squeezed through his clogged throat. "You have no idea how much this means to me!"

THE CONFUSION GROWS

The nightly excursions under the wall through the canal had already turned into a treasured ritual for Hori. Tonight he didn't expect a message from Nakhtmin, but being locked up tormented him. He craved the sense of freedom he experienced outside the walls. Out of habit, he headed for the spot where the rock marked the cranny. Almost there, a noise made him flinch.

A voice whispered, "Hori!"

Blood rushed in his ears; his legs buckled. This time they caught him, and now… Somebody pulled him up, grabbed his elbow and dragged him to a rugged rock wall. Then it dawned on him this couldn't be guards or the king's officers since they'd have taken him in a different direction. "Nakhtmin?" He rubbed his eyes in disbelief. "Boy, you sure gave me a start!" He embraced his friend. "It's good to see you. Working with the dead gets rather lonely."

Another person emerged from the shadows. "It's me, Ameny."

Alarmed, Hori blurted, "What are you two doing here? Did something happen?" He listened to their report spellbound.

When it ended, the priest added, "Nakhtmin thinks something could have happened at the banquet on Nebit's estate that might help us unmask the killer. Obviously he is to be found in the vizier's house, and I personally believe it's your friend Shepses."

Hori snorted.

"I'm not that sure," Nakhtmin contradicted. "Shepses isn't smart enough."

For a while Hori weighed the information in his heart, then agreed with Nakhtmin. "I loathe the guy, but he's just a show-off."

"Mutnofret thought the murderer could be a woman. Might not be as farfetched as it sounds, since a woman could approach the girls more openly than a man even if they knew him. I've compiled a list of suspects. We should go through them together and see if someone stands out or can be eliminated."

Hori found it puzzling how Nakhtmin's voice had changed when he mentioned Ameny's daughter. Was there something going on between these two? Oh my, the last thing he needed was mulling over other people's love life. They had more urgent problems to tackle. Hori admired Nakhtmin's methodical approach, except it didn't really help. Shepses or Hotep, Nebit or Sitamun, they all looked suspicious. Everybody had access to the murder weapon, but nobody seemed to have a reason to kill the young women.

Nakhtmin suggested taking a closer look at the vizier's service staff.

That seemed absurd to Hori. "A servant couldn't have walked this far into the temple of Amun compound. The royal gardens, where Ankhes perished, would also have been off limits. By the way, did you talk to the family of the fourth girl, Bastet?"

Nakhtmin and the priest looked at each other and groaned simultaneously.

"What? What is it? Did I say something silly?"

Ameny spoke first. "She was the daughter of Thotnakht, senior scribe of the king."

"Yes, we know that." Hori still didn't understand.

"Thotnakht attended your trial, more importantly, he heard what was said in the judges' chamber." Nakhtmin sounded excited.

Now, realization dawned on him. "No! No, no, you can't let Thotnakht in on this. If he finds out about my involvement—I doubt he'll keep our secret."

"Oh, come on. You've got to understand this might be a perfect way to find out what the vizier knows to have such a hold on the pharaoh."

"Sure, Nebit would have spread out the king's misdemeanors in front of everyone," Hori scoffed. "By the way, there's someone else you could ask about the discussion among the judges: my father. Don't you think he'd have objected if something so obvious had been going on between the king and his vizier? I might not rate highly in his esteem, but he wouldn't have put up with such an injustice." Burning liquid rose in his throat. The whole trial... What a farce! His head spun. "Please be silent, I've got to think," he hissed and covered his ears while recalling the events and trying to sort them. Finally he looked at the two men sitting opposite him on rocks. The low moon shone on their faces and seemed to cut them in halves, one light, one dark. He took a deep breath. "Ameny is right, that evening could be the key although two of the girls were murdered before. Therefore, I'll tell you everything I know about it." In detail, he described his impressions of the vizier's family. Reaching the point when Nebit retreated, he hesitated and met Nakhtmin's gaze. His friend shook his head ever so slightly. He too still felt ashamed having witnessed such a scene, so he only sketched his sensing jealousy among the brothers, then moved on to the tragedy unfolding in the tavern, ending with Neferib's death.

Ameny, hearing the prelude to the brawl for the first time, drew in a sharp breath. "Now I understand your reaction. I would have acted the same way toward Neferib if I'd been there."

A drawn-out howl rang through the night and made them start.

Hori laughed nervously. "Just a jackal."

Soon more animals joined in. The priest rubbed his arms as if spooked. "It's time for us to leave the world of the dead," he murmured.

Hori sighed. "I wish I could accompany you."

Nakhtmin hugged him. "I too wish you could come along."

"Give Mutnofret my regards," he whispered after the departing figures. On his way back to the high wall of the weryt, Hori chuckled to himself. Nakhtmin and the priest's daughter—should get interesting.

A FAILED ATTEMPT

After breakfast, Nakhtmin strolled into the garden and sat down at the peacefully smooth pond. Soon the daughter of the house joined him, and he endured her interrogation with a sigh. What had he found out yesterday? What had he discussed with her father? He wasn't sure how much he could tell her. Anything regarding Hori he had to omit anyway since she didn't know about his involvement and shouldn't. That required his full concentration. Once he almost slipped up and told her about the nighttime excursions. To his relief Mutnofret didn't notice his abrupt silence. She seemed deep in thought. Nakhtmin was glad to be spared her pointed remarks for once.

A high shriek made them both jump. One of the twins fell, hit his head and screamed as if his life were at stake. Nakhtmin ran to him and left Mutnofret behind at the pond.

The wound on Huni's forehead wasn't deep but bled strongly. "I should stitch you up," he said. Penu lurked nearby, so he called to him, "Quick, get me my doctor's toolkit. It's on top of my clothes chest." In the meantime, he pressed a piece of linen on the wound. How fortunate he had his own instruments now!

Gradually the entire household gathered around them, and the boy visibly enjoyed the attention after the first pain eased up. Penu returned with the leather wrap containing his instruments.

Nakhtmin fumbled the thin needle from the loop fixing it in place. He looked up. "Isis, I need a thread, ideally cleansed intestine of a small animal, but fine linen should do as well."

Mutnofret picked up the reel with the previous morning's work and handed it to him. He threaded the thin yarn into the eye of the needle where it jammed, since the small eye wasn't polished that well inside. Because of that general problem, intestine worked better. Annoyed he moistened the end with saliva and succeeded.

Huni had observed his every move with eyes growing wider. When he realized Nakhtmin wanted to stitch up his skin, he screamed at the top of his voice, kicked and writhed. The women held him, but Nakhtmin saw it wouldn't work that way. He had an idea. "Hey, Huni, aren't you always getting mad when people mistake you for Bata?"

The boy nodded.

"Listen, when I'm done, you'll have an impressive scar on your forehead. Everyone will be able to tell you apart at first glance."

A tentative smile spread over Huni's face. "Really?" He sniffed. "Will it hurt?"

Nakhtmin remembered the two rascals loved to play king's soldiers. "Oh yes, it will hurt, but I know how tough you are, like a real warrior."

The child nodded gravely this time. "Yes, I won't scream."

"That's my man." Nakhtmin hurried to make the two stitches.

Huni pressed his lips together but didn't make any noise.

"You are a true hero. And soon you'll have a scar to prove it."

Isis took the reluctant hero in her arms and went inside with him.

Bata gazed after them with visible envy and leaned his head toward him. "Can I have a scar as well? Please!"

Nakhtmin shook with laughter. Mutnofret squatted and explained, "Scars need to be earned. You don't want to cheat, do you?"

Bata shook his head.

"Besides, I promised Huni that you two will be distinguishable," Nakhtmin said. "He'd think I'm a liar if you also got a scar. You don't want that, do you?"

"No. Did it hurt very much?"

Nakhtmin pricked his finger with the needle. Bata screamed. "I'd rather not get stitched." He dashed away.

Smiling, Nakhtmin was about to roll up his instruments when Mutnofret stopped him. She pulled out one of the puncture needles and studied it. "Hard to belief a stab with this delicate tool can be lethal."

"If you hit the right spot, yes. However, it is a strange choice of weapon." Her inquisitive gaze demanded an explanation, so he obliged. "When the insides of a body are injured, vital juices seep from the vessels transporting them, very similar to the blood gushing from Huni's forehead. The bigger the wound the faster one dies. I wonder, though, if with such a tiny wound the victim would collapse right away."

She furrowed her brow. "Does that matter?"

"Imagine someone stabs you, and you know this person wants to kill you. What would you do?"

Her face lit up. "Of course! I'd scream for help."

"Exactly. The girls must have known who attacked them. Would they have remained silent if they lived long enough to tell?"

Mutnofret grabbed his hand. "Let's try!"

Horrified, Nakhtmin gaped at her. "I can't just jab a needle into someone's heart. Even the best doctor—"

"Stupid as a donkey!" she called and ran off toward the kitchen wing.

Nakhtmin stumbled after her. What was she up to now? At the stables she stopped, opened one of the wattle doors and slipped inside. A few moments later, she stepped out, pulling along a young goat with a rope around its neck.

"I believe tomorrow we're going to have roasted goat kid anyway."

"You're crazy!" he blurted.

"Oh, come on. I'll hold it." She bent forward and handed him the puncture needle.

Nakhtmin went down on his knees. If they wanted to learn something from this experiment, he needed to find the heart first.

"Meheheh," the goat bleated and jerked back. Mutnofret lost her balance and fell on her butt. The goat saw its chance and skipped away. Just in time, Nakhtmin snatched the end of the rope.

Mutnofret rubbed her bottom and snorted. "You beast. I'll eat you with pleasure tomorrow."

He suppressed a laugh. Finally she managed to hold the animal tight, allowing him to touch the trembling body. The hammering heart wasn't hard to find. He estimated the spot that might equate to the stab wound under the left breast of a young woman and jabbed the needle in.

The goat bleated with terror and jumped, rear hooves lashing out and connecting with Mutnofret's thigh. She yelped and let go of the goat, which absconded into the bushes.

"Just great," Nakhtmin barked. "You were supposed to hold it."

"Help me up, you chuff! You were supposed to pierce the heart. I think you only pricked the beast a little."

He snorted with indignation. "No way. The needle went right into the heart, believe me."

Their gazes locked.

"But then it's obvious," she said. "Such a wound doesn't kill right away."

Nakhtmin jumped up. "Come on, we've got to find it." The animal shouldn't suffer any longer.

They searched the neighboring grounds, but it took some time until Nakhtmin heard a meek bleating. Behind a hedge, he found the animal with buckled legs, unable to get up. Glad to have his instruments with him, he pulled out the flint knife and cut the young goat's throat. The blood didn't gush as strongly as he'd expected, but it spattered all over his shendyt.

Mutnofret put her hands on her hips and laughed. "Quite the doctor you are. At the moment people might mistake you for a butcher."

He grimaced. "And now?"

"Now you'll take the carcass to the kitchen," she said, turned on her heels and ran away.

Nakhtmin couldn't believe it. That woman! After dumping the animal in the kitchen and mumbling a stuttered excuse about medical experiments, he only wanted to wash himself, and he appreciated Mutnofret's absence. He'd had enough of her for now. The rest of the morning flowed at a sluggish pace allowing him to sort his thoughts in peace.

Their investigation had reached a dead end. The families of the vizier and the Amun priest had little in common and their social circles hardly overlapped. However, they needed eyes and ears on Nebit's estate to sniff out the killer. And now this discovery. The puncture needle alone couldn't be the murder weapon unless the villain held his victims tight until they died. Not very likely. Until he could make more sense of it, he wouldn't bother Hori and Ameny with news of his goat experiment.

The midday meal usually consisted of light food. Like most days, Ameny took a break from his temple duties to join them. Mutnofret did not show, which wasn't uncommon. She often simply munched some fruit before lying down for a nap. Conversation at the table centered on Huni's accident. Soon they all retreated to escape the worst heat of the day and seek refuge dozing in their cooler bedchambers.

Slamming of doors and hasty steps in the hallway jerked Nakhtmin awake. He must have been sleeping like a log since he felt numb and found it difficult to orient himself. The door to his room flung open, and the lady of the house poked her head in. "Is Mutnofret with you?"

What an absurd idea. Why should Mutnofret share my bed? Then the underlying implication filtered through to him. "What? She isn't in her room?"

Isis shook her head. "My daughter can't be found anywhere in the house. My husband is beside himself."

Nakhtmin jumped to his feet, quickly donned his shendyt and hurried after Isis to the great hall of the house, where Ameny instructed Penu and another servant. "Search every nook and cranny of the house and garden. Mutnofret has to be somewhere. She wouldn't leave the estate without telling us. She knows…"

"What does my daughter know?" Isis stopped in the doorway, and Nakhtmin almost bumped into her. He squeezed past her and stood beside the priest. The servants scurried off.

Ameny turned to her. His face showed embarrassment and alarm, but also his fear for his daughter. "It's just that I asked her not to leave the premises without Nakhtmin escorting her. Because of what happened to Hetepet. You know that."

His wife studied him with a doubtful expression. "Are you really telling me the truth? It's not like you to stir up the whole household just because the girl goes for a walk."

"And it's not like her to stroll off without letting someone know. She's aware of my concerns."

"…and she might deem them exaggerated, my dear. Maybe she enjoys escaping your vigil."

Yes, that would be typical for Mutnofret. However, the girl knew why she really needed protection. If she only wanted to make fun of Nakhtmin, it was a cruel joke for her father. He never thought her inconsiderate of other people.

Ameny seemed deeply shaken. He probably wanted to yell in his wife's face that Mutnofret's life was at stake. Nakhtmin admired the man's self-control when he answered in a calm voice, "The two of us will go look for her. I'm sure you're right." He headed toward the door, and Nakhtmin hurried after him.

Crossing the front yard, he profusely apologized to the priest for his failure. This shouldn't have happened. But how should he have prevented the young woman setting out on her own if she was determined? Nevertheless, Nakhtmin blamed himself and couldn't suppress a sense of dread. "We should start our search at the House of Life," he suggested.

Ameny grabbed his arm. "Why did I even hire you? What do you know? Did she tell you something, and you left her alone?"

"No, definitely not. She interrogated me earlier and I had to tell her all about Shepses and Hetepet. I should have known better. You know what she's like. If she wants something…"

"…she'll get it. Yes, my daughter always had a strong will."

Quite different descriptions popped up in Nakhtmin's mind: stubborn, obstinate, self-centered, spoiled and careless. If she really went to see Shepses, she faced great danger. Did it mean nothing to her that she worried everyone in the household, most of all her father? Likely she gloated over having fooled him—again. What good was he to Ameny if Mutnofret regarded it as a fun pastime to sneak away from him?

Ameny's words hit home hard. Indeed, the man might very well regret having welcomed him to his house. He could only hope nothing happened to Mutnofret, or else… He thought of his miserable hut in the paupers' quarter, the tough position in the House of Life he'd had to cope with before. If Ameny kicked him out, he'd be even worse off. Where could he go? The medical men in the Two Lands formed a rather tight-knit community. Without recommendations he wouldn't get a foot in the door. Until recently, he didn't even have his own instruments. Most likely he'd have to return to the small backwater village where he was born, where he'd be the only doctor among peasants, with no access to writings. His father had already died, but at least people knew him there. Cringing, he realized what a selfish, uncaring turn his considerations had taken. He worried about his future when the girl in his charge was in serious danger!

The priest picked up his pace even more, and Nakhtmin breathed heavily trying to keep up with him. Fortunately, it wasn't far to the temple. Soon they passed through the pylon. Nakhtmin hurried after Ameny across the yard to the gate of the House of Life, where Inpu blocked their way. "Venerable prophet, you're early today."

Ameny shoved the dignitary aside. "Where's my daughter? Have you seen Mutnofret?"

Inpu pursed his lips and wrinkled his nose, a sure sign of disapproval. "The young lady arrived awhile ago, indeed. She suffered from a headache and specifically requested doctor Shepses to—"

"Where? Where is she, man?"

"I do beg your pardon!" Sulking, the head of the House of Life pushed out his lower lip.

Nakhtmin took his former supervisor aside. "The prophet is deeply worried about his daughter's headache. You remember the tragic death of his youngest daughter, little Hetepet, don't you? Please forgive his rudeness."

Inpu nodded ungraciously. "Still—such behavior…" He clicked his tongue, another sure sign he was still miffed. "Shepses is in the third room to the left today. Whether your daughter is still with him, I cannot know."

Nakhtmin on his heels, Ameny dashed ahead and through the third door, only to find the room empty.

An opening in the opposite wall led to the temple garden—reserved for the priests of Amun. Nevertheless, a woman's bubbly laugh filtered through the linen curtain billowing in the wind. The door stood ajar. Nakhtmin nodded toward the instrument kit he'd seen during his previous visit. Ameny only glared at it, then took three long strides to the opening and stormed outside. With determination, he headed toward the voices. Nakhtmin ran past him and peeked behind a dense bush obscuring their view. What he glimpsed dealt him a blow: Mutnofret embraced Shepses with visible bliss. Ameny arrived like a raging bull, but Nakhtmin managed to restrain him. "She's fine," he whispered. The words tasted sour in his mouth but too much was at stake here. "Don't do anything rash."

He dragged the worried father behind the plant and carefully parted the twigs so they could see without being seen.

The priest snorted. "The cheeky windbag will taste my fist."

Nakhtmin felt with him. He couldn't understand why Mutnofret took such a risk. Shepses might be her sister's killer. How could she? Rage boiled inside him, too, except it was rather directed at the young woman. *May the gods forgive me. If she can't give us a very good reason for her actions, I'll personally spank her!* An oath he meant to keep.

"This is outrageous!"

The sharp voice made them spin around. Inpu must have followed them into the park, but unlike Nakhtmin and Ameny, he'd stayed on the path and spotted the couple after the next bend. Shepses and Mutnofret flinched and cast searching glances around. Nakhtmin bent lower and gestured to the priest he should stay hidden. "It's better if they think Inpu caught them, not you," he whispered, and Ameny nodded. Nakhtmin was glad the powerful man let him take the lead.

Mutnofret certainly meant to achieve something with her visit. As long as she was safe, he wanted to give her the chance to follow through with her plan—if she really had one. Heat coursed through his body. Was she attracted to Shepses? He'd always thought the long list of conquests Shepses liked to flaunt was much exaggerated. What if he was wrong? Maybe women were stupid enough to fall for this arrogant talebearer. He'd thought Mutnofret smarter than that. Whatever her intentions, a furious father could ruin everything.

The head of the House of Life had turned crimson with indignation by the time he reached them. "Shameless!" he ranted. "Shepses, I would have expected better behavior from you. And you, young lady, should know better, too. This is the garden of Amun, and you're not allowed in here. Get out, both of you!"

Hand in hand, the culprits ran over the meadow and into the doctor's room without glancing back. Thus, Nakhtmin and Ameny remained undiscovered behind their bush. Relieved, Nakhtmin took a deep breath. "Maybe you should go talk to Inpu, ask him not to mention you asking for Mutnofret. She's planning something. If it's what I think, I sure don't like the idea, but it might help us a lot."

Ameny grumbled something unintelligible but slowly moved toward Inpu while making sure he couldn't be seen from the house. Nakhtmin heard murmurs traveling back and forth between the men. Finally, Inpu nodded, and Ameny signaled Nakhtmin to follow him. They took a detour to the temple and entered through a different door. Nakhtmin recognized the corridor with the offices of the prophets. Here too, access was restricted to priests. As a doctor he'd reached the first level of consecration but had only been here once.

"I've asked Inpu to accompany her to the pylon. You should meet her there. I'll have to take care of my tasks now, although I'd like to give my daughter quite the scolding. You have my permission to thoroughly chide her before I come home. What poisonous vermin bit her to give me such a scare?"

Relieved that Mutnofret's solitary endeavor had no horrible consequences, he grinned from ear to ear. The prospect to upbraid her in the role of her father's representative delighted him and chased away the nausea caused by the view of Shepses's hands on her body.

Soon it dawned on Nakhtmin that Mutnofret neither felt guilty nor paid attention to his reproach. Chin held up high, she sashayed ahead of him and ignored his words like a mother her child's whining. Only the disapproving expression of her own mother caused her to lower her gaze.

"Since when is it custom in this house for people to simply come and go as they please?" Lady Isis greeted her.

"Forgive me, mother. My head ached, and I longed to stretch my legs."

Isis huffed. "Here we have a beautiful garden and even a doctor in the house, but you take to the streets. Your father was beside himself. I expect this won't happen again."

"No, mother." As soon as Isis was out of sight, Mutnofret grabbed Nakhtmin's hand and pulled him to her room. Laughing, she flopped onto her bed and spread her arms. "So, how did I do?"

Incredible! She seemed to be proud of herself. "Mainly, you took a great risk." Nakhtmin trembled with scorn. "Did you waste a thought on how you embarrassed me? Your father provides accommodation for me, so I can look after you. Had something happened to you, it would have been my fault!"

She waved his comment aside. "Don't make such a fuss. It's always about you. I've opened the doors to the vizier's house for us."

Baffled, Nakhtmin stared at her. He'd imagined she only wanted to charm information out of Shepses—groping and fondling *not* included.

"Naturally, you must be aware that we won't get anywhere if we sneak around outside Nebit's house like cats. Shepses has lost his bride and is looking for a new one. People say I look much like Hetepet, who had already spiked his interest so I thought…"

Her foolhardiness left him speechless. Then he barked. "Are you aware that all of Shepses's brides or even lovers tend to lead a rather short life? Think of Hetepet!" With satisfaction, he saw her lips quiver. Secretly though, he had to admit she was right. He'd come to the same conclusion already, but using Ameny's now only daughter as bait? The prophet would never agree to such a ploy. And he himself wanted to throw up when he thought of Mutnofret in the arms of that windbag. "You didn't let him seduce you, did you?"

"Jealous?"

He snorted. "No, I just wondered if you'd go as far as to join in passion with the murder of your sister."

Her eyes narrowed to slits. "Poison drips from your tongue. Take care you don't swallow it."

"And your tongue is so sharp I'm surprised you don't cut yourself."

She hissed and turned away from him.

He didn't want to let her off the hook so easily. "Besides the scare you gave us all, our plans for the afternoon are ruined."

She rolled onto her back, arms over her eyes, but said nothing.

Heavy breathing made her breasts rise and fall. That moment he wanted nothing more than to touch them. *Get a grip, Nakhtmin! That's what she wants.* Right, if he showed his reaction to her allure, she'd come out on top and stay there. He aimed for a placid tone of voice. "I actually wanted to take you to Thotnakht's house today, to find out more about the circumstances of Bastet's death. Now it should be too late to call on the lady of the house. Unreasonably as you've acted today, it's probably better if I don't take you along."

One eye peered out from under her arm, but he turned away as if to leave. He so craved to hear her beg. She shouldn't always keep the upper hand, noble family or not. He reached for the door knob when he heard her sitting up.

"Without me? Oh, come on, don't be like that. All this is so exciting. Staying behind all alone, I might die of boredom, and Father wouldn't appreciate that either."

He grinned inwardly, but managed a disapproving tone as he said, "You act as if these murders happened for your entertainment only. Shows how immature you still are. No, I can't have you around on this serious mission."

"Without me coming along, you won't even get into Thotnakht's house," she challenged him.

He turned to her. "Maybe your father can get me an invitation. He is not happy about your behavior either. Surely he'll forbid your leaving the house—either to see Shepses or the wife of the first scribe."

Her face showed undisguised horror. "But...I've set up everything so well. Don't tell me I let those slimy fingers grope me for nothing!"

He almost laughed with joy. She didn't care for Shepses!

"Oh please, Nakhtmin, you must convince father. You have to!"

And let Mutnofret walk farther into the lion's den? How much persuasion and arm twisting would it take to wrestle the permission from Ameny? That prospect made his triumph over her begging go stale.

"Never! I won't allow it. Mutnofret will set no foot near that miscreant." The Amun prophet paced along the back wall of his study like a caged lion.

"What if I promise to always stay close to her? You know for yourself: we won't get anywhere without her. We can't just accuse somebody, and there are too many suspects living in Nebit's house."

Ameny looked like a wounded animal. "You can't guarantee you'll be able to help her if necessary," he whispered almost inaudibly. "How quickly is the deed done? No. And that's my last word."

In Nofriti's Clutches

To Mutnofret's chagrin, Ameny stuck to his refusal. He only permitted her to accompany Nakhtmin when he called on Bastet's mother, but any further investigation he prohibited with such vehemence she didn't even dare to argue. Their visit didn't reveal anything new, though. The first scribe's daughter had been found lifeless in a public park. The mother, stricken with grief, didn't know anything about a possible lover and thus they had to exclude Bastet from their considerations—at least for now—since they couldn't detect any obvious connection to Nebit or his sons.

The priest's family had gathered at the breakfast table, and Nakhtmin noticed a certain restlessness in Mutnofret. He suspected she was up to something.

She cleared her throat. "Father, I haven't seen my friends for a long time. Isisnofret invited me over to her place. There will only be girls. May I go? Please! I'll take Nakhtmin along."

Nakhtmin admired the show. She begged like a child and batted her eyelids enticingly. *She knows how to get what she wants!*

Ameny's features softened. "Only women? Then go. Nakhtmin, you'll take care she doesn't expose herself to the sun for too long."

"Certainly," he said. What was the girl cooking up now? No way did he believe in a harmless reunion of friends.

The family rose from their chairs and started the day's work. He followed Mutnofret to her chamber. While sifting through her chest of clothes for something suitable, he asked outright, "What's this about today?"

She cast a glance over her shoulder. "Oh, come on, you wanted to make inquiries among the young ladies at court. This is your chance. They'll all be there…" Then she rattled off names, of which Nakhtmin only remembered plenty of Merits and Nofrets.

Ameny had forbidden any further involvement of Mutnofret in his investigations, and Nakhtmin was in doubt as to whether this development comprised a fraudulent evasion. The way she'd put it, he was supposed to ask the questions, and that would keep her out of it. Although he had no idea yet how to subtly sound out the girls, he hoped they might give him the right clue. At the same time, he dreaded the meeting since even one young woman made him feel rather insecure and shy. How would he fare among a whole flock—or rather, a pack? *I can only hope I'll get out of the gathering in one piece.*

Mutnofret had made her choice and shooed him out. "I assume I may change without supervision?"

A little later they mounted the palanquin of the house and were carried to the estate of the city provost and father of Isisnofret. Passing through the gate, they entered a notably lush garden. A true master of landscaping must have employed his skills here. Narrow paths meandered past flowers and bushes, every now and then presenting views of cozy nooks, where benches invited one to linger in the shade of trees with dense foliage. Sometimes cordons of wine, and other climbing plants lined the path, and Nakhtmin spotted beds arranged according to purpose, like medical herbs or cooking spices. A pleasant scent hovered in the air. From one corner of the garden, the clear laughter of the girls traveled toward them, and Mutnofret headed in that direction. The guests had made themselves comfortable on a reed mat at the pond and slurped refreshments, which attendants served. Delighted calls greeted the newcomers. Nakhtmin felt thoroughly scrutinized and hardly knew where to rest his gaze.

Since Mutnofret couldn't avoid introductions, she made a dismissive gesture. "This is just my personal physician. Father is so concerned with my health that Nakhtmin has do go everywhere with me. Simply ignore him."

Heat rose to Nakhtmin's head at these words. What was he to her? Hardly more than a servant? A convenient accessory? Well, she had compared him to a hand fan. The young ladies darted him furtive glances and giggled. He suppressed a groan. This certainly wouldn't be fun. How should he pick up new information if he had to keep his distance? Mutnofret should have considered that before clearly putting him in his place.

Despite the constraints of her tight-fitting dress, she elegantly sank onto the mat and sat with her legs folded, while he still stood like a log of wood. To make matters worse, the girls obviously had no inclination to ignore him, despite Mutnofret's advice to do so. Soon one of the Merits rose and led him away.

"What's it like under Muti's thumb? She can be quite the beast," she tempted him to gossip.

He assessed the round face of the girl, who cast a calculating glance at him. Only a beast would badmouth her friend like that, he thought and said, "Oh, I can't complain. I lead a pleasant life at the house of the prophet with little to do. Much better than treating an endless procession of patients, day in and day out."

She bit her lower lip, evidently a nervous tick of hers since the tender skin was chapped and scabby in places.

"I could prepare a balm of wax and aloe for you to smear on your lips. And you really shouldn't chew them so often," he recommended.

Her teeth released their grip. Beast-Merit seemed undecided whether to hiss at him or not. Eventually a smile that made him shiver conquered her face. "Good advice, and I'd love some of that balm. Do you know of more ways to emphasize a woman's beauty? Seems like you've already helped out Mutnofret. She looks resplendent, like the god Nefertem when he steps from the lotus."

"Oh, no," he denied modestly. "That's not to my credit. Lady Mutnofret is in love, which makes everyone glow." Glad to have found a great transition to what really interested him, he looked at Beast-Merit expectantly.

She straightened and lifted her chin a notch. "Lo and behold! Is that so? What do you know about it? I believed her still in mourning. Tell me more!"

He aimed for a conspiratorial smile. "But you won't tell anyone, right? It's young Shepses."

"Shepses!" Her face displayed envy, jealousy and triumph. "So he sweet-talked another one into it?"

"You know him? He's also a doctor."

She snorted with contempt. "Yes, and mostly young women seek his services. Despite..." She giggled.

"What?"

"Well, his horny viper seems to need treatment just as often as his female patients do."

"No kidding? You mean…? Don't tell me you too?"

"Certainly. An itch needs scratching, right? Muti shouldn't dream of ever keeping him to herself. In love, ha!"

Nakhtmin found this confession very enlightening. Shepses didn't simply brag. Still, some of the girls must have meant more to him, and those were now dead. Did strict Inpu know what Shepses was up to in his office? One thing puzzled him. "Aren't you and the other girls afraid of getting with a child?" The next moment the answer dawned on him. How monstrous! "He gave you contraceptives?" he guessed aloud.

The beast nodded and showed some propriety by looking ashamed. "In the worst case, he has the means to get rid of fruit growing in the womb. At least he says so."

Shepses sure knew how to put his medical knowledge to good use. Although contraceptives were allowed, they should only be prescribed to prevent a woman from carrying a child for health reasons. Life was sacred after all. Naturally, the harbor strumpets and dancers knew how to get them. Hardly any doctor would descend to an abortion. It was too dangerous for the woman and seldom successful. Nakhtmin shook his head. How many couples had come to him in despair because they couldn't conceive, and these spoiled young things reversed the nature of life. It seemed utterly wrong to him.

That moment, another girl joined them. She cast a meaningful glance at the beast. "You don't want to keep this attractive young man all to yourself, do you?"

Beast-Merit's eyes shot daggers. "Here you go; he's all yours, Nofriti." Sashaying away, she blew Nakhtmin a kiss. "Remember the balm."

And he'd thought Mutnofret was exhausting! Her friend gave him a once over and made him feel like a rabbit before a cobra. This Nofret sure looked on the hunt for a mate. She dragged him behind a tree and without shame entwined herself around him.

He stepped back. "I…uhm…I promised B…" He'd almost said Beast-Merit before he caught himself. "I just promised her a lip balm. Then we talked about Shepses."

"Shepses?" She cooed the name. "Your upper arms are much stronger than those of that weakling. And with your name…"

That's what he got for being named after the god of fertility. Strong Min—would these jokes never stop?

"I'm sure you know how to really take a woman." Her hand wandered down his shendyt.

His treacherous body reacted without permission. He gasped.

Mutnofret's voice rose above the background noise of chipper chatter and extricated him from the snares of lust, with which Hunter-Nofret had bound him. He'd lost sight of his charge despite his promise! His erection shriveled as fast as it had reared, and he peeked around the trunk. That moment, lecherous Nofret pressed herself against him and kissed him so passionately he lost his balance. Entangled, they both fell over. Hitting the ground hard, he found himself lying under her. *Oh gods! I bet they are all looking at us!* To his horror, Nofriti sat up straddling his loins, her hand trying to push aside all fabric still separating them. He couldn't believe it. The very idea of taking this girl in public, in front of onlookers, killed any residue of lust. And he certainly didn't like being used without having a word in the matter. Rather than him taking her, she was going to take him. Disgusted, he pushed her away and jumped to his feet. His searching gaze met Mutnofret's, in which he read nothing but reproach.

Damn, how could I have let it go this far? Nakhtmin cursed his body and his wretched self. He needed to get a grip. What would Mutnofret think of him now—or Ameny if she told him? His ears whooshed. He couldn't understand what the gaping and moving mouths of the young women uttered. Were they laughing? Mutnofret strode to him, and gradually the storm in his ears quieted down. Finally he could hear: they laughed. Then he found himself being dragged behind the tree again. Cajoling and cheers rose. Mutnofret's face distorted with scorn. He wished to sink into the ground.

"You doctors are all the same," she scoffed.

"Please, Mutnofret, I…" He saw her lips quiver and wanted to kiss her.

"Let's go. I can't take you anywhere. What a way to behave among other people!" Her shoulders shook.

"I…I'm really sorry. I didn't want that. She…"

Mutnofret didn't react to his stammering. With curt words, she took leave from her friends and pulled him along the path toward the gate.

"Look, she's put a rope around her donkey," one of the women called.

On the way, Mutnofret's face grew darker and darker.

Outside the wall, she couldn't hold back anymore and gave free rein to her feelings. Clumsily, Nakhtmin patted her twitching shoulders. It took him some time to realize she was laughing. Her whole body rocked with merriment until it ebbed into helpless giggles. He couldn't begin to understand what was going on with her. On wooden legs, he climbed after her into the palanquin. "Mutnofret, what…?"

She snorted more laughter. "You imbecile," she squeezed out, then a kind of whimper escaped her throat. "Nofriti of all the girls!"

Her amusement started to feel rather insulting. He must have done something incredibly stupid, but she wasn't mad at him. Could her earlier rage have been fake? In truth, she'd let him run into a trap she was well aware of. After all, she had to know her friends. This, he swore to himself, was the first and last time he accompanied her to these women. The next visit she'd have to do on her own or pass on it. He certainly wouldn't let her make a fool of him again. Hopefully Ameny would understand. "You could have warned me! I guess you knew this might happen." Another suspicion grew in his heart. Did she mean to take revenge because of her tryst with Shepses?

She still giggled. "Nobody is safe from Nofriti. I'm surprised she didn't take you right there behind the tree."

Stunned Nakhtmin asked, "What kind of a wild bunch is this? Are the noblest women at court supposed to act in such an outrageous way?"

"Not all of them are like that. Actually, it's only Nofriti, but the others like to goad her, cheer her on." Mutnofret sighed and placed her hand on his arm. It felt cool and for a moment seemed like balm on his hurt pride. He'd never been so mortified, except…

He banned the memory of his former lover who'd just played with him. To her, he had only been a convenient means to make prospective suitors jealous. He should have learned then to stay away from spoiled women of noble families. They knew no limits and didn't respect the feelings of others. He gazed at Mutnofret and wished he could silence his heart, which seemed to persistently beat her name.

DEATH AT THE FESTIVAL OF THE DEAD

Day 25 of month Hut-heru in Akhet, season of the inundation

Toward the end of the fourth and last month of the inundation, the ten-day festival in honor of Sokar, the god of fertility and death, was celebrated. It started with the ritual 'Digging up of the Land,' which renewed the fertility of the Black Land. Priests, wearing the falcon mask of the god, hoed the fresh, still-moist earth in a symbolic act since sowing would soon commence. Ameny was among those allowed to pour a sacrificial drink into the new furrow, while the public watched.

The next day, without public attendance, the secret purification and anointment of the god Sokar-Osiris took place, followed by sacrifices. Nakhtmin, as wab priest of Amun, held too low a rank to be allowed at these rituals, but he could imagine how they played out.

The day after, the ceremony of the Mouth Opening was performed, and this really constituted magic for him. During a night wake, the priests read the very long ritual text aloud in full length and brought the image of the dead god back to life. He wondered if Hori performed similar tasks on the dead in the weryt. What amazing power lay hidden behind those walls, and how easily it could be abused. Surely, there were spells with which to steal a person's ka soul and submit it to one's whims. No wonder such knowledge must remain secret.

The following day of the Sokar festival was dedicated to the protection of the mummies and thus fully committed to the dead. Again, Nakhtmin felt very close to Hori. Next, the statue of the god was carried to his bark in a great procession and taken up the Nile to its grave. At dawn the journey continued on the divine *neshemet* bark heading for Abydos, the holy city of Osiris. Nakhtmin had never taken part in this, but he knew Sokar-Osiris's enemies were ritually destroyed there, which guaranteed the god's survival. After mummification had revived the divine body, this act restored his powers.

Today, in the evening of the fifth day of celebrations, the Netjeryt festival lay ahead. While the god on his gilded *henu* bark merged with the setting sun, the people accompanied him across the Nile and moved on to the necropolis where the kas of deceased relatives waited for their offerings. All Itj-tawy residents were out and about, wearing necklaces of onions. The river bustled with watercraft of all types, small fishing boats as well as the barks of the high and mighty. Of course, Ameny's family had their own vessel, on which they stood in silence and stared into the starry sky still showing a tinge of lilac.

Somebody tugged on Nakhtmin's shendyt, and he looked down at one of the twins. In the dark he still couldn't tell Huni and Bata apart. He stooped.

"These onions smell bad," the child said. "Why do we need to wear them around our necks?"

Nakhtmin glanced at Ameny, who should rather explain the deeper meaning of the ritual to his sons, but his benefactor appeared deep in thought. He understood how difficult crossing the river had to be for the family this year. Their grief over losing Hetepet was still too fresh. "The onion is a magic plant," he explained in a low voice and sank onto the planks. He patted the wood next to him and both boys snuggled up against him, full of trust. "It is the only plant that lives above and below ground, in this world and the underworld. Its green leaves rise from the ground, and we eat them. The round bulb is also edible but grows in the earth. Doesn't it look like the sun? The god Sokar merges with the sun tonight and travels with it through the underworld. What happens with the sun in the morning?"

"It's reborn," they said at the same time.

"Exactly." Nakhtmin smiled. "That's why the onion is sacred to the god Sokar, because it travels through the underworld. And there's another reason. Its tang that makes your eyes water also wafts into the noses of the dead and breathes life into them."

"Hetepet's nose too?"

"Yes, it does that for Hetepet as well. Now you know why it's so important that you wear the onions. She'll receive new life from you."

Open-mouthed they stared at him in awe. "Yes," one whispered. "You're real smart."

The passage took quite some time since the necropolis of the dynasty's previous kings had been abandoned. The rocks surrounding it were too crumbly to dig tunnels into them. They passed the walls of the weryt, then the tall pyramids of the transfigured pharaohs Senusret I and Amenemhet I. Nakhtmin woefully commemorated little Hetepet and hoped the god in his form of Ptah-Sokar-Osiris, responsible for fertility, continuance and death, would safely lead her to the fields of the blessed. On many barks people sang, but overall the mood was rather subdued and melancholy like on the priest's boat.

Mutnofret eventually intoned one of the traditional songs. She had a beautiful, clear voice. Nakhtmin joined in, and together they greeted the dead while gradually the outlines of the gigantic pyramids, burial places for the god kings of ancient times, moved into their view. The current pharaoh's father lay under a pyramid upstream of the capital. Senusret III, however, had his eternal resting place built near the pyramid of his grandfather, Amenemhet II. Here were also the *mastabas*, in which the court officials were entombed. Hetepet had been taken to a chamber in the tomb of Ameny's parents.

The torch-lit path up an incline to the flat-roofed rectangular structures rising above the desert sand took them past a rock plateau. It wasn't easy to stay together in the jostling crowd of people coming from the piers. When, at last, they reached the chapel of the family tomb, the Amun priest made a sacrifice of drink and smoke. At the false door to the grave, they lay down their onion wreaths. Through this stone slab, shaped like a door, the kas of the dead could enter and leave their tomb and partake of the offerings brought by the family and by priests of the necropolis.

Together with Ameny, Nakhtmin recited the prayer asking Sokar to illuminate the countenance of the deceased. The onions symbolized the sun and its everlasting journey across the firmament. Nakhtmin placed one hand on the massive building blocks of Hetepet's resting place and also prayed the mighty god would take his parents and the other murdered girls on his bark. He found the towering walls of the burial site rather depressing. In silence, the family said good-bye to their beloved. Even the always-so-dapper twins Huni and Bata were dumbstruck.

The torches had burned down when the family joined the procession of citizens returning to the riverbank. In the dark, Nakhtmin tripped a few times over rocks and bumps in the ground. The path was so crowded, he more than once stepped on the heels of the man walking in front of him. The humid night air still smelled of onions since their odor clung to the festive collars of the courtiers. Despite the large number of people, it was eerily quiet. All of a sudden, a scream sliced through the silence. Movement stalled. News passed from mouth to ear, "Ahead someone collapsed."

Without thinking, Nakhtmin struggled through the bystanders until he reached a knot of people. "Let me through, I'm a doctor!" he called.

Sluggishly they made way for him. He bent over a young girl, almost a child still, lying on the ground. Last time he'd seen her on Neferib's lap. A dry sob erupted from his throat. It was the daughter of the *Golden Ibis* innkeeper. Somebody brought a torch, and in its shine he registered she still wore the same rags as back then. The girl was beyond help, his experienced fingers told him, but he didn't say so aloud. If he announced her demise, the priests of the necropolis would take her straight to the House of Death. However, he absolutely needed to examine her body before all evidence once again disappeared behind the impenetrable walls of the weryt. "She's unconscious. I'll take her on our boat and to the House of Life, where I can help her."

He glanced up at the bystanders and detected Ameny's face among them and sent a silent plea for his permission. The priest caught on quickly, gave a curt nod and stepped forth. Together they lifted the limp body and carried it the short distance to the pier.

On the family bark, they placed the body on one of the reed mats lying at the stern for passengers to sit on. Nakhtmin dipped a corner of the awning into the Nile water and acted as if he cooled his patient's forehead. Murmured conversation between Lady Isis and her husband drifted over to him. Obviously, she was too tired to puzzle over their strange behavior, just like the twins and Mutnofret, since she seemed to accept Ameny's curt explanation. Soon the gentle rocking of the boat put the women and children fast asleep.

The sun god sent his first rays across the horizon when the bark reached the harbor of the capital. Plenty of boats already bobbed up and down at the piers, and sleepy people staggered onto land. Nakhtmin also stumbled as he stepped on firm ground. He was so tired that it took him much longer to adjust to the lack of rocking motions underneath him. Ameny helped his wife carry the still-sleeping twins ashore. Trembling, Isis and Mutnofret stood on the planks, each a child in her arms. Nakhtmin sure appreciated the palanquin awaiting them. Even cheeky Mutnofret appeared lost and fragile this morning.

As soon as the bearers had carried off their human freight, Ameny said, "She's dead, isn't she?"

Nakhtmin didn't need to ask who he meant and nodded. "It's the daughter of the innkeeper of the *Golden Ibis*." Since Ameny showed no sign of understanding, he added, "That's the drinking hole where Shepses's brother died. Because of her, Neferib and Hori had that fight."

Ameny clenched his fists. "And again the thread leads straight to Shepses."

Nakhtmin thought along the same lines but wanted to make sure. "Wait until we've examined her. Only when we've seen the deadly wound will we know with certainty. That's why I didn't want to leave her there with the dead."

The priest pulled a grim face. "I'm already convinced. Quick, let's take her to the House of Life as if she were a patient before the other doctors arrive. We might finally get proof!"

Together they hauled the body ashore. Stiffness of death had already set in, and she wasn't as easy to carry as before. Nakhtmin glanced along the harbor promenade, but couldn't spot any palanquins for rent. Maybe that was just as well. Common people's superstitious fear of the dead might have led the bearers to reject such an eerie cargo. Fortunately it wasn't far to the temple. Still, a stretcher would have come in handy. With a sigh, he grabbed the girl's legs, while Ameny slipped his arms around her chest.

Inpu showed surprise when Nakhtmin and Ameny arrived this early with their 'patient'. Judging by his disparaging scrutiny of the girl's rags, he didn't send them to the yard where paupers were treated only because of Nakhtmin's high-ranking company. "Take her to the first room to the left," he ordered.

Nakhtmin stretched his back in relief as soon as they'd placed the corpse on the table.

Ameny, too, groaned and touched his lower back. "I'm getting old," he said.

It was still fairly dark in the room, so they lit one of the oil lamps with the flint stone and cinder lying next to it, then lit all they could find with the first one. The light reflected by bronze mirrors illuminated the room enough.

With expert moves Nakhtmin undressed the corpse. "Under the left breast," he murmured and bent over the naked body. His fingers couldn't feel an injury. "Hand me the lamp." He reached back and wasn't surprised when he felt the weight of the clay bowl in his palm, but then he realized he'd commanded the powerful priest like a servant. Ameny seemed not to have noticed or didn't care because he, too, was curious. In the light of the flame, Nakhtmin found what he'd been looking for. "There!"

Visibly excited, Ameny bent over the wispy body, while Nakhtmin illuminated the spot and pointed.

"Yes, I see it. So tiny. Are you sure this wound caused her death?" Ameny ran a hand over his face in confusion.

"I'm sure because Hori is. He'd held Hetepet's heart in his hands and described the injuries on it for me." Nakhtmin needed a moment to identify the strange noise beside him: the prophet ground his teeth. "Unfortunately we can't tell anyone about it," Nakhtmin continued. "And if *you* harbor doubts…" His voice failed. Indeed, how could they convince the other doctors that this small stab wound wasn't an insect bite? The girl's body showed a few of those. The strange discoloration in the shape of a blossom, which Hori had mentioned, wasn't visible here. His friend had speculated it might have developed later. On Hetepet's body, Hori had discovered it two days after her death, on Merit-Neith's forty days later. Of course, they couldn't keep the poor child here for that long. Then he thought of another problem. How should they explain to the Medjay why they had been looking for an injury in this particular spot? Nakhtmin's body went limp with disappointment. He'd placed so much hope on this new evidence, and now they stood here just as stumped as before. He sank onto the low stool next to the table.

Ameny's heart seemed weighted with the same concerns. "We have to try, at least. I'll go to the house of the Medjay right away and report this death as murder. Maybe someone there will believe us."

"Yes." At a loss, Nakhtmin asked, "What was she doing there, and why wasn't her father with her? If he'd taken his family to lay down an offering at the grave of his ancestors, why didn't he notice her disappearance? We should have encountered him at the pier, if not earlier."

"I guess we'll find out. Whether Nebit and his kin made the journey, we don't need to ask. They certainly brought Neferib their sacrifices. Even without a fresh death in the family, courtiers wouldn't miss this festive ritual. And they do own a splendid boat, unlike the innkeeper of the harbor tavern, I assume."

That sparked an idea. "Maybe the innkeeper coaxed a guest to take him and his daughter across the river to the necropolis. Many fishermen and ferry workers frequent these taverns."

Ameny lifted one eyebrow. A smile twitched around the corners of his mouth. "You know a lot about the harbor district."

Nakhtmin's face burned. "My hut is in that area..."

The priest had turned serious again. "No use procrastinating the inevitable. We'll just raise suspicion. Cover the body and take care nobody messes with it. I'll notify Inpu and go to the Medjay." Lips tightened to a thin line, he marched out the door. Nakhtmin heard him talk to the head of the House of Life in the corridor. A little later, the door flung open. Inpu as well as the head of doctors entered. Nakhtmin groaned. He sure wouldn't be able to convince Imhotepankh.

AN ARGUMENT AMONG FRIENDS

Day 26 of month Hut-heru in Akhet, season of the inundation

In the weryt, the Sokar festival was celebrated in a unique and, to Hori, rather strange way. All utu had to wear wreaths of onions, which got in the way of their work.

Kheper explained the reason, "It is of utmost importance to care for the dead in transition between life and death since they haven't reached the state of transfiguration yet. We need to recite particular blessings and spells for these, so they'll be 'justified of voice' after mummification and the opening of the mouth. Thus they can join the god Ra on his bark during this circle of the sun."

Now he knew why lector priests stood in every room in which the dead were treated, and rattled off their singsong. At first, Hori tried to understand the words, but soon gave up. The language they used was ancient, maybe even older than that of the god kings during the first dynasty.

Since the priests performed their secret rituals incessantly, even at night, he had to stop his excursions beyond the wall. It seemed too risky although they stuck close to the deceased. They took turns to get some sleep, so he might run into one of them anytime.

After the Netjeryt festival, this part of the rituals finished—much to Hori's relief. The last days of the Sokar cycle were dedicated to the continuity of the kingship, so he'd dare venture outside tonight. Unrest made him edgy. For too long, he'd gone without news from Nakhtmin.

He'd just reached the hiding place for their messages when he heard the voice of his friend. "Psst, Hori!"

His heart leapt with joy and excitement. "Nakhtmin! Are you alone?" He strode toward the rocks where they'd met before.

"Yes, I'm on my own. I simply had to get the news to you right away."

Hori's mind spun. What had happened. A new clue? "Come on, tell me. I'm dying with curiosity."

"Our killer has found his next victim."

All joy over the unexpected visit perished in Hori's heart. "Oh no. Who is it this time? Do we know her?"

"Yes, both of us know her. She's the *Golden Ibis* innkeeper's daughter."

"Nebet-Het! That's her name. They mentioned it at the trial... But how? Why?"

Nakhtmin sighed into the darkness. "If only we knew. Maybe the killer bore a grudge toward her because of what happened to Neferib? Whatever the reason, this murder also connects to the vizier's family."

"A grudge—yes, that might be. But why wait this long?" Hori found no explanation for the numerous puzzles.

"Every time we believe we've taken a major step forward, it turns out a step backward. Instead of finding answers to our questions, new ones pile on top of those we're asking ourselves. It drives me to despair. But let me tell you what happened..."

Breathless, Hori listened to his friend's account. When Nakhtmin told him how he and Ameny wanted to report the murder to the Medjay and to the head of the House of Life, he interrupted. "Imhotepankh of all people!"

Nakhtmin's low laughter spread from the shadows to his ear. "That's what I thought but the old fellow surprised me. As soon as I'd explained our suspicion, he took a puncture needle and pushed it right into the wound on the girl's body. It slid in as if her chest were made of tallow. That convinced him and his confirmation was enough for the Medjay to start an official investigation."

In his exhilaration, Hori grabbed Nakhtmin's arm. "Wonderful! At last!"

"Don't get too excited yet. If it hadn't been a barmaid but one of the noble ladies at court—rest assured the Medjay would have made more of an effort. Unfortunately, we couldn't tell them about the other three victims without getting you in trouble."

"What?" Hori felt like a wineskin drained in one big gulp. "Didn't they do anything?"

"Sure they did something. I tailed them and witnessed how they informed the girl's father, this fat Khonsu, of his daughter's death. First he broke into a big lament, then when he realized there'd be an official investigation, he shut his trap real fast. The only thing the Medjay could get out of him was that he let her make the trip to the necropolis with a friend and boatman, so she could perform the sacrifice for the dead in his stead."

Hori needed time to process the news. Pacing a few steps back and forth, he gazed at the flickering lights of the city of the living. The Nile's high waters had retreated somewhat. Soon the sowing season would start. He sighed. New life emerged everywhere, and he was trapped with the dead. "Maybe Khonsu is afraid the case of Neferib's death might be reopened. After all, he did give false testimony and there might be evidence to be found." He spun around to look at Nakhtmin. "If I were you, I'd try to find out if our killer had approached the girl earlier. He must have had a reason to intercept her after the ritual for the dead when nobody else was with her."

"Nobody?" Nakhtmin snorted. "You know how crowded the path to the burial sites is during the Netjeryt festival."

"Sometimes you're more isolated in a crowd than in the desert." Hori hadn't meant to sound so bitter.

"Of course you're right." Dismay and empathy carried in Nakhtmin's voice.

For a moment, Hori wrapped the sentiment around himself like a cloak. Only he couldn't afford the luxury of such comfort. They had important things to discuss.

"You're onto something here," Nakhtmin said. "Somebody from the vizier's household couldn't go near the tavern without drawing attention. I'll ask around."

"Hey, what's going on with Shepses and Mutnofret?" Hori could well imagine how hard it must be for his friend to know his charge was so close to that windbag. Only Nakhtmin still didn't seem to understand his feelings for Mutnofret.

He recalled when his friend fell in love with one of the patients at the House of Life and won the young lady's favor. For quite some time he seemed totally happy and was planning a future with her. Hori was there when the girl laughed at Nakhtmin. How could he possibly think she—born to a noble family—would marry a man without means from Upper Egypt, whose family nobody knew. From then on Nakhtmin retreated even more into himself. Hori hadn't noticed him venturing into new adventures with women and didn't believe there'd been any. Nakhtmin was too serious. If he got into another relationship, he'd probably seek full commitment.

Nakhtmin released a weird noise, half snort, half groan. "Nothing's happening between the two. Ameny immediately stopped them from seeing each other. Surprisingly, the girl conceded."

"Too bad. I'm afraid if Ameny doesn't dare risk Mutnofret's life, we'll need different bait." He'd chosen such a provocative phrasing to get a reaction, and Nakhtmin jumped to it.

"What? How coldhearted are you? Do we want to find Hetepet's murderer? Yes, but not at all cost!"

Hori's grin probably remained invisible in the dark and he appreciated it. "Could it be possible she means more to you than any other patient?"

"What's that supposed to mean?" his friend barked. "For several moons now, I've spent my days with her. Naturally, there's been a bond growing between us. But that...? No, certainly not. Mutnofret is a strong-headed and spoiled brat with more intelligence than is good for her. She's the last to tempt me."

"Oh," Hori said. "That's settled then. Nevertheless, we need a door opener for Nebit's house."

When they said their good-byes a faint resentment still lingered. Hori fretted over his carelessness. Why did he have to rile Nakhtmin? His craving to participate in the life of people across the river had made him surge ahead without thinking.

MUTNOFRET'S SECRET

No news of the Medjay's investigation reached Ameny's house. Nakhtmin admitted to himself it might have been smarter not to inform the pharaoh's law enforcement. These men had shown little interest in solving the murder of a child from a poor family although Maat applied to everyone: young and old, rich and poor, noble and common. On the other hand, he and Ameny couldn't let the chance to report these crimes pass. In the meantime, Nebet-Het's body had been taken to the House of Death, and he wondered if Hori took care of her. He was still a little miffed by his friend's insinuations he might be in love with Mutnofret. As if to prove him wrong, he went to see the young woman at her favorite place in the garden. She sat in the shade of the wall surrounding the estate.

He didn't mean to sneak up on her, but she only noticed him when he'd almost reached her. Startled, she stared at him and hastily hid something in the folds of her skirt. Then, as if she'd never been doing anything else, she bent over her stitching work, with which she had been occupied for weeks now. Her flushed face belied her pretense though.

"A love letter?" Judging by her looks, his wild guess hit home. The realization hurt, then a horrific suspicion crept up on him. "Don't tell me it's from Shepses!"

The mix of guilt and anger on her face said it all.

"I don't believe it! How can you be so unreasonable, so incredibly reckless? Didn't your father explicitly…"

She flashed her teeth and released that familiar hissing noise. "My father…" She emphasized every word. "…forbade me explicitly—as you call it so fittingly—to meet Shepses. He never said anything about letters."

"Cheeky!" He gnashed his teeth, bent forward and tried to grasp the message.

She reacted too fast and shoved it in the neckline of her dress. "Go ahead, dare to take it," she threatened.

"What then? You'll scream? I'd love to hear what your father has to say if he finds out what's been going on." With satisfaction, he watched her pale. "Hand it over, or I'll go to him straight away."

Reluctantly, she retrieved the papyrus from the cleft between her breasts and placed it in his proffered hand. He skimmed the lines and drew a sharp breath. Things had gone far between her and Shepses, too far. "How long have you been at it?"

"What's it to you?"

"Right, none of my business if you flirt with someone who may have killed your sister and three other women. What's it to me if you even plan to marry him! I really don't understand you." He couldn't decide whether the glittery shine of her eyes came from anger or grief.

"And I don't understand why you all think Shepses a villain. He isn't so bad and he certainly didn't murder my sister. If you knew what beautiful words he wrote to me…"

He rolled his eyes. "I can't believe this. He sweet-talks and you fall for it? Your father will never agree to this match."

"If all goes according to plan, father won't have a choice. Very soon the vizier is going to fulfill his son's wish—his ardent desire—and negotiate the bride-price and marriage contract with Father. Nebit does everything for his son." She pushed out her lower lip.

"One might think you wish your father would show as much indulgence toward you. But that would be a sign of disinterest and low esteem for you. Do you think your father is so callous as to deliver you into the hands of such a family, just to gain a little more prestige. Sure, a proposal made by the vizier can't be easily turned down. What an honor to marry into such a noble family. If Ameny hated you, he'd be more than happy to throw you to that murdering pack. However, he doesn't hate you…"

Tears rolled down her flawless cheeks, and left a trail of the kohl lining her eyes. "*I* hate *you.*"

"Because you know I'm right." He sighed. "I guess it's too late now. Shepses already announced his intentions openly?"

She nodded.

"You meant to enforce it and succeeded. I hope you'll…" No, he couldn't get himself to wish her well. "Just be careful. It's a pit of vipers."

All afternoon Nakhtmin wrestled with the problem of whether he should betray Mutnofret and tell her father what awaited him. He owed Ameny loyalty. At the same time his heart murmured insistently he shouldn't antagonize Mutnofret even more. If she saw an enemy in him, she wouldn't confide in him anymore. Her trust in him had never been more crucial. Had he paid more attention to her, he might have been able to prevent her taking things so far with Shepses. Could she actually be in love with the braggart? No, he didn't want to believe that. She wasn't so stupid. Then he remembered what a fool he had made of himself before—out of love.

Still, if the vizier's visit surprised Ameny, he might show his feelings. How could he explain his refusal to let his daughter marry the much-higher ranking vizier's son? At long last, Nakhtmin decided to take the bull by the horns. He went to Mutnofret. "Listen, I have to tell your father about the letter—and all the others."

"Of course, I should have known. Go blab your mouth; it's one of your best skills." She chewed her lower lip.

"I don't want to do it. The gods know I'd love to keep this secret from him because it won't be pleasant!" He paced the room. "He'll find out soon enough and should be prepared for the vizier's visit. And there's something else…" Taking a deep breath didn't make it easier to say the next words. "If you really want to follow through with this, insist on taking me along to their household as your personal physician when you move. Maybe that will help reconcile your father with the whole endeavor. But I'll only do it if you're going to be honest with me from now on. No more lies, no more secrets. This isn't a game."

Her almond-shaped eyes shot fiery looks. "Oh, you've come up with some nifty plan to provide for yourself. You're simply afraid father will kick you out."

Yes, Nakhtmin had taken his own future into consideration as well, to some extent. Once Mutnofret was married, there wouldn't be any use for him in the house of the second prophet of Amun. He was ashamed of his selfishness. How could she look through him so easily? Upset, he replied harsher than intended. "You underestimate me. My concern for your health and well-being is real, and I respect your father far too much to hold back on him under false pretenses. Well, your choice of husband shows how little you understand of human nature."

She paled with scorn. "You know very well why I'm doing this. It's certainly not for my pleasure."

"Really?" He lifted one eyebrow and cursed himself at the same time. Something about this girl kept riling him although he'd come to win back her trust. Instead, he felt the need to castigate her with words. He was older and should be able to control himself! "Mutnofret," he tried again in a conciliatory tone.

"Go away. I don't want to see you again."

With drooping shoulders he slunk away. What a mess he'd made.

As soon as Ameny returned from the temple, Mutnofret sought out Nakhtmin and changed her tune to that of reason. "You're right, we should tell father."

Her quivering shoulders made him realize how hard it would be for her to confess to her parent. Most likely she only reacted with such vehemence to his words because she'd acted against Ameny's express wish. He suppressed a snide comment. Surely she'd only come to him in hopes of support and backup during the storm of parental rage. He swallowed triumph and self-righteousness. No use bashing her because of it. Deep down he admired her courage. Would he have dared take such a risk? "Then let's do it right after the meal."

She nodded her approval. They both knew hunger would only make Ameny more irritable.

An hour later she timidly knocked on the door to her father's study, where he always retreated to around this time to revisit his day's work.

"Yes, what is it?" he called, words muffled by cedarwood.

She let Nakhtmin enter ahead of her, which made him feel like she was hiding behind his back. Ameny's eyebrows hiked up in an unspoken question.

Since Mutnofret didn't utter a word, he began, "Your daughter needs to tell you something." Stepping aside, he nudged her to the front.

As was to be expected after such an opening, her father's face furrowed. She hemmed and hawed. "You look tired. Maybe I should tell you tomorrow?"

When she turned toward the door, Nakhtmin held her back. "No, this can't be postponed."

"Young lady, you'll account for your deeds now. What do you have to confess?"

She lowered her gaze. "I've exchanged messages with Shepses." Her voice was so faint, even Nakhtmin, standing beside her, had trouble hearing what she said.

Ameny obviously had understood. His face turned a frightening crimson. "Tell me this isn't so! You disregarded my orders? Speak up!" He jumped to his feet and rushed to her.

She flinched but lifted her chin a notch. "No, father. You said I must not *meet* Shepses, and I didn't."

Ameny's breathing became so labored and wheezy, Nakhtmin feared for his employer's health. He added, "I only learned about this exchange today, my lord. Unfortunately, there's more to it…"

"Shepses wants to marry me, and I agreed." The words burst out of her as if she feared she might never be able to say them otherwise. She cast a glance filled with a mix of fear and scorn at Nakhtmin.

Now Ameny paled and swayed. Nakhtmin hurried to his side and supported him. Gently, he led the priest back to his chair and insisted he sit down. He poured water from the pitcher into a mug and handed it to Ameny, who emptied it in big gulps. He seemed unaware of what he was doing. Nakhtmin looked from father to daughter. He realized she wouldn't get another word out and he couldn't bear to hear more. However, the situation required thorough planning. No time to treat their feelings with care. "Soon, I'm afraid, Nebit will call on you to announce his son's intentions."

Ameny groaned and buried his face in his hands. "How can I deny his request without insulting the man to the core?"

"Well…" In Nakhtmin's heart grew the seed of an idea. "What if you pretend to accept? Much time will pass until the marriage contract is crafted and Shepses has his own household. Nebit will insist on celebrating their engagement with a big feast to which Mutnofret's family—all of us—will be invited. We can use this chance to look around the vizier's house. Afterward Mutnofret will be able to visit Shepses anytime without raising suspicions."

At this point Ameny released a dry laugh. "You want me to let the only daughter I have left go there on her own? You must be insane, Doctor."

Of course, Nakhtmin had anticipated Ameny's reaction and took no offense. "I was about to say she can take me along every time. People have become used to me accompanying her everywhere. This would allow me to make inconspicuous inquiries and to observe what's going on. It can't take much longer until our killer will slip up. As long as I'm watching over Mutnofret, he can't get close to her. I doubt he'll dare make an attempt at her life under his own roof." A foolhardy scheme but the best they could do under the circumstances. Mutnofret had created facts, and they had to deal with them. "I'll have to completely focus on never leaving her alone." Now he turned to the young woman. "Mutnofret, will you promise not to take any risks like sneaking away, but always stay close to me? No more solitary adventures, or I can't accept the responsibility."

Ameny gave a grim nod. "I have no choice but to go along with this plan. I'm very angry with you, my child. I guess you don't know what you got yourself into. And if we don't succeed in identifying the murderer and proving his guilt, you won't be able to take back your promise of marriage. Our family would lose face and all respect at court. Nebit is a powerful man. He could easily prevent me from ever ascending to first prophet of Amun. Have you considered this? No need to even talk about your prospects of ever marrying a worthy man."

Mutnofret lowered her head. The whole time she had been unusually quiet. "Father…I…" She sniffed.

"How could you have been so foolish? You've put all of us, the whole family, in severe danger. Indeed, you need a husband with much reason in his heart, or else I see your life painted in the darkest colors. I can only hope all will work out as Nakhtmin described. And now you'll swear to do as he asked."

She seemed very subdued as she made the requested vow. For the first time, Nakhtmin didn't doubt her sincerity.

"Now go to your chamber. I need to discuss a few things with Nakhtmin. Afterward I'll have to relay the great news to your mother. At least she will be happy for you."

Once Mutnofret had left the room, Ameny allowed himself a groan of agony. "She wouldn't have told me if you hadn't insisted, right?"

Feeling awkward, Nakhtmin pressed his lips together. He didn't want to get Mutnofret in even more trouble.

"Doesn't really matter anyway. At least I'm forewarned. It would have been pure torture to sit and talk with the vizier totally unprepared. I seriously doubt I could have concealed my feelings."

"My lord, I promise to watch over her."

Three days later, Nebit's visit was announced.

BINDINGS

Hori spent another long, exhausting day with the bandagers. He still couldn't fathom why he should learn this step of the mummification process as well since they, who diligently wrapped the corpses limb for limb in linen, made up their own group. They didn't mingle with the other utu, and Hori sensed a kind of rivalry between the different departments. He wasn't even allowed to try his hand at bandaging a body. Instead, he was supposed to tear old rags, which were collected by people for their mummy bindings, in strips.

With linen being expensive and precious, even wealthy households collected well-worn clothes and threadbare fabric in baskets to be used as part of their bandages. Hori ripped off strips in different widths and rolled them up with care. He needed to mark beginning and end of each piece. For the mummies of noble people, each digit was wrapped individually; while for those who couldn't afford this expensive procedure, each hand and foot was wrapped in one go. The bandagers performed their tasks in a rather artistic way, and the more bindings they added, the more the deceased's mummy resembled a cocoon, in places even with colorful patterns worked into it. Sometimes Hori received colored linen to process: red, yellow and blue. The dead lay on special racks, where only the head, bottom and feet touched the wood, while the rest of the corpse was poised. After the long drying period, the bodies were so stiff and light this was simple to achieve for easy access to the respective parts.

During the lengthy act of wrapping, the lector priests recited spells from the book of the dead. One priest wearing the mask of Anubis, the god of the dead, supervised the proceedings to make sure no part of the ritual was neglected. The bandagers worked in teams of two, one man wrapping the linen around body parts and the other handing him what he needed as well as picking out amulets and fixing them in the right spots. Some of these magic tokens were sewed on, while the man simply placed others on the bindings and held them until they were fixed by the linen. There were little figurines, signs of life, Horus eyes, *djed* pillars symbolizing eternity and much more. Each of the magic tokens protected the deceased in its own way. With bandaging finished, the body was wrapped in a linen shroud ready for the sarcophagus.

The previously removed entrails, now dried as well, were also wrapped up and placed into special jugs. Some were of clay, the more precious ones of stone or alabaster. Each organ had its own guardian deity watching over it, Hori learned. The human-headed Imsety protected the liver; Hapi with the baboon head guarded the lungs, jackal-headed Duamutef the stomach. The intestines were in the care of Qebehsenuef with the falcon head. The plugs for the canopic jars were often modeled in the shapes of the four heads of the guardian deities.

Soon Hori grew bored with observing the wrapping procedure. At first, he'd tried hard to keep up with the nimble moves of the bandagers' fingers, but soon gave up and turned his attention to his mind-numbing task. That gave him time to ponder more interesting questions, except his thoughts went in circles like the linen he rolled up. Had the Medjay discovered a clue to the identity of Nebet-Het's murderer? Had Nakhtmin found out something in the tavern? For days now, he'd received no news. Could he still be angry? It drove Hori nuts not to know what was happening across the river. He didn't even get the chance to examine the dead barmaid since Kheper assigned him to the bandagers on the very day she was brought to the House of Death. Likely he wouldn't have found out anything new examining her body. Still—it would have comforted him to get at least somewhat tied in with the investigation. *Huh, tied in!* He cast a disgusted glance at the bent backs of the men. He felt tied with mummy bindings.

The cool night air brushing over Hori's wet body felt pleasant after the stifling humidity at the bandagers', where the scent of resin and oil dazed all senses. The short bath in the canal had refreshed him. Sand stuck to his bare feet, but his body would dry fast. Hope for news made him speed up. Maybe his friend was even waiting for him? Although he didn't really expect it, he whispered, "Are you there?"

"Yes, over here."

Nakhtmin's voice startled him, but soon his heartbeat changed from startled turmoil to a happy dance. He wasn't alone anymore! Speechless, he embraced his friend.

"How did you know I was waiting for you?"

"I didn't, but hoped you would be. You can't imagine how slowly the days pass when you're so isolated from everything. Come on, tell me the news. Did you go to the *Golden Ibis*?"

"Yes, on two evenings, but I couldn't find out anything yet. I have to be careful. If I'm too keen while sounding out the patrons, the sleazy innkeeper will catch on, and who knows, he might think this information valuable to Nebit and therefore worth another reward. After all, the fellow might recognize me."

"And it might be a dead end anyway."

"Quite possible. At least I've found out this Khonsu treated his daughter worse than a peasant his donkey. The poor thing always had to be in attendance and wait on the guests. Some of the regulars went so far as to say she's better off now she's left the world of the living."

"Poor thing, indeed." Hori sighed. He hadn't done the girl any favor when he tried to save her. Without his interference, she might still be alive. He voiced his thought.

"Oh, Hori, we can't help everyone. You told me about a stonemason with a crushed finger, whom you treated during your exam. You had to send him back to his dangerous job, just as we release all our patients to the lives they've led before, good or bad. If you'd managed to tear the girl from her father's clutches, where would she have found shelter and protection? With you at your father's house?"

Hori had to admit his friend was right. Thinking of his father constricted his throat. "Have you...I mean, have you met my father lately? Did he talk about me?" He sensed more than he saw Nakhtmin shake his head. And why should the treasurer speak with Nakhtmin even if he ran into him? He probably had no idea who his son's friends were. For his father and the rest of the world he was dead.

"I need to report something else though." Nakhtmin breathed hard and fast. "Mutnofret and Shepses are promised to each other."

"What?" In his shock Hori had raised his voice, and its echo bounced off the rocks. He murmured the next question, "How could this happen? And why did Ameny acquiesce all of a sudden?" Poor Nakhtmin, he thought. How bitter this must taste for him.

Nakhtmin told him about Mutnofret's secret correspondence with the vizier's son and how the family couldn't do anything but deal with the consequences—make the best of it or rather avoid the worst.

"Gods, the girl has courage." Thinking how she'd have his poor friend under her thumb when they finally acknowledged their feelings for each other, he chuckled. Only then did the full extent of the situation hit him. If she married Shepses, she couldn't have a relationship with Nakhtmin.

His thoughtless amusement certainly warranted Nakhtmin's indignant reaction. "That's not funny. I don't know what you're cackling about. Quite the contrary, it's awfully dangerous. In two days, Nebit will host a large banquet to celebrate their engagement although he wasn't too excited about his son's choice of bride. Of course he didn't show it openly, but you know how he is."

Hori recalled how amiable the vizier could act, while his eyes said something else. Nothing in his household might be as it seemed at first glance. He grunted his consent. "Mutnofret was really brave to provide you this chance you've been desperate for. Don't be too hard on her."

This time Nakhtmin cackled. "Oh, we were hard on her. You can't imagine how docile the young lady can be when led with a strict hand. I hardly recognize her anymore. Maybe she only realized now what she's set in motion—and what consequences her thoughtlessness might have for her whole life."

Hori pondered this in his heart. Maybe it wouldn't be Mutnofret keeping the upper hand in their relationship after all. It dawned on him that these two wouldn't cut each other any slack. Well, there were more important matters than their chances of surviving as a couple. "If all works out as you hope, she won't have to marry him. Once the murderer is unmasked, the honor of Nebit's family should be so damaged nobody would hold it against Mutnofret if she revoked her promise of marriage."

"Yeah, once, when, if..." Nakhtmin raked his fingers through his wig. The stubbly hair on his scalp, which must have grown back since the morning shave, made a scraping noise. "But what are we going to do if we can't identify him in time, Hori? Or even worse: what if we find him, but he isn't a member of the vizier's family?"

He hadn't even considered this possibility. It could be, but— "Not likely. The blossom on the handle of Shepses's tools must be unique. I don't know any other doctor ordering such ornate instruments. Too expensive. As you well know, needles and hooks break or bend too easily and need to be replaced fairly often. Not even the king's personal physician would squander his resources like that."

Nakhtmin paced. Sand scrunched under his sandals. "A doctor at the House of Life could have snatched his puncture needle. Remember how Shepses had sought his pleasure with Mutnofret in the god's garden. Anyone could have sneaked in and stolen one of his instruments." Nakhtmin's voice rang with despair. He stopped right in front of Hori, pale moonlight shining on his face.

"Quite possible, however, there's something else connecting all murders with Shepses's family. Each victim had a relationship with one of the vizier's sons."

"But not with stuttering Hotep."

"Right, Hotep—why do I keep forgetting him?"

"Perhaps because Hotep doesn't have a tongue as smooth as those of his brothers? Perhaps because his own family tends to forget about him too?"

"The forgotten son…" That sounded all too familiar to Hori. He could well imagine how Hotep felt, always in the shadows of his older brothers. But he couldn't imagine committing such crimes out of hatred for his family. However, Hotep also had to suffer being mocked for his speech impediment, particularly by young girls, he guessed. He envisioned the brides of Hotep's brothers visiting the household, trying to chat with the young man, laughing at his ineptness, his failure. Yes, it was possible. "I'd keep a close eye on Hotep," he said. "Currently, he seems most suspicious to me, and he might have a strong motivation to kill the women." He explained his reasoning to Nakhtmin.

"Only Nebet-Het doesn't fit," Nakhtmin argued. "As the innkeeper's daughter, she wouldn't have laughed at such a distinguished guest. And she certainly wouldn't have visited Nebit's sons for a chat."

"Right." Hori sucked in his lower lips, pondering the flaw in his theory. "But he might have killed her for a different reason. No, that shouldn't exclude him as a suspect. Observe Hotep."

"I'll keep an eye on each and every one. If anything happens to Mutnofret…"

Yes, Hori thought, then not only her father would blame him. The worst demons lurked inside his friend.

They were saying their good-byes when Nakhtmin groaned.

"What is it?" Hori asked.

"I'm such an idiot. I totally forgot to tell you something else. It happened before the Netjeryt festival, and afterward other things weighed on our hearts. Maybe it's not important at all." Nakhtmin's voice trailed off.

"Perhaps we'll only find out later if it's important or not. At the moment, I think you should tell me anything that seems even slightly relevant. Go on, speak up." Hori sensed Nakhtmin's unease and guessed it might have something to do with Ameny's daughter.

His friend took a deep breath. "Mutnofret visited some girls, and I had to accompany her."

"Oh." Hori's fantasy created amusing pictures even before Nakhtmin began his account of the events. Imagining his friend at the mercy of sharp-tongued ladies was too funny. He chuckled.

"Sure, you go on laughing. I truly made a fool of myself. Mutnofret had fun—and revenge. But wait until you hear what one of them said."

Curious, Hori listened. "Incredible! Now I understand why Shepses is so successful. Contraceptives!"

"But I don't know how that knowledge might help us."

"Well, it presents more motives…" Hori started pacing to clear his thoughts. "An incensed father, an abortion gone wrong…"

"New motives and more suspects than we can count. I doubt it ties in with our murders, but it casts a damning light on Shepses. I'd totally pushed this issue aside with everything else happening." He told Hori about his encounter with Hunter-Nofret.

Hori snorted with laughter. "Nofriti! Truly one to watch out for. How mean of Mutnofret." He too had his share of experiences with the seductress. Fortunately, not all women were like that.

Nakhtmin slapped his forehead. "I forgot to tell you something else. About our experiment with the goat."

"Funny that you should think of a goat when I mention Mutnofret," Hori teased. Unfortunately it was too dark to watch his friend grimace.

"It was her idea to check if a jab to the heart with such a thin needle kills right away."

Hori paid close attention now. "Oh, that's an interesting question, indeed." Hetepet's heart—the wound had seemed strange to him as if it had festered for a while. He shook his head. *Impossible!* The killer couldn't risk letting his victims run around screaming. Nakhtmin told him about their failed attempt at the young goat's life, and the whole matter became ever more puzzling.

When Hori described the wound he'd found on the organ, his friend too shook his head. "As a doctor, I'm at a loss. This doesn't fit with what I know about injuries."

"Same here. However, neither of us has any experience with how wounds develop inside the body. After your experiment, though, we must assume a puncture needle alone didn't cause imminent death of the young women. Particularly since the heart of a goat is much smaller than that of a human being."

"Is that so? How big is a person's heart? And what exactly does it look like, feel like?"

Shocked, Hori realized he'd said too much. "Stop it, Nakhtmin. I'm violating the rules by leaving the walls of the weryt, but I'm no traitor. The secrets of the weryt—you don't want to know them. Such knowledge is far too dangerous, for both of us."

For a while Nakhtmin remained silent, then he said, "I won't ask again but rely on what you can tell me. Maybe the killer modified the needle somehow to make it deadlier? Dear gods! I'm worried about Mutnofret. What will happen to her if she really has to marry Shepses?"

These words stayed with Hori until he went to bed. Nights had turned too cold to sleep outside, but not much longer and he wouldn't be able to stand the small room. What would happen to Mutnofret? Although he hadn't told his friend, he feared a wedding was out of the question. They either found the killer and brought him to justice, or Mutnofret would share her sister's fate. The girl really took a big risk. Why? Was it simply the thrill of danger or something else that drove her to such fool-hardiness? Did she mean to impress Nakhtmin or seek justice for her sister or...did she truly like Shepses, after all? Of course, Shepses would exploit his position to make advances. No surprise there, but how audacious a method the guy used. Now he wondered if the head of doctors knew what his once-favorite student was up to. Oh, how he'd love to watch Imhotepankh getting the scales plucked from his eyes!

He kicked away the linen sheet that felt far too heavy on his heated body. Still, he found it hard to breathe. Shrouds, mummy wrappings—he was bound. Slowly, he drifted off to sleep.

SURPRISING REVELATION

The day of the big banquet approached frighteningly fast. Tomorrow it was going to happen. Nakhtmin had spent another night tossing and turning. Judging by how Ameny looked he hadn't caught much sleep either. Isis noticed, too. During the morning meal she leaned over to her husband with a concerned expression. "Are you unwell, my dear? I hope you won't get sick this close to the feast. Nakhtmin, why don't you take a look at him later?"

"I'll be happy to." He wanted to talk to the priest anyway, and Isis had already grown suspicious of their many meetings behind closed doors. Ameny had explained a friendship developed between them and they enjoyed discussing erudite texts. Nakhtmin appreciated this pretext. He held the lady of the house in high esteem for her quiet and gentle nature—so unlike her daughter. Having to deceive her troubled him more and more, although he knew Ameny only wanted to protect her and spare her unrest.

A short time later he stood face to face with the prophet in his study. Birdsong wafted through the airing slits as well as a cool breeze smelling of Nile mud. Sowing had started.

The priest pulled a lopsided grimace. "You look like you've also lain awake all night like I did."

Nakhtmin sighed. "I have to examine you. How would medical texts phrase it? 'I find a man deep in worry about his daughter. His eyes are dull, his lids heavy.' As doctor I prescribe sleep, as friend I know it's hopeless to even try." Only now did he realize what he'd said and felt alarmed.

Ameny rested a hand on his shoulder. "Friend, indeed. I certainly need one. I'm glad you're here."

The prophet's words moved Nakhtmin, but their troubles were too serious to take real comfort. Then he remembered why he wanted to talk to his host. "I'd like to speak with Shepses again, question him."

"Dear gods! You want to give it all away? What if he ...? No, I forbid it!" Ameny's chest rose and fell as he breathed heavily.

"No, I won't tell him about our suspicions! What do you think of me?" The prophet calmed down, and Nakhtmin continued, "The last time he mocked me and said I was jealous because of Mutnofret. I'll let him believe that and act the rejected suitor. Maybe I can find out why he chose Muti of all the young ladies available." For the first time he'd used her nickname. How soft it sounded, befitting a precious and vulnerable wearer. He swallowed.

"Yes, I'd like to know that too. Wasn't it enough that Hetepet..." Ameny visibly wrestled with his emotions.

More than ever Nakhtmin was aware of the seriousness of their situation. During their investigation, he usually worried most about the danger for Mutnofret and forgot about the grief and pain over the loss of their other daughter, burrowed deep into the hearts of Ameny's family. Maybe because, although he'd liked the girl, he hadn't really known her. *Strange how we don't mourn every loss of life with the same intensity. One doesn't really grieve over death, but the gap the loss of a per-*

son leaves in our lives. We rather pity ourselves. Nakhtmin pulled himself together. These idle thoughts he'd better keep to himself. "Maybe I'll find out something that can help us."

Directing his steps toward the House of Life again felt strangely odd. For almost half a year he'd been living at the prophet's estate instead of fulfilling his duties as doctor inside the temple walls. He caught himself stroking over the relief of god Amun on the inside wall of the pylon as if he greeted an old friend. This early in the day, there wasn't much activity at the House of Life yet. Most ailing sought help later. Only a few people sat in the courtyard on the mats placed in the shade of the wall, waiting their turn. That moment a servant stepped out the door and collected the next patient. He recognized Nakhtmin and greeted him with a smile.

"Is Shepses here?" Nakhtmin asked and gave a friendly nod in return.

"Sure, you'll find him in his usual treatment room. A lady patient is with him though." The servant led an old man inside the building.

Of course. Why should Shepses end his relationships with other women this close to his engagement celebration? Nakhtmin wondered whether he should burst into the 'treatment session' or wait until the girl left. He decided to wait, as his chances to get answers might improve if he didn't affront Shepses. Fearing he might miss the moment when the vizier's son was alone, he ambled along the corridor lined with treatment rooms until he reached the end, where he slid down the wall and settled on the floor.

After a short wait the door, behind which he'd found Shepses the last time, opened. A woman peered out. In the gloom of the corridor, he saw the contours of her face outlined by the light flooding in from the entrance. She darted quick glances around, then sneaked out as if she didn't want to be seen. In his dark corner he must have remained invisible to her. Nakhtmin, though, recognized the woman right away: lady Sitamun, mother of the young doctor. Her furtive behavior puzzled him. The day before an important feast, why shouldn't she visit her son? He shrugged the incident off. Something to mull over later. Now more important things lay ahead of him. He rose and went to the door, from which Sitamun had emerged. Should he knock? No, he was supposed to act the jealous lover, so he stormed in.

Shepses sat on a stool, arms resting on the tabletop, head buried between them. At Nakhtmin's noisy arrival, his head jerked up, eyes wide.

Like he saw an evil spirit, Nakhtmin thought, but quickly concentrated on his part again. He slammed the door shut, pressed his fists in his sides and yelled, "Why? Why did you have to take Mutnofret away from me?"

Shepses straightened. Nakhtmin waited for a snide remark or at least the usual arrogant smile—in vain. The vizier's son stared at him, or rather, right through him. Caught off guard, he wondered what had happened to the guy.

Finally a kind of smile slid over his features. "Because she was available."

"What? What are you trying to say?"

Shepses's gaze cleared, and Nakhtmin thought he really saw him for the first time today. "I didn't take her *from* you. *I* needed to get away, and Mutnofret was there."

Speechless, he wondered if Shepses had gone mad. Nothing he said made sense.

Still, he'd better stick to his role. "You knew very well that I wanted her, and you stole her from me anyway. You dog!"

"Mutnofret agreed. Made me think she didn't want *you*. Come on, Nakhtmin, did you really think you could marry into our noble circles? Have you forgotten who you are?"

That hit home. Dear gods, yes! He'd allowed himself feelings for someone far above his station. All his education, his medical skills, none of it made up for being from the province and of lowly origins. He rubbed his face with one hand. *Remember what you're trying to achieve here! Damn emotions.* Shepses was able to hurt him because of her. Not good. "I'm a doctor in the House of Life in the pharaoh's residential city. You're the same as I am. Where's the difference? Mutnofret would have chosen me if you hadn't come between us." He lifted his chin.

Shepses looked tired as if he'd already fought a strenuous battle. "Let it go, man. None of this had anything to do with you—or with her."

"You don't love her!" Nakhtmin's heart skipped with joy at this revelation.

"I didn't say that." Apparently, Shepses didn't want him to take such a message back to his employer's house. "I just want to get away from *her*."

"Huh?"

Shepses sighed. "Didn't you meet her on her way out?"

Now Nakhtmin understood whom he meant. "Your mother? But... I don't understand. The other day, at our graduation party—I saw how you..."

The corners of Shepses's mouth drooped, and Nakhtmin had a vision of how the young man would look in a few years. He suddenly resembled his father in a frightening way. Maybe it wouldn't be as easy as he'd imagined. Maybe Shepses hadn't found much satisfaction in being the object of his own mother's lust. He recalled the looks of Shepses's brothers. Envy, hatred, jealousy—he'd only read hurt feelings in them. Did lady Sitamun grant her favors according to her whims, play her sons off against each other? And where did this constellation leave Nebit? Was he blind? Nakhtmin didn't dare ask.

"You saw but didn't realize anything. You were blind like all the others!" Shepses jumped up and paced behind the table. "She controls everything and everybody, wants everyone to herself. If someone isn't infatuated with her—oh, woe to him who rejects her! My mother is pure evil!"

Pity welled up in Nakhtmin, but for a brief moment only, then he remembered Shepses's many love affairs. "Oh, and you're better than her? First Hetepet, now Mutnofret and in between—who knows how many others you seduced. You toy with other people, trample their feelings."

Despair shone from Shepses's eyes. "Nobody understands. I have to do that, have to forget. The girls, that's the only way I can escape *her*! I won't be safe until I've left that house of horror. Don't you understand?" Shepses stopped right in front of him, grabbed his shoulders and shook him. "Doesn't anybody understand? Only marriage can liberate me!"

Nakhtmin wrestled free of his tight grip. "You're hurting me. And you're out of your mind. I'll prevent your marriage with Mutnofret."

These words affected Shepses like a gush of cold water. He shook himself, then his familiar arrogance took over. "Oh really? I seriously doubt anybody will ask your opinion in this matter. You better stay clear. My father has the means to turn the life of a little guy from Upper Egypt into pure misery."

Nakhtmin shook his head. "You're insane! First you pray to get out of your parents' home, and now you threaten me with your father's power. Time to grow up, Shepses! Sort out our problems on your own. Don't drag others into this. Most of all, leave Mutnofret out of your mess." Head held high, he marched out the door.

On his way home, he wondered what just happened. He'd never seen Shepses like that. Did he get a glimpse behind the mask? If he'd spoken the truth, this doctor wasn't a boastful windbag, as he'd always thought, but a pitiable worm. Shepses's behavior didn't fit though. If Sitamun really abused him, why would he do the same to others? Not very convincing. And Shepses's mother—according to him it must be horrible to have anything to do with her. What did he say? 'Woe to him who rejects her!'

Hori had pushed Sitamun off his lap that night, then had been convicted of a murder he didn't commit. He'd become one of the utu never to return to the living. Could that have been Sitamun's wish? No, impossible. Not for such a small offense. But then the accident with Neferib happened—a much better reason for Nebit to scorn Hori. To some extent, Nakhtmin even understood the vizier's actions. Still, there was no excuse for such a blatant injustice.

What could have happened between mother and son before he called on Shepses? Presumably something that shouldn't be publicly known or else she wouldn't have behaved so secretively. What upset him most, though, was Shepses's off-hand comment he'd chosen Mutnofret because she was available. Why couldn't he pick someone else—enough young women of his acquaintance should be happy to comply. Drat! That's what he should have told the rich idiot to do. Why did such retorts always pop up in his mind when it was too late? He wished he were as quick-witted as Hori.

No, Shepses's choice of a bride wasn't as random as he claimed. Was it possible he didn't know why he wanted *her*? Of course! Nakhtmin had met Muti's friends. Nofriti or the beast—if the others were only half as disgusting as these two, Shepses would have gone from one horror to the next. Although Muti had a wicked tongue, she wasn't degenerate and perfidious like the rest of the noble ladies he'd encountered. Whether he was aware of it or not, Shepses had chosen a bride who was quite the opposite of his mother. What an abyss! One thing was certain: Mutnofret must not marry into this family.

Impatient, Nakhtmin awaited Ameny's return in the early evening. He could hardly wait to tell him everything. The priest must have read his eagerness to share news in his face since he postponed dinner.

Nakhtmin wanted to report in detail and in order, but soon realized Ameny wasn't aware of a crucial detail: Sitamun's relationship with her son or possibly all her sons. He had to tell the prophet about the events at the celebration in honor of the young doctors' graduation after all. Sitamun's misconduct was so outrageous— he felt ashamed to have witnessed those scenes. Nothing else for it, he couldn't remain silent any longer. Ameny needed to know so he'd understand why his mother made Shepses suffer so much. His cheeks burned, and he only raised his gaze when the unspeakable had left his mouth. To his surprise, Ameny seemed far less astonished than he'd imagined. Only his lips tightening to a thin line gave away his reaction.

"Go on," the priest demanded.

While repeating Shepses's words of this morning, Nakhtmin even tried to mimic his expressions so Ameny would be better able to make up his mind, considering all aspects. He did listen intently, without interruption. Finally, Nakhtmin ended his recount and asked, "Shepses is insane, isn't he? No matter how I look at it— Mutnofret must not marry this man."

"No." Ameny folded his hands over his stomach, leaned back and stared at the ceiling. A troubled sigh escaped his throat. Then he squeezed his lids shut and pressed thumb and forefinger over them as if to erase the images Nakhtmin's report had conjured up. "No, she will not marry him. We'll get through this banquet, but by all gods of the Two Lands, if we don't unmask the murderer tomorrow, I'll revoke the engagement right away, may it cost me my career, my position and my wealth."

Hearing this, Nakhtmin felt great relief. "But what do you make of it all?"

"Hard to tell." Ameny mulled over it for a while, and Nakhtmin patiently waited. "I've known Sitamun for a long time. She was the most beautiful woman far and wide. Every man at court, really, every single one of them, wanted her."

"You too?"

"I too am only a man! And she was rather generous with her affection." A shadow slid over his features. "She loved to have everyone at her feet. Grateful, you had to snap up each bone she threw. Oh yes, she knew how to drive men crazy." Ameny's voice sounded rather bitter than wistful.

"She only played with her suitors?"

"She was the master of that game! Not satisfied until all of them crawled in the dust before her—their hearts broken. I was lucky to realize in time what she was doing. I didn't take it as hard. Nebit however…" He snorted in derision. "Nebit was completely under her spell. Likely he still is. His desire to conquer her drove him to strive for the highest offices, since she'd never have been content with less."

"Why didn't you tell me all this earlier? That would have helped a lot."

Ameny burst out, "Like you did? What's been going on between Sitamun and Shepses—you should have told me right at the beginning! With regard to my history with this woman, do you think I find those memories pleasant? I've buried them deep inside my heart. Nobody likes to confess what a fool he's made of himself."

Nakhtmin recalled his former lover. He still didn't even want to think her name. Now he understood his friend and patron. Ameny had been young, made his share of mistakes. Contrary to Nebit, he'd learned his lessons.

The priest continued in a soft voice, "Then I met Isis, and she was a gentle song after a blustery storm, the scent of lotus after the stench of a cadaver, a soothing balm after emerging from a tangle of thorn bushes."

A smile tugged on one corner of Nakhtmin's mouth. A fitting description for Isis, but he'd likely never feel in such a way for Mutnofret. Was he in love with Ameny's daughter or did she simply attract him physically? He didn't know. There was something, though, and he'd better not stir it up. Whatever lurked in the shadows would only complicate things.

A MURDERESS?

This time Nakhtmin hadn't waited for him, but his message was longer than usual. Hori didn't even manage to finish it before duty called. Still, the portion he'd read provided plenty of food for thought. Today he appreciated the boring work at the bandagers.

The description of Shepses's breakdown was rather enlightening. He'd already suspected only the facade of the vizier's house looked pretty. So far he'd assumed Shepses enjoyed his mother's extraordinary attentions, though, while the hateful and disgusted looks of his brothers Hotep and Neferib spoke something else. Of course, they could have been jealous, but Neferib's behavior had rather shown disdain for Sitamun.

He remembered an event from his childhood when Sobekemhat was not at all happy with Hori's slightly older brother Puy. For punishment, he received five cane strokes—in front of the complete household. Father called it a deterrent example. Hori felt with his brother although he didn't like him much. Maybe it was similar with Shepses and his brothers?

"Hori? Are you dreaming? The men are waiting for the medium bindings."

The supervisor's words made him flinch. He'd been so deep in thought, he'd simply been rolling the same strip of linen back and forth. He jumped to his task but couldn't keep from mulling over Nakhtmin's message.

Shepses trying to escape his mother—what significance did this have for the case? Realization hit him. Of course! Shepses would be the last to sabotage his own wedding. Sitamun, however, if she wanted to keep her son to herself, she had a strong motivation to kill his brides or lovers.

That put Shepses's dealing with contraceptives in a different light as well. He'd certainly get generous rewards for providing them to the noble ladies at court. As a young doctor with a fairly small income, Shepses had to rely on his parents' support to afford his own home unless he ran some extra business on the side. The necessary ingredients were easy for him to get. Maybe he even tapped into the provisions at the House of Life without accounting for them.

Another way to escape from home was marriage. Custom demanded a bridegroom take his wife to his own house. In those circles—to which Hori had once belonged as well—the father usually contributed significantly to a home befitting one's rank. Nebit surely wouldn't have any problem providing for his son in such a manner. If Shepses was so desperate, why didn't his father give him the means to buy a house?

Hori regretted only having skimmed the rest of the text. Something had jumped out, but in his haste to get to the end before he had to run to work, it had slipped from his mind. Something about Ameny and Nebit—but those two had little in common. The day turned longer and longer.

After washing in the cleansing hall, he was glad to climb the ladder to the upper floor of his house. In his cranny behind the loose brick, a pile of messages had collected. Hori already had to scrape some of the adobe off the back of the slab to enlarge the space so it could hold them all. He found Nakhtmin's latest message right away, unrolled and straightened it. He started at the beginning.

Reaching the part where Ameny revealed his past with Sitamun, he sucked on his lower lip while he mulled over the news. If Nebit was completely under his wife's spell, as Ameny claimed, he certainly wouldn't go against her wish to keep her sons close. That meant Shepses had not only one guard at his prison of a home but two.

He recalled how Nebit had looked at his wife during the meal—as if she were the sky and stars to him. Later she'd silently commanded him to retire, and he traipsed off like a well-trained dog at his master's command. The vizier of the Two Lands nothing but a submissive instrument in the hands of a woman who knew neither morals nor scruples? What madness! And he'd wondered if Nebit didn't see or hear what was going on in his garden. Realization sunk in. He knew and let it happen.

Could it be? Was Hori's worst offense rejecting Sitamun's favors that night, not causing Neferib's death? Maybe Nebit was one of those men whose virility had lapsed, or… During his training he'd once witnessed an unusual treatment. The patient complained that only watching others having sexual intercourse aroused him—nothing else. He had come to the House of Life to get these demons exorcised. Hori never learned if the amulet and ointment made of fat and a bull's penis had worked. Maybe the same demons afflicted Nebit.

Hori sighed at such strange occurrences, when love between man and woman was so beautiful. How much he'd enjoy loving and marrying a young woman. Kheper's daughter Nut? No, she didn't stir any feelings in his heart. The women in the weryt belonged with the dead. The same fate would await his children if he wed one of them. Besides, when he thought of joining with Nut, he always remembered his teacher's remarks about the defilement of the female corpses. Unlike the women on the eastern side of the river, the daughters of the weryt had their purpose in life decided for them: professional mourners. Their whole life revolved around death. Hori still didn't feel like he belonged with the dead. As much as he valued Kheper, the weryt remained foreign to him, and he was regarded a stranger here.

He doubted any physician could help Nebit. The man's disease had burrowed into his heart, where medical skills failed. Only the power of a god might cure him. Nebit, however, didn't seem to be aware of any affliction and rather seemed to enjoy his life. Quite odd. If the vizier was so weak, how could he influence the pharaoh and the judges of the Great Kenbet to convict Hori? The more he learned about the man, the more puzzles turned up.

After these revelations, he couldn't maintain his suspicions against Shepses any longer. Of all the people in the vizier's household, he was the one who lost the most by these deaths. Shouldn't he wonder why three of his lovers, one of them his bride, had dropped dead? Oh sure, Shepses must harbor a suspicion. Hori ground his teeth. That son of a bitch didn't care if he endangered the lives of the women he got involved with. In the end, Shepses was just as selfish in everything he did as was his mother.

Only three suspects remained on his list. That should simplify their investigation if there weren't all those obstacles rising in front of them. He couldn't testify and raise and accusing finger. Nakhtmin and Ameny couldn't reveal their source of knowledge. The only official murder victim, the little barmaid, had no obvious connection to the vizier's family. Charging him with her murder would only draw a weary smile from Nebit. They had no evidence, and the killer was smart. He was hiding behind the position of the most powerful official in the Two Lands—and his role of judge at the Great Kenbet.

Hori lay down on his bed and crossed his arms behind his head. For a while Hotep had seemed the most likely killer of the three. The inscrutable youngster with the disturbed speech—he might be jealous of his brother and his success with women. Or he feared to be left behind, alone at his parents' estate, when Shepses founded his own household. But this couldn't suffice as motivation for such cruel deeds. Although he'd first lied at the trial, in the end truth had spilled from his mouth. So he couldn't be all bad.

Nebit. Hori chewed on the name. How he loathed the man! To commit such injustice in his high rank, to take revenge by sentencing an innocent man—he still found it hard to fathom. Oh, he'd love to point his finger at Nebit. However, he had to admit that now his own wish for retribution blinded him. He honestly couldn't picture Nebit sneaking through gardens and temples to stab his son's lovers. Why would he? He should be glad to get rid of one rival for Sitamun's favors.

Images of the orgy in the vizier's garden flashed before his inner eye. Shepses was more than one rival. The young doctor would occasionally invite friends, and his own personal experience had shown Sitamun didn't shy from seducing them. Hotep, though, certainly wasn't one to win friends easily. He had to be lonely. No matter what professional education he chose, his mates wouldn't want to take him along when they partied.

Instead of the two men, Sitamun took center stage in his considerations now. The secrecy and stealth with which the murders were committed seemed to rather fit with a female killer. And yes, he did think Sitamun capable of the cold-blooded calculation and diligent planning necessary to carry out the crimes. The once stunning lady was growing older as he could see for himself that night. Losing her beauty meant losing her most important means of capturing men. Maybe sleeping with the friends of her sons was a desperate act to preserve her youth. Or did she mean to prove she was still attractive? Sitamun's behavior sure was odd. She had a husband who loved her, and with Shepses, Hotep and her young daughter she had three healthy children left and a big household. What was wrong with her to act like that?

His grumbling stomach reminded him to rustle up a meal.

Stormy Weather

Although Nakhtmin now owned a selection of elegant clothes, he chose a plain shendyt and collar. He mainly wanted to observe and not draw attention to himself. Mutnofret's life depended on him watching over her like the falcon god Horus. How he'd have loved to discuss the situation with Hori again. After the previous restless nights, however, he desperately needed to catch up on sleep lest he doze off during his guard. So he'd only written a lengthy description of the latest events and taken it across the Nile. He couldn't have waited until late at night when Hori managed to sneak out of the weryt. Content with his outfit, Nakhtmin went to Mutnofret's chamber. Isis and a maid attended to her, so he only leaned in the door frame and watched the women decorate the bride. Like a sacrificial animal for the gods, he thought and shivered.

Mutnofret looked enchanting. Foreign and grown up—he'd never seen her like this. Sitting on a stool, she had her side to him, and he admired her profile. Now she lifted the polished bronze mirror and gazed at her reflection. For a brief moment their glances met in the shiny metal. He smiled at her.

A hand touched his arm. It was Penu, Ameny's attendant. "The lord wishes to speak to you."

Nakhtmin followed the lanky man, who showed him a little more respect these days. He'd always acted reserved and proper in the man's presence, hoping to convince him he posed no danger to his position of trust and wasn't trying to exploit the family's generosity. The door to his host's marital bedchamber stood ajar, and Penu pointed at it. Nakhtmin had never been in there before. Curious, he looked around. The large bed used up most of the space. Except for a small table, there was no other furniture, no chests with clothes. Strange. And where was Ameny? What he'd mistaken for a wall tapestry moved slightly. From behind he heard noise.

"You wanted to talk to me?" Nakhtmin asked in the direction of the fabric although he wasn't sure anyone heard him.

Indeed, the curtain swung aside, and his employer's face appeared between the folds. "I'll be right with you."

A little later, Ameny presented himself, wearing a sour expression and his best garb. Nakhtmin whistled his approval.

"So much effort for this charade! I wish I could just call it off."

Nakhtmin took a deep breath and expelled the air. "Unfortunately it's too late for that. I saw Mutnofret. She looks gorgeous."

"We have her to thank for all the trouble. If only she'd told us about her plans beforehand. Then we could have prevented it all." Fear for his only living daughter had carved deep furrows around both corners of his mouth.

"I'll watch out for her. She'll be safe."

The priest sighed. "Then let's fetch the women and head out."

The palanquin bearers didn't have to carry their burden far. Nakhtmin decided to walk since he didn't feel like squeezing in next to the twins. Marching along the full length of the wall, he realized how big Nebit's estate truly was. Before them, the gate opened invitingly. The hosts awaited their arrival already, and they followed the lit path to the main building. Nakhtmin's throat tightened when he heard the gate slam shut. Captured! These walls wouldn't offer any protection, not for Mutnofret. A cold breeze blew from the river. He shivered.

Nebit's servants led them to the same clearing where the last banquet had been held. Viewing the scenery, Nakhtmin recalled that fateful evening when everything began—at least for him. Once again he stood blinded by the rich table, the flower garlands and the lush garden. Once again, he felt like an intruder who didn't belong here. Hopefully the vizier had forgotten about that dratted attempt to bribe him. The bride's personal physician or not, he certainly wouldn't be welcome here.

When Nebit greeted the family of the second prophet of Amun, Nakhtmin closely observed him. The vizier's cordiality seemed forced; his smile never reached the eyes and froze completely when his gaze fell on Nakhtmin. *Damn, he recognized me! At least he didn't scream with outrage.* The vizier paused for a moment but didn't kick him out. Still, he seemed tense, like a bowstring right before the hunter shoots the arrow.

Nakhtmin's gaze wandered to Sitamun embracing Ameny. Shameless, she molded her body against her guest's. Ameny edged away and cast Isis an apologetic glance. Sitamun released a sparkling laugh but its disharmony reminded Nakhtmin of the sound of misfired pottery. Shepses took Mutnofret's hand, cast a sideways glance at his mother, then pecked his bride's cheek. Sitamun's smile seemed fake—or did Nakhtmin imagine that because of what he knew and had heard about the woman? He sure was happy to stay in the background.

Not only he lurked. Hotep, too, stood aside with a dour expression. What had Hori said? They should keep a close watch on Hotep. So far the young man only appeared annoyed by this social obligation. Neither hate nor envy shone from his eyes. Still, he'd follow Hori's advice. Maybe Hotep surpassed his kin when it came to hiding his feeling.

No guests besides the families of bride and groom had been invited, a number easy to keep track of. Nakhtmin appreciated his spot at the end of the table—far enough from his hosts. They certainly wanted to put him in his place that way, but he didn't care since he wanted to remain inconspicuous and not get involved in conversation. To his left sat the twins and across from them perched Hotep. The boy clearly held no high esteem within the family. His clumsy speech probably embarrassed the vizier. Light chatter at the table wasn't possible with him, so he had to sit with the guests' children although he was an adult. Nakhtmin, though, was content with his spot from where he had a good view of both families and could sound out Hotep without drawing attention—if at all possible with the stutterer.

The first course arrived: boiled lotus blossoms in a sweet sauce, served with fine white bread. Nakhtmin omitted the wine and went for pomegranate juice instead. He needed to stay alert to protect Mutnofret.

Nebit licked his fingers and told a joke. While Ameny and Isis laughed politely, Nebit's gaze flicked to his wife. Strange how she seemed to have waited for him to do so. Now she wore an impenetrable expression. Nebit kneaded the linen table cloth. Finally she smiled gracefully, and the vizier burst into a roaring laughter.

Nakhtmin felt like he'd just watched the performance of a well-rehearsed ritual. The most powerful man after the pharaoh needed his wife's permission to laugh at his own joke? That sure fit with what Shepses had told him. He'd love to hear more about customs in the vizier's house. Unfortunately, Shepses sat too far away.

After the platters had been carried away, servants brought the next course: roasted duck stuffed with dates and reed roots from the delta. Shepses helped himself to a piece of the juicy breast and started feeding Mutnofret with strips of meat.

Nausea gripped Nakhtmin's stomach, so he turned to Hotep. "A big night for both families. Shepses will soon move out and set up his own household."

Hotep shrugged. "W-won't ha-a-appen. Sh-sh-she'll ne-e-e-ver all-ll…" His face distorted in strange grimaces as if he had to chew the words like a big lump of gristle, then he fell silent.

She'll never allow it? Or what had Hotep meant to say? Well, that's what Shepses hinted at. It sure was a piece of work to get anything out of Hotep.

To make things worse, the twins gaped at him, then giggled. Nakhtmin sighed in resignation. Those two would start imitating him any time now. Indeed, Bata and Huni acted up moments later. Nakhtmin tried his best to rein them in, but they only turned wilder in their stuttering. How far could he go? If these were his children, he'd give them a thorough scolding, but he didn't dare reprimand his employer's sons. Isis looked toward them and frowned. She rose and walked over. Nakhtmin glanced toward Hotep, but his seat was empty. In his peripheral vision he caught movement. Just in time, he saw Shepses's brother run along the trail, away from them all. Should he follow him? Leaving the table would be rather impolite. He hesitated a moment. All eyes focused on the two children, so he should be able to sneak away unnoticed. This was his best chance to question Hotep. Slipping into the shadows, he scampered off.

A few steps beyond the torch-lit area, darkness enveloped him. He could barely see his hand right in front of his eyes, even less the path beneath his feet. Only the crunching noises told him he was still on it. Laughter filtered through the bushes. Mutnofret! He'd promised Ameny to always keep her in view. Wavering, he stopped. Between her brothers and Shepses, she should be safe. After all, Ameny and Isis sat right across from her. Although he'd given the prophet his word, wasn't it more important to find clues? He might not get another chance to scout out the premises.

His feet moved of their own accord. A gust of wind blew through the trees. Rustling and cracking noises all around him. Where was Hotep? In which direction had he turned? For a while, Nakhtmin simply kept following the path, then he painfully hit his foot on a stone edging. He suppressed a curse and glanced up at the sky. Thick clouds obscured moon and stars. The night was unusually cold for this time of the year. Taking more care, he felt around with his feet. The path seemed to end here. Beyond the stone lining he felt grass under his sandals and padded on in the dark. Soon he realized it was hopeless. Hotep knew the gardens and likely lay curled up in a spot where he felt safe. How could he find him on such a dark night? The wind shook the trees even more, drowned out the noise of the celebration. Nakhtmin stood disoriented in the pitch black. Where had he come from? Ears pricked, he turned full-circle, then released a bitter laugh. This couldn't be happening—lost in a garden! He had to get back. Heavy raindrops splashed onto his head and shoulders. If that wasn't a sign of the gods! South of the delta, the celestial Nile rarely watered the Black Land.

The dark grew even more impenetrable, although he wouldn't have thought it possible. Strong gusts drove him on. At last, he felt the gravel of a path under his feet again, and after a moment's hesitation, he turned right. After a bend, he saw flickering light and headed toward it. This had to be the main building. The others would have fled inside by now to escape the heavy rain. He picked up his pace and found himself in front of a small building. From chest-height upward, one wall was made of wattle. It looked like some kind of animal enclosure. Inside the small room, the flame of an oil lamp flickered in a nook at the back. The gusts of wind broke on the brick walls, so the fire didn't die. Curious about this strange cage building, Nakhtmin peered inside, but couldn't discern anything but a few big stones. At least the little house offered shelter from the cutting wind and lashing rain.

"Th-they d-d-"

Nakhtmin started. The voice seemed to come from nowhere.

"...don't c-come out at n-night. Th-they sl-leep."

Nakhtmin laughed in relief. "Hotep. I was looking for you. I'm sorry how the boys made fun of you. Just wanted you to know."

Hotep emerged from the dark and stepped next to him. "I'm u-used t-to it."

Nakhtmin registered Hotep's speech impediment was less noticeable now as if he found it easier to talk when his family wasn't around. "Still, it's wrong and their mother Isis gave them a good scolding."

In the quivering light, Hotep's smile rather resembled a grimace.

"What animals are kept in there?" Nakhtmin asked.

"Sn-n-nakes. M-my f-f-f..."

These words caused him more problems, Nakhtmin noticed.

"...f-father k-keeps k-ki-ki..." Hotep snorted in frustration then tried again. "K-king c-cobras."

"How strange!" And how dangerous. "Do you have a caretaker for them? A snake expert?" In Upper Egypt, every village had such a man. There were many snakes in the south, all of them poisonous. Adepts knew how these creatures lived and behaved. They traced them to their nests and killed the reptiles; the caves of scorpions they cleared out as well. This way the danger for the peasants during harvest was much lower. Some of the snake men had been bitten so often, the poison couldn't harm them anymore. The expert at his home village even kept a cobra. Nakhtmin had seen him milk the animal's poison, then dip a thorn in and push it under his skin. He did this once a year and thus survived when two cobras bit him on one day, or so he said. Nakhtmin hadn't believed him back then, but for all he knew, it might be true. In this spooky setting, anything seemed possible to him.

Hotep shook his head. "F-f-father d-does it himself."

"A strange choice though. The king keeps elephants and gazelles in his garden, but snakes... Does your father collect the poison?"

Hotep nodded.

"We should return to the house. I'm cold, but I lost my way. I'm sure glad I ran into you." Trembling, Nakhtmin wrapped his arms around his chest.

"Th-then c-come on." Hotep sprinted off, and Nakhtmin had trouble keeping him in sight in this ink black night. With relief, he saw the faint light streaming from the window slits of the house. They sneaked inside through a back door. Hotep went straight to a chest and rummaged in it, so this had to be his room. One after the other, he pulled out two shendyts, threw them on his bed and dropped the lid with a bang.

"F-for yyou."

Nakhtmin's teeth chattered. "Th-than-ks." How embarrassing! He could only hope Hotep didn't feel mocked. He cast a quick glance at the boy, but he only showed a weary smile. Grinning, Nakhtmin stripped off his wet clothes. Donning the dry ones, he was still cold but didn't dare ask for a cape. While the vizier's son also changed, Nakhtmin studied his surroundings. Nothing in this room was out of the ordinary. What his eyes searched for was easy to hide though. The killer might conceal the puncture needle anywhere. He, however, couldn't just start rifling thought chests and peeking under furniture. No, this way he wouldn't get any closer to the murderer. Mutnofret! It suddenly hit him what his actual job was here. "Are you ready? We should join the others."

Hotep opened the door, and Nakhtmin followed him through a corridor until they reached the big hall of the estate. Even before stepping into the light filling the room, he heard the voices of both families. Of course they'd fled into the dry house as he'd expected. The table had also been brought inside. Everyone had gathered there and feasted on the delicacies. Mutnofret laughed about something, and a large weight dropped from Nakhtmin's heart. She was well. It seemed hours since he'd strayed through the garden, but he and Hotep had only missed one course of the meal. When he stepped up to the table, Ameny's eyebrows knitted. A sign of resentment because he'd left or a question whether he'd found out something? Nakhtmin shook his head slightly. He and Hotep settled at their respective places, just in time to enjoy the last course.

Over the rim of his wine goblet, Nebit cast a disapproving glance at Hotep, then his gaze wandered to Nakhtmin. He took a swig, set down the chalice and set his fists on the table top. Rising, he swayed a little. The man was drunk, Nakhtmin thought.

The vizier walked over to Hotep and pulled him around. "Where have you been? What were you thinking, simply leaving the table and our guests?"

"M-m-m…"

"I asked Hotep to show me the snake enclosure. He'd told me about it, and I was curious. A silly idea in the dark, and then the storm moved in." Nakhtmin hoped his explanation sounded convincing since Hotep had suffered enough for one evening. Somehow he pitied the boy although his life looked great on the surface.

Hotep had paled, while his father's face reddened even more. Nebit hissed like one of his cobras. Hotep's desperate expression told Nakhtmin he'd only made things worse. Was the snake cage a secret? Why? Of course, it was rather eccentric to keep such deadly creatures but in no way objectionable.

The vizier's cold eyes stared at his son a little longer, then the patronizing smile returned. "Certainly, certainly. But that's not very polite, is it?"

"No, my lord. I must apologize. We should have waited."

Nebit waved dismissively. "I've forgotten all about it."

All of a sudden the man tried hard to play down the incident despite his earlier outrage. Nebit staggered back to his seat. Nakhtmin hardly tasted the nut-filled dates.

When the host snapped his fingers, musicians emerged from an adjoining room. Nakhtmin half expected the dancers of the other evening to appear as well, but for this occasion, the vizier had arranged for more sedate entertainment. Nakhtmin observed Sitamun. The lady showed no awareness of her behavior back then, nor of him witnessing her debauchery. *I'm far too lowly for her to associate me with the graduation party.* He looked at Shepses and their gazes locked. In the eyes of his colleague, he read disgust and scorn.

Officially ending the meal, Nebit invited his guests up to the gallery at the end of the hall. Hotep asked to be excused and his father dismissed him with a wave of his hand like an annoying fly. He sure didn't seem to value this son much.

Nakhtmin climbed the three steps. Cushions lay spread out on the floor, and the twins, as well as Nebit's young daughter Henut, already slept there. Isis settled near her sons. Smiling, she brushed the lock of youth from Bata's forehead. Nakhtmin sat against the wall. This way he remained in the background but could hear everything. The music was quiet enough for easy conversation.

Sitamun lounged between Nebit and Ameny, her back to Nakhtmin, who observed how she pressed closer to her guest, one hand straying. Ameny's back stiffened under her touch. He mumbled an apology and went over to Isis as if he wanted to make sure his sons were sleeping. Sitamun beckoned Shepses and Mutnofret, and the two settled across from the older couple.

The hostess leaned forward, and Nakhtmin had to strain his ears to understand what she said to Mutnofret. "You little vixen, think you've made a good catch? Don't rely on it." Mutnofret paled. She reached for Shepses's hand. Her groom appeared unaware of his mother's words. Mutnofret leaned over to him and whispered in his ear. Shepses nodded, rose and helped her up. Then he led her down the stairs and pointed at a corridor, likely directing her to the lavatory.

Nakhtmin cursed silently. She must not walk through this house on her own, under no circumstances, but he couldn't just storm after her. A personal physician had his limits, too. He slid over to Ameny. "I guess Mutnofret heads for the bathroom. I can't follow her. Maybe Isis…?"

The prophet jumped up. "Nebit, my friend, where can I relieve myself?"

And off he hurried like someone with a bladder full to bursting. Nakhtmin only relaxed when father and daughter returned together. Why was Shepses so impolite not to accompany Mutnofret? The two joined Isis and the sleeping children.

Nakhtmin's interference hadn't slipped Sitamun's attention. She turned to him. "So worried about your protégé? You're a brave doctor and bodyguard," she purred.

He edged away slightly. Why did this woman always have to act so intrusive? Her heavy perfume filled his nose and dazed him. A slight headache pulsed in his temples. "That is the task the prophet has hired me for. Mutnofret's life is especially dear to him." He hoped she'd take his words as a warning. The more he saw of this woman, the more he suspected her.

Sitamun laughed shrilly. "When a young man like you and such a beauty like her live under the same roof for so long… I'm sure you've tasted the fruit. Tell me, what is she like? Will my son have fire under his linen or only straw?"

"How could you insinuate something so outrageous? I'd never betray Ameny's trust like that!"

She slithered up against him, her fingers reaching under his shendyt, grabbing his manhood. He was so appalled, his body didn't show the least reaction this time. When she realized that, her head jerked back, and she laughed out loud. He wasn't offended though, would have felt more ashamed if her touch had aroused him.

"A limp dick. The priest chose wisely," she hissed. "At least we don't have to worry the cow might be with calf already."

Nakhtmin gaped at her. How vulgar she was. No, this wasn't a noble lady; the vizier's wife should never behave like that! "Mutnofret is a decent woman, who knows how to behave so as not to muddle her rank. She will be a noble wife for your son," he said.

Her eyes narrowed to slits. "He is my son."

What did she mean? That Shepses belonged to her or came after her?

Shepses turned around to them. At least the last few words must have caught his attention. "I will marry her, and there's nothing you can do about it." Triumph flashed in his eyes when she grimaced. "Next moon I'll take her to my home if it's only a simple hut I can afford."

The tension between mother and son felt almost tangible. From the corner of his eye, Nakhtmin caught a puzzling glimpse of Nebit sitting at some distance. The vizier listened intently to their exchange, fists clenched. *In this house only hatred dwells.* Nakhtmin thought even the walls might be soaked in snake venom. No wonder Ameny and his family sat apart from their hosts. A normal conversation with these people was impossible.

Now Nebit directly looked at him. His mouth stretched—was that supposed to be a smile? He beckoned him. Nakhtmin's legs turned to water when he rose and stalked over the cushions. He stood in front of the vizier, who grabbed his hand and pulled him down.

"I'm watching you, boy. Don't think I've forgotten your betrayal. You were smart enough to crawl under the shendyt of the second Amun prophet, but that won't protect you forever. Stay away from me and mine. And you better avoid the shadows."

Nakhtmin stared at him wide-eyed. Such an undisguised threat shocked him. This man could get away with almost anything, and he knew it. He tore away from the grip of moist fingers and retreated. Now he also settled near the sleeping children.

The atmosphere grew ever more discomforting. Good manners demanded staying at least until the end of the performance, and time dragged on—and not only for Nakhtmin. Absent-mindedly, he pulled down the dress of little Henut, which had hiked up her legs. She kicked in her sleep and revealed a birth mark on her inner thigh. It looked like a cobra! He jerked back. Truly, nothing good lived in this house.

When Ameny finally rose and started to take leave, all faces showed relief.

SNAKES

Hori could hardly wait to receive Nakhtmin's report of the banquet at Nebit's house. Although he couldn't imagine his friend having the energy to write everything down and come across the river, he'd have loved to dive through the canal to the other side and check. The storm however had stirred up the inhabitants of the weryt.

"A bad sign," the lector priests said. "The spirits of the dead are enraged."

All night long, prayers were said, and Hori didn't dare to undertake his usual foray. The night after, he sneaked out to their hiding place, though. Would Nakhtmin be waiting for him? He hoped so and wasn't disappointed. This time he discerned the outlines of two figures in the pale moonlight. "Nakhtmin? Ameny?"

"Yes, we've both come," Nakhtmin replied.

Hori heard suppressed excitement in his friend's voice.

"The three of us might be able to make sense of what happened the last few days." Ameny sounded tense.

How concerned he had to be as father. Hori wouldn't want to trade places with him but could hardly rein in his curiosity. "Tell me all about it. Did you find out something?"

"Yes, indeed." Nakhtmin began relaying events of the previous evening. Occasionally Ameny added a detail or things Nakhtmin didn't observe.

"Sorry, if this was quite a jumbled tale. We haven't had a chance yet to confer with each other," Nakhtmin said.

"Never mind, I get the picture. So you don't believe Hotep capable of these murders?" A gust of wind stirred the lonely copse at the riverbank and made him shiver. This year the cold had set in early, and at night temperatures dropped even lower. As always, he'd come here naked. Hopefully, they'd find the perpetrator soon since he'd have to give up his excursions in the cold season.

"No. I believe he's just a distraught boy. I noticed his stuttering lessens when his parents aren't around."

"Interesting." Could his speech problems be cured if he knew his parents far away? Hori pushed the thought aside. "I trust your judgment but I don't want to keep him completely out of our considerations lest we overlook something crucial. He might have followed his mother's orders."

Nakhtmin said, "One thing we can be sure of since yesterday evening: Nebit knows his wife cheats on him. He clearly saw her grab my manhood. The vizier doesn't seem to mind."

"Sitamun had always been like that. Insatiable." Then Ameny told Hori about his youth when he was in love with Sitamun.

Some of it he'd already read in Nakhtmin's message. Still, hearing the priest talk about it made a difference. His friend had omitted seemingly irrelevant details. At one point a thought flared but extinguished before he could grasp it. How he hated it when that happened! "Ameny, would you repeat every word that was said in Nebit's house in the right order? Please, also describe your impressions and how the family's faces changed."

"Sure, if you want me to…" He began.

Hori cowered so he offered less skin to the cutting wind and listened intently. He needed to form an accurate image so he closed his eyes and concentrated on the priest's voice since he also tried to mimic the tone of what people said. Gradually, Hori felt like he'd been there. He could envision everything clearly. Ameny's narrative reached the end of the evening and his voice trailed off. All three remained silent for a while.

Then Hori spoke. "Sitamun is the one controlling Nebit's actions when they are at home." He could only hope her influence ended at the walls of the vizier's estate but doubted it. "Whatever tickles her fancy, he concedes. I have the feeling he not only tolerates her misdemeanor but doesn't hold it against her either. Would you agree?"

"Yes," Nakhtmin replied.

Ameny grunted agreement.

"In the same fashion, she controls her sons. Shepses, however, wants to elude her."

"That woman is like a contagious pestilence," Nakhtmin confirmed. "Everyone living with her falls sick. The youngest, Henut, she even carries a birth mark shaped like a snake. If the girl stays in that house, she'll certainly be poisoned as well."

"No king cobra though?" Hori laughed. A bit far-fetched. Not even Sitamun could be blamed for birth marks.

"Those snakes in the garden," the priest said. "Dreadful! Who'd keep such deadly animals? So easy to get bitten. Or what if a cobra escapes?"

Hori recalled the horrible symptoms of a snake bite. The afflicted didn't die right away. The spot swelled, the venom paralyzed the limbs one after the other. Finally, the victims suffocated in an agonizing way, or their hearts gave out. During his studies he'd observed this a few times.

"Hotep said his father collects the reptiles' venom. I guess that makes them less poisonous although milking them is quite dangerous too." Nakhtmin told them about his experiences with snake experts in Upper Egypt.

"Any ideas what Nebit does with the venom?" Hori asked. Then he suddenly knew. Excited, he jumped to his feet. "It's Nebit! Nebit is our killer!" Blood rushed in his ears. Of course, it was all so obvious. While Ameny and Nakhtmin threw questions at him, he stood still for a moment and thought it over once more. Yes, it fit! Impatient, he started running back and forth. The words couldn't spill from his mouth fast enough. "Nebit gathers the venom. He has obtained one of Shepses's puncture needles and dips them in the poison. Repeatedly, I guess. I'd let one layer dry, then immerse the needle again until the surface is covered with a thick coating of venom. With this weapon, he approaches the girls. They suspect no evil; after all he's the vizier of the Two Lands and Shepses's father. They hope to marry into his noble family. Nebit takes care nobody observes their encounter, lures the girls to a place where they can't be seen or lurks in isolated places they frequent. Then he stabs them. The wound alone wouldn't be lethal right away as Mutnofret and Nakhtmin learned from their experiment with the goat. Maybe Nebit made the same mistake with his first victim. He or she might have run away."

"Goat?" Ameny asked.

Nakhtmin briefly explained their failed attempt at the animal's life.

"If you're right, why didn't this first victim report him before dying?" Ameny asked.

"Possibly, there was nobody nearby. Maybe Nebit attacked again? The victim would have been weak, likely collapsed. Doesn't really matter whether he used the cobra poison from the start, he sure did later. This explains why Hetepet's heart…" He swallowed. "…why it was swollen and darker. Usually one sees the effect of a snake bite on a leg. Nobody expects a heart to show the same, so I couldn't make sense of why her organ looked so strange. Now I know."

"But," Nakhtmin objected, "a cobra's bite doesn't kill right away either."

"Exactly. Venom injected into the leg isn't lethal right away. We bind the affected limb, so the poison can't travel up the *metu*, the vessels, to get where?"

"To the heart." Nakhtmin groaned and slapped his forehead. "As soon as it gets there, the patient can't breathe anymore and dies."

In his exhilaration over having finally solved this puzzle, Hori forgot Ameny's feelings.

The priest had sagged. "But why? Why did he do something so cruel to my little girl?"

Nakhtmin sat beside him and wrapped an arm around his shoulders. "Probably because Sitamun demanded it. Nebit is possessed by an evil spirit that has slipped into the body of his wife and feeds on him."

Ameny shivered. "First thing tomorrow, we need to share our knowledge with the pharaoh. Mutnofret is in great danger."

That moment Hori realized what it meant to confide in the king. Without sound evidence, his two allies had to reveal his involvement—and one consequence might be his death. However, he couldn't allow Nebit to carry on with his crimes only because he feared for his life. He owed the goddess Maat. "Yes, tell Senusret everything. I'm a dead man anyway."

Nakhtmin groaned. "Hori, no! We can't do that."

"We must! My daughter is in jeopardy."

"Ameny is right. You have to put an end to this. And who knows, the king might show mercy. Now get yourselves home. I'm freezing. Let's hope we'll meet again."

With wordless embraces, they took leave.

NIGHT-TIME ASSAULT

Nakhtmin paddled as if the crocodile god Sobek were on his heels. The moon had slipped behind a bulk of clouds, and he couldn't even see the water's surface. The paddle sank in with a slight splash each time. He could only hope he was heading for the jetty of Ameny's estate. "Can you tell if we're going in the right direction? How much farther to the riverbank?" The wind still blew in strong flurries, and he feared they might have drifted off course.

"I can't see my hand in front of my face. Oh gods, what a dark night!"

Nakhtmin's shoulder muscles ached with the strain. The distance had never felt this long before. At last the wind carried the rustling of reeds to them. It sounded very close. They'd almost reached the waterfront—but where exactly? The torch he always kept burning at the pier when he crossed the river had likely died. "Can you feel the jetty?"

The boat rocked heavily when Ameny shifted his weight. "The current drives us north, the wind south. I'm afraid the wind was stronger this time. We need to search farther downstream."

Nakhtmin paddled against the wind. For a brief moment, the cloud cover split and allowed moonlight to shine through.

"There, our pier!" Ameny called. "Just a small stretch downstream now."

And it turned dark again. Nakhtmin hoped he was heading straight for the small jetty. With a crackling noise the bulrush boat hit one of the stilts rammed into the water.

"Ouch." Ameny cursed. "Got my finger jammed. Hold on, I'll find the rope."

The boat careened as the prophet rose to his feet. Nakhtmin rowed gently so they wouldn't drift away. Then he hit the paddle against something hard. The noise sounded like wood on wood. What? Another boat was tied to the jetty. "Ameny, this isn't your pier."

"Sure it is. Ours is the smallest far and wide. I've got it. That's our rope."

"But there's another boat moored." Nakhtmin froze, then shouted, "Quick, Ameny! It's Nebit's boat."

The prophet leapt onto the planks, grabbed Nakhtmin's hand and pulled him up with such force, he thought he was flying. They hurried into the dark garden. Several times Nakhtmin tripped over obstacles and fell. Ameny didn't fare better since he kept releasing muffled curses. Where was the house? Like the night before, he lost his orientation, simply followed the sound of Ameny's steps. He obviously knew his own property well enough to find his way to the house even in such a gloomy night.

A gust of wind and a thud as if an open door slammed shut. As usual, he and the prophet had left through the door to the garden in Nakhtmin's chamber; they'd closed that door but couldn't bolt it. An unlocked door—an invitation to the killer. Nakhtmin cursed their carelessness. But who would have thought Nebit might sneak into the house at night? Of course! He groaned. Mutnofret was never alone. Either a family member or he kept her company. Nebit had to come up with a new method to murder her. What a stroke of luck for him to find an open door. As if the villain smelled it. Could he have watched them pull away from the jetty and seized his chance?

Another clatter sounded. Nakhtmin headed for the noise. He heard Ameny breathe heavily next to him. "He's in the house," he whispered.

He slowed and groped forward although he was agonizingly aware of the passage of time. Then his fingers touched the rough wall of the house. There, a door. But which one? It was closed. The next door kept slamming against the frame. Nakhtmin opened it and slipped into the room, which had to be his. He felt for the board holding the lamp, flint stone and cinder.

Nothing. No shelf.

Faint noises told him Ameny had found his way into the house. "This isn't my room," he murmured.

"What?"

"Let's find the lamp board. We need light."

While he groped the wall left of the door, Ameny felt along the other side.

"I've got it," the prophet said after a short while.

Nakhtmin heard him beat the flint stones against each other and saw the sparks fly. The typical smell spread through the room. If this wasn't his chamber, whose was it? No breathing disturbed the silence, no rustling of linen. Nobody slept in here. He dreaded what the lamp's light would unveil. They were too late.

At long last, a spark caught and lit the cinder. Gently Ameny blew at the flame and held the wick to it. "We're in Penu's chamber!"

Nakhtmin had never been in the small room where the mouse-faced servant lived. He recognized the lanky man's frame on the cot and felt for a pulse. "He's dead."

In the dancing light of the lamp, Ameny's features resembled a distorted mask of horror. "The killer has struck already. To my daughter, quick!"

Penu's room was close to the kitchen. Nakhtmin passed Ameny, who had to protect the flame, and ran along the corridor until he reached the large hall. Hard to believe, but he found his way in the gloom by heart. The lamp light behind him sufficed to let him discern the outlines of obstacles to dodge. He hurried into the hallway leading to the family's quarters.

Banging and screams. A fight. Nakhtmin burst into Mutnofret's chamber. A lamp sat on the floor and cast absurdly elongated shadows of two figures onto the wall: Nebit and Mutnofret. The vizier clutched her throat, his right hand ready to stab her, but she held his arm and pushed it up. Faint light reflected on the bronze needle.

Nebit didn't react to his entrance, had his back to the door, but Mutnofret stared at him, eyes wide with fear. Nakhtmin didn't think, lunged at the vizier from behind. His hands closed around the killer's neck. Nebit tore at his fingers, stumbled back. He must have released Mutnofret. Nakhtmin tightened his grip, squeezed harder. The vizier gurgled, pushed against him, forced Nakhtmin to step back until his back hit the wall. Nebit kept pushing against him, tried to slam his skull in Nakhtmin's face.

Energy draining, Nakhtmin cast a frantic look around for help. Then he saw the needle—still in Nebit's hand. The man stabbed at anything behind him. The slightest prick to his skin could be deadly. Nakhtmin wriggled to stay out of his reach.

His fingers slipped from Nebit's throat. He saw his end nearing when he heard a thud. The vizier's body went limb and slumped to the floor. With a clink, the needle dropped from his hand. Nakhtmin gasped.

Mutnofret stood before him, arms dangling, but in one hand she held a heavy vase of alabaster. "I hit him over the head with it…" The container clattered to the ground.

Incredulous, Nakhtmin stared at the slack body of the man they'd tried to convict for so long in vain. His gaze fell on the needle. He quickly kicked the murder weapon out of Nebit's reach. In shock, his teeth chattered. What a close call! "Arre you all right?" His legs hardly obeyed him when he stepped over the vizier's body.

She flung herself into his arms, and he held her tight. He'd almost lost her! Lifting her chin, he pressed his lips on hers. She responded with passion. A whole life in this embrace, although only a few moments passed.

"Hrr-hm," sounded from the door. "Shouldn't we bind Nebit before he awakens?"

For how long had Ameny been standing there?

Mutnofret immediately pulled away from Nakhtmin. "Father!" Sobbing, she sank against his chest.

As if to confirm Ameny's words, Nebit released a groan.

They had to act fast. "Where do I find a rope?"

Father and daughter didn't hear him.

He shrugged, tore a strip from his own shendyt and tied Nebit's hands behind his back. That would do for now. To err on the safe side, he fastened another strip around the man's ankles. Then he tapped Ameny's shoulder. "I'll go fetch the Medjay. The killer shall not tarry under this roof longer than absolutely necessary." All of a sudden, he felt dizzy. He sat down for a moment… Next to Mutnofret's bed stood a jar of water and a mug so he poured some.

Ameny pushed Mutnofret down next to him. "First, I think we all need a sip of wine."

Nakhtmin wanted to laugh, but instead, a sob erupted from his throat. Mutnofret snuggled up against him. He looked at Ameny. What would the priest think of him? That he'd seduced his employer's daughter? He inched away from her.

A smile spread over Ameny's face. "Boy," he said. "After Shepses, I'll accept any man as husband for my daughter, and you're not the worst she could have chosen." With that he left the room.

Had Mutnofret already talked to her father about marrying him? Speechless, he wondered if he'd have any say in this matter. He gazed into her pale face, touched her throat, where Nebit's hand had gripped her.

His relief that she was unharmed washed away his bout of anger. She lived, and he hadn't failed her. They embraced each other.

Before dawn, the Medjay arrived and took Nebit away. The vizier had regained consciousness after a while but had remained silent. Still mute, he now stumbled out the door, held by the forces of law and order.

"The Medjay will get the truth out of him," Ameny remarked.

Nakhtmin hoped he was right. So many questions were still unanswered. Why these murders? Why had Nebit entered through Penu's chamber and killed the servant? How much did Sitamun know? He gently wrapped an arm around Mutnofret's shoulders and gingerly pressed her against him.

As if she were fragile! She'd tricked him, established facts. That was so typical. *Oh you just wait, mischievous little tease. I won't make it that easy for you.* His heart, however, intoned a song of joy.

PHARAOH'S SECRET

Summoned by the king! Hands sweaty, Nakhtmin followed the messenger and appreciated Ameny's presence more than ever. "Why do you think his majesty—life, prosperity and health—requests our presence?" he asked.

Ameny shrugged. "It's not very common for the vizier of the Two Lands to be charged with murder. Most likely he wants to hear what happened."

That made sense. Nakhtmin was really glad they wouldn't need to mention Hori's involvement in the investigation. They'd caught Nebit in the act. So they had plenty of evidence to sentence the man. Except, he'd only be convicted of murdering Penu and attempting to kill Mutnofret. Was that the kind of justice the king's court owed to all the other victims? It didn't seem right to Nakhtmin. And what if Nebit somehow managed to talk his way out of the whole affair? Even worse: what infamous actions was Sitamun capable of once she lost her facilitator? This viper shouldn't get away without punishment. He took a deep breath. "We should tell him the complete truth."

"But…" Ameny checked if the pharaoh's servant was far enough ahead, then lowered his voice. "But we agreed to leave it at charging him for what he did to Penu and Mutnofret."

"That would be against Maat though. No atonement for Hetepet's murder, and the deaths of the other girls would never be revealed as crimes. What rankles most, Nebit will protect his wife. I want to see her punished for what she did."

Ameny grimaced. "A doctor has to teach *me* in matters of religion! You're right."

They stopped before the large double gates. The guard greeted them and let them enter without further ado. Obviously they were expected. Nakhtmin cast a shy glance around. Except for his testimony at the Great Kenbet and his visit to the royal gardens, he'd never been inside the palace. This time they didn't enter the large hall where he'd given his statement with trembling knees. Instead, they followed the envoy through a labyrinth of corridors that all looked the same. The bare, whitewashed walls were only broken up by doors, some of which were marked with symbols, for easier orientation, he guessed. Behind these doors the administration of the Two Lands was managed. Here flowed the juices of Kemet, the Black Country; here the officials managed every hamlet, every town, temples as well as farms. Nakhtmin felt tiny among the many people hurrying through the hallways with determination. He hoped somebody would guide them back outside since he'd be hopelessly lost in this maze.

At last they stopped before a door no different than all the others. "The heart of power," he blurted. How fitting that it looked just the same as the rest. After all, the country's body needed all organs in order to flourish.

The room they entered was as undecorated as the corridors. Pharaoh Senusret sat at his desk. In one corner Thotnakht, the first scribe of the king, had settled on a cushioned mat.

While Ameny greeted the pharaoh with many words, Nakhtmin only bowed. When he straightened up again, he spotted an ancient-looking chest with ivory marquetry—the only luxurious and adorned object in the room. Nakhtmin puzzled over this piece of furniture when he noticed Senusret had followed his gaze.

"This chest once belonged to the mother of Ameny, the founder of our dynasty. She was from the land of Kush and brought it with her when she married an Egyptian. I treasure it very much."

Embarrassed, Nakhtmin nodded reverently. His curiosity might come across as disrespectful. Senusret didn't seem to mind though. He turned back to Ameny. "This morning, the head of the Medjay called on me and reported Nebit, my vizier, was arrested in your house last night with you pressing charges. This is unheard of. Tell me what happened."

Heart pounding, Nakhtmin bit on his lower lip.

The Amun prophet appeared uneasy as well. Now he stealthily wiped his hands on his shendyt. "Your majesty, this will be a long story, which started several moons ago. The trial of Hori, son of Sobekemhat, is part of it as well. Before I reveal everything, I'd like to express my puzzlement over this uncommon verdict."

At these words, Senusret cringed. The king's eyes narrowed. Nakhtmin imagined he saw a bad conscience flinching.

Ameny continued, "I studied the protocols of the trial. Although I am no judge of the Great Kenbet, I do recognize injustice when I see it. I am convinced Nebit bribed several witnesses. Nakhtmin here can testify how the vizier approached him. Hotep, son of Nebit, revoked his original, false testimony."

Nakhtmin held his breath. Even the swish of Thotnakht's stylus silenced at the enormity of Ameny's allegation. The pharaoh placed one hand on the table as though he wanted to push himself up. "Answer my question, priest."

Ameny hesitated, swallowed with effort. "First I must know how this verdict came about when Neferib's death was clearly an accident. The attempt on my daughter's life is connected to it."

The prophet's persistence turned Nakhtmin's legs to water as if they wanted to flow down the Nile. He'd never have dared to talk to the king in such a manner.

The pharaoh, however, didn't jump up with indignation, as he'd expected, but placed his elbows on the tabletop and rested his head in his hands. "Thotnakht, you may leave." Senusret's voice sounded dull.

"My lord?"

The king straightened and looked at his scribe. "I have to talk with these two alone."

Without another word, the scribe gathered his utensils and rose.

"Stay close. I might need you later."

Thotnakht nodded and disappeared through a second door into an adjoining room.

This was very strange. Before them sat the most powerful man of the Two Lands, while they were only two humble subjects, and still Nakhtmin felt like their roles had reversed. The king behaved like a defendant. Nakhtmin said, "Your majesty, whatever you have to tell us, I for one swear a holy oath none of it will come across my lips. I'll bury your secrets so deep inside my heart, not even the utu will find them." He sank to his knees. "If you find out I lied, deal with me as you wish."

Ameny followed his example. "I too swear this oath. You can trust us without hesitation. May the underworld open up and swallow me if I speak a lie."

The king took a deep breath. His nose twitched. "I'll accept your oaths and place my fate in your hands. I once made a mistake, which gave Nebit the means to force my hand."

Ameny gasped, and Nakhtmin shuddered at the revelation.

"I'll tell you how this came about. My lock of youth had just been cut when my father sent me to the House of War to train as soldier. Like every man, I loved to party with my friends, and quite often we did so near the harbor. We particularly liked to frequent one tavern where the innkeeper offered rooms and girls for an extra fee."

Nakhtmin could well imagine. Senusret must have seen thirteen or fourteen inundations then. Many young men made their first sexual experiences at that age. Nevertheless, he immediately thought of the night at the *Golden Ibis*.

"I'd already imbibed serious amounts when I asked for a girl to be sent to the room. To my surprise, a mature woman awaited me, one of exceptional beauty! She sparked a fire in my groin like no other had done before. That very first night, I fell in love with her." The king shook his head as if finding it hard to fathom his youthful folly now. "Every evening, I was drawn to her. My bliss lasted two moons, then I marched with the army against Libu. When I returned, I couldn't find her."

"You never saw her again?" Ameny asked.

The king released a bitter laugh. "Oh, I did. Soon after my return, I was allowed to sit next to my father during a state banquet for the first time. We celebrated our victory, and my darling sat at the king's high table since she was the vizier's wife."

"Sitamun!" Nakhtmin blurted.

Senusret raised his eyebrows and nodded. "Sitamun. And she was pregnant—with my child as she told me."

Ameny groaned. "Adultery."

Confused, Nakhtmin looked from one to the other. "But what was she doing in such a tavern, she could have…"

Ameny cast him a pitiful glance. "I know all too well Sitamun hunts wherever she likes."

"You too?" Senusret looked flabbergasted.

"She was still young then. Who could have resisted her? I paid dearly a long time ago."

The king shook his head. "What a gaping abyss! The child, however, a little girl, was born a few moons later."

"But—she is Nebit's wife. He might have fathered the child," Ameny argued.

Pharaoh shook his head. "A whim of the gods. The girl carries my mark." He rose and came around the desk, then bared his thigh.

Nakhtmin sucked in a sharp breath as he recognized the snake mark.

"Let's all sit down." Senusret waved to the mat, where Thotnakht had sat earlier. "You've seen the sign on little Henut?"

Nakhtmin nodded.

"Well, it turned out lady Sitamun had been well aware for whom she acted the harbor harlot. At first I thought her husband must have forced her. I begged her to divorce him. How she'd laughed! 'And then what? Will you take me as your second wife? I want to be at the top,' she said. I refused. Degrading my sister Sherit to a lower place than she was entitled to? I wasn't that infatuated with her. Soon I realized she was anything but her husband's victim. At first, she and Nebit promised to keep my misconduct secret."

"But that wasn't the end of it?" the Amun prophet surmised.

"No. When my father set out on his journey to the Beautiful West, Nebit called on me even before the time of mourning was over. He demanded I confirm his appointment as vizier. Or else…"

"What an abomination!" Nakhtmin tried to put himself in the king's situation. What would he have done?

"This affair had troubled me for a long time already. I knew Nebit could accuse me of adultery any time, and then I would have to confess. Apart from that, my crime weighed heavy on my heart. However, I was the successor to the throne, the only son of my father. If I'd already had a son then, I might have taken the risk."

Ameny interjected, "Most likely you'd have been acquitted since you were not aware of the woman's marital status."

"Possibly—when I was only co-regent, maybe. Nebit picked the time for his coercing wisely. How could the king be both defendant and his own judge? I'd have felt obliged to sentence myself. Well, keeping him as vizier didn't seem such a bad thing. I'd likely have confirmed him anyway. He didn't ask me to do something that violated Maat, so I consented." The king's shoulders sagged forward. He buried his face in his hands. "I thought I could accept this crime against Maat, the adultery. May the adjudicators at the Judgment of the Dead decide. The Two Lands needed me. Who'd have benefitted if I sentenced myself to death as it would have been my duty?"

At a loss, Nakhtmin looked at Ameny. What a horrible predicament. "How did Sitamun manage to cast her netting so far and wide without ever getting accused?" he asked. "After all, I saw for myself how she had sexual intercourse with several men."

Senusret cast a brief glance at the ceiling as if the answer might be written there. "The law says only the betrayed spouse or the head of the family can file charges. As long as Nebit doesn't voice allegations and her lovers are unmarried or able to keep a secret, she's safe. Besides, most cases of adultery aren't even tried. Hurt feelings quickly send the offended party to the Medjay to press charges. As soon as they've calmed down, they shy from public scandal. Nobody wants to be mocked as a cuckold. Often the couple reconciles before the next court day. Then the legal complaint is withdrawn. Or there's a clandestine divorce. Likely the punishment for adultery is so severe to make people think twice before taking a case all the way to its bitter end."

"Is this the only reason for such horrible sentencing? It does seem strange."

Nakhtmin's question made Ameny laugh. "How young and ignorant you are. Imagine you wouldn't know if your wife's children are yours. What if she gets a divorce? Would you want to pay for another man's brats? Should these children split your heritage among them? Even worse: would you want to rely on them to perform the sacrifices for the dead when you set out on your last journey?"

"Oh." No, he wouldn't want that. Fortunately, he could depend on Muti. She wasn't like Nofriti. Whoever might take her one day… He forced his thoughts back to the matter at hand. "Still, I don't understand these men. What a risk they take." Nakhtmin recalled the night of the graduation banquet, the drunken frenzy. His friends probably hadn't been able to think straight anymore.

"But let's hear the rest of your story," the priest said. "I assume Nebit demanded more at some point?"

The king sighed. "Yes, he did. He wanted Hori sentenced to death. I kept telling him what an offense to the divine order this would constitute. None of the other judges would have convicted Hori. Sobekemhat pleaded for his son's life. And I...I couldn't order the man's death. It wasn't easy to convince Hut-Nefer, the mer-ut, to accept Hori into the closed world of the weryt. In the history of the Two Lands, no king has ever interfered in matters of the weryt."

"Thus Hori became the dead, who was allowed to live," Nakhtmin mused and couldn't suppress a grin. This man was king, but by the gods, his cunning matched that of a trader.

Senusret returned his smile. "It's a relief to share this burden. Now I'm hungry and thirsty. I guess we still have plenty more to discuss?"

Ameny nodded. The pharaoh called an attendant from the adjoining room and ordered refreshments.

The priest led up to the second part of their discussion, "We've promised to keep your secret. Now we must ask you to return the favor, because what we will report could mean our deaths—and Hori's."

"You arouse my curiosity. I'll give you my word. Or are you going to confess crimes?" He gave each of them a stern look.

Worried, Nakhtmin glanced at Ameny, then took over. "The thing is, at the weryt, Hori discovered a crime. Murders that would never have been recognized as such if his trained physician's eye hadn't detected faint traces. He found a way out of the weryt so he could send me a message."

Senusret gave an incredulous snort. "There is no way out of the weryt!"

When Nakhtmin told him about the canal, the king burst into laughter. "Dear gods, I'll believe you, though I'd never have thought of it."

"Hori neither, but one night the goddess Maat appeared and showed him the way."

At once, Senusret turned serious. "If Maat takes on physical shape, she must be seriously off balance. This is a matter of utmost importance. Keep talking!"

Gradually Nakhtmin laid out the events before the king. The names of victims, who'd definitely fallen prey to Nebit, made Senusret groan.

"Ankhes, my ward!"

"And my daughter Hetepet," Ameny added.

"That's why the second prophet of Amun agreed to help me with my search for the perpetrator. I needed his support because Nebit had thrown quite a few obstacles in my path as doctor. As revenge for my speaking the truth at the trial instead of repeating the same lie as the other bribed witnesses. But listen where he found his next victim."

Nakhtmin described how they'd discovered the dead barmaid, then relayed Mutnofret's bold actions and how they only learned about them afterward.

"Your daughter is a brave woman!" Senusret burst out.

"Inconsiderate, I'd call it. She almost died." Ameny finished their lengthy report with the events at the banquet and those of last night.

"I'm sure you understand why we need you to remain silent. Revealing that Hori left the weryt would cost his life—and ours. Who'd believe we didn't learn any secrets harbored behind these wall, nor wanted to know any."

The king leaned against the wall and stretched out his long legs, uncovering part of the snake mark. A muscle in the king's leg twitched and it looked like the worm wriggled under the fabric.

"I still don't understand one thing," Senusret said. "You didn't need to tell me about Hori. All of you would have been safe, while Nebit would have been convicted anyway."

"It's because of the goddess. Maat herself wants atonement for the dead women." A shiver ran down Nakhtmin's spine as he spoke these words.

Ameny rolled his lower lip between thumb and forefinger. "What are you going to do, my king, if Nebit tries to force your hand again? Your predicament is still the same."

All three of them fell silent. Ameny spoke the truth. Coercion was a despicable crime. What could they do? An idea germinated in Nakhtmin's heart. "We could give him a taste of his own poison! If he threatens you, put even stronger pressure on him."

Senusret's relaxed pose changed into the tension of a predator before the attack. "Explain!" he demanded, eyes flashing.

"I studied Nebit like a scroll in the House of Life. The man loves his wife beyond all reason. Not only would he do anything for her, but he leaves her free rein, no matter how disgusting her behavior." He told the king of the incestuous act he'd witnessed. "If Sitamun desires something, he gets it for her. What she doesn't like, he takes out of her way. It displeases her if one of her sons wants to go his own way, even worse if he prefers another woman—no matter how revolting this seems to us. Therefore Nebit kills those girls, who mean more than a temporary pastime to Shepses." He heaved a deep breath. In his fervor he'd talked faster and faster. "Threaten him with death, and he'll only grant you a weary smile. If he retorts with the menace to reveal your adultery, tell him you'll not only charge Sitamun with the very same crime but also with her involvement in his crimes. In consequence, a burial would be denied to her, and her ka soul would belong to the condemned for all eternity."

Senusret's features brightened. "Excellent idea!"

"You forgot one thing though," Ameny argued.

"What's that?" the pharaoh and Nakhtmin asked in chorus.

"The wench also knows of the adultery. She might try to force you to drop charges or else she'd make Nebit accuse you. Although she'd risk her life with such an attempt, she knows very well you've got more to lose. Believe me, she has never set her heart on anyone but herself."

"Then I'll strike her there, in her own heart. What threatens me, threatens her. She won't dare to pressure me."

"What if one of them takes the risk?" Ameny didn't give up.

"Guarantee her exemption from punishment for Nebit's deeds," Nakhtmin suggested.

"But only then!" Ameny blurted. "I want to see the bitch bleed for all the evil she has done!"

Nakhtmin squeezed his hand. "Me too."

Senusret lay his right one on top and said with fervor, "And me even more so!"

INTERROGATIONS

Their discussion with the king had lasted until the afternoon. Afterward it had been too late to give an official statement at the Medjay, which would serve as the basis for charges against Nebit. Nakhtmin and Ameny took care of that the next day. At the same time, the pharaoh personally interrogated his vizier.

As long as Nakhtmin didn't know for sure what Senusret achieved with Nebit, he stuck to the version a noise had awoken him at night and he'd caught Nebit in the act. Mutnofret's statement, he knew, would support his story. She'd described the dramatic events to the Medjay scribes the day before already. None of the king's law enforcers needed to know he and Ameny had crossed the Nile that night, which would certainly have astonished them.

After they took his statement, Nakhtmin waited impatiently for the king's return. Fidgeting, he sat on a bench in the small anteroom of the office where witnesses were interviewed, and counted flies on the wall. The sound of an opening door made him flinch, but it was only Ameny, who sat down next to him. He too had given testimony. Nakhtmin sensed the tension in his older friend. Much depended on how reasonably Nebit reacted.

"Fifteen flies," Nakhtmin said.

An amused smile on his face, Ameny lifted his brows. "One must have escaped then."

They both laughed.

A man in the attire of a royal servant entered and announced, "His majesty wishes to see you at the palace. Please follow me."

Ameny murmured, "Nebit's interrogation can't have lasted long if the pharaoh is already back at the palace."

The king sat on the mat and gestured for them to settle and forgo formalities. Nakhtmin spotted a plate with refreshments on a small table. His tongue stuck to the roof of his mouth. No matter how much he craved something to drink, he didn't dare take anything.

Senusret must have noticed his gaze, since he invited them to help themselves.

Nakhtmin poured a glass of fruit juice and took a gulp before scrutinizing the king's face. *Doesn't look like he succeeded, the lines around the corners of his mouth are even more pronounced.*

The young pharaoh rubbed his face with one hand and moaned. "Nebit's a piece of work. Like a rabbit, he darted this way and that."

"Did he get caught in the snare we designed yesterday?" Ameny picked up the comparison.

Senusret shook his head. "The man has the nerve to make demands. He wants to speak to Sitamun, alone, or else he won't say a word."

Incredulous, Ameny asked, "Didn't you tell him what's in store for Sitamun?"

"I sure did. At first it seemed like he might take the offer: exemption from punishment for Sitamun if he doesn't accuse me of adultery. I confronted him with all his crimes including those which hadn't been recognized as murders. That unsettled him somewhat."

"But you didn't tell him Hori detected the traces he left?" Nakhtmin asked in panic.

"Of course not."

"I'd hoped we could negotiate everything with Nebit. Now we need to persuade Sitamun." Ameny looked resigned.

Nakhtmin didn't place much hope in his plan either.

"I have an idea that might help us," Senusret said and winked like a mischievous boy. He refused to enlighten the two friends though. Instead he asked them to accompany him to the house of the Medjay later.

"Why didn't we just stay there?" Nakhtmin asked. Ameny shook his head ever so slightly. Shocked, Nakhtmin realized his impropriety. They'd become so familiar with Senusret, he'd forgotten who the man was.

"I need to prepare and make some arrangements first. Besides, I thought you'd like to have a bite to eat instead of sitting around in that little room."

Nakhtmin blushed. "Very considerate of you. Thanks."

Ameny and Nakhtmin stood in a cramped coop. The narrow room directly adjoined one of the interrogation rooms, with airing slits in the joint wall. One could hear every word spoken on the other side without the questioned person knowing. To anyone unsuspecting, it would appear like the street were on the other side of the wall.

A door slammed shut. Someone must have entered the room. A Medjay's voice, "As requested, Lady Sitamun, your majesty."

"I greet the Strong Bull of Kemet," Sitamun purred.

A muffled snort escaped Ameny, and Nakhtmin touched a finger to his lips. They could be heard on the other side of the wall, too.

"Fine, you may retreat," Senusret said.

Another slamming of the door. The Medjay must have left.

"The two of us alone… Remember?"

"Let's cut to it, Sitamun. Your husband has been caught red-handed as he tried to kill the betrothed of your son Shepses. He'd already killed one of the servants of the second prophet of Amun. Nebit will face a murder trial. Nevertheless, he dared to remind me of my earlier misstep with you. Nebit can't seriously expect me to simply sweep these charges against him under the bulrush mat."

Nakhtmin heard unidentifiable noises, then the sharp voice of the pharaoh cut in. "No, let me finish! Should Nebit decide to accuse me—and therefore you as well—of adultery, you should know his trial will come first. With such severe charges, the Great Kenbet is likely to take all day only for the one case. Until the next Great Kenbet, three moons will wax and wane, and by then Nebit will have been executed and fed to the devourer. He won't be able to accuse me himself. Therefore the board of judges will have little choice but to drop adultery charges against you and me."

Nakhtmin wondered why Senusret wouldn't simply risk this scenario. It would make for a much simpler solution. Then he realized Nebit wouldn't have any reason to confess in that case, and the king's conscience wouldn't allow him to perform such a deceit. He'd be misusing his power since Maat demanded his adultery trial to happen first. Senusret's words might trick Sitamun, though. Someone so rotten would assume others had no qualms either. He concentrated on the muffled words exchanged on the other side.

"You, however, will be charged with complicity in Nebit's crimes. I offer you exemption from punishment for your abetting if you convince Nebit to keep our adultery secret and to confess all the murders he committed. I know you wield such power over him. Now you may speak."

"How smart you are, my pretty prince. Some time ago, you wanted to make me your second wife…"

"Stay away from me. You're old, Sitamun. Nothing about you still tempts me."

A hiss filtered through the slits as if a snake were in the next room. "I've got nothing to do with the crimes of that old fool. I knew nothing. You find me completely clueless. You won't be able to prove anything."

"Some time ago, a woman taught me how an innocent man can be turned guilty. Take this as a promise from your king, who will be your judge."

Breathless, Nakhtmin strained to hear her response through the thin slit. If only he could see Sitamun's face.

"So you promise exemption from punishment if I influence Nebit? What makes you think I have the power to do so?" Her voice sounded cold and calculating.

"Oh, I know you hold absolute sway over your husband. He'd walk over burning hot coals for you. A little bird sang in my ear, he doesn't even dare to laugh without your permission. What a miserable creature!"

Her throaty laugh made Nakhtmin envision how she slithered up to the king once more. How did Senusret manage to control himself? He'd have gripped the viper's throat already.

"Very well. I'll do it. Then I'll remain unchallenged and can enjoy my husband's inheritance. Give me a written guarantee!"

A long silence ensued. Nakhtmin guessed the king was writing. Then he heard a faint rustle of papyrus being rolled up.

"I want your seal on it lest you claim I forged the document."

Senusret sighed, and Nakhtmin gritted his teeth. She thought of everything. More rustling.

"Now, go, Sitamun. Your husband is craving your visit. You will see each other for the last time before the Great Kenbet."

A door opened. Muffled words were followed by silence. A few moments later, someone knocked on the door of their tiny chamber. Ameny unbolted the lock, and they both slipped outside.

"You've heard it all?" Senusret asked.

"Every word," Ameny confirmed with a grim look on his face.

Nakhtmin couldn't suppress a grin. "Very clever twist with the trial dates."

Senusret winked. "And she doesn't know there won't be any inheritance left after the sentencing. The culprit's possessions will pass to the crown. Hopefully, Nebit will fess up tomorrow when the Medjay question him again. I'll attend as well." He walked ahead and they followed him outside the house of the Medjay, where the monarch's guards waited. "I'll keep you informed. My servant will take you to the palace tomorrow afternoon. Then I'll let you know if the plan worked."

Ameny couldn't neglect his duties at the temple of Amun any longer, so Nakhtmin directed his steps toward the prophet's estate, which already felt like home, and mulled over the intense last few days. After they'd been groping around in the dark for so long, everything happened incredibly fast. How he'd love to talk things over with someone. Hori! He wouldn't want to trade places with him. What a torture it must be for him, not knowing what happened. Tonight he had to cross the river again. Yesterday, he'd been too wiped out after the sleepless night in the aftermath of Nebit's attack, or else he'd have delivered the good news: the killer has been arrested! His heart leapt at the thought of Mutnofret waiting for him. Most of the previous day he'd been out and about, and when he did see her, they were never alone. No chance of a private word. Later, exhaustion had taken its toll. Could she really be in love with him? It felt so unreal. The girl sure had a strange way of showing her affection. He felt bartered away like cattle. At least, he could deal with that right away.

He passed through the gate and headed for the corner of the garden where she usually sat with her needlework. No, it was too cold for that. The storms of the previous days had cooled down the air significantly. Muti had to be inside. He found her in the company of her mother and a few maids, organizing the pantries. Grinning, he leaned against the doorjamb and enjoyed the view of her gorgeous backside as she bent over.

"Oh, Nakhtmin, you're back," Isis greeted him.

Mutnofret straightened and turned around. Her bright smile chased away all doubts. She liked him! Had she told her mother yet? Then it would be really true. He held Isis in high esteem. Quiet and inconspicuous as she was, she led the household with a strong hand. Although her voice wasn't heard often, he'd come to the conclusion she set the tone in this house. One thing she'd passed on to Muti... He grinned again. Both women gazed at him, then burst into laughter. Likely, he looked like a lovesick donkey.

"Off with you two. I'm sure you have much to talk about," Isis said and winked at him.

A rock dropped from his heart. He seemed to have smoothly ascended from poor employee to welcome future son-in-law. Surely, his rescuing Mutnofret must have played a role in her ready acceptance, but he hoped to have earned her respect in other ways as well.

Mutnofret took his hand and pulled him away to her room. Laughing, she threw the door closed behind them. He, however, fended off her embrace and crossed his arms.

The mischievous spark in her eyes died. "Has something happened?"

"You tell me." He enjoyed her dismay. "Let me summarize: You got engaged to Shepses behind your parents' backs. As soon as the marriage contract was sealed, you threw yourself into my arms—out of the blue—and your father talks about marriage as if it were a done deal. Did any of you ever think of asking how I feel about it? Or did you think little Nakhtmin from Upper Egypt will be so grateful he doesn't need to be asked? Have you ever considered I might not want you?" Her lips tightened into a thin line, but he continued. "Truth is, your father can be happy if you'll ever find a husband. I've never before met a girl so stubborn, irresponsible, arrogant..."

146

She leaned close and whispered in his ear, "I know you love me."

His arms flopped down. Dear gods, yes! He was madly in love with her. Hold on; having seen all the havoc mad love can wreak, he really shouldn't. He grabbed her, kissed her hard and urgently, threw her on the bed.

This time, she fended him off. "I'm still promised to another man. We should wait until the engagement is officially revoked."

"You're right. Holy Bastet, let Ameny hurry up with it! I can hardly wait."

"If you hadn't been such a yokel, we could have had this much earlier. I gave you enough signs."

He sat up. Signs? Scenes popped up in his mind when she teasingly lured him. He'd been so sure she'd only laugh at him if he took the bait. "Woman, you should learn to write. Nobody could have deciphered those signs of yours." He snorted.

She pulled a face and playfully hit his upper arm. "I certainly know how to write. Maybe you should learn to read?"

These eyes! How could he ever mistake her teasing for vicious ridicule? Actually, he rather enjoyed matching wits with her. He sealed her lips with a kiss, but she shoved him away.

"Why don't you tell me what you and Father have been concocting with the king all this time."

He lifted his eyebrows. Concocting! He'd have to get used to her disrespect. Remembering his promises to the pharaoh and Hori, he told her as much as he could without betraying their trust. No easy feat.

"You're keeping something from me," she complained.

"Only what I'm not allowed to reveal. State secrets."

She huffed. "Aren't you important! Give the guy a kiss and an audience with the king, and he thinks himself the most senior keeper of the royal seal!"

Ameny's return spared him a response. What was he getting himself into?

BITTER REALIZATION

"I couldn't have made it through another day without news from you." Hori shivered in the cold night air. Nakhtmin's embrace warmed not only his heart.

"Here, I've brought you a cloak. You can hide it under the rock later."

Grateful, Hori wrapped the warm fabric around himself. "Now, tell me," he demanded. "What happened?" The clouds had moved on, and an almost full moon illuminated Nakhtmin's grin.

"He has been caught!" he exclaimed.

"Tell me—was it Nebit?"

"Yes, Nebit. And it was great, so great, that you unmasked him. When we returned from our last visit to the Beautiful West, Nebit was on a nocturnal prowl." He reported what happened that night.

"Caught in the act! He'll never be able to talk his way out of it."

"No. At dawn the Medjay arrested him. The ph...uhm." Nakhtmin stalled.

"What?"

"The prophet."

"Yes, what about Ameny?" Had Nakhtmin meant say something else? Was he hiding something? Did he not trust him?

For a moment his friend seemed at a loss, then his features relaxed. "The prophet will soon be my father-in-law," Nakhtmin blurted.

Hori wrapped an arm around his shoulders. "Really? How did that happen? So, you and Mutnofret? And I thought you couldn't stand her because she likes to tease you. Well, I've been suspecting you two might become an item for quite a while now."

"He-he, very funny, these jokes at my expense. Muti is showering them on me. Earlier today, she called me a yokel because I didn't recognize the clues she gave me." He relayed how father and daughter had taken him by surprise.

Hori shook with laughter. His friend really was rather clumsy when it came to women. He'd probably never have approached Ameny's daughter, might not even have acknowledged his feelings to himself. The thought of how the girl had not only showed Nakhtmin the door to happiness but had to push him through was hilarious.

"Are you done yet?" Nakhtmin was the emblem of hurt pride.

"I'm sorry, my friend. I don't have much reason to laugh and it felt real good."

Nakhtmin pressed his lips together and only uttered monosyllabic responses. The feeling he was hiding something sneaked up on Hori again.

"You'll hear from me when I learn more," Nakhtmin said and took his leave.

Hori watched him march off. What was wrong with his friend? He should be singing with joy. Hori buried the cloak and hurried back to the weryt. The nights were really too cold now! He braced himself before diving into the chilly stream of the canal. Huffing and puffing, he broke through the surface on the other side of the wall and climbed out of the shallow water. Good thing he'd hidden a linen cloth in a cranny. He quickly dried himself off and wrapped the fabric around his trembling body.

What was that? A crunching noise like footsteps on sand. He froze. No, he must have imagined it. This wasn't the first time he'd felt watched during his excursions to the outside world. Illusions. If someone had spotted him, there'd have been an immediate outrage. His door to the world was only visible from a few houses. Maybe a sleepless wanderer? In the silence of the night, sounds traveled far. Nevertheless, he stood still for a while longer. Once again his senses had played a trick on him. Shaking his head, he trotted toward his house.

When he lay in bed, it dawned on him that Nakhtmin hadn't mentioned the king's reaction to the arrest of his vizier or Sitamun's fate. He jerked up. And what about himself? Had his involvement in the investigation been mentioned? Had Nebit confessed the other murders as well? Actually, Nakhtmin had hardly told him anything.

Then he realized Nakhtmin had no more reason to meet him now that the villain had been caught. The very thought hurt. He'd uncovered Nebit's crimes, but his life wouldn't change. Inside the walls of the weryt, life followed its daily course determined by the rhythm of death. He remained a beggar at the table of life, having to contend with the crumbs others threw at him. Only now, he became fully aware how much he'd hoped success in clearing up these murders would better his own fate. The acknowledgment brought on more pain, much more pain. Was that the reason for Nakhtmin's omissions? Did his friend know something he couldn't tell because it would only make things worse? Had he seriously hoped the pharaoh would quash his judgment when Nebit was executed? Had he even thought that far? At a loss, he stared into the darkness of his chamber. No. It was time to be completely honest with himself. He knew the secrets of the weryt. Nobody would ever let him leave this place.

ENCOUNTER WITH THE GOD OF DEATH

Day 8 of month Ka-her-ka in Peret, season of the emergence

Nakhtmin turned away from Hori and hastened toward the river, where he'd tied up the small boat. He'd almost slipped up. His heart urged him to tell, but his oath bound him. He wished he could reveal everything to Hori, from their discussion with the king to Sitamun's interrogation and Senusret's cunning trick. As soon as he mentioned one bit, though, he'd have to reveal it all.

Senusret hadn't said a word about doing anything to help Hori. Leisurely, Nakhtmin paddled across the river. How many times more would he be able to do this? Moist, cold air rose from the water and chilled him to the bones. Visions of Mutnofret's warm body flashed in his mind. His heart grew heavy. Once he was married to Muti, choosing between her fiery embrace and that of the Nile god would be tough. With a start, he realized she knew nothing about Hori and must never learn about his involvement. How could he possibly keep that from her and still visit his friend? Muti wouldn't pester him with questions for long; instead she'd simply sneak after him until she received answers.

Soon he would have to part with his friend for good. No matter how much he liked Hori, he was dead to the world—and he, Nakhtmin, lived. Hori couldn't expect him to risk his life and happiness for his sake. Saying good-bye wouldn't come easy to either of them, though. His throat tightened; a tear rolled down his cheek. Annoyed, he wiped it away. Too early to mourn their friendship. There was still hope!

The next morning, the king's envoy fetched Nakhtmin and the prophet. As before, he took them to the pharaoh's office. This time, Senusret sat at his desk and looked up when they entered. A smile softened the hard lines in his face. Hopefully that meant good news, Nakhtmin thought.

Senusret lifted the papyrus he'd been reading and flicked his index finger against it. "This is Nebit's full confession."

Ameny heaved a deep breath, and Nakhtmin too felt a heavy burden drop from his heart.

"The full confession of all murders?" the priest asked.

"All of them. There's even one more than we thought. Bastet too, the daughter of my scribe Thotnakht, fell prey to him."

"I thought so!" Nakhtmin blurted.

The king furrowed his brow. "You knew about it?"

"I…yes…no." Nakhtmin shrank under the king's threatening stare. "We suspected she might have been part of the series, but she'd died too long ago. Hori had asked the utu about young girls being taken to the weryt with no obvious cause of death visible on the body. Two names came up: Bastet and Ankhes. I did my research, found a connection between Ankhes and the vizier's family, but nobody could give me any clues about Bastet. According to her mother, she was found in one of the public parks with several scratches on her as if she'd run through shrubs."

"Hm." Senusret rubbed his chin. His beard stubble made a scraping noise. "This fits with Nebit's statement. Bastet was his first victim and he hadn't yet thought of covering the needle in snake venom as he did with the others." Senusret shuddered. "She didn't die fast enough for him. He stabbed her, but she was still able to run away."

Nakhtmin recalled their experiment with the goat and told the pharaoh about it.

"By the gods, you are thorough!" the king called. "That explains why Nebit couldn't risk his victims running off. They might have encountered someone and revealed his identity." Again, Senusret shuddered. "That man is totally crazy! He has no conscience, knows no scruples. He reveres only one religion and that is Sitamun. She is his goddess and high priestess of her own cult."

"Didn't Nebit realize his wife surrendered him to his judges?" Ameny asked incredulously.

The king snorted. "Like I said, he's crazy. He's fully aware of what's going on but sees himself as a sacrifice on the altar of their love. He's more than willing to do it." Senusret seemed exhausted. The interrogation must have been a strain.

Nakhtmin nodded. Just like he'd pictured the vizier's insanity. That left only one question, although deep down he knew the answer. "Did he admit Sitamun knew of his crimes?"

The pharaoh shook his head. "He knew what displeased her. She didn't have to say it out loud."

Then Nakhtmin remembered something else. "Did you ask him about Hori's trial?"

A slight smile played around Senusret's lips. "Oh yes, I did. He confessed to bribing and intimidating witnesses. Not that we really needed a confirmation. Before Nebit is tried, I'll call on the Great Kenbet to convene in secret and revoke Hori's sentencing."

Nakhtmin jumped up with joy. "But... That's fantastic!"

Senusret calmed him down. "Unfortunately, that doesn't mean Hori can walk out of the weryt a free man."

Ameny groaned. "The weryt is final. Nothing may leave its walls—no secret and certainly no bearer of its secrets."

Everything inside Nakhtmin rebelled, but he knew these men were right. The laws of the weryt were untouchable—above the king's rule. It had been an extraordinary feat to get Hori accepted into the community of the utu. Only one way to leave the weryt: as a mummy.

After a knock at the door, a servant stuck his head in. "Your majesty! He whom you are expecting has arrived." The man looked ashen around his nose.

"Show him in," the king commanded.

Neither Nakhtmin nor Ameny were prepared for what they saw. The god of the dead, Anubis in the flesh, stood on the threshold and scrutinized them with his lifeless eyes. Nakhtmin sank onto one knee, and the prophet beside him followed suit.

"This is Hut-Nefer, the mer-ut," Senusret explained.

Nakhtmin almost cracked up. It was a mask! Of course, only a mask. But it was so well crafted he'd fallen for it. He rose and stood on watery legs.

"This is the second time you ask me to enter the realm of the living, my king." The voice sounded dull but distinct.

Maybe the mer-ut was only allowed to leave the weryt in this attire so he

151

couldn't approach anyone and nobody would want to get near him. Everyone in the Two Lands feared the jackal-headed god.

"And I want to ask the same thing of you only in reverse."

"Explain yourself."

"Soon the judgment against Hori, son of Sobekemhat, will be revoked. The plaintiff confessed to bribing witnesses. The court issued a wrongful conviction, and Maat demands its revision."

The black head lowered in agreement. "I understand your wish. Alas, Hori must never leave the weryt except as a dead man."

Nakhtmin wanted to cry out, "But right now he is dead!" He knew, though, it couldn't be that easy.

"This is your last word?" the pharaoh asked.

Again the mask lowered.

Nakhtmin despaired. There was no negotiating with a god—this god. Still, there had to be a way!

"Hori must become an akh to leave those walls. This has never happened to anyone, whose heart was still beating, except for the mer-ut."

Nakhtmin couldn't hold back any longer. "Is there no way for Hori to live and be dead at the same time? I mean—now he is a dead man who lives. Can't he be turned into a living man who is dead?" He knew how absurd all this sounded, but he so wanted to help his friend. The masked head of the god of death whipped around to him. Nakhtmin froze.

"Leave this room! Now!" the mer-ut thundered.

Ameny flinched just the same as Nakhtmin. Both turned to the king, but his face revealed nothing. The mer-ut was obviously in charge here. Wordlessly they retreated and closed the door behind them.

Standing in the hallway, Nakhtmin asked, "Did I say something wrong?" He was shaken to the core.

Slowly, signs of understanding brightened Ameny's face. "No, my boy. You said the exactly right thing."

"I don't understand."

"And you must not. If it is what I think it is, powerful magic will be at work. Only the highest ordained priests know it. Not even I am entitled to such dangerous knowledge, but maybe someday. Have faith."

Easier said than done.

Abducted

Three times, Hori waited for Nakhtmin in vain. He didn't even find a message under the rock. With nights getting colder, he had to restrict his nocturnal forays. Tonight he fell asleep with a sense of bitter disappointment.

The walls of the weryt moved closer. They bound him and threatened to suffocate him like mummy bandages. He couldn't move, couldn't breathe...

With a jolt he flung open his eyes. This wasn't a dream! His whole body was wrapped in linen. Strong hands slung bonds around him. He wanted to scream, but a gag stuck in his mouth. Only a gurgling noise escaped his mouth. He was lifted and carried down the ladder.

They found out! I'm busted, and now I'll die. Need to escape! He twisted and turned in despair. His captors lost their hold, dropped him. He fell. His head hit the floor hard. He groaned, then blacked out.

The nightmare didn't end. When he came too, his head throbbed and the ground beneath him swayed. He heard the splashing of water. Where was he? On a boat? He was still wrapped from head to toes. The ties cut painfully into Hori's limbs. He tried sitting up—in vain. Once more, he lost consciousness.

Voices. A singsong filtered through the linen. The sounds echoed. Hori felt like he was lying in a burial cave.

"Osiris! Firstborn!

Oldest of the divine Ennead,

Founder of Maat on both shores."

No! They mean to bury me alive, immure me in a vault! Hori tried to scream.

"Your mother conceived you

From your father Atum,

When no sky existed yet,

When no earth existed yet,

When no gods existed yet,

Nor humans,

When death did not exist yet."

These verses sounded somewhat familiar. He gave up trying to free himself and listened to the voices in silence. Maybe they held a clue? The singsong was from the great myth of Osiris and Seth, but there was more. The men continued the story beyond anything he'd ever heard. Although he'd been robbed of his sight, images appeared before his eyes.

He completely immersed himself in the tale, became one with Osiris, the King of the Two Lands. Oh! Glorious times for the country at the Nile. The fields bore many times more crop, people suffered no austerity, and he enjoyed happiness with his wife Isis.

He loved his brother, although Seth begrudged him his luck. Seth wanted to be king himself, so he killed Osiris. Thus death entered the world. However, his death was not enough for his brother. Hori suffered with Osiris the agony of dismemberment at the hand of his envious brother. In every limb, he felt the pain, as Seth took each piece and threw it away—spread out over the Black Country. He heard the lament of his sister wife Isis. Her lovely voice was like balm. She found his limbs, every single one of them, and reassembled his body. His lover turned into a female sparrow hawk. And oh, how beautiful she was. Life returned to his body, lust made his phallus swell. Gentle as a breath, Isis settled on him. With bliss, he poured his semen into her and knew he'd overcome death.

"I give birth to you a second time,
So you may wander among the everlasting stars,
Elevated, alive and rejuvenated,
Like Ra himself every morning."

This wasn't the voice of Isis, but that of his mother Nut. It was the promise of eternal life. Together with the sun god Ra, he climbed onto the golden bark, night after night, and passed through the underworld. He was elevated to King of the *Duat*, the realm of the dead, while his son Horus ruled over the living.

Gentle hands removed the fabric from his face. Hori opened his eyes. The blackest darkness surrounded him. Was he blind? He felt strangely weightless as if he floated in an endless dark ocean. Now he became aware of the gag in his mouth again. How thirsty he was! The cloth sucked up the saliva in his mouth and seemed to grow bigger and bigger. He gurgled.

"Shshsh."

A deep voice intoned a ritual in an ancient language. A piece of metal touched his lips. The gag was removed, and someone trickled water into his mouth. Grateful, he swallowed.

"Shshsh," the voice repeated.

Again, he felt metal on his lips, and the singer's bass roared. Brightness spread around him, first a small flame, then he was bathed in glaring light.

"Shshsh," the voice said for the third time.

With a jolt Hori recognized the god of the dead, Anubis. He bent over him, holding an adze in his hand. Then he knew. *They are performing the ritual of mouth opening on me!* He truly must have been sentenced to death. Gratitude flooded him, because he was granted this ritual anyway. He'd be able to use his senses in the underworld.

The deep voice came from the snout of the jackal god. The ancient magic of his words coursed through Hori. Once again, his lips were touched to return his hearing. Strange thoughts occupied him. Although he hadn't been able to see or talk, he had heard everything. Was that because the voices of the gods were always audible? Or had he not heard, but experienced, the words? A shudder ran through his body. He was witnessing an incredible mystery.

Had hours or days passed? All of a sudden, Hori realized he was naked. Could all this have been a dream and he'd been lying in his bed the whole time? The lightness he'd thought to have experienced was gone now. Heaviness of the flesh burdened his limbs again, and his head throbbed as before. Blinding brightness had been replaced by impenetrable darkness. He was alone. The gods had left.

With care he touched what was under him. A wooden stretcher, not the sack of straw he usually slept on. He felt his head and grimaced when his fingers touched a large bump. So he hadn't been dreaming. He had been brought somewhere else. Fear gripped his heart. Buried alive after all? He sat up and let his legs dangle from the stretcher. His feet touched bare rock, rough and uneven. He stood and thought he was falling, found no holds. Where was the stretcher? It had disappeared. His knees hit the floor hard. Wincing with pain, he crawled on all fours. There had to be an exit!

"Hello?" he called. "I'm here." His voice bounced off the walls he couldn't see or feel. He sobbed. Never would he have imagined his punishment for leaving the weryt so terrible, so cruel! If only he hadn't done it.

"Hori, why do you harbor doubts?" The woman's voice sounded warm and gentle.

He thought to see the goddess Maat. "Where are you? What shall I do?"

"You have to be reborn. Follow the way I showed you."

He crawled toward the voice. His hand found no ground anymore. What was that? A water basin? No, a canal. Numb, he shook his head and immediately regretted it. Colorful sparks hurled before his eyes. Was this the weryt?

"He emerges from the birth canal.

Reborn is he who was dead.

Awakened to new life

By his mother Nut."

Where did the voice come from? It wasn't Maat who spoke. He strained his ears but couldn't hear other people breathe. Was he in his mother's womb? The water wasn't cold but pleasantly warm. Hori had nothing to lose. Maat showed him the way once again. He sank into the stream, immersed himself completely and dove under. Gasping for air, he surfaced. The canal narrowed more and more. Hori followed it to a wall. The water flowed through a small opening barely large enough for a sack of corn to fit through. He reached inside the tube. Not made of rock, it felt soft and yielding—like flesh. This truly had to be the birth channel of the goddess!

Fear choked him the same way as when he'd dived under the wall of the weryt for the first time. This was narrower, more dangerous though. If he got stuck, he couldn't be saved. He'd drown. But did he have a choice? He took a deep breath, then squeezed head and shoulders into the opening. His legs kicked at the ground to propel him forward, farther into the unknown. Arms stretched out, he groped the soft casing, but found no grip. With a last kick he slid completely inside. His ears swooshed, he thought his chest would burst. Someone took his hand, pulled him forward. He struggled on. A second hand grabbed him.

In a gush of water he slid into the arms of—whom? His eyes were closed, he didn't care. Inhaling deeply he cherished precious air. Linen was wrapped around him. He sobbed, then he lost consciousness.

Hori saw the light before he opened his eyes. He blinked. Where was he? His left upper arm hurt, but at least the pounding in his head had eased to slight pulsing. Hunger and thirst plagued him so he had to still be alive. Or not? His breath caught. Lined up against one wall stood some of the most important gods of the Two Lands: Anubis, Amun, Geb, Horus, Seth. A swishing noise from the other side of the room made him turn his head. There stood the goddesses. Besides Isis and Maat, he recognized Mut, Nephthys and Nut. He lay in the middle of the room on a cot. Looking down his body, he saw he'd been painted green—the color of Osiris symbolizing fertility. Hori understood nothing. Geb and Nut stepped up to him and took his hands. He jumped up and walked with them. They brought him face to face with Anubis.

"Behold, Anubis, judge of the dead, this is our son Osiris, who was dead. At your court, you declared him as one whose voice is justified. Now he is one who lives and is fertile in the Two Lands."

Anubis lowered his snout to demonstrate his agreement. "It is Osiris. He was dead. Now he lives and rules over the Duat."

They led Hori to Amun, the highest of gods, also called the hidden one. "Behold, Amun, king of the gods. This is our son Osiris, who rules over the underworld like you rule over the world of the divine. He has been reborn although he was dead."

Amun nodded his head with the heavy feather crown. "Welcome, Osiris, ruler of the Duat. May your fertility vegetate the Two Lands. The Nile is your semen. It fertilizes the fields of people."

One after the other, the gods bowed to Hori. The most ludicrous thoughts popped up in his mind. Was this the court of the dead? Had he turned into Osiris? If he had died, though, why did he feel pain? Why did he crave food?

At last, the goddesses and gods led him through a gate. Glaring light blinded him. He had to narrow his eyes and shade them with his hand to see he was in a temple yard. No reliefs revealed which god was worshiped here. This sacred site was completely unfamiliar to him. He wasn't in Itj-tawy anymore.

They took him to a water basin in one corner of the courtyard. There they washed the green paint off his body and rubbed ointment on his skin before they dressed him in a shendyt of finest linen. A man stepped from the temple building and walked toward him. The king!

Hori sank onto his knees, but Senusret gestured for him to stand. The pharaoh bowed his head to him. "Hail, adept. You experienced the greatest mystery of the Two Lands. From today on, you are a dead man, who lives, and a living man, who is dead. As a symbol of your level of consecration, you received the ankh cross." Senusret pointed at Hori's left arm.

He gazed down and saw the sign of life cut into his upper arm and traced with ink. So that caused the pain. Involuntarily, his gaze wandered to the king's arm. He too bore the mark. Hori still didn't understand the meaning of all this. Senusret led him back into the temple. This time, they entered a room, in which a large table was richly laden in a festive manner. Behind them, some men and women followed. Only now did he recognize the first prophet of Amun. He rubbed his eyes. A moment ago, he stood face to face with this man wearing the feather crown of the god! He also had the sign on his arm, just like everyone else present. They were all adepts and—now Hori understood. Of course! These were the first prophets of the gods they had represented just now. And he, Hori, was now one of them, one of the few who knew the great secret of Osiris. Anubis entered the room last. He was the only one who didn't take off his mask.

Then it struck him what the ritual meant for him. The king had sentenced him to life as a dead man. Now that he was reborn like Osiris, did that mean…?

The king asked them to take a seat, while he remained standing. He unrolled a papyrus scroll and read aloud, "On the thirteenth day of month Ka-her-ka in year one of Senusret of the Sedge and the Bee, Strong Bull…"

The many titles rushed past Hori's ears. When he heard the word 'judgment', he perked up.

"...against Hori, son of Sobekemhat is void. The plaintiff, Nebit, confessed to bribing witnesses to ensure aforementioned Hori was convicted of murdering his son Neferib. This judgment violated Maat and now stands corrected."

Hori's heart jumped in his chest with joy. The pharaoh settled next to him and gestured for him to eat. Hori needed no second invitation, but first he asked, "How long...I mean...have days or weeks passed since I've been brought here?"

Senusret laughed. "I remember very well when I was consecrated. You lose all sense of time and space. The ritual actually took three days and three nights."

Hori gulped and greedily grabbed a piece of duck meat. It tasted delicious! The wine, too, caressed his tongue like nectar. The food filled the void inside him.

The king stopped him when he wanted to drain his mug. "Strict rules apply to the adepts. No word must ever slip from your mouth about what you experienced. Never ever. You can't even talk about it with other adepts because this is the sacrifice you have to make as Osiris for the Two Lands."

Mute, Hori nodded. The cold eyes of the god of the dead fixed him. Was he really Osiris now? At least he felt like he'd shared the god's fate and pain.

Anubis leaned toward him. "As Osiris you are allowed to wander between the world of the dead and that of the living."

Comprehension glowed inside Hori. Effervescent bliss coursed through him. Could it be true?

"Beware. Nobody is allowed to reveal the secrets of the weryt. The worst curse will rest on the traitor."

Hori laughed and wept at the same time. Then dizziness enveloped him. He slipped from his seat.

When he opened his eyes, he gazed at the familiar cracks on the ceiling of his bedroom. He bolted upright. His head ached. Images flared up and faded again. Slowly his memory returned. What a dream! He turned his head left. Reality struck him. The mark! It was there.

Heavy pounding made him don his shendyt and slip into his sandals before he hurried downstairs and flung the door open.

"Hori, the mer-ut wants to see you," Kheper blurted.

So it was true! Hori grinned.

His teacher gave him a puzzled look. "What trouble did you get into?"

"I'm free, Kheper. Free!" He wanted to sing out loud.

Kheper shook his head. "You speak in riddles. And you've got a nice bump there. Too bad that you're our doctor."

A short time later, Hori sat across from Hut-Nefer, who fixed him with a stare. "You have friends in the highest circles, I hear."

He sounded reproachful, and Hori's cheeks burned. The old man likely felt his authority trampled on. Hori had already disturbed the order of the weryt when he arrived. Would the mer-ut allow him to leave?

"As Osiris you are entitled to walk between the world of the dead and that of the living. But I warn you, nobody is allowed to reveal the secrets of the weryt. The worst curse rests on the traitor."

He'd heard these words before. Surprised, he stared at the old man. His gaze slid to his left arm. The ankh sign had faded but was still recognizable. "Anubis," he whispered and lowered his head in reverence.

"Since the beginning of time, the mer-ut is also the first prophet of Anubis." A smile spread a web of fine wrinkles over the man's face. "I know we can trust you."

"Yes, you can. What happens in the weryt stays in the weryt." Woefulness sank onto Hori's heart. "Does that mean we have to part forever?" Despite everything, he'd miss the utu, particularly Kheper. Most of all, though, he'd miss gaining further insights into the human body.

"My boy, you don't have to return, but you can. As Osiris you are permitted to move between the world of the dead and the world of the living. Yesterday you saw all the adepts of Osiris. A distinguished circle. So far, I was the only one allowed to enter and leave the weryt. For the first time since recordings started, there are two keepers of the secrets of death."

Hori bowed reverentially. "I will prove myself worthy of the knowledge I've been entrusted with and use it for the welfare of the people in the Two Lands—and in the service of Maat."

"So be it." Hut-Nefer patted Hori's hand. "So be it."

HONORABLE RECEPTION

Nakhtmin's trust was sorely tried. Ameny had barred him from crossing the Nile again, to leave a message for Hori.

When asked for the reasons, he replied, "Not even I do know the specifics, but as second prophet of Amun, I have an inkling what the mer-ut and the pharaoh—life, prosperity and health—had in mind. We absolutely cannot endanger Hori's status now, nor distract him. I believe he's facing a hard test."

Nakhtmin appreciated the distraction of work and wedding preparations. Although he still lived with Ameny, he'd returned to his practice at the House of Life. Mutnofret no longer needed a bodyguard but a respectable roof over her head. He had no illusions. To gather the needed wealth would take a long time. Likely, Ameny would consent to giving him Muti's dowry in advance to buy a stately home, but his pride rebelled against that. He wanted to achieve it on his own. Maybe Muti would content herself with a humble house in the artisans' quarter?

At least his position in the House of Life had much improved. After Nebit's arrest and the extent of his crimes had become known, Imhotepankh had personally taken care he could treat patients who'd reward him generously.

He bandaged the wound on a cook's finger and sent off his last patient with good advice. Deep in thought, he brushed over his instruments. They were made to heal the ailing, not for killing. He folded the leather inward, below and above the tools held in place by loops, then rolled up the kit. A knock startled him. He sighed with reluctance. Another patient running late? The door opened.

"Are you Nakhtmin the physician?" The man wore the insignia of royal servants around his neck: an amulet of the double crown.

"Yes, I am."

"His majesty the king of Upper and Lower Egypt—life, prosperity and health—wishes to see you. Would you follow me, please?"

While Nakhtmin loped after the man, he had no peace of mind to appreciate the glorious view of the boulevard dipped in evening light. What could the king want with him? Did he have news of Hori's fate? He sure hoped so—and feared it. The mer-ut's voice hadn't inspired any confidence.

They passed through the double doors, and Nakhtmin's feet wanted to turn toward the labyrinth of corridors, where the administration offices were located, but the envoy headed in a different direction. Curious, Nakhtmin followed him. The man strode past the large hall and entered a broad hallway. In this part of the palace, Nakhtmin had never been before. The servant knocked on a beautiful door of painted wood. Although Nakhtmin heard no response from inside, his companion opened the door and motioned for him to enter.

The room was larger than he'd expected and featured a gallery like the one in the large hall with a throne and several resplendent chairs. This had to be the small hall of the king. He was alone but not for long. A door at the back of the room opened, and the king entered, flanked by several dignitaries. Before Nakhtmin flung himself onto the floor, he recognized scribe Thotnakht among them and, even more surprisingly, Sobekemhat, Hori's father.

At a knock, another person entered the room. Since Nakhtmin had to keep his face turned to the floor until the king allowed him to rise, he only saw the feet of the new arrival. The man threw himself to the ground a step behind him.

Somebody tapped a staff against the floor. "His majesty, the king of Upper and Lower Egypt, Strong Bull, of the Sedge and the Bee—life, prosperity and health—accepts your reverence. You may rise, Nakhtmin, son of Nakhtmin, and Hori, son of Sobekemhat."

Nakhtmin jumped up as if stung. Indeed! Next to him stood his friend. Hori winked at him, a subtle smile on his face. Questions upon questions stormed at Nakhtmin. Only, now wasn't the time to ask them. A slight cough drew his attention to the royal gallery.

"In recognition of loyal services rendered, the doctors Nakhtmin and Hori are appointed personal physicians of his majesty."

Confused, Nakhtmin looked around. Did Thotnakht really mean him?

The pharaoh's scribe descended the stairs, holding two papyrus scrolls with the royal seal in one hand. Sobekemhat followed with a strongbox of dark wood. Thotnakht handed him one scroll and gave the other to Hori—their certificates of appointment. The king's physician—no doctor in the Two Lands could strive for a higher honor.

Sobekemhat opened the lid of the box, and Nakhtmin thought himself caught in a dream. Dazed, he lowered his head as Thotnakht placed the gold of honor around his shoulders, a precious collar that would easily buy him a great estate for Muti. His cheeks flared up with embarrassment. How could he think of exchanging the venerable gold! Reverentially, he stroked the smooth metal slowly warming on his body.

Hori, too, received his decoration. Nakhtmin noticed Sobekemhat's hands trembled. The old man gazed at his son in silence and rested one hand on his shoulder. Before he could retreat behind his desk on the gallery, the king stopped him.

"Stay with your son, Sobekemhat. I have another appointment to announce."

Thotnakht received another sealed scroll from the ruler of the Two Lands and proclaimed, "A loyal official of the treasury, Sobekemhat, son of Weni, has served his majesty well. From today on, he shall be removed from his office. Instead, he will serve the pharaoh as vizier and assist in governing the Two Lands."

The face of Hori's father turned crimson. He bowed several times. "What an honor! I thank your majesty for your trust."

"Know that you owe your elevation to your son."

Sobekemhat lowered his head. "I will do my best to serve you and the Two Lands."

To Nakhtmin he seemed abashed. He didn't know much about the relationship between father and son, only that they weren't close. Hopefully, Sobekemhat would hold his youngest in higher esteem from now on.

"One more thing. Your oldest son Teti will succeed you in your position at the treasury."

Thotnakht handed Sobekemhat the last scroll.

The king dismissed his officials and asked Nakhtmin and Hori to follow him. They walked through the pharaoh's private living space into the lush, blooming garden. The whole way, Nakhtmin had been bursting with curiosity and now he couldn't hold back any longer. "Hori? Dear gods, is it really you?" He touched the shoulders and face of his friend as if he might be a phantasm.

Laughing, Hori fought off his hands. "Yes, it's really me."

Nakhtmin scrutinized him. How unfamiliar his friend looked now that he was wearing a doctor's wig again—so grown up. "Why...?"

Senusret interrupted. "Never ask how this came about. Hori must keep the secret forever. This is all you may know: Besides the mer-ut, your friend is the only human being allowed to enter and leave the weryt. However, he must guard its secrets."

Nakhtmin looked from the pharaoh to his friend. The two seemed strangely familiar with each other, and he felt left out although he'd been the one to report to the pharaoh and stay in contact with Hori. He should be the link between the two men. Straight away he felt ashamed of his pettiness. His hand touched his chest, where the decoration of his majesty lay heavily. Royal physician, gold of honor, Hori—for a moment it all became too much for him. He walked to a tree, leaned against its trunk and closed his eyes.

"In two days the Great Kenbet will convene to try Nebit," Senusret's voice announced.

Nakhtmin wiped a hand over his face and looked at the king. "In two days already!"

"The earlier, the better," Hori said.

Senusret gave a grim nod. "You, Nakhtmin, might have to testify if Nebit asks for witnesses to be heard. Since we have his confession, there's no need to mention Hori's involvement in the investigation of his crimes."

Nakhtmin exhaled in relief. Hori might be a free man, rehabilitated and guiltless—still, nobody should find out they'd met. Hori hadn't betrayed the secrets of the weryt, but would anyone take his word for it? Best to keep the whole affair to themselves with only Ameny, Hori, the king and himself knowing it ever happened. "May I ask how the two of us earned the honor and trust to become your majesty's personal physicians?" he asked.

A smile softened the young king's rugged features. "I've made some inquiries. One of you..." He nodded toward Hori. "...likes to explore new ways and knows how to connect what he learned with what he encounters. The other is thorough and methodical. He misses nothing. His instructors also say he has the gift of seeing beneath people's skins to detect what ails them. It would be stupid not to avail myself of such skills."

"Has his majesty told you our new positions include estates in the quarter of courtiers?" Hori asked. "You and I will be neighbors."

"That means I can take Muti to our new home?"

Hori laughed. "You only think of women!"

Day 27 of month Ka-her-ka in Peret, season of the emergence

As Nakhtmin entered the palace on the day of the trial, a throng of curious people gathered before the double gates. News had spread about which high official had to answer for what crimes today. Excited voices swirled around Nakhtmin's head. The vizier a murderer? No common occurrence.

The hall was full of people. Were all these officials and courtiers here to witness the event? So typical. As long as a man held power, everyone bowed to him. Woe to the mighty who falls from grace! Nakhtmin had to fight his way through the crowd to the front. If some of the judges weren't different today, he'd feel transported back to that day of Hori's sentencing. Today, however, Nebit stood there as the accused instead of sitting next to the pharaoh. Hori's father now occupied that place of honor. Nakhtmin's gaze wandered to where Sobekemhat had sat the last time. The young man in the treasurer's chair had to be Hori's brother Teti. He appeared excited. No wonder. His first time as a judge, and in such a sensational case, too.

Thotnakht rose, and the buzz of voices ebbed. Nakhtmin saw the pain in the eyes of the first scribe. Now he knew how his daughter had died. With trembling fingers the man unrolled the arraignment scroll, but his voice was firm. "Nebit, son of Amunhotep, you are charged with numerous crimes. You are accused of..."

Nakhtmin didn't want to listen to the long list of victims. Instead, he wondered if Hori was here and turned to search the crowd behind him. Fairly close, he spotted the brothers Shepses and Hotep. Would they be called as witnesses? Where was Sitamun? Then he saw Ameny and weaved through the people toward him.

Thotnakht had reached the end of the indictment. Now, the king directly addressed his former vizier, "Nebit, son of Amunhotep, you have already made a confession. Law demands you repeat it in front of your judges."

Nakhtmin stared at the defendant's back. While his shoulders had drooped before, a tremor ran through is body now. "Bastet was the first..."

"Speak up!" the king ordered. "You are talking of Bastet, daughter of Thotnakht?"

The scribe's face had paled.

Nebit nodded. "Bastet was the first." Now his voice sounded triumphant, challenging. "But it almost went wrong. So I had do improve my method."

"How did you kill her?" A hoarse voice had spoken the question. Thotnakht's? For a moment, Nakhtmin had averted his gaze.

"I had a doctor's instrument kit made for my son Shepses. The needles it contained seemed very suitable to me. I took one of them and stabbed Bastet with it, straight into the heart."

"Bastard!"

Who had called that? Nakhtmin looked around. Scorn distorted Shepses's face.

Nebit didn't seem to have heard since he continued unmoved. "I believed the jab to be deadly, but she ran away. I chased after her to prevent her telling anyone who had injured her. Then she dropped dead."

"Why did you kill her in this manner?" Senusret asked.

"I wanted to harm her where she'd caused me pain."

"How could Bastet hurt your heart? Did you love her?"

The accused snorted in disgust. "How could I have loved a stupid girl like her? She messed around with my son, and that displeased the one to whom my heart belongs."

"You're referring to your son Shepses and your wife Sitamun?"

"Who else?" Nebit half turned his face to the audience in the hall. A devious smile showed on his face. "And it had to look like a natural death."

Thotnakht lowered his head. A tear rolled down his cheek. "My poor daughter.

Nobody had the slightest idea."

"Yes, I was smart. And I refined my method by dipping the needle in the venom of a king cobra."

The pharaoh interrupted him. "Where did you get the poison?"

Nebit held his chin up high. "Your majesty wears the cobra on your forehead for protection. It adorns all your crowns. I kept the royal snakes for my protection." Such presumptuousness sent a ripple of disgruntled murmurs through the crowd. "I milked them so their bite wouldn't harm me. As a welcome side effect, I always had a sufficient supply for my improved weapon. Soon I got the chance to make sure it worked fast and deadly. Shepses dallied with Ankhes, and the Great Royal Wife talked to me about joining those two in wedlock. I could not allow such a thing to happen."

The king grimaced in pain. "Why couldn't you allow it?" he squeezed out between clenched teeth.

"I've said it already! Sitamun wants to keep her sons around her. She will not tolerate it if one of them tries to leave and set up his own household."

Nakhtmin watched people around him shake their heads in disbelief.

"I caught Ankhes in the royal gardens. Using the pretext of wanting to talk to her about the engagement, I approached her. It was easy. She died between one heartbeat and the next. And again, nobody suspected foul play."

"This was not your last crime?" Senusret prompted.

Nebit sighed. "The boy, Shepses, he simply didn't get it. Behind our backs he got engaged with Merit-Neith. I had to make haste getting her out of the way. With our boat tied to the pier of her parents' house, I lurked in the garden until she was alone. Next came Hetepet. I noticed right away what was going on between the two when I saw them together. This time I nipped romantic entanglement in the bud. She used to pick up her father every day."

Ameny clutched Nakhtmin's hand and squeezed it so hard it hurt.

"You are talking of the daughter of the second prophet of Amun and the vestibule of Amun's temple? That's where she was found."

Nebit gave a dismissive wave of his hand. "No challenge for me. Nobody saw me arrive, nobody saw me leave. Killing the little tavern harlot provided far more obstacles. Who'd have thought she, of all people, was never to be found alone?"

"He means Nebet-Het, daughter of the innkeeper of the *Golden Ibis*," Thotnakht explained to the other judges.

"Why did Nebet-Het have to die? Don't tell us Shepses wanted to marry her," the king said.

The former vizier gave a wry laugh. "It was her doing. The slut! Because of her, Neferib died. That aggrieved my love. Our son, our oldest!"

"Silence!" the pharaoh thundered. "The judges of the Great Kenbet have recently ruled Neferib's death an accident. He died because of his own fault after he wanted to violate the girl Nebet-Het."

The audience whispered excitedly. Nakhtmin could hardly believe it himself although he'd known for a while now. Hearing it all in context fully exposed the vileness of this family.

"Slut!" Nebit growled. "I caught her at the Netjeryt festival. She was among those visiting the dead in the necropolis. Nobody recognized me in the crowd. With this deed I honored my dead son. I sacrificed her to him as was his due."

Such sacrilege silenced the people in the hall. With that alone Nebit had condemned himself.

Senusret dug deeper. "Tell us about the crime when you were caught in the act. The murder of Penu, servant in the house of the second prophet of Amun, and the attempt on Mutnofret's life, his second daughter."

Nebit turned around and let his gaze wander over the faces until it met Nakhtmin's. "There!" Nebit pointed a finger at him. "This guy always accompanied Mutnofret although she was promised to my son. Because of him, I never met her alone."

This time Nakhtmin squeezed Ameny's hand.

"I sent one of my wife's maids to Penu, servant in Ameny's house. She seduced him and promised to return to him that night if he left his door to the garden unbolted." Nebit laughed as if he'd told a great joke. "It was not she who embraced him but death. What a gloomy night it was! I couldn't find the girl's chamber right away, needed a lamp. In the kitchen of the house, I found one. When I finally reached the right door, the minx was awake. She recognized me in the flame's light and fought me as if she knew my intentions."

Nakhtmin sighed with relief. Fortunately, Mutnofret really had known.

"This bodyguard of hers appeared and apprehended me." Again he pointed his finger at Nakhtmin.

All gazes turned to him and he proudly lifted his chin. Even if Muti had actually struck down the villain, he'd done his share in catching this dangerous criminal. When the accused ended his confession, the hall turned very quiet. They've all had enough, Nakhtmin guessed. He wasn't the only one to feel relief over Nebit waiving his right to call witnesses to speak in his favor. The judges saw fit to render judgment without calling witnesses for the prosecution. The man had thoroughly convicted himself.

Consultation took little time, and the sentence was cruel, but not unexpected: death by fire.

DEAD AND DAMNED

Day 29 of month Ka-her-ka in Peret, season of the emergence

On the eve of Nebit's execution, Hori had arranged to meet with Nakhtmin. They already had an opening knocked into the wall between their two estates, so it was a short trip to his friend. With a shudder, he recalled how he used to endanger his life every time he tried to see Nakhtmin. A spring in his step, he entered Nakhtmin's new house through a backdoor.

His friend embraced him. "Welcome at my table. My previous dwelling was no match for this one. Oh, you've never been there."

Hori slid onto the offered chair and let his gaze wander over the dishes. "After the long moons in the weryt, even simple peasant food tastes wonderful, but all this looks delicious."

"Don't tell me you weren't well provided for over there! I always thought the king supplies the weryt with everything?"

Hori grinned. "Hey, if we wanted a bite of meat there, we had to eat the dead. Just don't tell anyone."

Nakhtmin jumped up. "What? You can't be serious! That… No, I don't believe you." He clamped a hand over his mouth as if he were about to throw up.

Hori cracked up with laughter. "Sorry, but your lame attempt to find out more about the living conditions in the weryt called for that. You should have seen your face."

"Just great. Now I've lost my appetite," Nakhtmin grumbled. "I didn't mean to sound you out. Keep your secrets. They taste like maggots in my mouth."

"Oh, come on." Hori grabbed a stuffed vine leaf. "Delishoush," he mumbled. Fortunately, Nakhtmin recovered quickly from the gruesome joke, and they feasted and drank sweet wine stored in the pantry. "When will you bring Mutnofret to her new home?" Hori asked.

Nakhtmin looked up and dipped his greasy hands in a bowl of perfumed water. "I don't want the execution to cast shadows on our first days as a married couple, so we'll wait a little while longer."

Hori nodded. "Has the engagement with Shepses been officially dissolved now?"

Nakhtmin gave him a puzzled look. "Of course. I mean—dear gods! I don't know. I would think so. After all, it never was a real engagement, only pretense."

"Still, there's a sealed contract. Does Shepses even know his bride never wanted him? He's now the head of the family and can insist on compliance with the contract."

His friend groaned. "He still lives with his mother. His wish to get out of there set everything in motion."

Hori thought of the verdict. As soon as the judgment was executed, the royal treasury would confiscate Nebit's possessions including the magnificent estate. Sitamun would only be allowed to keep whatever assets she brought into the marriage, and that would have to suffice to find new accommodation for her and her three children. Shepses couldn't seriously expect Mutnofret to marry him under these circumstances. His inheritance was gone, and he wouldn't be able to afford his own household in the near future. Unless… "I don't like this. Sitamun knows all the secrets, which are supposed to die with Nebit tomorrow. I don't trust her. With her knowledge, she could still cause major harm. With Shepses presiding over the family now, he could press adultery charges or threaten to do so."

Nakhtmin froze. "By Seth's balls! Would she dare?" He brushed the tresses of his wig out of his face. "No, Shepses wouldn't go for it. He hates his mother."

"And he loves her—somehow." Memories of Shepses's mother giving him sexual pleasure flared up in Hori's mind. He had sure enjoyed that. "You should talk to your father-in-law as soon as possible."

"Ameny will have taken care of it. I hope." Nakhtmin shook his head. "While we're talking about fathers, have you spoken with yours in the meantime?"

Groaning, Hori leaned back. His father was a constant thorn in his flesh. He waved dismissively. "Let's not ruin this beautiful evening with unpleasant things."

"Oh. You thought the question about Muti's engagement with Shepses more pleasant?"

"That's not what I meant. It's only—I had high hopes placed in my acquittal and appointment as the king's physician. But he chews on it like on gristle. He loathed having to thank me for his promotion." Hori tried to ban the ugly scene, with little success. His brother Teti had thrown his arms around him with gratitude and happiness. Sobekemhat, however, had acted as if he were entitled to the appointment. He regarded Hori's conviction as just punishment for his unsteady way of life. At least his father was glad to see him free and rehabilitated if only because his reputation wouldn't suffer any longer. His mother, though—she had been truly happy for him. All things considered, Hori really appreciated having escaped the paternal regimen, which would have felt like another prison after his time in the weryt.

Neither Hori nor Nakhtmin wanted to attend Nebit's burning. Ameny, though, needed to witness the punishment of the man who killed his daughter. That evening Hori accompanied Nakhtmin to the estate of the second Amun prophet. A young woman flung her arms around his friend in exultation. Hori pursed his lips as he appraised her. Mutnofret was a beautiful woman, and he could see how much she was in love with Nakhtmin.

Ameny was still a little pale around his nose but had composed himself. Still, Hori would have waited another day before asking Mutnofret's father about the engagement. After the meal with the whole family, the men settled on cushions in the living space of the house.

"So, he's dead?" Hori began.

Ameny lowered his head. "Dead and damned. I witnessed the king's men scattering his ashes to the four winds. Nothing remains of Nebit, and he won't bother us with his presence in the underworld."

Hori saw Nakhtmin trembling. Goosebumps had spread on his arms. Knowing how much care was taken with the embalming and the efforts made to ensure an afterlife for the dead, he couldn't imagine how the vizier managed to face such a fate with such calm. Or had he not? "How bad was it? The flames? Did he step up to the stake without protest?" He'd seen the smoke rising on the western shore of the river. The execution site in a mountain gorge was a place nobody in the Two Lands visited voluntarily. Powerful protective spells had to be cast before anyone could enter. The ka souls of the damned—sometimes he'd heard them howl in the night when he lay on the roof of his house in the weryt.

Ameny released a noise, half sobbing, half moaning. "It was horrible. You should be glad you didn't see it. The screams, the stench—"

"Let's forget all about this criminal. Everyone should do so, forever."

None of them dared to speak the man's name. His ka roamed the world without a home. To imagine they might draw him to them with the sound of his name. How dreadful.

Nakhtmin clenched his hands. "And she who is responsible for it all, walks free. The criminal has paid a high price for loving her."

"I wonder if it isn't punishment enough for her to be who she is. Now that she's alone and without means…"

Ameny interrupted Hori. "Believe me, that viper will soon have found somebody else to keep her warm. She isn't one to stay alone for long. Still a seductress, she'll find a new husband soon, even though it might not be the vizier this time."

Hori laughed at the notion of Sitamun slithering up to his father and finding him a hard nut to crack. Sobekemhat didn't even feel tender love for the mother of his children. Somehow, Hori doubted his father was even capable of such emotions.

Nakhtmin cleared his throat. "Uhm, Ameny. I'd like to soon take Mutnofret to her new home. There are no reasons against it, are there? You've sorted out matters with Shepses?"

The prophet groaned. "Dear gods! I forgot!"

Nakhtmin jumped up and showered his future father-in-law with reproach. How strange, Hori thought. In their hearts, both men never seemed to have considered the contract a binding legal document. His father's death didn't void Shepses's claims. Both parties had to agree on revoking their promises to each other—in front of witnesses. "Shepses will surely understand that circumstances have changed. Let's go talk to him tomorrow and settle things before they have to clear out of the estate," he suggested.

The men's agitated voices fell silent. Sometimes Hori was rather glad he had never felt so strongly for someone. On the other hand, it would be nice to belong with someone who cares. Kheper's family had welcomed him more than his own. Hori shook off his longing. Love made one vulnerable, and his father's rejection hurt enough already.

The next morning, they met at Ameny's house again. Together they walked the short distance to Nebit's former estate. Ameny clutched the marriage contract scroll. The gate stood open.

From afar, Hori spotted palace servants carrying valuables from the house and loading them onto donkeys. "The pharaoh wastes no time," he said and bit his lip. Although he'd never thought much of Shepses, now he felt sorry for him. Last time he'd come here, Shepses was able to blind him with his family's riches. Today, he ranked higher than his colleague.

"Where's the family? I only see servants of the palace," Nakhtmin asked and looked around.

They stopped in front of the house. Ameny held up one of the workers about to disappear inside again. "Where do we find doctor Shepses and lady Sitamun?"

The man shrugged. "We found the gate open. The previous inhabitants haven't shown their faces. I guess they've left already."

The prophet groaned. "Just great. Now I'll have to search all of Itj-tawy for the fellow."

"Never mind," Hori placated him. "You should find him in the House of Life. Since we're here, however, I'd like to see the snake enclosure. Can you take me there, Nakhtmin? Or do you think the king's men have already cleared it?"

His friend shook his head. "It was pitch dark that night. I can only guess. Likely the building is located in that direction, close to the river." His finger pointed north.

Hori set off. The garden was very large, and even in daylight, this jungle was a maze easy to get lost in. After awhile he heard reeds rustling in the wind. The river had to be near. He rounded a man-high pomegranate bush with almost-ripe fruit and found himself on the edge of a lawn. A shack stood on the opposite side. The snake enclosure? Then he spotted a slumped body in the grass. A woman. She looked like she needed help. Hori wanted to run to her when he heard a hissing noise. A long shape slithered through the grass. "Stay back!" he called to Nakhtmin and Ameny, who'd been following him. "The snakes are free." His heart pounded.

"Is that Sitamun?" Ameny asked.

"I think so, yes. Who else could it be?" Would Sitamun still have any maids in the house? They'd surely have fled the moment they learned of her husband's crimes.

"Cobras only bite when they are aggravated. If we take care not to startle them, we're safe," Nakhtmin explained and set one foot onto the lawn.

"Are you crazy?" Hori tugged on his arm, but his friend shook him off.

"No hasty movements. Very slowly. We're doctors. We have to do something for her!"

Shame flooded Hori. Whoever lay there, she might be beyond all medical cure, but she suffered. Since when had he become such a coward, while Nakhtmin took the risk? He drew a deep breath. "All right, let's recover her. Ameny, you'll have to be our eyes when we carry her."

Cautious, they inched forward until they reached the still figure. Hori grabbed her ankles, while Nakhtmin lifted her shoulders. Gently, they turned the woman around. It really was Sitamun, and she breathed, if barely. Hori found the snake-bite wound below her knee. The flesh was swollen and discolored. Served her right, he thought, then remembered Hetepet's heart.

"She's so cold, must have been lying here for hours," Nakhtmin said.

With care, they carried Sitamun to the path, where Ameny stood and monitored all movement in the grass. As soon as they reached the gravel with their burden, they dared to strike a faster pace.

"Did you see? The door to the enclosure stood ajar," Ameny said.

Hori looked up. Who'd release such dangerous animals? Had that been an accident, an oversight? Possible. On the other hand...Sitamun in her despair might not have seen any other way... No, that wouldn't fit her personality. She wasn't capable of self-reflection and remorse. Or... Hori mulled over it. "What was the exact phrasing of her arrangement with the king?"

Ameny recited the conditions.

"So they didn't discuss her burial?"

"No."

Sitamun moaned; her eyelids flitted.

"Could she have been searching for an easy way to regain her youth, beauty and power in the underworld?"

Ameny shook his head. "She'd certainly like that but I doubt she'd have the courage. Taking her own life is still murder. She couldn't hope to fool the Judgment of the Dead with such a scheme."

Hori recalled the ruses he'd learned in the weryt, the heart scarabs and assertions. But Sitamun wouldn't know that.

Nakhtmin sucked in air. "Shepses," he murmured. "He'd found a way to free himself after all."

"Just as well it might have been Hotep," Ameny argued.

They laid Sitamun down near the house. Not much longer now, and she wouldn't regain consciousness anyway. A cobra's bite was pretty much always lethal, and in her case, any help would come far too late.

Nakhtmin said, "Does it even matter? I, for one, feel no urge to find out the truth in this case."

Hori looked at him in silence and nodded.

"Same here." Ameny brushed a blade of grass from Sitamun's cheek and studied it. "I think she might as well die here all alone."

Day 14 of month Shef-bedet in Peret, season of the emergence

Hori's first official act as royal physician was to examine the Great Royal Wife. "I don't have to tell you what you already know, your majesty. Your husband's seed grows inside you."

Sherit clapped her hands with exultation. "May the gods grant us a son this time."

Smiling, Hori bowed. The queen had already given birth to the daughters Senet-Senebtisi and Menet, two healthy little princesses. He accompanied Sherit to the royal nursery. To his surprise, he found a third girl there, a little older than the other two.

The queen noticed his puzzlement. "This is Henut. His majesty has taken her in as his ward after the poor child has lost both her parents."

With big, brown eyes, the girl stared at him.

Shuddering, Hori turned away. The king had a good heart. Would he have had it in him to raise the viper's brood together with his own children? Later he'd ask Nakhtmin the same question—if his friend found some time for him. Two days ago, Mutnofret had moved in with him.

After his mother's death, Shepses immediately agreed to dissolving the engagement. He'd taken his share of their mother's inheritance and headed for Waset. Best thing he could do: start afresh in a city where nobody had heard of the horrible events here. Hotep had gone with him. Time might heal the wounds their parents inflicted on the brothers.

Besides the pharaoh and the executioners, only Hori knew the woman's corpse had been burned like her husband's body. Both were denied a life in the underworld, and that was exactly what they deserved. Maat would be satisfied. Whistling, he left the palace and strolled home.

Appendix ~ Egyptian Deities

Amun – *the hidden one.* Originally the local god of Waset (Thebes), he gained importance when the city became the capital of the 11th dynasty. First he was the god of wind and fertility, displayed as a human with a feather crown. Since the ram was his holy animal, he was also depicted as a ram-headed god. Later the deity merged with other gods of the Egyptian pantheon (syncretism). As Amun-Ra, he incorporated the characteristics of Amun, Ra and Min.

Anubis – *the crown prince.* Jackal-headed god performing the rituals for the dead. He has special significance at the Judgment of the Dead when the hearts of the deceased were placed on scales and weighed against the feather of goddess Maat. This procedure assumes good deeds make the heart lighter, while bad deeds literally burden it. The dead recite all the things they did not do in their lifetime, for example lying, stealing, killing. If the scales tipped to the side of the heart, it was fed to the devourer. Since the Egyptians thought mind and memory resided in the heart, this meant a second and ultimate death. If the deceased passed the test, they were granted eternal life in the underworld.

Horus – *the distant one, who is above.* Falcon-headed god of the sky, mythical son of Isis, who conceived him when she transformed into a sparrow hawk and mated with the mummy of her husband Osiris. Horus was one of the most important deities of the Egyptian pantheon and strongly associated with the kingdom.

Isis – *seat, throne.* Mother of Horus and sister as well as wife of Osiris. She was patroness of mothers and lovers and depicted in human form with a throne on her head.

Maat – *justice, truth, world order.* Maat is rather a concept than a goddess. The word's meaning is a mix of justice, order and truth and signifies the ideal course of the world, where the sun rises every day anew and people treat each other fairly. The feather was her symbol, which she wore on her head as human-shaped goddess.

Min – God of procreation and fertility, who was always depicted in human shape with an erect penis. He was also called Min-Kamutef, bull of his mother, which refers to the insemination of his divine mother. Min is father and son at the same time; he can create himself.

Monthu – Falcon-headed god. Originally, he was the main god of Waset (Thebes) before Amun surpassed him in significance. As the god of war and protector of weapons he was particularly worshiped in the 11th dynasty, which also influenced the names of pharaohs.

Nefertem – Youthful god of the lotus flower, ointments and scents. Nefertem is strongly linked to the myth of creation since the lotus flower emerged from the primal waters Nun.

Nut – Goddess of the sky. Egyptians imagined Nut arching her body over the earth represented by the god Geb. Every evening, she swallowed the sun, which then traveled through her body to be reborn from her womb in the morning.

Osiris – *seat of the eye.* The god of the dead, depicted as a mummy with a feather crown. According to legend, Osiris was murdered by his brother Seth, who begrudged him his throne as ruler of the world. Additionally, he chopped up the corpse and spread the parts all over the earth. Osiris's sister and wife Isis succeeded in finding all parts, and reassembled them. She reanimated the corpse and conceived their son Horus. From then on, Osiris ruled over the underworld and was depicted as a mummy. Abydos (Abdju) was the sacred place of this deity, and pharaohs as well as common people wanted to be buried there—if only in the form of a cenotaph, an additional, empty tomb. The myth of Isis and Osiris meant a lot to Egyptians.

Ptah – Human-shaped primary god of Men-Nefer, the patron of craftsmen and creator god. He took part in the ritual of mouth opening and was depicted as mummy.

Ra – or Re. Sun god and father of all gods. The cult of the god, worshiped in On (Heliopolis), was strongly associated with the kingdom. The solar disk adorns this human-shaped god.

Sekhmet – *the powerful*. The lion-headed goddess was responsible for war, diseases and epidemics but also for healing.

Seth – *creator of confusion*. God with the head of a fabulous creature, brother of Osiris. He's regarded as the god of the desert and all foreign lands, of evil and violence but also as patron of the oases, god of metals and god of the dead, who picks up the deceased.

Sobek – Crocodile-headed god of water and fertility.

Sokar – Initially the god of fertility. In the course of Egypt's history, he also took on attributes of the god of death. He was worshiped west of Memphis, and the name Sakkara probably goes back to him. He played an important role during the mouth opening ritual. Later he merged with Osiris and Ptah into a powerful god of the dead.

Thot – God of the moon, magic and knowledge. The Egyptians believed Thot had brought them scripture. He was depicted as ibis or baboon.

Appendix ~ Places and Regions

Abydos (Abdju) – The city of Osiris, the god of the dead, was located on the western shore of the Nile, about 100 miles north of ancient Thebes. In addition to the pharaohs of the first dynasties, many Egyptians arranged for their burial there or at least had a stele, a stone slab with inscriptions or reliefs, set up to become part of the resurrection ritual of god Osiris.

Khent-min – Today Akhmim, was about 125 miles north of Thebes and the main cult site of the god Min.

Itj-tawy – *encompassing the Two Lands* – Amenemhet I erected the city between the delta and Upper Egypt. The exact location is still unknown, but most likely it was close to the necropolis El-Lisht, where the first two kings of the 12th dynasty were entombed.

Kemet – *the black*. That's what Egyptians called their country.

Kush – or Nubia, the land south of Egypt (today Sudan). The territory starting at the first cataract (granite barriers in the Nile) was called Kush. Because of its rich gold deposits, the pharaohs undertook many expeditions and military campaigns into the southern neighbor's country.

Libu – Nomads living in the desert west of Egypt.

Men-nefer (Memphis) – also called Inbu Hedj, the white walls. With a strategic position at the Balance of the Two Lands, Men-nefer was the capital of Egypt during the Old Kingdom. At the Sed festival run, the pharaohs had to circle the white fortification walls and thus prove their strength. Throughout Egyptian history, the city played an important part, among other things, as cult site of several important gods.

Waset – (Thebes, today Karnak/Luxor) The capital of the 4th Upper Egyptian nome gained major importance when it became capital of the Two Lands during several periods of the Middle and New Kingdoms.

Appendix ~ Glossary

Akh – The transfigured, an ancestor's spirit, the part of the human soul created after death. Ba and ka are part of the soul while a human being is alive. At death, they leave the body. When they return to it, they merge and create the third component of the human soul, the akh. Nevertheless, they still exist individually. The akh, the spirit soul, ascends to the sky and turns into a star. Together with the sun god, it travels through the underworld. The akh is as good or evil as the deceased had been while still alive. It can influence the world of the living and harm these. Therefore criminals were denied a proper funeral to prevent their components of the soul creating an akh.

Ba – The ba is also called the excursion soul or free soul of the Egyptians. It's the part of the soul depicted as a bird with a human head. During life, it's confined to the body, but when death occurs, it can separate from the body and fly around. However, it stays connected to the body and unites with it from time to time. The Egyptians believed the ba could be caught, injured and even killed.

Balance of the Two Lands – The place where the Nile branches out into the delta, the border between Upper and Lower Egypt.

Ben oil – Oil produced from the fruit of the horseradish tree, also known as Moringa oil. Grown and harvested in the Middle East, the oil was imported from there even in the times of the Old Kingdom. It tastes sweet and was used for cooking and as osmophore to carry the scent in perfume oil and ointment cones. In embalming, it found a special use.

Deben – Ancient Egyptian weight unit, its value varying in the Middle Kingdom. A copper deben was twice as heavy as one of gold. Besides barter trade, these pieces of precious metal served as a means of payment and for determining the value of goods. Deben were shaped in bars or rings, which allowed one to break off smaller bits.

Duat – Name of the netherworld. It consisted of the subterranean region and the celestial realm named Aaru. The two touched each other at the horizon. While the dead had to face various horrors in the underworld and needed to pass their judgment, they could reach the heavenly realm of Aaru afterward and enjoy a kind of paradise. Unlike in the garden of Eden, they had to work, though, farming the fields among other things. To avoid manual labor, Egyptians had little figurines called Ushabti entombed with them. These 'answerers' were to jump to work in their master's stead at the gods' summons.

Eye of Horus – Symbol of the god Horus. In their fight over the throne of Osiris, Seth ripped out his nephew Horus's left eye. The god Thot healed it, and since then it symbolizes medicine. In addition, mathematical fractions were based on the proportions of the eye, and these ratios were used for dosing the ingredients of remedies. Painted onto the hull of a boat, the eye was supposed to protect against dangers lurking in the water.

False door – An element of Egyptian graves that looked like a door. They were either a relief or painted on and allowed the ka soul of the deceased to leave the tomb.

Heri-Heb/Heriu-Heb – Lector priest/lector priests. High-ranking priests who played an important role during mummification and funerals since they recited ritual texts, litanies and songs.

House of Life – One might call it a kind of university, where the higher professions like scribes, physicians, artists and priests were educated.

Ibu – Place of purification. First stop for the deceased in the embalming process. There's no archeological evidence for these constructions. Judging by the few surviving paintings, they were made of light wood and mats.

Ka – A part of the soul. The ka leaves the body of the dying and continues to exist independently. As a double of the deceased, it serves as its guardian spirit. It inhabits a statue erected specifically for it in the tomb of the dead. It feeds on the sacrifices placed before the statue.

Kenbet – Board of judges, which consists of dignitaries with jurisdiction over property claims and crimes. Besides these local courts, there was the Great Kenbet with the vizier and the pharaoh as chairmen.

Lock of youth – In the Old Kingdom an iconographic mark of the king's children. In later times, the lock of youth was also worn by the children of noble families. While the rest of the head was shaved, one braided curl hung from one side to the shoulder. Since the Horus child is also depicted in this way, it can be assumed these children were equated with the divine child. When they reached adulthood (at the age of 13 in ancient Egypt), the hair was shaved off. From the earliest dynasties on, noble Egyptians covered their heads with wigs. In the course of time, fashion changed and so did the headdress made of real hair or plant fibers. Certain professions wore a specific type of hairstyle, which made them recognizable. Wearing a wig was a status symbol, but originally the custom likely had hygienic reasons.

Mastaba – Arabic word for bench. The kings of the first dynasties established the tradition to erect these large structures as their tombs in Sakkara. Starting with Djoser, pharaohs chose pyramids as their burial chambers. Until the Middle Kingdom, officials and noble people were entombed in these so-called bench graves, which were rectangular structures built with adobe or stone. Inside lay the dead. During the New Kingdom, graves were dug into rock, likely because then they couldn't be robbed so easily.

Medjay – Law enforcement, mercenary-soldiers from Kush or the desert tribes.

Mer-ut – Head of the embalmers.

Necropolis – City of the dead.

Pharaoh – In old Egyptian, 'Per-Aa' was the term for the seat of the king's government. In Greek times, the word became a synonym for the king, who from then on was called pharaoh.

Pylon – Large gateway made of stone, built in front of temples.

Sedge and the Bee – (Nesw Bity) Part of a pharaoh's title. The bee symbolized Lower Egypt, the sedge Upper Egypt. A pharaoh had five different names in total. The nesw bity name was the throne name a pharaoh chose in addition to his birth name. Another name, the nebty name (the two mistresses) also showed the dualistic attitude of the Egyptians: the vulture goddess Nekhbet represents Upper Egypt and the snake goddess Wadjet Lower Egypt. Both animals adorned the pharaoh's crown to protect the king. Additionally, the king chose a Horus name and Golden name.

Senet – A board game depicted in numerous murals since the first dynasties. Two players tried to place their pawns on a certain field on a board of thirty squares. The Romans adopted the game. It might be a precursor of backgammon.

Shendyt – A knee-length wraparound skirt or kilt.

Sibling marriage – For the pharaoh it was common to marry his biological sister as it was believed the king's divine blood was only transferred to daughters, who could then pass it on to their offspring. Likely the reasoning behind this was that only the mother of a child could be determined with certainty, while fatherhood might be doubtful. In the Egyptian language, the word for 'sister' developed into a synonym for 'beloved'. Marriage of siblings mostly happened in the royal family until Greek-Roman times when they are also documented for common people. Otherwise incest was frowned upon early on like in most cultures.

Strong bull – The king was often equated with a bull since the animal represented virility, power and strength.

Sycamore – also called sycamore fig or mulberry fig. With its protruding canopy, the tree made for an ideal shade dispenser in Egypt, where few deciduous trees prospered. Many parts of the sycamore were used as food or cures, and in Mennefer (Memphis) a holy sycamore was worshiped as embodiment of the goddess Hathor.

The Two Lands – Upper and Lower Egypt. Even in prehistoric times, the fertile Nile valley had been a popular place for different cultures to settle. The population of the marshy delta in Lower Egypt had been a different one than that of Upper Egypt. The mythical king Menes, however, managed to unite the two kingdoms. For Egyptians, this event retained immense significance throughout history. Their language reflects the duality in many ways as a consequence of previous individuality. Particularly in imagery, the unification was symbolically reenacted over and over again.

Ut/Utu – Embalmer. Little is known about this professional group, neither where nor how they lived. Presumably, the art of embalming was so secret that hardly any information was passed on. The sparse knowledge mostly stems from Greek authors of the Late Period, who had their own particular view of a culture so strange to them.

Wab priest – The wab priests were the largest group within the priesthood of a temple. They ranked below the prophets in the temple hierarchy and took care of a major part of the daily offering services.

Weryt – Embalming hall. What the weryt looked like or how its interior was made up is fairly unknown. In Memphis, an embalming hall for Apis bulls was discovered, and it can be assumed the weryt for humans was designed in a similar fashion.

CALENDAR AND CLIMATE

Early on, Egyptians had a fairly exact calendar based on the annual Nile floodings. Additionally, they observed the course of the stars. When the morning star Sirius, Sothis in Egyptian, rose with the sun, the Nile floodings were about to begin. This marked the start of the year. The Sothis year and the solar year diverge slightly. Every 126 years—approximately—a one-day difference needs to be figured in.

One peculiarity is that the first month of inundation started earlier in the south than in the north, because the floods arrived there about two weeks later. I've used the later dates in this novel, because Itj-tawy was located quite far north.

Egyptians knew three seasons with four months of approximately 30 days each.

Akhet was the season of the inundation, lasting from about mid-June to mid-October. Then Peret, the season of the emergence, followed from mid-October to mid-February, and finally Shemu, the season of the harvest, from mid-February until mid-June. The names of the months changed in the New Kingdom. I've used the older names in this novel.

Akhet (inundation)

Wepet-renpet – June 19
Tekh – July 19
Menkhet – August 18
Hut-heru – September 17

Peret (emergence/winter)

Ka-her-ka – October 17
Shef-bedet – November 16
Rekeh wer – December 16
Rekeh nedjes – January 15

Shemu (harvest/summer)

Renutet – February 14
Khonsu – March 16
Khenti-khet – April 15
Ipet-hemet – May 15

The day was divided into 24 hours, with 12 attributed to the night and 12 to the day. The day began at sunrise and ended with sunset. This close to the equator the hours of daylight varied far less than farther north or south. A week encompassed ten days, the year consisted of 36 weeks, plus five leap days called Heriu-renpet. In early times, these were regarded as dominated by demons, later they were dedicated to the gods. These leap days came right before the new year.

Julius Caesar adopted this very exact calendar, and it formed the basis for the Julian calendar. Thus our calculation of time, to a large extent, goes back to the calendar of ancient Egypt.

POSTSCRIPT

In this story, the embalming of the dead in ancient Egypt plays an important role. Egyptian mummies are well known, not only from museums but movies. Although Egyptians in general liked to record many things, there are no written sources available about mummification, and archeological findings help very little. Greek writer Herodotus visited Egypt in the 5th century BC and expressed his puzzlement over this culture, which seemed rather strange to him. He described mummification explicitly in his histories.

However, in his time, mummification had already been practiced for millennia. Naturally, the craft had changed and evolved. Since the 18th century BC, the country at the Nile had also been ruled by varying peoples, who brought their own cultures to Egypt. In consequence, the insights of Herodotus were very different than those of someone who might have described the techniques during the period of the Middle Kingdom around 1900 BC. In addition, his viewpoint is that of an outsider, who found the Egyptian burial rites quite peculiar.

Mummies have been examined by modern researchers. They show much of what Herodotus described, but also how the art of mummification had been honed with growing experience. Presumably, Egyptians discovered in prehistoric times that bodies buried in the desert sand didn't decompose but turned into natural mummies. The hot, arid climate helped the process. Preserving the body was very important because Egyptians believed a part of the soul stayed inside the corpse, so their deceased needed to be preserved for all eternity. They discovered how particularly the inner organs tended to decay and rot, so they removed them and preserved them separately. Using potash and natron, they dehydrated the bodies. Fragrant plant parts, ointments and oils not only preserved, but also provided the magic breath of life reviving the deceased through their noses.

Organs had to be buried with the dead since the body had to be complete. The heart, usually placed back inside the body, was more important than any other organ since it played the essential role at the Judgment of the Dead.

Egyptians imagined the heart contained intellect, thoughts, emotions and memories. The significance of the brain was completely overlooked. It was the only organ not just removed, but totally destroyed and tossed away. This view was not as absurd as it might seem to modern readers because the heart beats faster with excitement. Love, fear, anxiety—all these things we still attribute to the heart today since it reacts perceptibly to these emotions.

After embalming, the body was bandaged with much effort. Amulets were added to the bindings. The procedure lasted seventy days and was accompanied by numerous rituals, since sending a deceased off to the afterlife involved magic. This may be the reason why so little is known about it today. In ancient Egypt the processes must have been top secret. Such knowledge could have been easily misused. The fear a stranger might take possession of a part of the soul and use it for evil purposes must have been great. Where and how the embalming was performed we can only assume. A painting of a purification tent in a rock-cut tomb in Meir survived. These light-weight structures were not built for eternity, though, so we can only make assumptions as to what happened in them and what they looked like.

They had to be set up near a water source in any case. The embalming hall weryt, however, must have been made of stone. The hall built for embalming the sacred Apis bulls has survived through the millennia. For this novel I decided on a closed off area with a surrounding wall, and I sited the place of purification within the compound. Water was supplied via canals built under the wall.

Whether the laws of the weryt were as strict as I described them is unknown. To a large extent I also made up the inauguration ceremony of Osiris. Osiris mysteries existed, but how they unfolded exactly has not been passed on through time. The Sokar festival is known at least in its general proceeding. Onions were indeed a symbol of the sun and became an integral part of the Netjeryt festival.

Sexually, Egyptians were rather permissive, but within well-defined limits. The position of women was singular in the ancient world. They could learn a profession and operate their own business. Marriage contracts determined how, in the case of a divorce, wife and children would be provided for, likely one of the reasons why adultery was severely punished. In case of allegations, both guilty parties, man and woman, were sentenced, sometimes even executed. Apparently, this didn't occur very often though. Sex before marriage was allowed although illegitimate children were frowned upon and certainly posed an obstacle when it came to finding a suitable husband.

Contraceptives existed and they may have been fairly effective: a kind of diaphragm soaked in spermicide preparations. Since life was held sacred, contraceptives were usually only prescribed for medical reasons. Likely, a flourishing black market existed. Medicine was fairly advanced in Egypt. Still, for religious reasons with strong beliefs in how the afterlife was achieved, dissecting the dead was off limits for medical students. In consequence, the Egyptians never understood the vascular system. Instead they assumed canals provided the body with blood, air and water. Another set of canals served as outlets for feces, slime, urine and semen.

Money and monetary compensation did not yet exist, only barter trade. Pieces of copper, silver and gold served as a precursor of actual currency. These deben were either shaped in bars or rings so that smaller pieces could be broken off. Services like medical care were rewarded with more or less valuable presents. The House of Life was not only a kind of university, doctors practiced medicine there. In case of an emergency, they also made house calls. Apparently, the concept of independent medical practitioners did not exist. It is certain, however, that the poor also had access to health care.

I have bestowed the symptoms of a narcissistic personality disorder on lady Sitamun. A person afflicted with this disorder can easily dominate and influence family relations.

I thank forensic doctor Stefan Potente, who made me aware that a simple stab into the heart with a thin needle wouldn't be fatal immediately. The wound would bleed into the heart sac, which would cause a cardiac tamponade. It might take quite some time for the heart to stop. Our killer found out when his first victim ran away, which forced him to refine his method. Any errors with regard to medical aspects or embalming are my own, however.

A special thanks goes to Edith Parzefall for killing every German word of my novel, transfiguring the text and breathing new life into it via the English language. And I'm grateful to Rebecca Rasmussen and Les Tucker, who helped polish the prose and weed out typos.

I hope to have provided a suspenseful, entertaining and interesting insight into the world of ancient Egypt. More adventures of Hori and Nakhtmin in Maat's service are to follow.
If you enjoyed this novel, please leave a review. Nothing can motivate a writer more than the reader's appreciation.

Berlin, Germany, August 2014
Kathrin Brückman